M000211015

Projections

TOR PUBLISHING GROUP BOOKS
BY S. E. PORTER

Projections

AS SARAH PORTER

Vassa in the Night
When I Cast Your Shadow
Never-Contented Things

Projections

S. E. PORTER

TOR

TOR PUBLISHING GROUP
NEW YORK

PROJECTIONS

Copyright © 2024 by Sarah Porter

A Tor Book
Published by Tom Doherty Associates / Tor Publishing Group
120 Broadway
New York, NY 10271

www.tor-forge.com

Tor® is a registered trademark of Macmillan Publishing Group, LLC.

The Library of Congress Cataloging-in-Publication Data is available upon request.

ISBN 978-0-7653-9677-8 (hardcover)
ISBN 978-0-7653-9679-2 (ebook)

Our books may be purchased in bulk for promotional, educational, or business use. Please contact your local bookseller or the Macmillan Corporate and Premium Sales Department at 1-800-221-7945, extension 5442, or by email at MacmillanSpecialMarkets@macmillan.com.

First Edition: 2024

Printed in the United States of America

0 9 8 7 6 5 4 3 2 1

For Vesper, star of my heart,
my first book of your life

Though I am old with wandering
Through hollow lands and hilly lands,
I will find out where she has gone,
And kiss her lips and take her hands;
And walk among long dappled grass,
And pluck till time and times are done,
The silver apples of the moon,
The golden apples of the sun.

—William Butler Yeats, "The Song of Wandering Aengus"

Projections

Catherine Suspended

If only Gus Farrow had not fled so precipitously on murdering me, or indeed if he had fled to any refuge but this one, I might have found peace.

There my body lay on the riverbank, cooling like so much stale porridge, mud-smeared from my struggle. And there he stood above with his darting eyes, his mouth still befouled by proclamations of what he had called *love*. Had I been in any condition to speak, I might have disputed that the sentiments of my murderer deserved such a name. But I could not form words.

Please do not infer from this that death had left me voiceless. On the contrary. I knew that I was dead; I have never been disposed to avert my mind from facts, however disagreeable. With a certain stunned detachment I noted the body so lately mine: now silent, limp, and filthy, its petticoats mingling with the muck. Nonetheless I was still screaming and found I could not stop.

Gus jerked his head and clapped his hands to his ears, so I supposed I was in some manner audible, if only to him. With his movement I realized where I was.

His hands were cottony with my ghost, though I do not think that Gus perceived me wound about his fingers. For my part, I assure you I had no desire to cling to him. Ugh, how had I become so entangled? The result was that in covering his ears my scream drove through his head, and he yanked his hands away and gaped with hounded eyes.

Then he began running.

Had I not been in a state of shock, I would have guessed at once where he was going. But even then I could not have known what it would mean for me to be carried, poor shredded ectoplasm that I was, to the city of sorcerers.

To Nautilus.

If he had stayed on the green earth, then in time I might have disentangled myself and floated free, released into the sweet blue sky and sparkling river that I have always regarded as my truest home. Or I might have come loose without any effort on my part, and dissolved into serene unbeing. But Gus allowed no interval for that. Like some unholy rabbit, he reached a burrow or gap he knew in the fabric of our dear world, and down he went. There was a wild spinning-about of which I was but dimly sensible, and after some time a landing.

And then I, who had always regarded magic as the most noxious presumption, who had certainly never felt the slightest desire to see this city so imbued with it, found myself in Nautilus. I could see why Gus had grown infatuated with the place, all pearly grandiosity and unsettled forms. There was hardly a straight line to be seen anywhere, nor a surface that did not warp and scroll, as if, in their arrogance, these sorcerers had petrified the wind itself. If I had still been possessed of my body I would have been seasick simply from looking at the architecture, and even bodiless I felt a fierce distaste.

Gus had fled, of course, hoping to escape the consequences of his guilt. So far as the rope that would have awaited him under ordinary laws, he succeeded. But he was still very young then, and very foolish. I knew quite well, for he had told me that he had won his citizenship in Nautilus only a week before: he was nearly as much a stranger there as I was.

So it seems likely that he was as astonished as I by what followed.

My scream, which had been a thin and nagging wisp of sound before, grew markedly louder; so much so that the extravagant denizens of the city began to look at him askance as they passed. He glowered back at them, lifting his chin. But I could feel how he quaked at the prospect of being challenged by those with strength and experience far beyond his own. His heartbeat quickened, too, at the realization that in Nautilus my scream was not reserved exclusively for his ears. I suppose he had regarded it a mere figment brought on by his guilt, likely to fade once he composed himself.

And then there was the matter of my spirit. On being yanked so rudely from my person it had unspooled like a ball of yarn batted about by cats. In such disorder had my unsuspecting killer carried me to Nautilus.

The atmosphere of Nautilus is not at all the fresh and wind-scoured air of my home. Instead it is a positive miasma of enchantment, as unwholesome as the breath of a fetid marsh. And its effects, as I then discovered, are hardly predictable.

My spirit battened on that uncanny wind, or perhaps there was a sort of reaction analogous to those of chemistry. Again, this was through no desire of mine, or indeed of Gus's. Neither of us could have foreseen the dreadful consequences of his actions. Only a few hours previous, my intentions for the day had been to inform Gus of my engagement, then set to the week's baking and study my Thucydides while the dough was rising. Writhing up as a wraith, pulsing endlessly back and forth across death's threshold, had not been among my plans.

But so it was, and so I was. A sinuous female figure, recognizably my own, spun up from Gus's hands as he flung them protectively before his face. My lower extremities caught on the back of his spine, and there they stayed, so that I flapped above his head. I could see my own hands, sleeves, billowing skirts, all winking frantically between a white-limned darkness and a black-shot pallor. Gus shrieked in wild dread, and I myself was put out by the development. My father's church and the Spiritualists seemed to be equally misinformed on the question of what life after death was like.

If I am honest, I was as much offended by my scream as Gus seemed to be; it felt too much like an admission of hurt, of vulnerability. I would have liked to insist that nothing he did, *nothing*, not even my murder, had the power to distress me, but my scream said otherwise. If such feelings sound absurd in retrospect, nonetheless they were mine.

Gus twisted his head so that we faced each other, or nearly so, our confrontation torqued and oblique. We stood in a shimmering alley, pressed between two curvilinear walls as finely fluted as a river skirting boulders. I had known that morning that any future meetings I might have with Gus would be awkward, but this was rather worse than expected. How had I ever regarded that pointed sallow face, those pale green furtive eyes, with affection?

Gus's scream and mine hung entwined for a moment, but then his voice ceased with a gasp. He leaned back on the wall, one foot propped on its alabaster froth, and crossed his arms over his chest—a very impudent pose, I thought, given the enormity of his guilt. I did not slide into the wall, as popular tales had taught me to expect. Instead the wall's curve pushed me over his head, so that I draped willow-like into his view.

"Catherine," Gus said at last. "Do you see it now? Do you see the mistake you made, in failing to love me? Why else have we been granted this reprieve, unless to give you another chance?"

All sorts of furious rejoinders occurred to me, but I was sadly unable to pronounce any of them. As I have noted already, I could not stop screaming. Looking about me, it seemed that this city was built in its entirety of change, of volatility, trapped in awful stasis, and so it seemed to be with me. I remained seized by my dying scream, unable to resolve into silence. I hung flickering on the brink. Nautilus preserved my death but would not let me die.

Abhorrent city.

Gus had the small sense to take my scream as a refusal, for he nodded curtly.

"You say that now, Catherine. You say that now. But I am no longer that frail and gentle boy begging for your notice. I have come into my power, as you see. And my quest for power—it was *always* for you. It is *still* for you. This great love of mine, which endures beyond death itself—what else is my power for, but to bring love to its full flowering?"

His love endured beyond *my* death, he meant. Ah, but would it endure beyond his own? I wished to propose that we make a trial of it, then and there. My scream again proved a great humiliation, for it blocked my throat of all else. As if I were a wordless thing, empty and bellowing, and not still and acutely myself—

Gus, meanwhile, considered my apparition. I billowed like a flag some feet above him, my colors flashing from dove to crow, and would have given anything to sit sensibly by the hearth and resume my reading. He worked up his courage and passed his hand through me. I made the disappointing discovery that I could not corrode his flesh with the acid of my anger. He was unharmed.

It did occur to me, though hazily, to wonder why I interacted differently with his matter than that of the walls. I learned in time.

"But what are you, after all?" Gus mused.

Was it not obvious?

"What is it I love? I suppose you were attractive enough, but my love is plainly not conditional on your person."

Since my person lay dead, he meant. I thought of how Old Darius had mocked me as *the object*. There is nothing as utterly object as a corpse, its materiality distilled by the subject's deletion. Gus, in short, had found me not *object* enough, and had amended that deficiency.

"No: Catherine is an *essence*." Gus had begun to pace the alley, head bent and hands laced at the small of his back. My reluctant ghost dragged along with him, a black-and-pale flame that gusted and bobbed. "And the nature of that essence is that Catherine can and must love me! There are other qualities, of course: a refusal to accept the world's terms, a certain brisk clarity. But the love, the love is *definitive*. If Catherine did not love me, it was only that she failed to be her truest self. No wonder I found it necessary to set aside—that particular framing of Catherine, then."

Set aside? It took me a moment to understand. His theft of my life, my future, the quiet tenderness of Thomas's arms, that was a *setting aside*? All at once my scream felt less like confession, more like intention.

"And if that essence did not inhere in her living body, does it not follow that I can find it elsewhere? If *this* Catherine failed, might not another succeed? Can her fault be redeemed, but in a different form?"

I could hardly parse the implications of this speech. What, did he mean to hunt down girls of what he considered my model and extract love from one of them, and as *redemption*? Did he think he could slake his pride with someone elected as my substitute? The idea was so ridiculous that I rocked in disbelief. It was no wonder that I had accepted Thomas Skelley in preference to Gus; Thomas surely considered me an end in myself.

He twisted again and looked at me. He looked at me, and I, who could not speak, looked back. People speak of the language of the eyes. Well, their vocabulary is cruelly limited.

But hatred my eyes could convey, quite clearly. Gus recoiled, which only pitched me toward him. He let out a gratifying shriek.

Then he recovered himself.

"I can do it again," he said, with a certain flat viciousness. "Catherine, I'm warning you."

What, kill me? I could not burst into bitter laughter at what struck me as a difficult undertaking. Then, oh, then I understood.

"If I can find you again in others, if I can grant you anew the opportunity to correct your fault—then I can also kill you again if you disappoint me. Do you understand? I can still be merciful. But that mercy must be *earned*."

On hearing these words, on understanding that my personal murder was not enough to satisfy him, rage buzzed through me. It swarmed like a cloud of insects dense enough to blacken the skies. I was not literally blinded or deafened by my feelings, but I might as well have been, for I forgot everything that my private darkness did not encompass. I forgot Gus's voice, even while he prattled on, forgot the shining architecture, forgot even to pine for the pulse and twinkle of a flock of sparrows bursting from the grass. I felt myself transformed into an explosion of black heat that swept all else away.

For some timeless time, I hovered in the nearest approximation to a swoon that a ghost can attain. But as you may have gathered, that state of unconsciousness wasn't nearly as permanent as certain other states I might mention.

My story emerges now from death. It comes in search of its own ending, hated reader.

And it comes in search of you.

Angus at the Door

There has to be a reason I do these things. My eyes sort of slur into waking. I'm upright, a backpack hunched over my shoulders and my hand lifted, forefinger up and eager—not what you'd expect for someone who's been asleep. I didn't just ring the doorbell next to this pale green, rust-mottled door, did I? I have a feeling that maybe I did. So it might be good if I could remember what I'm doing here before somebody opens it?

Something's clutched in my left hand. Phone. I swing it reflexively in front of my face, and there's a text message bubbled blue on the screen. It's from someone named Tom Monroe, and I don't think I recall anyone with that name, unless maybe I do? *Angus hey buddy heard you're in Chicago! My mom's friend Carmen has jobs in her warehouse. 2021 West Street. Just show up.*

Below that there's a reply, which I presumably typed myself: *Thanks buddy. On it.*

A job! What a valid, incontestable, normal-person reason to be standing here. I love it.

This is definitely a warehouse in front of me. Those skanky mylar parallelograms are clearly marked with *2021*. And Chicago? That seems like useful information too. The clouds hang low above, sallow and heavy with September heat.

The door jerks open. A woman looking fifty-some is standing there, all square jaw and boxy shoulders and giant puff of hair as thick and sticky-looking as freshly poured tar, but with more gray. Brilliant blue eyes screwed into a censorious scowl. "Carmen?" I say, but it's obvious she can't be anyone else. "Tom Monroe sent me. He said you need workers? I'm Angus Farrow."

There. I'm pleased with myself for getting it together so quickly, for acting so much like people are supposed to do.

But Carmen throws back her head and laughs. "*You're* Gus?" It's a hilarious piece of information. She laughs again and looks me over, shaking her head in what seems like disbelief.

I laugh, too, just to cover the awkwardness of it all. "I really prefer Angus. I guess Tom told you about me?"

Another head shake. "*Angus.* Well, in that case you're hired, little boy. Come on in and we'll get you settled."

"Just like that?" I say. And then, "Settled?"

"Just like that," Carmen agrees, already walking away into a mush of vague shadows. I hurry to follow her. "And settled, because the job comes with an apartment. Nothing too nice, but it'll keep you in the running. That plus minimum wage. I don't expect an argument."

"Are you sure you don't have me mixed up with someone else?"

Carmen laughs again. "You're Gus Farrow. It's a small, stale, indigestible fact. Not something I'm likely to find confusing."

Angus, I think. But it seems like I've already lost that argument. She's walking away, and I scamper after her.

"It's not that complicated of a job," she says without looking around. "You follow instructions, you don't screw it up on any kind of major scale, and you don't bitch where I can hear you. Why would I waste time interviewing you over *that*?"

Catherine at Home

To call my removal to Nautilus an unsettling transition would hardly do it justice. I had lost my life and my person and become a shrieking hant, flapping unwillingly after my sullen murderer, and besides that been dragged to a city I found highly uncongenial. From a lovely day in July, 1859, from my insignificant little town in western New York, I had passed to its luminous nowhere, its bleary nowhen. Time as we know it does not apply in Nautilus, so I cannot say how long it was that insensate rage took up all my attention and spared none for my circumstances. I seemed to spin in my own flashing black and shine, detached from all external happenings.

But at a certain point, I woke from the violence of my own feelings and looked about me, a bit numb and drained at first: at the pearlescent city, and at Gus's doings within it.

However harshly I assessed my old friend's character, even I could not call him lacking in diligence. Gus had secured a large room—I gathered from scraps of conversation that money as I knew it was not required for that purpose, only the same uncanny powers that had obtained his citizenship—and set to work.

"I have the advantage, dearest Catherine," Gus hissed at me, as if continuing a conversation that had never truly stopped. "You see, I age only when I leave Nautilus. If I make my visits sparingly, I can endure here for centuries of ordinary time—more! In that span I can achieve anything."

Of his ambitions, I knew only what he had told me on my arrival here: that he meant to extract love from young women he deemed my surrogates, or scatter death among them if love was not forthcoming. On the former count he was right to think me skeptical. On the latter I did not have the luxury of doubt.

He paced, yanking my spirit after him. His pivots set me wagging like washing on the line. How I hated the bend of his neck with its pale bristles, the sharpness of his steps, the pretended wisdom of his somberly shaken head! Around us the glowing walls rippled and light spun in their depths, but even then I had glimpsed enough of Nautilus to guess that his room was modest by local standards.

He had not bothered with furniture, nor had any been supplied beyond a pallet on the floor. His clothes lay about in heaps of variable cleanliness, and he had an ill-fed look that made his pointed face positively vulpine. The diffuse glow of the room erased every trace of shadow and made his dirty underthings appear to float, dimensionless and bright. It also showed the stains with eerie emphasis, like a sort of reverse phosphorescence.

"Look!" he exclaimed, pointing across the room at what appeared to be a hovering blot near one fluid wall. "See what I can do already!"

The blot was not on the wall, but perhaps a yard before it. It was low and hunched, like a child with its arms wrapped around its knees. Rather than being flat, as I had first supposed, the thing was sculptural and translucent, a shadow inflated into rounded cylinders and bulges. My insubstantial being churned with terrible cold, though I did not yet understand what I was seeing.

Then the blot raised its head and looked up at me with eyes like greenish dewdrops, its mouth wide and imploring. I would have liked to scream at the sight, but had no way to differentiate that shriek from the one I was emitting already.

I knew that face. The pointed nose, poking far forward of both brows and chin, the round eyes tinted with the palest green arrogance, the tow-blond bristling hair that no brush could induce to lie smooth: I was looking at Gus himself as he had appeared at four or five years of age.

The child-apparition opened its mouth as if to keen, but no sound came out. The air tensed with its silent plaint. The grown Gus turned from the mournful little thing to me, his head nodding with furious satisfaction.

"You observe, Catherine? I *made* that. With nothing but the abilities you reviled, I made the semblance of a living being!"

I would have liked to inform him that this ghost of his own past was so evidently miserable that even I, who wished him all the ill in the world, nonetheless pitied it.

Why had he made it, though? What use could he find for this creature?

Gus was staring fixedly at me. I realized he was inspecting my flickering visage for indications of what he considered proper awe, and found it wanting.

"Future versions can be made more substantial," Gus told me in defensive tones. "I'm still practicing with appearances, but once I've made them thoroughly persuasive I can begin collecting materials to give them all the solidity of actual persons. I've seen what masters of the form can do with these projections; no one uninitiated would ever imagine they were anything but living men and women. *No one,* Catherine. No matter how clever she thought herself."

Tethered together as Gus and I were, had I seen such beings before? I tried to search my memory, but it was no use; I had been too remote, too obliterated, to recall any examples of what Gus might mean. But now I was back, aware, and curious. I found that I wanted to act again, to put my arms around his creature, to claw out Gus's throat. My bodiless state mocked me, restrained me at every turn. I could neither embrace nor assault.

Gus had said that he would age only outside of Nautilus, in the warm and breathing world now lost to me. And he had intimated as well that he meant to live a very long time. I considered the possible uses to which embodied echoes of himself might be put, and felt an icy clenching. I thought he wanted emissaries, beings who could return to the world in his stead, and I feared I could guess why.

But a child? How could this dismal boy, all jagged features and inaudible whining, serve Gus's purpose?

Gus was nodding again as he turned his back on me. He approached the huddled child-thing with a few curt steps, and I of course billowed along with him. Gus dropped to one knee and stretched out a hand to his feeble simulacrum. For a moment I entertained the hope that he meant to comfort it as I longed to do. Enemy or not, *human* or not, the sight of a wretched child was unendurable to me.

"Here, Angus! Come to me at once."

The little Angus showed a marked reluctance to obey. Meanwhile I considered how Gus had never allowed anyone but Margo to call him by his full name.

Gus leaned forward impatiently. There were no corners to the room—nor to any other in Nautilus—but its scrolling contours still served to trap the little wraith in a hollow. A *projection,* Gus had called it. An image that might be made flesh.

Gus grabbed it by its shoulder and yanked it forward. It writhed and thrashed, but without much energy. Perhaps it knew already the futility of resistance.

Gus's two hands spread on the dim head and chest; he had always had very long hands relative to his build, blond and deft with prominent bones: a pianist's hands. The Angus's small shadowy mouth opened in hollow protest, and I flapped above in the futile conviction that I must do *something* on the instant.

Then Gus's hands squeezed in. The apparition crumpled. It looked for a moment like strange glassy paper with the image of a terrified child printed on it, or like a child-shaped balloon of fine silk deflating. I could still see one green dewdrop eye staring directly at me in voiceless longing, as if I were its last hope.

Gus wadded it up like a handkerchief and stuffed it in his left trouser pocket. I had a last glimpse of dim fingers clutching at his wrist, then it was gone.

My scream remained the same, much as I would have preferred to scream more loudly.

Gus glanced at me over his shoulder. "The creation of such beings is demanding," he explained, and I detected a note of embarrassment. "It draws much less on my resources if I reuse the power invested in the old ones to make the new."

It was at this juncture that a knock sounded, oddly resonant. It was not a knock at the door, for I realized in surprise that no such thing could be seen in the room. Rather there was an area of wall defined by a lintel and doorstep but otherwise identical to the rest, and under that lintel an opalescent light spread in concentric circles that pulsed in time with the knock. The wall then wavered and admitted a figure.

A minotaur. In a dandyish frock coat of bright peacock blue. Had

I been able I would have burst into uncontrolled laughter, and tears as well, at such a visitor arriving so soon after the unfeeling destruction of the shadow-child. Was it still aware, still in some way itself, where it sat crushed against Gus's hip?

The minotaur recoiled slightly and turned an appraising gaze on me. "No wonder no one will take the rooms near yours, Gus," he said, nearly shouting over my permanent clamor, then gave a low chuckle. "How could they possibly sleep with all this racket? It would cost a fortune to be forever paying for silencing spells; no one would put themselves in such a position if they could help it. And it must be exceedingly awkward at parties. There's nothing worse than a woman who doesn't know when to shut her mouth, eh?"

With that he clapped Gus on the back with loathsome bonhomie. The blow reverberated from Gus's shoulders into me, so that I pitched windily beneath the ceiling.

"Oh, I can go *nowhere*. The number of invitations I've had to turn down, only because she can't be quiet—" Gus waved his hands as if all these unattended dinners and balls hung about him like a cloud of gnats.

"I'm sure. Your talent has attracted attention already. In Nautilus power is the only currency, and if you are not rich yet, it seems likely that effort will make you so in time." The hairy mouth bent into an ingratiating smile, quite human in character. I could not justify the conviction, but I felt certain that I was looking at a man, albeit one with magical abilities like Gus's, and no authentic monster.

"I'm not pursuing my studies in the interest of anything as coarse as wealth or social position," Gus said loftily, contradicting the complaints uttered only moments before. "I have a calling."

He raised his chin. In the vaporous glow of his room his profile stood out, sharp and brittle as the edge of a broken plate. How thin he was!

For the first time it occurred to me that Gus's death might spell release from my unspeakable suspension. I looked at his sunken cheeks with new interest. What could I do to hurry matters along?

"Of course you do," the minotaur soothed. He cast about with bobbing horns as if seeking someone to gore, though I suppose he only wanted a chair. He shifted uncomfortably. "But what you are attempting is no simple feat, Mr. Farrow. If I understand your objectives correctly, a projection that lasts only a few days will not serve. Neither will one that lacks bodily substance. Even more difficult, you will need to endow your creations with minds of their own, with a certain amount of education, and with enough memories to convince them of their own reality. It might take dozens of attempts before you have one ready to commit to the field, even assuming that you can obtain the materials."

The word *materials* was delivered with a slippery emphasis I did not like.

"I don't see why they require independent minds or memories," Gus rejoined fretfully. I noted that he had no argument with the other items listed. "The appearance should suffice."

"It won't." The bovine eyes rolled toward Gus's dingy pallet with a look of combined longing and revulsion. That gigantic horned head was no doubt burdensome.

"Why not?" Gus demanded. "I have work enough to do on their appearance and durability without worrying about what they *think*. They belong to me, and they have only to follow my orders."

"You told me that your Catherine was clever. Clever above all else. A poor girl who taught herself Latin and Greek, who was fascinated by natural history. Or did I misunderstand you?" The creature at last stopped swiveling about and settled for leaning on the nearest wall, then glanced at me again. I noted that the wall now supported him; was it permeable only where there was a suggestion of an entrance? His immense nostrils narrowed. "I grant that she gives no particular impression of wit at present."

Didn't I? Well, the minotaur gave the impression of carrying an absolute labyrinth of self-satisfied dullness about with it, as a snail transports its shell.

"Oh, she was! Catherine was a lighthouse in the wastes to me. She was the flash that glides through the dark, that looks *through* in any direction. The excitement I used to feel when she had trained her attention on any question at all, as I waited to hear what she would say—it was exquisite."

Oh, was Gus still moved to lyricism on the subject of my perfections? How nice to be remembered so fondly.

"And you are seeking to win her love, are you not? At least, the love of some reasonable facsimile, since hers is no longer"—the snout vibrated delicately—"a realistic goal?"

"And?" Gus was beginning to fidget. His left hand contracted in his pocket and the fabric bulged as if his fingers were worrying something inside it.

"The heart of such a woman won't be won by a puppet. That ought to be obvious. Your projections will need freedom of thought and action and a fair conviction of their own humanity, or these not-quite-Catherines you envision will recoil at the first word they speak."

Gus's shoulders slumped and his eyes turned skyward, with exactly the exasperated air my mother would have assumed at the sight of a freshly washed nightgown flung into the mud.

"That will require an entirely separate course of study."

"Indeed it will." The minotaur looked at me again, his mouth contorting in a bestial approximation of a smile. He presumably imagined that his form conveyed all the terror of myth brought to life, but to me he was never more than a cow in a coat. "Hardly anyone has achieved a truly independent mentality in their projections—and most of the claims that *have* been made don't hold up on examination. You can expect decades of labor ahead of you."

A huffle escaped Gus's lips; he sounded like an expiring horse. "Then what course do you recommend? If what I intend is really so difficult—but I can't let that put me off!"

"Oh, your dedication is admirable, no doubt. Continue practicing with children; their minds are simpler. Once you've mastered the projection of a thinking, dreaming child, you can turn your hand to young men, even change and refine their faces if you like. A pity you can't consult Catherine as to her preferences."

Practice. I wondered how many infantile wraiths Gus had already crushed like sketches that hadn't come off, and how many more would cringe away from him in vain. I thought I could feel the little thing's suffering like a vibration humming in his pocket, fancied that I caught the glint of a welling eye.

Gus, meanwhile, drew himself up, no doubt offended by the insinuation that I might have liked him better with a different appearance. He flashed a glance at me that was positively plaintive, as if my ghost might be persuaded to stop screaming long enough to reassure him of his personal attractions.

"And there was already the bother of obtaining the materials." Gus was fretting outright now.

The minotaur's lips flattened as he repressed a smile. This was the moment he'd been anticipating, I realized; he had induced Gus's weariness at the prospect of his undertaking on purpose, so that any offer of assistance would be received eagerly.

"Possibly I can help you there." An outright grin opened on blocky teeth. "The occasional Athenian youth isn't too much to spare for my friends."

Gus looked sharply at that, as indeed did I. "On what consideration?"

"Nothing just now. Possibly you can repay the favor in the future."

Gus was not so easily put off. "I cannot possibly spare talens for you in any significant amounts. My own projects require every drop I can muster. Already I barely sleep. Instead of resting I'm always *drawing* from myself, and using all my concentration to do so."

"As to that, you have a tremendous source of wealth close at hand." The tone was not lost on me, jocularity half concealing the fervent intent behind.

I could not guess what source he was referring to until Gus glanced up at me, his lips pursed in distaste. "That would be most unseemly. Possibly even dangerous, if I understand the mechanism correctly."

The minotaur smiled. "Well, then, we can forget the question of payment for now—though many ghosts make an excellent wellspring, depending on the type. All that bottled fury packs a punch!" Then his eyes rolled sidelong at me and his lips flattened in concern. "The walls *do* repel her, I assume? She doesn't pass through?"

"Through the walls? No, she doesn't. I hadn't considered—"

"The walls recognize anyone—or anything—seeping magic. She's definitely generating talens, then."

Gus gave a startled laugh. "The walls mistake her for a *citizen*? They think my poor Catherine is paying *taxes*?"

"She is, in effect," the minotaur said with studied carelessness. "Not that it alters her legal status, and that's very much to your benefit. Ghosts are nonentities under the law, so you can do as you like with your Catherine. Shall we meet at the Nimble Fire soon and discuss this further?"

"That would mean carrying her through the streets. It's only when I return to the unworld that no one seems to hear or see her. She's quieter in my ears there as well."

The *unworld*. In all its beauty, intricacy, splendor, that was what he called it. A single fallen leaf, a bit of robin's eggshell in the grass, I rated more precious than this whole enchanted city. The sheer waste of it all choked me: the waste of my life, of the child, of vast power turned to nothing good or useful.

The minotaur shrugged. "I advise you to give up your seclusion regardless. You are hardly the only citizen encumbered in such a manner. Charles Rollins, for one, has a minuscule sky-blue child, no bigger than a lizard, forever attempting to wring his neck and wailing. So Charles wears a muffler and gets on with his business."

Naturally he did, I thought. So many things were different here in Nautilus, but society's habit of winking at monsters—that was quite unchanged.

Gus was nodding in acknowledgment of the minotaur's wisdom.

They exchanged more pleasantries, more assurances, and then our visitor left, the wall rippling behind him.

"Terrible vanity," Gus muttered at the wall, and then confirmed all my guesses regarding the minotaur's original form. "Imagine the expense of keeping up such an excessive appearance—an entire bull's head, and probably improvements to his physique as well! It must drain his magic at a dreadful rate. One would think there were no *serious* matters to attend to."

I would have liked to tell him that he was mistaking his own cruelty for gravity; that everything he himself did was as senseless, as wasteful and absurd, as that bull's head.

There was a brief lull while Gus shifted about, oddly furtive, as if there were something he wished to do unobserved. Several times he glanced at me, perhaps hoping I would do him the courtesy of disappearing. He was so frank on the subject of his proposed crimes that this new discomfort baffled me. What could he intend that was so much more vile than what I knew already?

And here a change in my own outlook struck me: I was *anxious* what Gus meant to do. I cared, and cared to see if I could, what? Stop him? I understood then that withdrawing as I had was no longer an option for me. Perhaps I could do nothing, but that was irrelevant. I must observe, must consider any avenues I could find.

I must try. Thrash, flail, or fail as I might; it was all as nothing compared to that child's green eye squeezed between his fingers.

At last he sighed loudly and began stuffing his soiled linens into a sack.

"My mother and father are away," Gus informed me. "Visiting for a few weeks with my Hathaway cousins. We're going to see Margo." He paused, scowling. "Don't *look* at me like that!"

Oh, Margo! So she was spending her old age scrubbing her fugitive nephew's underclothes? I could not scream with laughter, so I simply screamed.

Catherine in Hiding

I've alluded already to the friendship with Gus that animated my childhood. Those memories now appear to me transformed, their homely fabric ablaze with anger, though at the time I know I felt very differently. Can I still give an honest accounting of those hours, one unsinged by retrospective rage?

My father groomed the Farrows' horses, my mother took in their laundry, and I myself was always popping in and out of the hedge that delineated their lawn. The Farrows and their house were grand in a small way, enough to put them among the preeminent families of our middling town. It was the sort of small grandeur that twists and yaps like a small dog, predisposed to bite when it feels itself impinged upon. When their young son formed a stubborn attachment to the daughter of their servants, it was a positive trodding upon the unpleasant beast's tail. But this is getting ahead of my story.

I cannot recall when Gus and I met, for we were no more than infants then. So many of my earliest memories include him that I cannot put an order to them, or say with certainty which came first, so I will begin with a recollection that gains its primacy through vividness rather than sequence. It finds the two of us hiding behind a large leather armchair in a corner of the Farrows' library—for their small grandeur swelled far enough to include such a haven—poring together over the colored plates in a book, rustling the protective veils of tissue. It was a volume on marine life, and the illustrations were of polyps and medusas, jewel-toned and frilled and looking not at all like animals as I then understood them. They seemed too fanciful, too wonderful to be real. I observed as much.

"They're only bits of jelly bobbing in the sea, though. That's what my father says. If they were *really* wonderful they'd be the size of cart horses. And they'd fly." Gus delivered these words in lordly tones that made my admiration feel too cheaply bestowed, so that my gaze lingered on the images with a certain shamefacedness—as if I ought not to love them so dearly, as if that love showed me poor and ignorant, awed by those things that Gus could take for granted—

There it is, my dead woman's rage refracting through the past. At the time, though, Gus appeared to me colored by the brilliance of the medusas, for it was through him that I had access to such marvels, and the wings he wished to give them seemed to sprout from his own shoulders.

"Are there any that fly?" I asked him, with undue faith that he must have the answer.

He lifted his chin in a way that I later learned meant he was concocting nonsense, and he was about to reply when we were interrupted by the whisper of oiled hinges. A step sounded in the library and we caught our breaths and huddled closer, knowing that his parents would not be pleased to find me there. But the snappish cadence of those footfalls calmed us an instant later, and we jostled and tittered.

"The mice are nibbling knowledge again," Gus's aunt Margo observed, not bothering to peer behind the armchair, "as they no doubt did even in the Garden. The Good Book neglects to inform us what became of those wise mice, fat on the windfall of good and evil. But you may be certain that their stomachs pained them mightily."

Gus and I both were stifling our laughter by then, and rather unsuccessfully. We knew from experience that Margo's assumed severity was nothing to fear.

"Dreadful animals," Margo pursued, "such mice grown too knowing for their own good. Why, I find it necessary to stop their mouths with gingerbread or they will cheep their sophistries without ceasing! Here, mice!"

At that inducement we tumbled out from our concealment, climbing over each other by turns. The book thudded out with us, and Margo snatched it up and looked it over.

"The tissue covering this plate is creased. Your father must not see that his fine volume has been damaged, my bright boy. I will put it right with a touch of the iron."

Gus was habitually cool and distant with his parents, who reciprocated his reserve with a chill of their own. But his arms were already wound around Margo's knees and his face nuzzled into her skirts. I stood near the chair, bashful now that I felt myself hemmed in my own singularity—the eldest Bildstein girl, who ought to have been in the kitchen—rather than part of the protective tangle Gus and I formed together. I fidgeted under Margo's sharp pale gaze, which held me as if its immaterial rays were so much steel.

"You will discover that the world suits you poorly, Catherine Bildstein," Margo observed at last. I was taken aback by the softness of her voice, for Margo's speech was habitually a snapping, springing thing. "A girl of too much daring, who hungers too much after the sort of truths that don't get the washing on the line. What will you find to do with such a spirit except lose it?"

I did not fully apprehend Margo's meaning, but I surely caught her menace. It seemed a betrayal that she had coaxed me from my hiding place with gingerbread only to jab me with this bleak, incomprehensible warning in its stead. It felt to me as if, had I only stayed concealed behind the leather chair, neither Margo's words nor their import could have reached me. An inarticulate wish for eternity bubbled up in me: to stay enclosed in my naive moment, in the must of leather and the glint of colored inks, where I would never have to decipher the cold codes muttered by adults.

I reared back and glowered at her with childish resentment. "I helped hang the washing already!"

Gus pulled his face from her skirts and stared from her to me, and back again. "What do you mean?" he demanded. "What are they going to do to Catherine?"

"Only what they do to every girl like her." Margo's usual tone was back, all brusque plucked strings and leaping catlike rhythms. "Especially ones from working families, as she is, and I was as well, though of course we don't speak of that old *misalliance* where your mother and father can hear us, Angus, my dear. Now, children, if you proceed with me to the kitchen you'll find gingerbread fresh out of the oven, and no one will presume to tell me that I must slice it thin."

But Gus was not to be put off so easily—though for my part, I would have been glad to set her uneasy words aside. "Then I won't let them! *Whatever* it is. They'll just have to do it to somebody else instead."

Margo gave a half smile, as if she were pleased at Gus's fervor—as I very much suspect she was. What exquisite amalgam of charity and spite was it that moved her, young as Gus and I both were, to begin this careful nudging of his inclinations? At that time I knew only that Margo was an inmate of the Farrows' house, and that she brought to it her own disruptive vividness. Later I would come to know that she had married Gus's wayward great-uncle Clement who had then died and left her a young and childless widow, awkwardly dependent on the family, stuffed into odd corners like the unwelcome legacy she was. And so she had remained.

I did not understand what made her spark so, as if she were always in danger of setting fire to their placidity. Now I would hazard that the quality of her fury in life was not so different from that of mine in death. She knew a bit too much of the eternal stasis that now rules me, and that I was once foolish enough to wish for.

That is, she was already dead in her own way, and it lent her a paradoxical vitality.

"And what will you do to stop them, my dear boy? Here is the world given to us, and rather more of it is given to some than to others. A plant can't grow large in too small a pot, can it?"

I parsed her meaning somewhat better now. My cheeks flushed hot and my eyes were veiled by watery distortions. I cast about for ways to escape the fate Margo threatened; could I be a teacher? I was about to voice this novel ambition when Gus interrupted, and I saw that his eyes brimmed with tears.

"But Catherine can't be small! Can I—give her enough—I mean, a big enough flowerpot?" His words were fumbling, but his meaning still came through. And, however naively, I felt as if Gus had rescued me. Not with the promised flowerpot, for I shied from the image. But the words *Catherine can't be small* affected me like an unlooked-for reprieve. With his gaze on me, I felt an intimation of scope.

No one else in my small world would have seen in me a potential for largeness—or if they had, they would have wanted to suppress it. I looked gratefully at Gus's tear-streaked face.

"Can you?" Margo asked pointedly. "You will need a will of steel to do so, my dear."

It was on that strained note that we three slipped down to the kitchen, where Gus and I were fed the promised gingerbread along with blackberries and cream. I watched Margo with a distrust wholly new to me, one that I later came to know was misplaced—for Margo surely considered herself my ally—then yet later I knew to have been very apt—for her alliance betrayed me at my core—and may revisit still again, here in my death undying.

For all that nothing significant ever changes here in the awful brightness of Nautilus, for all that my dying will not resolve and my scream keeps tossing like a beaten rug, changes of thought and perspective are still possible for me. I keep my secret mutability, like that of a dream.

Consider this paradox, my pitiful one: even dead and captive in my twin prisons, I possess far more freedom and more possibility than you do. You can go where you wish, do as you like, but you can't know what you are—whereas I, who can't take a single step, have had ample time to study the ways of my own heart.

Self-knowledge is a map, and no true journey is possible without it.

Angus Searching

The room is on one side of the warehouse, windowless and grubby. I have a new Smurf key ring clutched in one hand. I've gotten a grip on some of the basics now: I'm Angus Farrow, nineteen years old, recent high-school graduate from Clayton, Missouri.

But I can do better than that. I also know why I'm here.

I mean, to get a job and take a stab at independence, obviously, in a real, exciting city. But it's not just that.

I chose Chicago because I had an overwhelming, absurd, completely unjustifiable blast of intuition. It told me that *she's* here.

She? Oh, don't be dense. You know who I mean. I mean love-of-my-life, girl-of-my-dreams, my particular, personal, extra-twinkly star out of all the billions of stars in the sky. So what if assuming she's here isn't logical? I'm stupid and brilliant and nineteen and extremely likely to live forever, and I can go anywhere.

And the way that intuition came to me—it was like a message coming from the past and future at once. So certain, so absolute. As if someone had whispered it straight into my ear. *Chicago. She's out there. Find her, Angus. Claim her love.*

I will, I said. *I will, I will, I will.*

My next stop will be a bookstore, I decide. I need the kinds of books that will impress her when she sees me reading them, sensitive-intellectual books. Because one thing I know for sure about her, she's very, very smart and probably arty.

There's a sharp rap on the door, and Carmen swings it open before I have a chance to react. I'll have to remember to start locking it. "Forgot to give you these, boy-o."

She's holding out a couple of boxes, stacked. The one on top is a matchbox, and the bigger blue box beneath has an illustration of stumpy white emergency candles on it.

"I don't think I need those," I tell her.

"You do, though. We have lots of problems with the power here. Outages almost every night. Just take them, Gussy."

Gus wasn't awful enough for her, I guess.

"Thanks," I say, and lean over to grab the boxes. For some reason, though, I really don't want the damned candles. I have to suppress an impulse to shove them back in her face.

Then she's gone. I drop the candles and the matchbox on the yellow table and hurry to turn the lock before she decides to barge in again.

I sit cross-legged on the mattress and just feel it: *her* presence wheeling through the city outside this crappy warehouse. She grooves the darkness in my head with orbits of trailing light, and then I don't even care what I do or don't remember because I feel so absolutely certain that everything I'm doing is right, that the world is turning just for me and the sky is spinning to snap everything into place, and that my one true love is drinking her coffee right now and watching the sheet of muggy sluggish clouds through a window. She's wondering why she feels like she misses somebody she's never met, and whose name she doesn't know. Misses him intensely.

Don't worry, I want to tell her. *I'm here, I'm coming, and I'll find you before you know it.*

My eyes flutter closed, and I could swear I feel her lips against mine; my kiss is fierce, devouring, while the rush of a river floods my ears. There's a paddling noise, a roar where wind becomes coursing blood, where blood leaps high to become a scroll of red wind. There's a river here in Chicago, of course, but I get the feeling that we're somewhere else, another time and place. As if I've always known her, a hundred years and more before either of us was even born. As if that kiss rumbles through decades, rolling so quickly it blurs, circling around her wherever she goes. A sweetness that always rhymes with itself, and that always makes her mine.

Catherine in the Unworld

Our visit to Margo that evening—for our emergence through Gus's accursed rabbit hole found us bathed in sunset—was surely not the first, only the first of which I was sensible. My screaming voice softened on the instant, and I was surprised by the vibrancy ringing through every note of birdsong. The scent of fermenting apples clouded the golden air. Damson shadows streaked across the grass, and where Gus stepped the grasshoppers burst in such abundance that they nearly gave the impression of splashing water.

Shadows. What a luxury this juxtaposition of violet and amber was, after the diffuse pallor of Nautilus! How marvelous the scattering of tiny creatures, the small lives tumbling along their secret ways beneath the soil! The suspended life of Nautilus seemed a dull and deathly thing in comparison.

And Gus called this the *unworld*. Were the people here therefore *unpeople,* unwomen and unmen? But of course, I realized, that was what Gus thought. Besides himself, only Margo had ever been real to him; I surely hadn't. When my own independent reality had infringed too much on his awareness he had killed me in retaliation.

For being real, and no mere projection.

Gus promptly quit the orchard and its adjacent gardens in favor of slinking along the edge of the woods. The underbrush snarled at his legs, for the only path ran through the grass outside this dusky verge. He tramped on determinedly, cursing under his breath. Even concealed by the scrim of the trees, he twisted often to look over his shoulder, to peer around the trunks for some fancied mob waiting to drag him to justice.

It was in this craven fashion that we drew in sight of the Farrows' house, with its white and petty grandeur marked by dark green shutters, its yellow roses, its maple tree flaring crimson above the east wing's gabled roof. A stooped figure clung to the balustrade in front of the parlor, whose French doors hung ajar. Margo scanned the woods with hawklike expectation, then caught sight of Gus with a visible jolt.

In that small movement I read that her love for Gus was no longer unadulterated. But that was not what startled me.

Gus had murdered me on a fine day in early July, and from all I could see it was now late September or early October. Without giving the matter much thought, I had inferred that three or so months had passed since my death. I had dared to hope that I might glimpse Thomas or Anna, if only at a great distance; that they might sense me and look around, searching for the source of a sweet ache resonant with my name; that my love could somehow translate through the air and brush them with solace.

But with a hundred yards still between us and Margo, I knew at once that not even grief could have aged her so much in such a short time. When I had seen her last she had been an upright, stately woman, old but willowy, her movements swift and definite. Now her posture had a fractured quality, as if the inner force that had sustained her had been flung against a wall. It was clear that time must have allied with heartbreak to bring Margo to this state.

I knew then that I had been dead for years.

I can't say why it mattered to me so much—whether my body was months or centuries in the earth, my life was gone for good—but the realization stung. Time would have done its work and dried the tears of those who loved me long ago. The sense of my presence would mean, not comfort, but a miserable reminder of old grief, best put aside. Thomas might, perhaps, have married someone else; he might have a babe in arms. While I knew I should wish myself utterly forgotten for their sake, I could not find in myself enough generosity to do so.

I wanted to see longing in their eyes, and feel that I remained linked to anyone other than my killer. The pleasure of returning home twisted and struck me with renewed pain.

Gus broke into a run, racing across the lawn to his aunt, and scrambled over the balustrade. His bag of dirty laundry thudded down. "Margo!" he breathed.

"If all your sorcery can't get the stink out of your underclothes, then what use is it, I'd like to know?" Margo sniped by way of greeting. Of course she could not hand off his laundry to a washerwoman, or not without provoking questions.

"Magic is as finite as all other sources of power, Margo. One must consider carefully how one expends it, not waste it on domestic minutiae. If you have an army at your call, you do not set the cavalry to embroidering cushions."

"These greater ends of yours. You haven't seen fit to inform me of what they are, have you, Angus, my boy?"

"Is this how you welcome me home?" Gus rejoined with fond reproach, and swept his aunt into an embrace. She was smaller than formerly, her wispy head resting on his collarbone, though Gus himself was of only middling height.

It galled me to observe any redeeming qualities in my murderer—I would have preferred to keep my loathing pure—but his tenderness for Margo was undeniable. He enfolded her as if her bony frame were some rare and delicate flower, kissed her brow as softly as petals falling. I saw a tear well in Margo's glittering gray eye. She pressed close, though only for a moment.

So she still loved him. Against her better judgment, no doubt, for she must know what he had done. The conjunction of my cooling corpse and Gus's abrupt flight, and on the day after my engagement, was hardly equivocal.

"Come in and eat your supper before you waste to nothing," Margo said, and pushed him away. "I've packed some things for you to take along with you, too, though it's never enough to put any flesh back on your bones. Your magic is eating you alive." She turned away, tugging him through the French doors into the parlor—and in contrast with Nautilus, here I flowed through the wall above the door in just the fashion stories had taught me to expect.

Behind her back, Gus was grinning at her solicitude. Nautilus was a city of many pleasures, I supposed, but coddling was not among them.

His meal was set out on a low table before a cold grate—the evening was too warm for a fire—and it was extensive, roast beef and kidneys, potatoes and stewed peaches. Gus sat and attacked the food at once, and Margo stood watching him with an expression I could not decipher. Sunset gold streaked across the room, knelt against the wall, plumped on the cushions.

Gus kept eating, ravenously. I wondered if the meal had been meant for Margo—she could hardly demand an extra supper from the cook before sending her out of the house. It did not seem to occur to Gus that she might have gone without for his sake.

Margo had not once glanced in my direction, I realized, nor given the slightest flinch at my admittedly subdued screaming. Outside of Nautilus, then, I was both invisible and inaudible to all but Gus, just as he had said. Small wonder that visiting the *unworld* gave him such an appetite. How unconcerned, how happy he looked as he shoved forkfuls of beef into his bulging cheeks!

Margo's hands behind her back knit busily at the air. Something was troubling her, I thought—something more immediate than the strangling of a girl of nineteen however many years before.

"It isn't only for my own plans, you know, that I need to conserve my powers. It's also for your sake that I economize, and in every way I can. It's a disgrace how my parents have—*relegated* you, as if you were nothing but a heap of worn-out skin. I mean to get you out of this dull place. To elevate you to your proper condition."

Margo gave a small start, from which I gathered that the idea was new to her. "Transport me to your fairy-tale city, you mean, Angus? The one so exclusive, as you can't seem to stop telling me, that only sorcerers are allowed to sniff its rarefied air? Why would it take in an old lady with nothing to recommend her but a talent for bitterness? I might as well attempt to reclaim Fort Sumter."

I did not catch the reference. Later I would grow used to experiencing history in a pattern of dashes and elisions, skipping from one year to another. The trick, I find, is never to be surprised.

Angus had lifted a forkful of scalloped potatoes halfway to his mouth. But at this he dropped his fork and leapt up to clasp Margo by her shoulders.

The fork did not fall. Instead it maintained a wobbling levitation, though the potatoes escaped and splattered on the carpet. Gus was oblivious.

"You are a queen among rabble," he informed her somberly, his lichen-green eyes fixed on her face. She kept her own gray gaze stubbornly lowered. "Margo, I beseech you, don't make the mistake of seeing yourself as these—these squabbling goblins see you! In Nautilus you would envision yourself truly, I'm sure of it. That's the reason I must bring you there, as soon as I can manage it."

A *queen*. Gus had often described me in terms similarly exalted. My realm had proved to be bipartite: a span of air hitched to the shoulders of a murderer and a span of cold clay dancing with grass. I did not suppose that anyone envied me my rule.

Margo tottered, slightly but noticeably. Was she feeling faint?

"I don't anticipate becoming a witch, Angus, able to turn frogs into castles or whatever else might impress those examiners who approve your city's new arrivals. Not in the time I have remaining to me."

The word *remaining* was etched in acid. I understood at once, but Gus seemed not to notice.

"You need not worry about time! Once I take you to Nautilus, all this nonsense of aging and illness will stop where it is. As long as you never set foot outside the city, you can endure as long as it does." He laughed, and the notes were jerky with nerves. Margo pulled from his grasp and started at the sight of the hovering fork. Fragments of scarlet sunset winked on its tines.

"*Angus.* There's a catch to bringing off your delusions of me as some grand old Morgan le Fay in the making. Remember, won't you, the citizenship requirements you like to boast about? I don't meet them."

"I'm aware that you don't—though you might develop a slight magical capacity with enough effort. But Nautilus is like anywhere else in that respect. Officials can be careless with the paperwork."

The minotaur had said that magic was currency in the sorcerers' city. I understood at once that Gus would have to save up a great deal, however that task might be accomplished, to pay a bribe of this magnitude. So, of course, did Margo. She'd always had a fine ear for matters related to human corruptibility.

"If properly persuaded, you mean. Letting in an old lady with no more magic than a mayfly has in her—that won't come cheaply."

"What wouldn't I pay for your sake? No one else alive is worth a fig to me." At this Gus noticed the suspended fork with precisely the irritable cry of a miser who finds he's left the candles burning. The fork dropped with a clatter. "I did not even mean—ugh, and these small expenditures add up so quickly! I must be more careful."

Margo laughed, quite as horribly as I might have done. "And are you rich, in that unnatural city of yours? What vast wealth do you have to fling in their venal faces? Angus, my dear boy, I know your intentions are loving. But they're also ridiculous."

"I am not rich yet." Gus had started pacing, his supper forgotten. Beyond the balustrade, I watched the last traces of crimson sunset submerging into blue. "But I have both natural aptitude and unparalleled perseverance combining to make me so, and you are not so old that we need be in any rush. Soon enough I'll be able to offer you the life you always should have had—where wishes are horses indeed, and even sprout wings! You will ride above the glowing towers—"

This speech was also familiar to me. Now that I was expired, it seemed, Gus had cast the feverish visions once reserved for me around Margo's stooped shoulders instead.

She stood shaking her head with marked impatience while Gus attended only to his own mania. But at last he seemed to truly see the gesture.

His eyes widened, full of liquid light, and his face went gray with understanding. It had taken him long enough.

"I will see nothing, my boy, except the cracks in the ceiling over my bed. Perhaps the shiny pink snout of some hired nurse, snuffling about me. And even that much won't be mine for long."

Gus's hands were clenched. "That can't be. I won't allow it."

"You seem to believe that the sun requires your permission to set, and the corpse solicits your approval before it rots." Margo had caught hold of the back of that sofa where Gus had been sitting. She looked very pale, a white rag straining to keep hold of human form.

"They do! Or they will, at any rate. Margo, you have no idea of the feats that are in my reach. Once I carry you to Nautilus—it isn't timeless in the strict sense, but the time we have there is not the kind that slants toward the grave! And if I cannot pay the fees at this very moment, I— My other endeavors can wait until we have you comfortably established, I will sacrifice even my mission for the time being—"

Margo kept her gaze fixed on the sofa's melon-colored brocade. I could feel how desperately Gus wanted those gray eyes turned toward him, warm and confident and flooded with gratitude. He would say anything, I knew, spout any lie to secure that look, and then attack nature in an attempt to twist his words true.

"Angus. I will soon be dead, my boy, and making myself at home in some suitable perdition—for I don't suppose there's ever been enough charity in my heart that the beyond will spare any for me. The world will roll along well enough without me, and you will be obliged to accept that death isn't yours to command."

Gus's lips tightened in a smile at once pained and vicious. "It was once. Why shouldn't it be so again?"

Margo at last looked at him. "I seem to recall that only worked in one direction."

"Ah." He bared his teeth in a strained grin. "That was over three years ago. My abilities have improved since then."

Margo laughed darkly and spun toward the window; I recognized the yearning in her gaze as it met the sky's glassy indigo, for her feeling was not so different from my own.

"I've always admired your arrogance. It takes a certain spirit to be so blind to reality."

"Margo." He approached her again, embraced her again, this time from behind. His lips brushed her white hair. "I will determine what is, and is not, reality. At least where you are concerned. You will live, and live as a queen, in a realm as bright as pearl. I ordain it so. I give you my word."

Catherine in the Orchard

We were perhaps eight or nine, in the Farrows' orchard. Petals fell so thickly that the wind wrapped us in restless lace. Gus caught my shoulders and yanked me down into a hollow among knuckled roots.

"The king will kill us," Gus whispered urgently, "if he finds us before our transformation is complete."

"Yes," I agreed. An image flared in my mind's eye. "We're like a caterpillar in its chrysalis. If something tears it open before the right time, it dies."

I had recently found that out for myself, and I was still distressed by the experiment. I'd meant no harm, only to peek into the mystery, and now I could not dispel the thought of the sticky liquefaction that had spilled across my hands.

Gus considered, and approved. "We are together in the chrysalis of our power! Soon, no one will be strong enough to stand against us. The king knows he must strike now!"

It occurred to me that there was a gap in the narrative. No one ever attained exaltation by crouching behind a tree. "So what do we *do*? To complete our transformation?"

Gus relied on me for this sort of pragmatism, but it irked him nonetheless. I watched him sulk, then recover. "The ritual."

He ordered me to lie flat on the grass, and I complied. Then he gathered an armful of branches and arranged the plucked blossoms in lines: down the middle of my face and body, then along each of my limbs, as if he meant to diagram me in bloom. Carefully he set a circle of flowers around my head, a ruffling diadem. I shivered. I could feel power lambent at the base of my brain. It wicked inside my skin, hot and nervous, until my fingertips jumped against the grass. I felt as if I could rise into the vaulting blue, and Gus gave a sharp cry.

"What is it?" I raised my head and flowers tumbled down my cheeks. Their soft tussle confused my vision for a moment. But there, at the edge

of the woods: wasn't that another movement? Shoulders angled in retreat, a head drawn back, gone before I could see them properly?

"I almost thought—" Gus shook his head. "You do me, now."

"Someone was watching!" I hissed. I thought of my unspeaking father,
colored gray by disapproval. He would not want to punish me in front
of his employers' son, but I could see the scene through his eyes in all
its pagan defiance. It was all too plain that Gus had been arraying me
as some sort of vernal queen. *None of that—that—*my father would say
once we were alone, then fall silent and stare at his gnarled fists. *It's not
for you, understand?*

He wouldn't beat me. But he might well order me to stay up half the
night oiling tack. Our town was not so far distant from Hydesville,
where the Fox sisters had lately begun communicating with rapping
ghosts. The atmosphere was a ferment of heresy, and young girls were
especially suspect.

Gus had a different king in mind, of course. He looked alarmed, then
furious.

"The king has sent out his spies!" Even as Gus pursued the game,
his face flushed and his eyes welled. "He'll do anything to stop us from
changing! He can't stand for us to be *more* than he is!"

This frustration was one we held in common; we both yearned for
some nebulous *more,* for a sort of levitation of the spirit that would let
us gaze down on our dull town with confidence that we were not, and
never would be, of the same base material as its inhabitants. And if such
yearnings are commonplace—indeed, if they are themselves base—we
were blissfully unaware of the fact.

I felt a rush of resentment I could hardly put a name to, much less
justify. It seemed to surge outward from my feet in concentric waves, and
I closed my eyes and turned my face toward the sky. I felt brilliant and destructive and immense, as if I had traveled far beyond whatever anyone
thought me. I heard Gus exhale, long and amazed.

What had I to fear? I was queen, and I was burning.

"Together," Gus said, under his breath. "That's the only way."

Angus in the Smoke

Bookstore! I'm standing out front, a little vague on the process that brought me here, but I remember the important thing: it's part of my mission.

Book-stacked tables and Babar onesies hanging behind the register and a blue-haired boy with narrow glasses looking bored. But out of all these thousands of books, which is the one that would impress *her* most? I have no idea.

A journal, I decide. If I'm writing in a journal, it's open to interpretation; for all she knows, I could be jotting down the most amazing ideas. She'll have to talk to me to find out.

So I pay the blue-haired boy for a classic black Moleskine, the fattest one they have—because I must have a lot to say, right?—and keep wandering. Pick up some pens at a drugstore. There are girls on the street, and I check them as they pass, waiting to feel the zing of *her*-ness, but I don't look that hard because I can already tell there's no point.

If she came within a hundred yards of me, I bet I'd know it. Even blindfolded, I'd sense that she was there.

Afterward, I window shop, ogling these beautiful sparkly guitars and wondering if I ever learned how to play an instrument. When I try to remember, there's a glass-fine flash of my hands flying over a keyboard, then nothing but a sharp sensation like a bead of blood welling on my mind. Like, it literally hurts my head when I push too hard at an image.

One piano in particular comes back to me: the keyboard is a row of blocky teeth and the whole thing is densely covered in short golden hairs, a beautiful, lustrous coat. But it's a real bitch of an instrument, jumping and scuttling until I smack it hard in frustration.

I can practically feel the piano's hide under my fingers, and my head throbs. It's as if I peeled a pretty shadow off the ground, then discovered the hard way that its edges were sharp enough to cut. Anything else, then; *think about anything else.*

Fifteen minutes later I'm staring up at Carmen's warehouse again, a take-out bag in my hand. I guess I stopped somewhere?

"I'm here," I shout once I've entered. No one answers. There's a single clip-on work light beaming from an exposed pipe on one side, but all it does is punctuate the dark bloat of the place. Cracks in the floor ravel like negated lightning bolts barely visible against a lifeless sky.

So I hurry to lock myself in my room, sit at the little yellow table. I blather in my journal, or at least I assume I do because the pages seem to be filling pretty fast. Get through most of the decent burger and the distinctly mediocre, squishy fries before there's a *fizzip* noise and I'm dropped into utter darkness. It's so overwhelming, so hard and flawless, that for a moment it's as if I were embedded in a solid block of black stone. My heart judders and I sit paralyzed, completely forgetting how to move.

A beat later, I realize it's just the power outage Carmen promised me earlier. The two boxes are sitting inches from my hands, and I can get out a candle and light it and send my panic packing with no trouble at all.

I fumble a candle free of the packaging, slide the matchbox open, and strike up a tiny flame on the second try. Then I use a few drops of molten wax to fix the candle to the tabletop and light it. I seem to remember that these candles are way more expensive than they look, and I should use them judiciously; no more than one at a time. The flame flings its bobbling light around, sloppy as a drunk throwing punches.

In the exact same instant, my lamp flares back on. I lean in to blow out the candle.

The smoke wreathes up. God, it's beautiful. Who needs TV when you can just light candles and blow them out over and over, and watch those incredible feathery filaments doing their air ballet? The smoke scrolls and weaves in midair until I start to see pictures in it. Forms.

A face. It's not a face I'd ever *choose* to see.

The smoke twists into the half-scrawled portrait of a creepy, hateful old man. Diaphanous, looping, but not nearly vague enough. I stare at it, appalled, and see two green-white eyes staring right back at me, even while the lampshade behind glows right through them.

It's just smoke, though; I'm obviously imagining things. I swing my hand to disperse it. Maybe in a convulsive kind of way, if anyone was watching.

But his lips are already moving. There's a puff, barely distinct, like the sigh of an extinguishing flame. *Find her, Angus.* Not even a real voice; it's more like a suggestion breathed into my ears. *Claim her love. Carry my—* Then there's another word I can't quite make out. Was it *kiss* or *curse*?

Kiss seems bad enough. I'll go with that.

And anyway, that did not just happen, that did not just happen, there is no *way* that happened.

The smoke is just a soft white blur rising gently toward the ceiling. Shapeless and silent. I gape up at the haze where it's settling under the bumpy plaster, and there is no trace of anything weird about it.

I need something normal. Grounding. With a sort of flailing reflex, I realize I'm calling my aunt Margo. She's the top contact in my phone. No surprise there.

"Angus, darling! If I hadn't seen your name, I'd think I had some masturbating pervert on the line. All that labored breathing. What's troubling you?"

Hearing her voice knocks the dread right out of me. "Margo, I am so, so happy you answered! I—" Margo's open-minded enough that I can trust her to evaluate what just happened to me. I do my best to describe it all, the smoke, the face. Before I'm halfway through the story I can feel the bemused shake of her head transmitting over all the miles between us.

"You're an excitable boy. If that brain of yours gets any more high-flying, you're going to flip clear off your trapeze, Angus, my dear. Try descending to Earth once in a while. Spend some time with us poor, tired, gravity-bound mortals."

"Oh, Margo! You're right. I was getting carried away." The smoke-face was lingering in my head, clinging all over my mind's eye. But Margo's brusque tone swings through it like a broom and sends the wisps flying.

"You certainly were! Otherwise you would have taken a gander at the time before you called me. Why, I'd been fast asleep for two hours already."

Shit. Of course. I didn't even consider what an early bird Margo is.

"I'm sorry, I forgot—"

"None of that, Angus. Get your wooly head to bed and see if sleep can do anything to improve it. Personally, I have my doubts."

Great, now even Margo's insulting me.

So why do I put up with this crap? For her, for *her*. For the one who slides into the definition I carry in my mind. I'll know her the moment I see her.

A refusal to accept the world's terms, a certain brisk clarity. Snappy, impatient realism. Pragmatic, intellectual, merciless. The perfect complement to my burbling soup of romanticism and impulse.

The perfect fulfillment of an unfinished dream.

Catherine Considered

Further acquaintance did not make me fonder of Nautilus—and indeed the reverence I saw in Gus's eyes as he gawked only heightened my distaste. The buildings rippled and rilled, rising in fantastical contortions around alleys so narrow the inhabitants could barely skirt one another, and every surface partook of the same nacreous glow. Towers spiraled up in wanton disregard of gravity, carving bright trails into a sky that never showed anything but twilight. Those inhabitants who did not mind indulging in a continual expenditure could use their magic to create any appearance they liked, and a great many of them strolled about in permanent masquerade. Faces glittered with tiny turquoise scales, or antlers rose in a diamantine mist, or pearly draperies flowed like Greek statuary pursued by restless winds. Gus stared and marveled, his mouth twisted into eternal self-congratulation that he was here among these chosen ones.

For my part, I would have preferred tossing in muck with the pigs.

Even in his awe, Gus seemed hurried and distracted, charging through the streets and then reeling to unexpected stops to gaze up at the sky before rushing on again. I supposed that the recent revelations as to Margo's poor health were to blame.

We came to a place where the word *Immigration* was gouged into the wall in phosphorescent script, and I noted a lintel above it. Lintels, I now knew, marked those places where a citizen could penetrate the walls, a lit or two of magic extracted as a toll as they went. Gus shoved directly in. I was forced to tip sharply backward in order to slide through the permeable zone, the bright letters bannering and then bursting against my eyes. There was a queasy whitening of the view as if we were drowning in a butter churn, a resistant suction, and then a yielding gasp. We were through.

Into what, even here, was clearly an office. It was a very small room, the sort allotted to someone of correspondingly small importance. Most of the cramped space was taken up by an enormous desk of battered wood, so discordant inside these luminous walls that I knew at once it must have been brought here from what Gus called the unworld. On the floor nearby was an enormous china basin painted with tiny violets and filled with dingy water.

Papers and stamps were strewn on desk and floor alike, and so were what I took for the wet prints left by the inmate's feet; that is, once I realized who the inmate was.

There was a severe wooden armchair behind the desk, but no one sat in it. Instead a very large frog spread its warty folds amidst the papers. The creature was quite circular apart from the bulges of its legs, and some two feet in diameter. A mouth ran around nearly half its circumference, which gave it the look of a cushion with its seam coming undone. Its hide was a dirty blue dotted with emerald-green bumps of a disquieting brightness.

It looked at Gus through a pair of pince-nez, which finding no nose to pinch were simply balanced atop its head.

"Well," said the frog. "Have you the requisite, then?"

I was accustomed to persons of odd appearance, of course, but this was extravagant even by the city's standards. If the frog was an altered human, it was surely spending quite a bit of magic to maintain an aspect so removed from its former one. I supposed its salary did not suffice to meet the bills.

"Not yet." Gus exhaled, out of breath. "I thought perhaps an initial payment, to be followed at intervals by—"

The frog turned away. This was a prolonged procedure involving lumbering haunches and undulating flesh, which ended with the frog's profile spread before us. "No."

"I am presently able to draw on my own mind at a rate of nearly three talens for every unworld rotation! I can put down two hundred on the spot, and—"

"You are not *in* the unworld, Mr. Farrow. What passes for time in Nautilus is not so reliable. Your flow here might not be either."

"I can remove myself there between payments, in order to ensure a steady supply."

I knew by the rolling of Gus's eyes how much this offer terrified him, and how handsome he thought himself to make it. In the unworld he risked being arrested for my murder, besides which he would age there like anyone else. His life was the currency he wished to hoard most of all.

"I would find the wait too onerous, I fear." The frog's delivery was laconic, drawling, and I began to enjoy it. Owing to my scream, my mouth lacked the flexibility for an appreciative grin.

"Do you not hear me? Within a single unworld year, I could meet your requirements. Even with interest!" Here Gus stamped with all the petulance of a child.

"If only you were not subject to taxation, you mean? All citizens must contribute to the city's maintenance. These talens you boast of are bleeding even now to feed the common atmosphere." That observation startled me. The minotaur had mentioned taxes, and said that even I paid them involuntarily, but I'd given little thought to *how* they were paid. Of course I saw that the magical outlay necessary to create and sustain all the cold marvels of Nautilus must be enormous.

"Then—call it a year and a half. I could—"

"No. You are perhaps aware that bribery is a crime punishable by exile, Mr. Farrow."

"Yes, of course. But for Margo's sake I would risk nearly—"

"It is not the risk to *you* that concerns me, Mr. Farrow." A single eye, scarlet and black, rotated to gaze at us sidelong. At this angle, the lens of the pince-nez did not cover the eye at all but rather twinkled beside it like a small mirage. "Every time you visit this office, it could be remarked upon. The more visits, the greater the chance that I will live out my days in a manner—uh, ugh—not of my choosing."

At this I grew quite certain that the frog had indeed been human, and moreover a woman. My interest in her flared with such heat that it took me by surprise. I had settled into a comfortable contempt for every Nautiluser, I realized, as if there were nothing to choose among them. But perhaps there might be some—

"Then we can find an intermediary. I have a friend—for a percentage, at any rate, I believe he would help. You could meet Asterion anywhere you found convenient."

"The minotaur?" The frog expressed her feelings at this suggestion by continuing her sluggish turn atop her paperwork until we confronted a green-spotted rump. "Certainly not."

"Miss Anura, I beseech you to reconsider!" Gus here forgot his manners to the point of rounding her desk and thrusting himself into her field of vision. "My aunt is very ill. I must bring her here immediately, on any terms that can be arranged. For a greater consideration—you need not feel bound by your initial mention of a thousand talens—I would be delighted to increase the figure."

I noticed for the first time that her front legs did not end in the splayed paws of a frog but rather in miniature human hands, dusty blue, and about the size of a two-year-old child's. I supposed they made it easier to sign and stamp.

"A thousand, Mr. Farrow. Paid in advance, and on the condition that you leave now and don't come back without it. Another intrusion like this one, and no amount will suffice to move me."

Gus began sputtering, leaning much too close to her. Rather than continue her laborious shuffle, Miss Anura seized on the expedient of shutting her scarlet eyes. Two globes of blue wrinkled skin faced Gus and would not part again for all his blustering.

Miss Anura was hopelessly corrupt; that I quite understood. She was abusing her position as a public servant for private gain. When I was alive I would have considered such venality unforgivable, revolting.

Here in Nautilus, I found I rather liked it, and her, and not merely because of the consternation she produced in Gus. Had death made me so amoral, then? Perhaps it had.

Gus at last drew a deep breath, closing his own eyes in sheer frustration. The frog opened hers and looked. Not at him, but at me.

It was nothing new to me, of course, to be stared at in my ghastly condition. I had no way to hide what I was; I could not mask my billowing and flashing as one might a disease of the skin. Instead I must submit to a constant and degrading examination as a waving, shrieking spectacle towed about against my will.

But Miss Anura's look was of a different character. She met my eyes with a morose, unblinking *knowing*. It did not quite rise to the level of sympathy, perhaps, but it was still an acknowledgment of my person-hood.

"Good afternoon, then, Miss Anura," Gus managed. His words were sharp-edged, snipped like so many paper dolls from crisp resentment.

"A good afternoon to you, Mr. Farrow." There was no such thing as afternoon in Nautilus, but such phrases are not easily extinguished. Miss Anura did not lower her gaze as she spoke, but kept it on my flickering visage. "And to you, Miss Bildstein."

Gus jerked on hearing this, as indeed did I. For of course we both realized at once that it was the first time since my death that anyone had addressed me—apart from Gus himself, who prattled at me as a child would to a favored toy.

On an impulse I moved to bow myself down to Miss Anura. I don't know what I hoped to do—perhaps I would have tried to kiss one small blue hand. My bodiless form inclined with more alacrity than I had expected, though the part of me corresponding to feet remained firmly anchored to Gus. Like a candle flame bent by the wind, I swooped straight at the frog's bulging eyes.

Even in Nautilus, it seemed, such behavior on the part of a ghost was deemed alarming. The frog flattened herself to an improbable degree across her desk. She quivered, her emerald spots blazing with anxiety, and spat at me. I recoiled and pitched to-and-fro above Gus's head again, and Miss Anura, released from the pressure of my looming presence, sprang into the air with shocked agility and splashed into her basin. Her webbed hind feet and human hands paddled at the unclean water while she glowered at me.

I wished I could apologize; I was very sorry to have frightened her. But my scream would not allow room for words.

"She's never done such a thing before!" Gus yelped. "Miss Anura, I hope you won't allow this, this *fit* of Catherine's to change your mind. She probably was not even conscious of her own movement—it was likely a kind of reflex or spasm triggered by her name. I realize she may not have made the best impression, but as a rule she's quite docile. No trouble to me at all."

Docile. My longing for vengeance compounded at the word, though I knew Gus's claim to be untroubled by me was a lie.

"She can't possibly make a worse impression than you do," Miss Anura groused. "She's calmer than you are, and far more well-spoken."

With that, Gus nodded, his face crimson, and we backed out of the office with a pop of violated wall. He stomped a short distance, and even the worn folds of his coat seemed to seethe with frustration and spite.

Then he stopped and leaned against a wall. I had time to wonder how Miss Anura had learned my name; her casual knowledge suggested that Gus and I were of more interest to the local gossips than I would have guessed. I had time to worry that I had squandered her goodwill, broken that frail thread of connection that had spun from the meeting of our eyes.

What was it I was feeling? Why was my loneliness so much heavier now that she had breached it?

I found Gus's eyes had lifted while I was lost in thought. His head was craned back so that he could take in nearly the whole of me, and so he remained, contemplating me in the way that a pickpocket might the bulges in a rich man's coat.

Catherine in Memory

Gus slept on his pallet, the icy glow of the walls making a blot of his face until he looked something like a stand of fir trees heaped with snow. I hovered over him, sleepless as death, observing the nervous saccade of his eyes beneath the lids. At the same time, I was back in my own cottage, rolling out biscuit dough. It was the thought of snow that had returned me to that particular memory: the windows showed a seethe of white.

I don't suppose I was older than eleven in the memory; my mother's strength was already failing then and I'd taken over cooking for the family. And Gus sat watching my flour-caked hands. He'd brought along a volume of fairy tales purloined from his father's library, but it annoyed him if I divided my attention while he read aloud, and the book sat closed beneath his elbow.

"If your mother can't cook anymore, why can't Anna?" Gus asked. "School is wasted on her. She ought to stay home and do the work, and free you for"—and here Gus's gaze swung about, as if seeking a suitable object for my freedom—"higher things."

"Anna is clever in her own way. And she must learn to read!" I said. I did not admit that I enjoyed cooking, as that would evoke disapproval on Gus's part. "She's much too little to manage everything at home, but I can get our meals ready and study besides."

But I lowered my face to hide my smile as I argued the point. I was shamefully dependent on Gus's opinion of me as somehow out of the ordinary. While my father and our teacher Miss Gryson observed that I was quick enough, they did not share my ideas of my own distinction. Why should they? The implied insult was none too subtle: I wanted to be distinct from *them*.

Should I blame that girl-child and all her febrile yearnings, then? After all, it was longing that made her vulnerable.

Oh, why? There are plenty of people eager to condemn girls such as I was without my contributing to the chorus.

Gus fell silent, which surprised me, for he was not one to readily re-linquish a quarrel. I'd begun to cut the biscuits into the diamonds Anna preferred, waiting the while for Gus to insist on my general superiority. When he did not, I looked sharply at his knitted hands and drawn brows. He glanced back, then closed tight his eyes.

"Gus? What's wrong?"

"I know I've sometimes told you tales. I meant nothing by it, no harm, only—sometimes the truth didn't seem *good* enough to tell."

"I know," I said indulgently. Gus tended to embroider rather brighter tapestries where he found the underlying cloth too plain. "I'm used to picking out what parts to believe."

"That's the trouble!" Gus was nearly shouting, and he jumped up, lip quivering. "Now, when I have something important to tell you, you'll—pick away at it, and say it's true and not true, until there's nothing left! Why can't you just believe everything?"

It struck me as a somewhat unjust demand, coming after he had con-fessed to habitual lies. But seeing his agitation, I fell back upon habits of my own. I soothed.

"Of course I will, Gus, if you tell me you're serious. What is it?"

Gus bit his lip, but he sat down again. His flaxen tufts stood outlined on one side by the chill daylight and on the other by the fire's ruddy blaze, and when he nodded those tufts bobbed comically. I was glad he could not observe the effect.

"Old Darius."

"What of him?" Old Darius was a vagrant who sometimes appeared in our town, flaunting a knowing air which made him seem quite mad. He claimed to have been an actor and liked to recite from *King Lear,* which did nothing to diminish the impression. He hung about on the bridge by the mill and stole the occasional cake or cheese, and was sometimes chased away, sometimes tolerated, depending on inexplicable shifts in the town's mood. For my part, I preferred it when he was absent, though I would not have cared to admit that he frightened me.

My childish wish was that Darius should be afraid of *me.* The cer-tainty that he was not made the mention of him galling.

"I saw—I don't think he noticed me, but what if he did? I'm sure he didn't want to be seen, not doing—something no one can do! Oh, Catherine, what if he comes after me? What if he can hear me telling you this *right now*?"

I was sorry to have pledged Gus my belief, for this was just the sort of dramatic flight I most distrusted in him.

"Even if he's hiding outside there's no way he can hear you, not with the wind the way it is. Did you see him stealing? Everyone knows that he does that sometimes."

"I saw him burn the snow."

There was a pause as I tried out possible interpretations of that unlikely phrase. I found none that suited me.

"Burn it? How do you mean?"

"I mean—I was on my way home yesterday when it was getting dark, and I'd just come around that clump of willows where you can see the bridge? Darius was there, looking down at the ice spinning in the current. And you remember, the snow was starting in earnest then."

I'd been inclined to doubt the story when Gus began it, but there was something in the telling that changed my mind. A staggered rhythm of hesitations, as if he were afraid to come to the point. When Gus lied, he lied with vigor and enthusiasm.

"It was terribly cold last night," I agreed, in tones newly hushed. Gus leaned closer.

"It was. I was shaking; I wanted to rush home. But when I saw Darius I knew I couldn't pass over the bridge."

A detour to the next bridge down would have added nearly three miles to Gus's walk.

"But—burning the snow? You can't mean he lit a bonfire on the bridge! It would catch."

"I *don't* mean that!" He was fitful again, his voice a dangerous whine. "I mean the falling snow, the flakes all around him. They were alight! Everything else was dim, but he stood in a sort of cone—or an upside-down whirlwind—made of spinning flecks of fire. None of them touched him, I don't think, or the bridge. In all that whirling white, there was this terrible golden interval."

Were those really the words he used, a *terrible golden interval*? That is how I remember his speech, even now, and he was precocious in his use of language. Say then that this eleven-year-old boy vented such overheated poetry.

"That doesn't sound"—I mulled the word *possible,* then flipped it over to look for a different one beneath—"natural."

"No. Obviously not. I've thought about it all day, and it must have been"—and here Gus quite palpably rejected a word of his own—"something else."

Witchcraft. Sorcery. Neither of us said it aloud, but the thought fired between us.

It was not a thought I wished to entertain. "What?" I said, and my voice lightened into something nearly mocking. "Just to stay warm? He must have known someone could happen by."

Gus scowled. "It was very cold. And there are holes in his coat."

He might use magic to mend it, then, I thought. Of course, I had no way to know at the time how very specialized sorcerers tend to be, or how often they scorn to put their magic to uses they deem beneath them. Gus now goes about in tattered clothes as well.

"So what did you do?" I asked instead.

"What do you think?" He was still angry with me. "He was turned away from me, but I thought—if he could do *that,* who knew what else he could do? I almost thought I could feel him looking at me with his back, a spot near the shoulder blade. I crept away as softly as I could, and then I ran. Oh, if he knows I *know,* what will he do to keep me quiet?"

In theory, we lived in a rational era, its heartbeat tapped out by telegraphs. In theory, the execution of suspected witches had been relegated decisively to the past. But the past has a way of circling back. Of haunting.

"Nothing," I said. At once, I was surprised that Gus couldn't see it. "He'll think it's funny to watch you pull away from him, that's all. It's not a story anyone would believe. Not coming from a child." *And noted liar.* I skipped that amendment.

"Oh—but you're right. They'd all be too stupid to believe me if I tried to warn them."

"But in this case it works to your advantage! You don't need to be afraid that Darius will try to hurt you, even if he did somehow know you were there. There's no reason you should speak to him again."

I'd meant to be comforting, but Gus sighed and tipped his head into his hands.

"No—I must! Even if he kills me for it."

If I did not consciously believe in Gus's strange account, my body seemed to believe it. Dread coiled in my stomach. "Why would you approach him? You got well away."

"Catherine, don't you see? If we're meant to be different, different *together,* this could be our chance!"

Alarm quickened inside me at this intention—I wanted to throw my arms around Gus, pull him back from some sickening danger—but I had no time to challenge him. The door flew open with a spray of white and my two little brothers tumbled into the room, snow-cakes splitting at their elbows and crumbling from their limbs. I leapt up to herd them just outside and brush them off before they could soak the whole house.

Anna was crouched under a tree nearby, pressing pine cones and needles, dead leaves and twigs, into the snow. Her tiny reddened fingers wove a design of branching, radial lines, and she'd cast aside her mittens for precision's sake. I paused to watch her. So absorbed was she in her task that she seemed not to notice the cold.

By the time I turned back to Gus, he was shrugging on his coat. He never spent time with my family if he could help it.

"Gus!" I said, with too much emotion for an ordinary goodbye.

"I must get home. I have a new piece to learn before my lesson tomorrow." Already Gus displayed a striking gift for the piano. I both loved and envied him for the readiness with which music came at his call.

I wanted to argue, but none of the things I meant to say were allowable in my brothers' hearing. Gus and I were constrained to an exchange of meaningful looks, and who can say if they meant the same things to both of us?

I walked back to Anna and observed her for a moment. Her design evoked something, some ragged-edged memory, but I couldn't place it. Loose channels of white meandered between patches of bursting lines sketched in woodland debris.

"What is that pattern?" I asked her. "How did the idea for it come to you?"

Anna bit her lip. "I saw it," she announced, halfway between bashful and defiant.

"Where? Do you mean you saw it in your mind?" But then I realized that she was pointing silently upward, and I looked to see the spreading crowns of trees separated by just such white channels, only made of sky instead of snow. It moved me in a way I could not name, and I knelt down and embraced her. Her warm little head leaned against my cheek.

If school was wasted on her, it was not at all in the sense Gus meant!

Angus in the Morning

In the morning I find Carmen sitting in—is it an office, or a lounge, or the dreariest conference room of all time? A big fake-wood table dominates the center, and then there are more folding chairs and an olive vinyl sofa dragged kicking and screaming out of 1979, and another mini fridge, and—I focus on it to the detriment of all else—a coffeemaker burbling serenely on an end table, next to a box of donuts.

"Breakfast, boy-o," Carmen says, following my gaze. And then she turns back to the two people she's talking to.

I take it as an invitation to help myself, because at least it wasn't a direct order to get lost. And once I've found a mug, I turn to perch on the fridge, three donuts in a wobbling tower on my knee, and really observe Carmen's visitors for the first time.

One is a very tall, slim, exceptionally dark-skinned Black man with buzzed hair and severe features and an elegant, flowy dove-gray suit. Cheekbones like silver scythes, narrow skull. He glances at me with zero interest, but then his gaze backs up and he peers harder, just as I bite into a donut and a blurt of gory jelly splatters my cheek.

The other is a truly beautiful old woman; realistically she's probably close to Aunt Margo's age but she's a completely different kind of creature. She's golden brown and has long silver hair in a ponytail and a straight black dress to her ankles. Huge, searching brown eyes. A delicate necklace made of beach pebbles drilled through and linked with silver hoops. I'd like to flop down and rest my head in her lap and ask her to adopt me. She's gazing at me too.

The sleek, suited man breaks out in a crooked smile. It's not aimed at me, and it wouldn't seem friendly if it was.

"Beamer?" he asks Carmen. Say what?

She smiles back. "I knew you'd catch it, Julian. Want to guess?"

He spreads his hands. "Surprise me."

"*That*," Carmen says, and clocks her head sharply my way, "would be

Gus Farrow." Did the word *beamer* refer to me, then? What sense does that make?

"Um, hi," I say. "Carmen, I don't mean to sound unappreciative, but I really prefer Angus." But it's like I didn't speak at all. Julian's eyes do a sort of ironic pivot in my direction, then his shoulders roll back and he cackles. What exactly does he think is so funny?

The beautiful silver-haired woman amps up her soft-focus attention. I think she likes me.

"*Gus* Farrow!" Julian says, with bone-dry amusement. "Still working it out, then, I take it? He didn't hew too closely to tradition either. There's quite a look of embellishment to this one."

"Working what out?" I ask, keeping my tone as polite as I can. "You know, I am right here."

"That's what he does," Carmen agrees. She and Julian both have stopped looking at me. I've progressed from inaudible to invisible, and only the silvery woman still keeps her brown gaze hovering around my face. "Works it out, and out, and out, ad nauseam. Lots of juice, not a lot of what you'd call new ideas. But as far as that particular trick goes, you know he's invented most of the major innovations."

It almost sounds like a very confusing compliment, but what trick could she be talking about?

"And that really doesn't concern you, Carmen?" the silvery woman asks. Almost tenderly. "You don't have any objection to participating in that?"

Carmen does one of her inimitable dismissive twists. "It's his way. Not like I could stop him even if I wanted to, and I don't see why I'd bother. Besides, he's making it worth my while."

"Stop me?" I say. I'm still trying to sound calm and mature, but my voice is getting prickly. "From what? I haven't done anything!"

Julian gives a huffing chuckle of pure disdain, and Carmen flicks me the smallest possible fraction of an annoyed glance. "You can run along now, Gussy boy."

Hell yes, I will, I want to say. *I'll run straight out of this dump, and you can find someone else to spew your incomprehensible rudeness at.*

But then the silvery woman stands up, steps closer, and holds out her hand to me, graciously waiting for me to shake it.

"Hello, Angus," she says. "I'm Dolores Rojas. You can call me Lore for short, but I promise I won't ever call you Gus."

And just like that, I completely forget about storming out. Instead I hurry to wipe jelly on my pants and reach out for her slim, strong hand, her fingers heavy with carved-stone rings.

"Hi, Lore. I'm happy to meet you!" It's such a relief to make eye contact after the way Julian and Carmen have been acting that I decide not to be hurt anymore by what she said, the *You don't have any objection to participating in that?* part. "Carmen hired me yesterday to help out here. I'm going to do my best to be a good worker."

It sounds defensive, because I'm still not sure if she thinks there's something wrong with me.

"Yes," Lore says. "I'm sure you're bringing the best of intentions to everything you do."

Her gaze, though, expresses something different. Something under shovelfuls of warm brown soil. I just can't tell what it means.

"Lore," Julian breaks in. I'd like to give him the benefit of the doubt, but there's really no mistaking his tone. He's disgusted. Disgusted that she's *touching* me? "You know what that is."

"Angus is an innocent boy," Lore retorts. But the whole time she's holding my eyes, not looking back at Julian at all. "And he deserves better than this."

Thank you, thank you, thank you. Someone, at least, thinks I should be treated like I'm human.

Carmen shrugs. "Run along now, Gussy. Can't you mop, or something?"

"It's my lunch break," I snap at Carmen, and then I swing toward Julian. "What's a beamer?"

His teeth set on edge and his eyebrows shoot up, like he can't believe I'd have the gall to speak to him.

"Just tell me," I say. "You want to get rid of me so badly, all you have to do is answer one question. If I'm going to be insulted for no reason, I'd like to at least know what it means."

He thinks it over for a few seconds. Smiles like an iron spike aimed at my skull.

"Think of movies, Angus. Do you like movies?"

Even with the derision in his voice, I feel a flutter of pleasure. "Yeah, I do." I love them: the sweeping emotions, the involute intrigue, the sheer scale of the drama. What I despise are tiny, twiddling conflicts, *whose turn is it to take out the garbage* and *why didn't you say you were running late,* and the cramped, romance-depleted love that goes with all of that. I'm a believer in bringing it on, all of it, whole towers of it balanced on war elephants. A goddamn stampede.

"Well, then think of the beam of the projector, traveling through the darkness. *Beamer* alludes to that. To projection."

"Oh," I say. Not that I actually understand, but I don't want to sound dim in front of this guy. Not when he already looks down on me. And I like the idea of seeming like a movie: luminous, vibrant, and larger than life. I glance at Lore for confirmation, but her face is sad and watchful, not giving anything much away. "That doesn't sound so bad."

"Indeed not, to you. Now think of the end of the movie."

Now I really don't understand why he thinks *beamer* is an insult. The end is the thrilling part, victory and kisses. You go through all the misery and danger, you earn the payout. Why would I mind that?

"Then I guess we're good," I tell him after a moment. "I can be a beamer, if that's all it means."

"You have little choice in the matter," Julian tells me, and he's still smiling. A revolted smirk, as if I were some kind of thousand-legged spider, but at least he's looking at me. Lore, though: she isn't smiling at all. "Now. Carmen told you to go away."

I think about it as I go. A movie. A light in the darkness, carrying visions from long, long ago. It's a beautiful idea, actually.

If I'm a movie, then I hope I'm something classic. Old. Black and white. A love story, naturally, full of grand passions and heartache and doom and ultimate triumph.

And, of course, there just has to be a kiss! One that goes on and on, or maybe again and again.

A kiss like snow, eternally falling.

Catherine Drawn

The victors write the histories of wars. Great men pen their memoirs without wasting ink on the villages they burned or the washerwomen they raped. And the living, of course, have rather a monopoly on telling tales of ghosts.

Even I, who was never fantastical or morbid by nature, had once listened with pleasure to accounts of pale women groaning on parapets or drowned children eternally beckoning beside lakes. I had not wondered how such apparitions might tell their own stories, if anyone had cared to solicit their version of events. Now that the shoe was on the other foot—though my lower extremities were so nebulous that feet were impossible to distinguish—I found I had a great deal to say regarding my own history and condition. My mouth thirsted for language until I felt a dry crackling all down my insubstantial throat. My fingers twitched to hold pen and paper. It was a useless craving. On the rare occasions that such articles came within my reach, I could not grasp them. Not even make them stir.

Gus suffered from no such constraints.

As a general rule, he was solitary and disciplined in his habits, dedicated to his magic to the point of austerity. After his conversation with Miss Anura, he spent nearly all his time hiding in a garden shed behind his parents' house. He sat on the dusty floor, his back rigid and his eyes squeezed shut in tense meditation, and paused only rarely to devour the food Margo hid behind a shovel.

I quickly realized that he must be employed, for all his apparent stillness, in collecting magic from the workings of his own consciousness. *Nearly three talens per unworld rotation,* he had said, with a pride that made plain he thought it an impressive figure. From the agonized pinching of his face, I was sure he was striving to increase his output. How were such magical dribblings gathered, in what manner of purse were they stored? I learned such practical details later, but at that time I was still ignorant. He slept in brief snatches, curled on the same splintery boards, and his discomfort was to me a very minor pleasure.

No: for me the salient fact was that every day, every minute Gus spent in the unworld brought him nearer death. I fluttered above him, savoring the taste of expiring time. And since he kept silence during these vigils, the inequity between us—that he was alive, and I not; that he could tell tales, where my voice produced only one burning, wordless threnody—was not so glaring. Then we were just two wordless minds crouched in a shed, each scheming against the other as best we might.

I saw my father once through a gap in the planks, somehow become an old man with sunken eyes and swaying head. I thought I glimpsed Anna once in the distance as Gus made his way to the hedge where he relieved himself, but she was so tall and so far away that I could not be certain. My fantasies—that my survivors might somehow sense my nearness and my longing—were not borne out, try though I did to project my urgent love across the air. My cries were silence to them, my love extinct.

I never saw either of them again.

Even Gus's self-discipline was not limitless, and after perhaps ten days he faltered. The night came when he slunk home to Nautilus. When he, indeed, got drunk.

We met Asterion the minotaur in a large common hall where comfortable chairs and settees in intimate groupings dotted a cavernous space. A fireplace taller than a man and wide as a heifer blazed with flames that, even at a distance, had a distinctly unnatural aspect. Uncharacteristically for Nautilus, an immense pair of doors with the appearance of molten silver stood directly opposite the fire. The furniture was mostly finely carved wood of various periods, upholstered in velvet or brocade: luxurious, yes, but likely imported from the unworld and looking somewhat out of place against the restless glow of the walls, the eerie writhing columns.

Asterion was already nestled in a large armchair of azure silk. He heard my screaming the moment Gus passed through the double doors and craned around the chair's back to wink at us; a scattering of other heads, human and otherwise, turned along with his, then nodded and returned their attention to their companions. The faces present showed every tint imaginable, deep brown brows and creamy cheeks intermixed with verdigris and violet, and all the unworld's languages coasted on their breath. Some had what I took for familiars perched on heads or shoulders: ravens with iridescent blue plumage, tiny golden lizards with lion's faces. I noticed, too, a subtle haze, and a stink like burning violets wafting among the company.

As we approached the minotaur, I noted the bottle of lilac-colored cordial on a small table, the two glasses, and understood that Asterion did not care to leave Gus fully possessed of his faculties.

Gus's eyes flicked around and his shoulders hunched. "It might be better to return to my room," he said, not bothering with a greeting. "Catherine will make it impossible for everyone here to converse."

"Oh, they can block out her squealing for just a lit or two; it isn't expensive magic as long as you don't need to keep it up for terribly long. The Nimble Fire is open to all citizens, however encumbered. And there's nothing like the scent of seeping magic, when so many of us are gathered together! Have you savored it before?"

Gus wrinkled his nose in reply. So that was the smoldering floral stench, the blur that feathered distant faces: it was magic *bleeding to feed the common atmosphere,* as Miss Anura had put it. It was startling to realize that I was smelling a system of taxation.

Asterion leered at me, then patted the chair drawn close to his. "Come. Try to relax. You're among—colleagues, at least. How goes your work with the beamers?"

I had never heard the term before. After a moment's reaching I realized it must refer to that translucent child whom Gus had made and then destroyed, and to all similar beings.

"As to that," Gus said, and stopped, chewing the inside of his cheek. He remained standing, his long hands curled like dead spiders on the back of the chair Asterion had indicated. It was covered in cut velvet, midnight blue, with an acanthus pattern. "I regret that I've been obliged to suspend work on my great project. Temporarily, of course. I need to save every talen I can toward a, a personal expense."

The minotaur's brows shot nearly to his horns. "What could possibly deflect you from your purpose? I tell everyone I know that nobody equals

Gus Farrow for dedication, and here you are simply dropping the whole undertaking?" The reproach in the beast's voice rang false and tinny. "I did not think you were so fickle."

"I'm not!" Tears of frustration swelled in Gus's eyes. My whole being felt like a pair of twiddling thumbs; how could Gus, so intelligent in some things, be so obtuse in the face of Asterion's manipulations? "I assure you, I would not abandon my work for any but the most pressing reasons! But now I find myself at the mercy of the unworld, with all its insulting indifference to everything I hold most precious."

"The vagaries of the unworld should be behind you."

"Indeed they should, and they are! Except in this one matter. I am disgusted, outraged that it, it *impinges* so—"

Asterion filled two glasses and held one out. "Sit *down*, my poor young friend. Tell me everything. Whatever is the trouble?"

Hesitation crimped Gus's face. He was not given to being overly confiding, or not to anyone but Margo and me.

Then he accepted the glass and swung himself into the midnight chair. "My aunt—great-aunt, really. She's ill, and I don't know how long I have until her illness claims her."

The minotaur's expression suggested that the impending death of an elderly woman could not possibly be of much concern, and that therefore the real problem was yet to be stated. He turned his palms up, a gesture of waiting. Gus stared at him quite blankly and tossed back his lilac cordial. It had the smell of a bonfire on a spring night, similar to and yet distinct from the enveloping fug.

"Ladies in the unworld do have a way of expiring, given a bit of time," Asterion observed at last, pouring more liquid into Gus's cup. "I can hardly remember when such deaths seemed worth regretting, if they ever did."

"But Margo is no ordinary lady!" The words burst from Gus like steam from a kettle. "She has that piercing vision that sees through all the obfuscations of society, that fine understanding—I believe that, if only she had found the right mentor in her youth, if only she had been *cultivated*, then she might have been one of us indeed. To let her simply die, as if she were no better than some veiled spinster always muttering at the back of the village church—it would be indecent. She ought to be one of us, and she ought to be *here*. Death is not for such as us, and it is certainly not for Margo!"

How very like Gus, I thought; since he considered himself the most exceptional of mortals, it followed that anyone he loved must be similarly anointed. Margo was quick and acerbic enough, no doubt, but when did that let anyone off the grave?

Of course, I had personal reasons for bitterness on the subject.

"Not everyone here tries to avoid dying," Asterion pointed out idly. "There are those who maintain double lives, here and in the unworld, knowing though they must that aging and death will follow. Even your old mentor Darius, eh, though he's had the sense at last to give it up? Personally I find it terribly wasteful." He shrugged as if to say there was no accounting for tastes, especially a taste for April sunshine and springing grass.

"Well—let them. If they choose to squander their own immortality in that fashion, no one will stop them. But Margo—"

The minotaur let out a great whickering sigh, rolled his wet brown eyes. "Margo, Margo. If you are so determined, dear Gus, we should examine the matter practically. There are obstacles in the way of Margo's immigration, I take it?"

"That amphibious bitch! I pleaded—offered her everything I could! For work she could complete in a matter of moments. It's nothing short of extortion."

The wide bovine mouth compressed in clear warning and the globular eyes swung meaningfully about. Gus flinched and fell silent. And I? I found myself unaccountably imagining what it would be like to sit with the *amphibious bitch* on one of the nearby sofas, laughing softly, her small blue hand in mine—never mind that I had no body to sit, or laugh, or touch.

"Allow me to sum up your position. You need funds, and quickly. You are already fully exploiting your inner resources, and finding them inadequate. Am I correct so far?"

"I've managed to collect forty-two talens in the last ten days. *After* taxes, at that. If only I knew for certain that Margo's illness would not progress too quickly, it would be an excellent rate."

"It would, but you don't. And so you need a second source."

And here they both confirmed their murderous tendencies. In this case the victim was ambiguity, which they dispatched by gaping up at me in perfect unison. It jarred me from my daydreams.

"A true sorcerer," Asterion observed, "knows how to turn his burdens into opportunities."

Gus threw back his drink. The minotaur's hands were so deft, so nearly invisible, that I hardly caught their motion before the glass was filled again to the brim. Well, a few lit worth of legerdemain would be a fine investment.

"If I understand correctly, I would be drawing magic from Catherine's consciousness, assuming she can still be said to possess such a thing. Or from whatever unconscious processes she has in place of thought. But either way, her processes are something that might be better left alone. Involving her could be dangerous."

"Dangerous? Ah, so it could," the minotaur said. He let the words stand as a dare.

At that Gus gulped his brimming glass and the hands blurred again.

"I'm not conversant with the method, though I've heard it discussed a bit. I understand that specialized equipment is involved."

"It requires a heartstring—not the commonplace design, but one made for the purpose. An *umbrastring,* they're called. Rare things, produced by a refined art. Not many of them kicking around, and not many sorcerers who have the craft to pull one off. Ghosts aren't a popular specialty. Personally, I can't understand the squeamishness, when they have the same legal status as—a hat, or any other object."

Ghosts. It now occurred to me to scan the company for others of my kind, and I thought I spotted two in the distance. In one case, a pallid gentleman by the fire appeared to be quite literally skewered through his heart by a vaporous, weeping girl-child with African features, though he chattered on unconcernedly. And there, in the far corner: did that woman made of flickering blades not wear a boneless, translucent young man draped like a stole around her shoulders?

"*Rare* and *refined* have a habit of running up the bill, don't they? It would be another expense I can ill afford."

At this the minotaur drew something from its florid waistcoat. At first glance it appeared to be a sort of tuning fork, if such an implement could be made of tightly wound spider silk: translucent, glistening, the color of rain on an autumn night. There were two slim prongs that curved to merge in a single stem, and an ebony handle with a long and barely visible thread trailing from it. Set into the handle was a pearly dial not much larger than a pea, its swinging black hand hair-thin. Excepting the tail, the whole was not more than five inches in length.

"You could borrow mine."

I regarded the object without enthusiasm. My mind was all that was left to me. The prospect of my murderer siphoning from that mind— what? A rippling magic current generated by my thoughts, a stream of primal being?—was enough to make my whole being flex with rebellion.

Gus looked from the thing to me, and back.

"For a percentage, I assume?"

The minotaur did not immediately reply. He was too occupied in watching my convulsions, pleasure shining on his face.

"Look at how she flashes! It's a promising sign; the more active her reactions, the better her likely output. Oh, your Catherine hears us, plainly enough. She wishes to register an objection to our plans. Well, little miss, if you insist on hanging about you should expect to be put to work. Eh?"

Gus twisted to watch my furious winking, scalding white inverting to the black of an abyss and back again at terrible speed. For a moment his look was distinctly sheepish. He knew me well enough to understand that to me such a violation of my mind was even worse than a violation of the body. He knew, and some stitch of ancient loyalty yanked tight inside him.

Then he deliberately turned to the minotaur and forced a smile.

"Objecting is what Catherine does best, it would seem." He paused, mastering his unwanted sympathy. "What percentage?"

"Even half would leave you much richer than you were previously."

"A third."

"With a very active, productive ghost—as your Catherine seems to be—we can sometimes collect as many as seven talens per unworld rotation!

Nearly double your own rate. And in a state of high excitement"—here he eyed my involuntary signaling, its precipitous blink from ghastly white to jet—"it could go even higher."

Now that Gus was engaged in haggling over my rape, he kept his gaze curiously averted. "A third. I'm the one who must always be listening to her carrying on. I should reap the benefits."

The minotaur inclined its shaggy head with such a travesty of graciousness that I knew it had attained its goal. It had cultivated Gus entirely in the hope of exploiting me.

"Shall we begin?"

Gus drank again at that, priming himself for the violence at hand. The minotaur's glass was untouched, of course.

"How is it accomplished?"

Hidden somewhere in his words was a question: could he avoid watching while the operation was performed?

"The fork is inserted, anywhere at all; you will see that it embeds itself in Catherine just as securely as if she were fleshed. The thread rests in your mouth. You will find it easy enough to draw on her, and you can pay me my share when we are done." He paused. "If you prefer not to be observed, I can throw up a quick deflection so that no one looks at us for a bit."

"The fork doesn't go in her head? I suppose she has no brain anymore as a seat for her mental processes."

"Exactly." The minotaur nodded at me. "Whatever cognition she has is evenly distributed."

How can I describe what I next experienced? To speak of bodily sensations is at best analogy where a body is lacking. The silken fork was jabbed into what once would have been the fleshy part of my calf. At once the area felt thicker, stiffer, something like when blood swells the site of an injury. As the minotaur had promised, the fork stuck quivering in me, though in every other case I was incapable of interaction with material things. Excepting the walls, of course; but they were not material in the ordinary sense.

For some reason, the minotaur had not thought to mention the pain. It was different than bodily anguish, but pain was the only word for it. It was the sun's glare on a sheet of ice, but rendered in cold pricklings; it was a rain of needles, each of them hungry, parasitic, and sipping at my mind. And it was neither of these, but something like the first slap of bereavement: a cruel visitant that strikes and then passes through, deducting from one's essence as it goes.

Whatever it was, I buckled and flashed, quite unable to defend myself. And Gus held the thread in his mouth and sucked, his gaze fixed on his knees.

It went on until I felt myself whirl and bend, my black and white yanked from their usual alternation into a moody swirl; until so much of my consciousness flowed to power Gus that I folded into an uncertain dimness, nothing left to me but my scream. When I thought I could bear it no longer, Gus let slip the thread, and I heard his voice join with the minotaur's in cries of celebration.

"Ten! No, nearly eleven. Of course, she may not be so generous always. But nonetheless!"

"I did tell you that Catherine's mind was remarkable. I suppose it's only to be expected that she continues to be—a great inspiration. A muse to me, in death as she was in life. Oh, my regard for her was not misplaced!"

I sagged above them, a limp and wrung-out ectoplasmic rag. Not since the immediate aftermath of my murder had I felt such obliterating despair. Meanwhile they crowed and their glasses clinked while heads antlered and scaly continued their intimate babble all around us; the deflection had worked, no one had seen. But didn't they see me now? All the living present in this glimmering hall were human, I believed, or had been once. But no one felt the least compassion for me, or for those other poor wraiths for that matter? Did no one besides Miss Anura believe that I was still *myself*?

Gus and the minotaur drank and laughed while they laid plans for an ongoing project of mind-rape. They meant to meet regularly, I understood, going forward. Gus's laughter in particular was uproarious; it brayed and brawled, the notes of it knocking one another about. I had known Gus all his life, and never had I heard him produce such sounds before.

Now and then he brushed away tears. After some indeterminate time, he pitched from his chair onto the floor and lay quite still.

The minotaur arranged for an army of glistering silver-blue beetles to carry Gus back to his room. I did not doubt that he would extract the fare from Gus later, with something over for himself. I sailed above while Gus slid prone through the alleys on the rattle of ten thousand chitinous feet. Gus's eyes were closed, the lids lacquered in sweat.

Gus slept a long time, rousing only once to vomit purple fluid in a corner. Slowly I recovered myself, reared and flashed again.

When he woke and washed he kept his eyes stubbornly turned from me, while I did my best to flap into his line of sight. Given our peculiar relations, it was the nearest we could come to a quarrel.

"For *Margo*, Catherine," Gus muttered at last. "You must see reason! I will only inconvenience you until we can bring her here, of that you may be sure. We must both give our utmost, spare ourselves no effort or discomfort, if only Margo can be saved."

We. An outlandish construct, and a brutal one, that *we*. I tried to express as much with my scream, but it sounded the same as ever. Who was more isolate than I, a dead woman trapped among the living? I could not be packed into a *we* by anyone, least of all by my killer.

If everyone I'd loved had gone on with their lives and left me behind, then the only *we* I could conceive was the purest fantasy: a small blue hand in mine.

At that moment I would have gladly bled a thousand Margos to slow death, if by so doing I could have tasted my own life again. The realization surprised me: I hadn't been an outstandingly *good* person while I lived, perhaps, but to feel such driving malice toward anyone? That was a new development in my character.

Death, though it rots the body, usually has at least the virtue of sparing the spirit from further corruption. But it had not spared mine.

Catherine in Flames

Gus found me weeping on the riverbank. It was the spring of my thirteenth year, and life had begun its drumbeat of disappointments. He kneeled nearby, regarding me somberly, but did not touch me. Only after several minutes did he venture to speak.

"Oh, Catherine, I'm so sorry! But she's been suffering so long, no one should have to endure that. It might be a mercy, in the end."

It was a very natural misunderstanding, and after a moment I grasped it. "My mother? She's—she said she felt stronger this morning, even sat up in bed! Had a few bites of toast. She isn't—"

The opening leaves were thin and pointed as birds' feet. Their shadows clawed the ground, slipped on lamellae of ice. How cold it was for April!

Gus flushed. "Then what's wrong?"

"Miss Gryson. I went to her, I *begged*—I suppose the spiteful witch enjoyed it, because she let me plead on and on—"

His head tipped in bafflement. I hadn't actually told him of my intention to appeal to the teacher of our local school—I'd hoped to conceal the humiliation if she refused me. But her satisfied smile had made it all too clear that she would spread the story herself. There was no use trying to conceal what had happened.

"Begged for what, though?"

"The high school in Rochester. I can't go without a scholarship, but she could recommend me. She said it's hardly the education I seem to need, and that the best education for me would be the kind that comes from duty."

She'd also said how shameful it was, that I sought to flee my family even as my mother lay dying. Who, pray tell, did I think would watch the younger children in my absence, who tend the house? I omitted reporting that part of her commentary, since I knew that this woman I loathed was at least partly right. My father, certainly, would have considered it a cruel betrayal if I had succeeded in leaving.

I had confided my plan only in Anna, and she had urged me to go. I had cooked and nursed long enough, she'd said, and she would gladly take a turn. I'd promised to come back for her when I could, but I knew it was a kind of abandonment nonetheless. I *knew* that, and I loved her dearly.

Honesty demands a confession: such considerations wouldn't have stopped me for an instant. But Miss Gryson could, and had.

Gus leaned in. I watched white pouches of ice-caught air shift under the pressure of his foot. "Rochester? Of course you can't go. I can't believe you'd even consider it, I'd hardly ever see you. But Catherine, listen—"

"You have a tutor! You'll go to college! And my education will end completely in two months! You'll never know what it's like to be, oh, to be cut off from *yourself,* from the person you know you ought to be. To see her in the distance and know you have no way to get to her."

I had not dared, before that moment, to formulate the problem so clearly, even to myself. Hadn't allowed for the possibility that I might not find a way to escape what Margo termed my flowerpot.

"But going to Rochester wouldn't let you achieve your *real* transformation at all! If you'd only talked to me first, you'd— Never mind. Catherine, listen, you don't need anything Miss Gryson could ever give you, so there's no reason to care what she thinks. It doesn't matter a bit."

"I can see it doesn't matter to you!"

I'd never taken such a furious tone with Gus before, and he recoiled. "You aren't listening to me! If you care so much about conventional education, then I'll lend you all my books, I'll teach you whatever they teach me. But it's beside the point, really."

It wasn't what I wanted; I glossed my longings with the euphemistic *education,* when in truth distance, independence, escape all had an equal share in my desires.

But if Gus helped me, I might find another, albeit longer, way to achieve such wild dreams. "Gus! Do you promise?"

"Of course I do!" Already Gus gave me his books, as often as he dared, and then informed his parents they were lost; it was owing to him that I had, at this juncture, the rudiments of Latin. However much his father groused at the expense, he still replaced the missing volumes. With that in mind, I was ready to believe Gus—and with better Latin, Greek, mathematics, perhaps I might someday secure admission to one of the new female colleges! My despair scattered in a gust of fantasy. I half rose on my knees and turned to him, starry with gratitude; in another moment I might have violated our habitual reserve together and thrown my arms around his neck.

"But Catherine, what we really need is Darius. He's back in town, I saw him in the distance just this morning, in the lane near our house. This time I won't let him get away without *demanding* that he teach us everything he knows!"

Darius. The name slumped me back on my heels.

How sick I was of the subject! For two years Gus had fretted over Darius, dogged the old man's steps whenever he showed his face in town, dragged me along with him; then sputtered, faltered, said nothing in the end. And if I'd half-believed Gus's story of the fireflakes at the time, well, time had eroded my belief. We lived in an age of unseen forces when nearly anything seemed possible, but I thought that, at nearly fourteen, I'd learned to distinguish which *sorts* of forces were credible. Animal magnetism, electricity, mental energies were the currents sweeping us toward the future—or at least they might be.

But magic seemed too bare in its absurdity. Gus, I thought, ought to know better.

"What do you think Darius could do for us, even if he wanted to?" I tried to keep my voice relaxed, but exasperation drew it taut. "Say I learned to set fire to a snowstorm, what *use* would it be? Do you think I should throw my dough up in the air, and hope to have bread when it lands?"

Gus was shaking his head. "There must be more to it than that! Much more. Where do you think Darius goes, when he isn't here? He might—he might have a palace on the moon, he might be a nobleman there. You're sitting here talking about Rochester, and how I'll go to college, but I can tell you already I don't intend to do anything as ordinary as that! And when I do go to, to *wherever* it is, I'll bring you with me. I swear it, Catherine."

I'd known that Gus's reveries of magic occupied a good deal of his mental territory. I hadn't guessed that their conquest was so absolute. Why suppose that Darius went anywhere except to the next town over, or to an abandoned shack somewhere? The thought that Gus could no longer distinguish dream from reality stopped the mockery in my throat. My friend plainly needed help, not teasing.

"So you see now why you don't need Miss Gryson," Gus pursued. He was calm, patient; gravely unaware that he was uttering absurdities. "You don't need my books, either, though you're welcome to them if they amuse you. I'll look at them just enough to humor my parents, but no more."

There is no need to point out how near Gus's childish fantasies came to the truth—how grimly prophetic they were, indeed, even as I took them for utter delusion. It's not as if I've lacked the time for reconsideration.

"Gus!" I cast about, rather wildly, for the right thing to say. "It's very good of you to want to help me. And I know that you wouldn't just run to the moon and forget me here—"

"Of course I won't! I would *never* go without you. Everyone here thinks they can degrade you, drag you down to their miserable level. I'll lift you up—"

"But I think you might be getting a bit ahead of the facts—the definite facts—that we have in hand. All we know for certain of Darius's magic is what you saw two years ago now."

"No," Gus said.

"No?" I was not aware of climbing to my feet. But at this I found myself standing. Tense, knees slightly bent, as if I meant to run. We were in a narrow fringe of woods between the river and a fallow field belonging to one Mr. Clay. I could see its grass silvery in the cold light, its beckoning waves of shadow.

"Catherine, I haven't told you everything. I didn't just see Darius this morning. We—talked. He asked me to speak to you. Before he offers you a demonstration." Gus was standing, too, very close, his slight figure a slash against the field's shimmer. It was inconceivable that he meant to block my path.

"A demonstration?" I said. The twinkling of the grass now seemed wrong for the sunless day. A play of scattered gold, like sparks, flitted over its tips. I clapped my hands. "It's getting late. I should run home and start supper." I did not always mind the little ones as I should have done, and Gus knew it, but still it was indisputable that they must be fed.

Or so one might have thought.

"No!" Gus said again, and his manner turned abruptly from tender to imperious. He grasped my arm. "No, Darius said that you *must* see—" And there the old man was, square in the middle of the field. I hadn't seen him approach as I gazed that way. All around him birdlike forms flitted with a disquieting brightness. Lambent. *Burning.*

It could not be magic I was witnessing—Darius was nothing but a common vagrant, and it was beneath me to think otherwise—but fear sent shivers like emissaries down my limbs.

I tore my arm away.

Gus gawked as if I had committed some unspeakable betrayal. I felt his shock like a charge on the air, felt my own anger rise over a flush of guilt.

"I must get home, Gus!" I hissed. "I have more to do than listen to your ridiculous tales!"

With that I lunged out of the woods, ignoring as best I could the sense that Darius's regard dabbed at my every movement with a thousand delicate feelers. There was nowhere to go that would not take me past him, but I was quick, the field wide, the road just on the other side of it. Surely I could reach it before he caught me.

I didn't get far.

From the grass directly in front of me a serpentine *something* floated up. In form it was rather like a pollywog balanced on its tail, bulbous at the head and dwindling to a point at the bottom. The head—for such it was—was golden, translucent, and the size of a newborn's, but the thing brightened and blued along its length until its lowest extremity seared my eyes with azure.

The whole hideous thing was made of flame, bobbing and dancing, and its face was recognizably my mother's. But it was her face wizened, rotten, and infantile, as if someone had carved her likeness into an apple and then left it for days in the sun. It leered, and I could see the fiery gums shrunk back above the minute jets of flame that were its teeth.

I screamed and reared away, hands upflung. My thoughts whirled with blurring rapidity, but a tiny lucid core remained. And in it was the awareness that what I'd heard of Darius's magic involved fire.

I dodged to my left, hoping to break around the horror in my path.

A second blazing snake bounced up on the instant, this one bearing my Anna's angelic little visage turned crumpled and wicked. Her jaws worked as if she barked and snarled like a dog, but no sound came from her mouth. And when I whirled to the right another appeared, and another, closing off my retreat. The heat from those frisking serpents stroked my skin, smoldered in my cheeks. My eyes stung, as when one draws too near a bonfire.

How I fought against myself, then, for the small clarity persisting inside my terror informed me that the fire-snakes were nothing more than twitching marionettes. I was nearly certain that I could break through their ranks with no consequence worse than a singed sleeve.

Nearly. But my doubt and dread were enough to make me waver. And in the margin of my hesitation Old Darius came walking up behind me. When he was nearly on me, I caught his approach from the corner of my eye and jumped to face him.

I was entirely ringed in the faces of those I loved, all of them transformed into prancing, grinning grotesques spitting with heat.

Darius leaned on the fiery serpents, one forearm atop the other, as if they were a picket fence. Their frolics calmed as they steadied to support him, and he did not seem to burn. He leered at me, and I thought that his own vileness had served as his model for the faces surrounding me.

"Fear is a pretty thing, isn't it?" Darius asked me. He stank of ancient sweat and soot. "Fear shines where everything else goes dark. Its light shows the path, if you will but follow. Look at you dancing there with the firelight on your pretty hair! Look at you, looking at your fear, eyes so bright. Ah, but will you look closer? That's the question of the moment. Your little friend will, that's a given, but wouldn't I rather have you?"

"Let me go," I said, and was at once annoyed with myself. The utterance seemed both trite and futile. "I must go home."

Gus must have been watching the whole time, and now he came running, red-faced and breathless.

"Leave her alone!" he shouted fiercely; the effect was diminished by his fluttering yellow tufts. "Don't frighten her, or she won't want to—" Here Gus seemed to realize how the situation failed to align with his projections. "I was the only one who watched you on the bridge that night!" With that, Gus sounded nearly plaintive. "Catherine wasn't even *there*."

"What night?" Darius asked, and laughed. "There's the one that wants, and the one that fears. But the fear shines brighter. It shows me more. The power that frightens her? It isn't mine, I'll tell you that. What she sees reflected in me, now, that's another matter."

"I'm *not* afraid of you!" I put in—at least half a lie, but I felt truth in it too. If Darius was terrifying he was also ridiculous. Both of them ignored me.

Gus paused a moment, flummoxed. "I mean the night you set fire to the snow! It was just me. I only told Catherine about it afterward. But now she sees for herself that you're a sorcerer, I'm sure she'll, uh, recognize the potential of what you can teach us."

This last sentence was delivered like an offering.

Darius straightened, lifting his arms off the blazing snakes surrounding me. "A sorcerer? Am I really? Am I really, little boy, with so much disdain already in your eyes? The sun's not bright enough for your tastes, is it? And the ocean's far too dry."

"Of course you are."

"And would you like to hear a proper incantation now? *Oh piggledy south, a fart in your mouth. Oh flabberdy gee, a piss on your knee.*" He raised his hands in a gesture more flail than flourish, and the blazing snakes stretched high and thin. "Now, that's what I call magic!"

Darius cackled and Gus hung back, nonplussed by this performance. Such vulgarity hardly comported with his expectations of how a sorcerer should behave.

"I set fire to the snow whenever the cold nips my old ass," Darius added. "So I can't *imagine* what night you'd be referring to."

His flaccid mouth twisted into a smirk, which made it plain he was lying. And I? I felt rage lift at the base of my brain, felt something there tug loose. My teeth set in an unbidden snarl, and, so quickly that I could not tell what was happening, I felt my thoughts transformed into *something*—a scythe? The unseen shape slashed out, and the snakes hissed, loudly, then extinguished in a feathering of ash.

Darius looked momentarily startled. Then he grinned until his cheeks bulged.

The grass showed no mark, no hint of char, where those hellish manifestations had been. My way was clear now if I chose to run. Terror thumped inside me, and I longed to grasp Gus by his elbow and pull him with me in a frantic dash up the road. But Gus would not come, I knew. He had solicited this encounter, badgered and nagged for it. Why then should I not leave him to its good graces?

No. I could not abandon my friend. Gus looked dazedly at the falling ashes, so intent on screwing up his courage that he seemed not even to wonder what had quenched the fire.

"You promised to teach me!" he managed at last. "I can do it. I bear it concealed within me, the Great Secret waiting to be told!"

Presumably he was trying to nudge Darius toward a more suitable tone.

"And I think you do, indeed," Darius agreed, surprising me. "Some native ability. Take the filthy straw of your little-boy thoughts and spin it into something worth having, shall we?" But then he looked at me. "Didn't I hear you say that you won't go without her, though? I don't mean to be greedy, but you can't blame a poor old man for taking an interest."

His fingers worked the air, and I took a step backward.

"Catherine?" Gus said tentatively. "You can't think of the school in Rochester now, can you? Now that you see we're meant for so much more, for realms far beyond—everything we've ever known? And this is our chance!"

If I'd been able to articulate my thoughts in that moment, I might have said that Darius, with his bullying and staring, did not represent any *beyond* worth pursuing. Rather he seemed like more of the same, a dreary oppression I sought to escape, only in his case amplified by magic. But I had as yet no words for such intimations, and all I managed was a sharp shake of my head.

"I only scared you to *show* you, Catherine," Darius coaxed, now all lilt and courtesy. "It was just a little friendly teasing, no harm in it. I held up the mirror for you, that's all."

Did he think to win me over with this sudden change of tone? To me it was no change, but as disgustingly familiar as his rougher tactics had been. It was the same voice my father's cousin used, attempting to lure me under a hedge; the voice of the well-dressed old stranger who'd cornered me on the way home from school when I was only eight, and tried to force a kiss while I gagged and kicked. Only the lucky distraction of a crashing branch nearly on the man's head had enabled my escape.

"No," I said. "Gus, don't you see he's—all wrong? Whatever power he's offering you must be wrong too." Darius and I stayed fixed on each other as I spoke; he seemed surprised to find me less than charmed. Well, so had my father's cousin been. I caught Gus by his sleeve. "Please come away with me!"

Gus hesitated only briefly. "I *can't* turn him down. How else will I save you from this place?"

Should I have objected, in that moment, that I did not require saving?

Possibly I should have. Possibly what I required was not, at that age, clear to me. I stepped back, tongue-tied by obscure fury and frustration— for it seemed that I should somehow save *Gus,* and I saw no way I could without his participation.

I backed away a few steps, my legs weighted with reluctance. Darius saw it and chuckled.

"You can come to me when you're ready, pretty Catherine," Darius crooned, one hand creeping toward me. "I've got lessons enough for the both of you."

I sprang back in reflexive horror, then turned and ran. And Gus stayed behind. He seemed confident that he was safe with the ragged old sorcerer, and I did not imagine Darius would harm him physically. The danger I sensed was of another kind.

Gus stayed with his own unknown future, with his wild becoming that was an unmaking as well of all that was best in him.

I was temperamentally unsuited to magic, certainly, but there was more to the revulsion it inspired in me. I'd seen that magic was real, and at the same moment seen it allied with the forces that constrained me. I could not conceive of it as a friend.

The Rising

—Anura

Once in a hayloft, turning up the straw,
The gold unspun that scattered lightless motes,
I touched an empty pouch, a humanskin,
Its fingers limp as desolated hopes.
I raised it up and knew it for my own,
Then bore it to the fire and cast it in.

If fire is water, let it rise!

Once in a pond, forgotten as the drowned,
I glimpsed sky through a window hemmed in reeds,
And someone swam above, whom once I'd loved,
Yet who was now but greenly memoried,
Warped as the surface, blustered as the glow,
Till all that floated sank beneath the flood.

If time is water, let it rise!

Once in a city spiraled by our dreams,
With towers swift and mutable as thought,
I swallowed down a pearl, and felt it grow
Into a dome so vast that I was caught
In mazy whorls of what I had become.
No lung holds back the breath, no cloud the blow.

If mind is water, let it rise!

You called me sweetheart, I called you my dear,
But that was when I wore another shape.
When turning new I grasped my primal limbs,
I met your stricken gaze and mouth agape.
Who loves me as I'm not loves nothing mine,
So let new eyes of welcome take me in.

If heart is water, let me rise!

Angus in the Rain

Rain taps down, just a first few exploratory drops like dead fingers, but the air is sagging under the weight of all the drops to come. I've been looking for her all day, and I'm almost ready to say she doesn't exist and go sit in traffic.

There's a café across the street called Bluebell's. I've gone in a couple times and it's cozy, with mismatched slumpy chairs and a carousel horse wound in plastic ivy. A nice, warm, smoky smell, like Lapsang souchong and oak and leaky sofa stuffing. So, fine. I will go there, and order a cocoa, and write something pissy in my journal while I resent the universe for the intolerable way it's let me down.

The downpour starts for real just as I cross the threshold. Naturally I don't have an umbrella, because today is dedicated to making me miserable. There's a long line, because *today,* and some professorial dude cuts in front of me, because *today.*

At last, though, I reach the front. There's this cute touch where they have an antique roulette wheel on the counter, and if you win the spin your order is free. I scowl down at its red and black pie slices marked with golden numbers, because why even bother?

Then I look up at the girl taking everyone's orders. While I was still in line my view of her was blocked by the pastry case, but do I ever see her now!

Choppy, floppy, slept-on hair hacked off around chin length. Faded sunset streaks in her dark tangles, which more than compensate for the sunset that just got wiped out by the storm. Softly brown skin, lighter than Lore's but darker than mine. No makeup except for a few stray flecks of purple glitter in peculiar locations, such as her upper lip and neck. Huge hazel doe eyes, an exaggerated nose, a wide sweep of plump lips, a receding chin. She's nobody's idea of a beauty.

Except mine.

I stand there smiling like a maniac, expecting her to recognize me too.

"What can I get you?"

Gruff voice, but with a secret sweetness to it. Her gaze lands right on my face, and I don't see anything light up in her eyes. She really doesn't know that I'm me?

"Large cocoa?" I sound like a puppy snuffling for scraps. "And a piece of the lemon poppy-seed cake?"

She jots down the drink order, and it doesn't seem to bother her that she's stopped looking at me. "That'll be eight twenty-eight. Want to spin for it?"

Her hand is out, and I almost take it in mine. Then I see she's just offering me a blue-and-red marble to drop on the roulette wheel.

My hands jerk back and up. Defensively. That startles her into lifting her gaze my way again. "No. No, thank you."

"No? If you win your whole order is on the house."

"But, I mean—" How can I explain? "I've had way more than my share of good luck for today already. Trying for more would just be unappreciative." I dig in my wallet and hand her a ten-dollar bill.

That gets me a semi-huff of laughter. "No problem. What name?"

"Angus," I tell her. She nods and scribbles my name below *cc lg,* then slides the slip down to the barista. I drop my change into her tip jar while she levers my cake onto a vintage plate with the logo of a defunct railway on its rim. And then I'm completely out of excuses to keep hanging around the counter and staring at her.

It's me, I want to tell her. *It's me, it's me, and you don't have to wait any longer.*

Strategy! I choose my table carefully: one where she'll have a sidelong view of me. But I sit with my back mostly to her so I won't gawk too much. I want to give her a chance to recognize me too; to surreptitiously study the lines of my neck and shoulders, the way the lamplight traces my curls, and think, *You know, there's something about that guy! Why didn't I notice before?*

Then I open my journal and slowly, deliberately eat my cake, taking my time as I lick frosting off the fork. Maybe she'll bring my cocoa over herself, use it as a pretext to start a conversation.

"Angus!" a voice calls. But it's a guy's voice, not hers, and its tones are sodden with indifference. When I stand up to fetch the mug she's talking with animation to another girl across the counter, her big mouth leaping through vivid smiles and grimaces. She doesn't look at me at all.

So she needs a little longer. I go back to writing, trying hard not to feel hurt. But as the minutes tick on and she doesn't come over something starts poking in my chest, like my heart is growing porcupine quills.

I run out of cake and cocoa, and I must have flooded a dozen pages with illegible babble by the time I feel a presence near my shoulder. So warm, so right, so full of gruff, sweet life that I don't even need to look. I glance up as casually as I can.

"Hey," she says. "It's almost ten. We're closing."

When I first saw her I was so overwhelmed by her face that the rest of her escaped my notice. I look now. She's wearing a worn-out T-shirt with the legend FREE KITTEN and a snarling cartoon tiger. Necklace and bracelets made of brightly colored pom-poms on strings. Slouchy torn jeans, navy sneakers. I love her so much, and it's not socially acceptable to tell her so. How long do I have to wait? Is a week enough time?

"Okay," I say, because what do you say in a situation like this? Stand up, shove my journal in my back pocket. "Have a great night."

The rain has stopped. All that's left is a checkerboard of puddles under the dark sky. Where the traffic lights blink, green and red shadows criss-cross the pavement like drawn knives.

Catherine in Mind

From his point of view, Gus's merciless exploitation of me was a roaring success. He still huddled in the garden shed much of the time, drawing on his own consciousness to supplement the greater wealth he derived from me. Whatever else might be said of him, his anxiety that Margo might die before he could buy her redemption was sincere. But he allowed himself more rest than formerly, smiled more, and lingered sometimes by the Nimble Fire with a drink in his hand. The thrum of agitation that had sung through all his limbs grew subdued.

When I knew he had collected nearly the thousand talens required for purchasing Margo's citizenship, I felt an unexpected brightening, a lucent anticipation. Even the torture of the umbrastring took on a biting joy, and I yielded to it with new eagerness. In truth, I was beside myself at the prospect of seeing Miss Anura again—for however unreasonably, I considered her a friend. My only friend, indeed, in that dreadful place.

I was rational enough to understand she did not, could not, share this valuation of our negligible relations. I knew that, if she saw me as more than an object, that very *more* might appall her. I knew I had no way to communicate with her, nor to tell her of my regard. My last attempt had been a notable failure.

All that uncompromising awareness did nothing to stifle the hope that I might find a way to make myself understood, and to understand her in return.

When Gus met the minotaur to draw the last eight talens he required from me, I leaned into the pain with gratitude at what those talens would buy me: a few moments' nearness to a talking frog. Hope is a habit that outlives life itself.

Gus left the Nimble Fire upright on this occasion. From there he wove through the sinuous alleys directly to that framed patch of wall where *Immigration* was inscribed in letters of a sharper glow than the general hazy ambiance, and burst through with arrogant suddenness. The startling effect was undoubtedly enhanced by my scream. Miss Anura sprawled atop her papers, pen in hand, and looked up annoyed—and there was something closed in her expression as well, the contraction of slight embarrassment. Gus's momentum sent me pitching in that narrow space so that I swooped close to Miss Anura's papers before she could cover them. I saw a series of short lines, the dark clusters of stanzas, and saw as well that they were signed simply *Anura*. I resolved at once to drop the *Miss* from my thoughts and style her as she styled herself.

She was a poet! I yearned to read more—what a delight it would have been to peruse even dull, indifferent verses after my long deprivation! Gus no longer read at all, so I had no opportunity to peer at books over his shoulder. But I had at once the feeling that Anura's poetry was something more than dull.

Her small blue hand yanked official papers over the page before I caught more than the opening words. *Once in a hayloft . . .*

It need hardly be said that haylofts were a scarce commodity in Nautilus. It tended to confirm my guess that she came from the unworld just as we did; that she had not been born here, nor whipped up in some frenzy of conjuring. I wondered what had brought her to this place, what personal history darted unseen in her depths.

"I have it!" Gus proclaimed, loud and impetuous, as if the matter were every bit as important to her as it was to him. "The whole thousand! I can make the transfer to you now, then bring back my aunt to be certified in front of your witnesses. Shall we proceed?"

She looked at him in silence for some moments, blinking her scarlet eyes. I found that my previous urge—to kiss her hand—was still very much present, impossible as such an act would be for me.

"I did not expect to see you again so soon, Mr. Farrow."

"No," Gus agreed. He deflated before her dearth of enthusiasm. "No, of course. I should have knocked. I found a way—to speed matters to this happy conclusion."

Her lemon-shaped pupils narrowed and rolled up to my face, and I felt myself pulse in response. Would she address me again? My bright and dark were still in that sickly ebb and swirl that came after Gus's sessions draining me. Anura's level gaze was as good as saying that she knew quite well what *way* Gus had found to his windfall, and that she did not approve.

If she dismissed Gus on my account, I thought it likely that Margo would die in the unworld, and fairly soon. She had not been looking well. I will confess that my spite toward Gus was enough to make me prefer Margo dead, if only to watch him suffer. Toward Margo herself I bore no ill will.

(I have examined my last statement, and found it less than true.)

"How convenient for you," Anura drawled at last. With that I knew that while she might enjoy provoking Gus, she would not refuse a bribe that was for the most part cruelly extracted from me. Why did I at once forgive her?

Forgive her I did, with an impetuous fullness of heart that was quite unlike me. If I examine the question cynically, I suppose I couldn't afford anger at the only person in Nautilus who was ever kind to me. I told myself it was better that the talens go to her than stay with Gus.

"And for you as well," Gus sniped. "Isn't it?"

The ruby eyes blinked in acknowledgment. A device was brought forth from a tiny drawer in the desk, unwound with ceremonious care. It was similar in some respects to the implement that Gus used on me: it consisted of a thread like gleaming spider silk with minuscule dial that might at first glance be mistaken for a dewdrop dangling near one end. What was missing, of course, was the fork that regularly skewered my fleshless flesh.

By then I had seen enough to know the delicate trinket for a heartstring. It appeared to be the ordinary kind used for ordinary transactions— Gus sometimes paid for drinks with a similar, if cruder, one—though I guessed that Anura's must be in some way spelled to conceal her bribe-taking.

Gus and Anura each took one end in their mouths. Gus's face turned pale and queasy at once, while Anura's battened visibly around a slow smile—which in her case encircled half her body, as if satisfaction clasped her in a tender embrace.

And then something occurred that I think no one present had anticipated. It was subtle enough; to this day, I'm not sure if Gus noticed anything. For me there was a sudden roll, a shifting and yaw to my view, a smeary doubling. I still saw Anura crouched on her desk, but at the same time I saw Gus sickly and teetering, his hair in jerky peaks above closed eyes. And above Gus I saw *myself*: lightning white and the slick black of decomposition throbbed together around the void of my screaming mouth, topped by a lashing halo of hair.

My disorientation was a mad and flailing thing, but driven through it was a single pin of understanding. I knew that I was looking through Anura's eyes. More than that, I felt her muscles tense at a sudden sense of *invasion*. An alien presence brushed against her mind, featherlight and not screaming at all.

What she felt touch her thoughts was none other than myself, and I am sure she knew it. Not the whole of me, of course, but a torn-off wisp, an outlying fiber. It was a sentinel of self that thought with me, felt with me, for all our separation.

Hello, I said, or rather thought. She shuddered, and I felt a bursting release at finding I had crossed that uncrossable barrier between myself and all other thinking beings. It hardly mattered that it was only a single word. A word to me then was a universe of possibility.

But having come so far, the hope of more urged me on. I must speak, and quickly; I did not know how long this odd connection would persist. While she held the heartstring in her mouth? Or not even as long as that?

I was and am very grateful for your kindness in acknowledging me, Anura. To one in my condition, such recognition is everything.

A pause. She had been afraid at first sensing me. Now she reevaluated, and found her fears misplaced.

I am well aware of what recognition *can be worth, Miss Bildstein.*

We were conversing! In the excitement of my speech coming un-dammed, I would have babbled on with excessive animation—I wanted to ask about her literary labors, about her life, about everything. But here Gus reeled back and the heartstring dropped from his lips.

With that small slippage, my ability to speak dropped away as well. The rush of words backed up with a choking sensation. What on earth had happened, I wondered, and how could I contrive to make it happen again?

"A thousand! There you have it, Miss Anura. I'll go fetch my aunt and we can conclude our business. Can you muster up your witnesses on short notice?"

Anura stretched her hind legs, and her gaze stayed stubbornly lowered. On the instant I feared that I had offended her somehow. Why else did she avoid looking at me?

"For the pleasure of concluding business with *you*, Mr. Farrow, I would have my witnesses dragged from their beds." Previously I would have enjoyed the implied insult, but now it cut—for if she wished never to see Gus again, it meant she also had no desire to see me.

"Well, then," Gus sputtered. "I will return as soon as possible."

He headed for the wall, his chin up in a poor attempt at dignity. I had no choice but to drag along behind him. But I could twist myself to face Anura, and I could lean in her direction like a sapling in the wind.

Now that Gus wasn't watching, Anura gazed up at me. She smiled, rather sadly I thought. And then I saw that she was holding up a paper hastily scrawled.

Courage, Miss Bildstein.

Then the moment was past, and we were through the wall and hastening toward one of those rabbit holes back to the unworld. His steps were stumbling, veering, from the shock of giving up so much magic at once. Who would wash Gus's laundry, I wondered, once Margo was brought here? Who would feed him roast lamb and potatoes? But I gave those questions only idle consideration, for there was another that compelled my attention.

How had we communed, Anura and I?

Gus had made other transfers of magic, of course, though only in grudging amounts. On those occasions I had not felt myself sweeping against the consciousness of the recipient, nor had I spoken. I had not thought to try, admittedly. But it seemed likely that the immense sum of a thousand talens, most of it drawn from the workings of my mind, had been enough to carry a scrap of me into Anura—though I had been able to speak only while the transfer was in progress.

This, I realized, was the *danger* that Gus and the minotaur had spoken of: that using me might in some small way free me as well.

Gus popped up by the orchard, now white and luxuriant with spring blooms in the rising sun. The air twirled with birdsong. And what had seemed such a marvelous development, such a bubbling-up of hope and sweetness, reversed its flow and sucked again into the mud.

It had taken a *thousand talens* poured all at once into Anura's mind before I could speak a few desperate words. A thousand! When would Gus yield up so much wealth again? Especially, when would he yield it up to her? When could I ask her anything, or receive the fleeting touch of her sympathy?

The answer, plainly, was *never*. There was no other living person whom Gus loved; for no one but Margo would he pay such an exorbitant bribe, or any bribe at all. Therefore I would never have another chance to speak to Anura. I would see her briefly while she fussed with Gus's paperwork, and that would be my last glimpse of her unless we passed her in the street. Oh, I had lost everyone I loved while I was alive, and now this new connection was ripped away almost in the moment it was formed!

The exhaustion, the despondency this thought induced was nearly enough to pitch me back into a state of oblivion. My vow to stay alert was not sufficiently strong to keep me from craving that self-erasure into which my first ghostly span had vanished.

What *did* stop me was the memory of Anura's scribbled message. *Courage.*

I would have liked to ask her what had made her write such a thing. On what possible grounds should such as I choose courage over helpless lethargy?

I did not think Anura was one to induce false hopes.

It followed that there was a way, if only I could see it.

A way to avenge my murder, and with it achieve my release. That it might be release into nonbeing troubled me not at all. At this thought Gus neared the end of his path, and the Farrows' house flashed, dawn-pinked, through the fluttering lace of blossom.

A possibility struck me: I'd considered myself cut off from all other minds. But my thought-collision with Anura proved that was untrue: I'd entered her via Gus!

I understood, then, that some essence of myself infused him every time he drew power from me. That was—interesting.

Gus lifted his aunt tenderly from her bed with the same hands that had throttled me. He bade her dress while he shoved a few of her effects into a carpetbag. She looked weak, her eyes wandering, but she obeyed him.

I had been generous with self-pity since my murder, and I defy anyone to say I bestowed it without justice. But as I watched Margo hustled with hat askew through the hallways and down the stairs, I had as yet no idea how much pity was owed to *her*. The old lady offered her beloved nephew no resistance. She suffered him to drag her off to Nautilus and thereby save her life.

Had she refused to go with him, had she insisted on staying to meet her death, she would have saved something far more precious.

Catherine in the Crowd

Understand, dreadful reader, that the middle of the nineteenth century was an unquiet era. The urgent questions of abolition and women's rights beat the air like wings; the ghosts who'd merely rapped and tapped for the Fox sisters appeared to be growing ever more numerous, forceful, and expressive. The old Calvinist doctrines, so eager to toss dead children like coals on the fires of hell, were shaken by new beliefs in universal salvation. Nowhere was this tempest of change wilder than in our region of western New York, and so for me Darius's magic took on the character merely of one more gust—or so I told myself.

It was a different blast, a few months later, which brought me Margo's invitation via my father's hand. The trance speaker Nora Downs was to give a talk in our town's small hall, Margo's note said, as if we could possibly be unaware of an event so fervently discussed on every corner. Would I kindly accompany Gus and herself to see Miss Downs speak?

A pleasure in petty tyranny surely informed Margo's selection of my father as her messenger. She must have known how much he, a good and rather rigid Methodist, would recoil from its delivery. Known too that he was not in a position to refuse her. When I read the note aloud, he could not meet my eye.

"The apostle Paul said women aren't to speak so, in public. If this girl's wrong to speak, I don't see how it can be right for you to listen. I told old Mrs. Farrow that, and she said it's not the girl doing the speaking at all, but the spirits using her to be their vessel. Well, what are the spirits doing out of the hereafter, then?"

This was an extraordinarily long and intemperate speech by my father's standards.

"I can take what I hear with a grain of salt," I reassured him—neglecting to mention that my salt would be of a very different flavor from his own. My reading was quickly leading me to that most unacceptable of ideas, materialism, and I no longer believed that the spirit survived the body, or at least not with its individuality intact. "We wouldn't want to offend Margo Farrow."

I still incline to the belief that the spirit *should not* survive, even if I'm not in a position to deny certain evident exceptions.

"Just be sure you don't, don't—" my father mumbled. I did not kiss him, only nodded as soberly as I could, since too much warmth would give away how my heart was racing.

They said Nora Downs was only fifteen, hardly any older than I was; scarcely literate, in which I flattered myself we were poles apart; the daughter of farmers. Yet she stood up in front of large crowds and spoke with the eloquence of angels. Extempore, at that: she would be informed of her subject only once she arrived in the hall.

I was desperate to see her, and I'd told Gus as much; after a brief chill following the episode with Darius, we were often together again. And he, in turn, had told Margo.

The next night I stood sweating between Gus and Margo under smoke-black beams; such was the crowd that they'd taken out the benches. Heads clustered thick as August blackberries in the airless murk. A man mounted the podium and announced that Miss Downs would speak on the virtue of obedience—a topic obviously chosen to trip her up. And with that, he yielded his place.

A flash of many colors broke from the shadows beside the stage. Miss Downs had not tried to cloak the indecency of her public appearance in dourly modest clothes, as the abolitionist women did. Instead she wore a dress brightly striped: cherry, dawn pink, feverish moss green. Her coffee-colored ringlets trailed long and loose around a pale face; her eyes were closed as if in rapture. Ribbons flaunted from her wrists.

Her neckline was so low that I felt a throb of agitation at the sight. Her shoulders shone, bare and vulnerable, in the light of an Argand lamp suspended over the stage.

This unlikely creature climbed the few steps with dreamlike slowness, all alone. Her eyes remained shut tight, but she did not grope or stumble when she reached the stage. Instead she advanced serenely and then turned and folded her hands atop the podium—and how could she find it with such an assured economy of movement in this strange hall, when she could not see?

The crowd gasped. A great many of those present took it as proof that spirits escorted her, and the rest at least wondered.

"The spirits have brought me here to speak on their behalf, so that what is known above can be known below, and guide the conduct of those who await their own ascension." Her voice seemed too light and girlish to carry well, and yet it sounded close and intimate in my ear. Her lids fluttered like a dreamer's, and the shadows cast by her long lashes quivered on her cheeks. "And above, as below, there is no virtue dearer, more essential to the happiness of all, than true and perfect obedience."

The crowd's reaction cleaved predictably between the customary recipients of obedience and those obliged to dole it out. Approving murmurs, grunts of anger. I suppose my dismay showed on my face, because Margo smiled at me sidelong and pressed my hand: as much as to say, *wait*.

"But how shall we distinguish true obedience from false? Therein lies the difficulty at the source of all the great and pressing problems of the day. There are many, too many, who insist that the Creator arranged humankind in a hierarchy, wherein each of us owes obedience to those above: wife to husband, slave to master, the poor to the rich. But tell me, was there ever a husband who made his own wife from the clay? None of you are Pygmalion. And if God did not delegate the *creation* of woman, neither did He delegate the command of her conscience!"

I felt my heart go still.

There was no greater blasphemy, Miss Downs continued, no fouler sin, than to exact false obedience. To do so was an assault on God's will, a usurpation of his place.

And *any* obedience delivered from one human being to another was false. Surely no one dared propose that the all-powerful Creator was too feeble, too negligent, to speak directly to each human heart? We were each, equally, God's holy revelation, the manifestation of His word; we must therefore be equally free to act on the truths we embodied.

If I had been drifting toward atheism, Miss Downs' astonishing re-ordering of religion was nearly enough to drag me back. How neatly she turned divine authority against anyone who harnessed it in support of oppression!

It was not lost on me that Miss Downs was among those who stood to benefit, if the wisdom of her spirits was generally applied. So, of course, was I.

It was not lost on me that no one would have paid the slightest attention to her, if she had admitted to speaking for herself.

It was not lost on me that she played at passivity to hide her own fierce will.

The crowd listened now in silence, and if certain white men and women flushed with shame and fury, the larger part of those assembled— the dark-complexioned men, the tattered ones, most of the women of all hues and classes—took on a proud radiance.

An hour later, Miss Downs had established that *obedience* necessarily entailed the radical equality of all humanity. Then she went limp. Her head dropped forward and she rubbed at her eyes with her fists, like a sleepy child.

She looked from under her lashes with a shy smile. "Hello. Whatever have I been saying? I— Please excuse me, I think I had better sit down."

A lady rushed to help her off the stage. There was a stir and flutter and the dimness went pale with handkerchiefs patting away the sweat beading on every forehead. It was some time before the press of bodies carried us into the open air, but then I was met by a night that seemed vaster, looser, than any I had known before, by stars so bright the air seemed to shake with their applause.

"What more proof do you need of spiritual inspiration?" a man said to his companion. I looked and saw that it was Dr. Lewis and his wife, who were every bit as prominent as the Farrows. "A poor, ignorant country girl who hardly knows what a word like *equality* means? It's inconceivable that she delivered such a speech on her own!"

Gus cocked his head at that, considering, then shook it decisively. Margo smiled at him with such burning elation that I knew her, with a shock, for a complete convert to Spiritualism. But none of us spoke until we had crossed the unassuming town square and reached the quiet road that led to my family's cottage, where we stopped and perched on a stone stile. The moon was gibbous and very bright, sketching our faces in silver.

"She's a fraud," Gus announced brusquely once there was no one in earshot. "That is, she isn't what she claims to be. Did you see her absurdly overdone innocence, when she pretended to wake from her trance? I don't see how anyone could fall for it." He paused. "It's possible she could be—something else, though."

I knew he hadn't yet told Margo of his secret apprenticeship, so I let the implication wisp away.

"A genius, then? To speak so well, untaught, with no preparation whatsoever?" Margo asked. She positively glittered. "And you, Catherine? Do you think that sweet girl could be a fraud, or is she a conduit for the spirits, as she claims?"

I hesitated to answer. I had, in fact, very definite views of what Nora Downs was, and what she was doing. But I didn't know how to cast those views without impugning her character.

"I think the ideas she voices are her own," I said at last. Gus snorted in triumph, and Margo arched her brows. "But that doesn't mean her trance isn't genuine—or that she isn't truly inspired. She is, only by something in herself."

I did not mention how much I would have liked to throw myself at Miss Downs' feet.

(I was hardly alone in this. I would learn later that she batted away marriage proposals like so many mosquitoes. If I had been young in a later era, would I have recognized my feelings for what they were?)

I did not mention how, if there were any fraud involved in compelling the world to *hear* her, it was a sort I would have very much liked to perpetrate myself.

Nor that her deceit, if it was such, was nothing compared to the imposture of the men who daily claimed an undeserved superiority over the rest of humankind.

"I knew Catherine would see through her nonsense!" Gus crowed— though I had neither said nor meant such a thing. Margo gave me a long and searching look.

"So you never question your father's beliefs, young Catherine? You're quite sure the souls of the dead stay glued either to heaven or hell, like flies mired in honey, and can't come anywhere near the living?"

In that time and place, in the person of a girl of fourteen, my true beliefs were inadmissible. I suppose it was owing to the influence of Miss Downs' intoxicating openness that I admitted them.

"No. I don't believe in the immortal soul at all! There are no angels or ghosts, and the only spirit we have is in the present moment! If there is to be a *better world* we must make it ourselves, now, and not wait for a heaven that will never come."

I spoke with breathless passion, then stopped, appalled by my own honesty. I didn't entirely trust Margo; if she repeated my incautious words I could expect to be roundly denounced, rejected by nearly everyone. My father too; he would be heartbroken. Margo gazed at me, brows hiked, but her mouth showed a twist of amusement.

Gus went uncharacteristically quiet. I knew him, felt his tension bowing the air beside me: it was not the silence that comes from having nothing to say, but rather from having too much. I meant to ask him later what was on his mind. When we were alone.

"A skeptic, then," Margo said, smiling so slyly that I was nearly persuaded she would not betray me. "But what if you witnessed evidence of the spirit's survival for yourself?"

To you, I imagine, the significance of Margo's question may be obscure. But in western New York, in the year 1854, there was only one construction I could put on her words.

Margo was inviting me to a séance.

Assuming the séance would be held in the Farrows' house, I could not imagine that Gus's mother would tolerate my presence. I was about to say as much when running footsteps sounded on the dirt road, and all of us turned to see a small figure pelting toward us at frantic speed.

"Catherine!" Anna shrieked. "Oh, Catherine, you weren't there, she asked for you but there wasn't time to go and search—"

How long did it take, the revolution of my thoughts from denial to understanding? It was endlessly slow, and yet so fast the moon blurred into a stream of milky light.

Our mother was dead, and only moments after I had denied any hope of her salvation.

Angus Gets a Ride

Stay calm, I tell myself. *It's a process. You can't expect overnight results.* If she was just going to find me annoying, why would so many factors work so perfectly to bring us together? Short answer: they wouldn't bother. And that's why I'm back at Bluebell's in a collapsing brocade chair, inhaling cocoa and shortbread, while closing time creeps up on me.

Something weird that I hadn't totally registered before: I can't seem to read my own writing. As in, at all. My hand seems to be full of enthusiasm for the creative process, but my eyes flinch at the wriggling ink. I have to assume I'm writing about her?

But she doesn't show, she doesn't show. And after a while the counter dude comes to kick me out. His piercings bayonet the innocent air, and we hate each other.

The instant I'm back in the street I get the feeling that things aren't entirely right. I need to be on the lookout, but for what?

For *what*? My mind starts to sing with alertness in a whole new way; I didn't know I was capable of it. That mailbox on the corner, for example: it's as if I'm watching it from every angle at once, holding it suspended in my mind like some kind of 3D rendering. I can rotate it, inspect it inside and out. I can breathe in the traffic vibrations sliding through its metal sides.

The mailbox checks out. So do the fifteen squares of sidewalk between me and it. I walk that far, then stop again. *Step on a crack, break your mama's back,* and even though I'm not particularly close to my mom I stick to the squares. The bookstore's display window glows on my right, limning the mailbox and a sapling in soft gold. The excessively pierced jerk from the café walks out behind me—I don't need to look to know it's him, because even his scrubby little beard prods my consciousness on a hair-by-hair level—locks the door, and glares at my back for a few beats before he turns away.

Bye-*bye.*

Shit. Something else is moving; it's my fault for letting the café guy distract me. A twitchy paper-cut of a motion somewhere near my left shoe.

A thin black line is fidgeting an inch above the ground. I stare, and it looks like an optical illusion, like the kind of artifact that might jump around on your retinas after you gazed at a bright crack for too long.

A *crack*. I understand it's a significant detail before I grasp why. Not a line.

Oh. It's one of the cracks that surrounds my square of pavement. It's lifting free of the sidewalk and ascending the air with spasmodic little jerks. Higher and higher. It's like a slim drain made of pure darkness, and my mind is sliding into its dancing suction.

Shit, shit, *shit*. That is not a metaphor. The line is drinking me down.

I reel back, but they're all around me now. Black sidewalk cracks prance on all sides, slurping on the edges of my mind. They gouge my view of the tree trunks across the street, gash the parked cars, carve into the bright jackets of the books gleaming behind glass. There's a straining in my skull as my consciousness tightens like cloth yanked in every direction at once.

They're going to rip me apart and feed on the scraps. Spew my remnants through to—somewhere, crumple me, chew me into compost. Why do I get the feeling it's happened before, this mashing down, over and over? Why am I sick to death of being recycled? It's not a great moment to dwell on the question. I scramble up onto the mailbox, clinging on all fours to its blue metal lid, but the cracks keep on with their inexorable twitching up, and up, and up.

Even though the cracks are about to devour me, I'm impressed. This is an advanced stunt. I feel, I don't know, a sort of professional admiration for it, though I know that makes no sense. *Somebody* did this to me, that much I get. It follows that somebody hates my guts.

There's a shredding pain along my left thigh. I'll never get to kiss her now, or even touch her hand.

A silver-blue car shrieks to a stop beside me. The crack jitters in front of it, crossing out the shimmering paint behind. The darkness is accumulating now like a heap of sticks, but I can make out the car's passenger door swinging open.

"Angus!" A spill of long silver hair, warm brown eyes. Whose, again? "Angus, get in!"

Lore. But the crack separates me from her car, a hungry midair moat. It wobbles, it craves.

"I can't get to you!"

"Leap over it! And pull your feet up!"

I can see what she's thinking, but it seems challenging. That dark dancing crack is already a good bit higher than the mailbox's top. I'll have to spring way up and out at the same time from my slippery blue summit, and I can barely get traction.

It's that or have my psyche drawn and quartered, sucked straight from my skull. And I have to do it *now,* or I'll have no chance of getting over that thing.

I scramble my feet into a steadier position, crouch, and propel myself up into the night. There's a sharp streak of pain deep in my head as if a strip of glue had torn away, taking brain tissue with it—the bitch of a crack bit me!—but then I'm crashing down. My shins hit the edge of Lore's car and my upper body topples through the open door and onto the seat.

She's dragging me in by the shoulders even as I'm swinging my legs in behind me. I wind up in a tilted fetal position while she leans over me to slam the door, her foot already pounding down on the gas.

It takes me a moment to catch a first breath and straighten myself out, and several breaths more before I can speak. My head is screaming and my heart jabbers like a cage full of monkeys. When I twist around to look behind us, my odd heightened sense of perception is gone, and I don't see anything but ordinary street and electric-frosted night.

"Lore," I manage, "Lore, you're so great! Thank you. Those things would have killed me." Then I turn back to her. Her profile, weary but still strong and defined, her golden-brown skin ribboned in bluish light, her brown eyes fixed on the road. We're peeling away at wild speed, heading down streets I haven't seen before. It's already getting leafier than I would expect in the middle of a city; are we entering some huge park?

"They would," she agrees. "You would have been destroyed barely a week after your appearance here, and it would have been due to your own carelessness. Angus, I absolutely expected you to do better than that!"

"You're criticizing me for almost getting murdered? That seems pretty unfair. I have no idea why some stranger would try to off me!"

Shit. I'm almost whimpering. There's a flash in my head, not quite a face. Turning away under a spill of honey hair and smiling pure loathing. *Who?*

Lore's scolding has such a warm, motherly tone, though; it's almost like she's chewing me out because she cares about me. The car is zooming now down an alley of vastly arching mossy trees, a primeval tangle of night-stained green.

I watch Lore nod in the mirror, moonlit reflections waving on her deep eyes—not an agreement nod, a so-that's-what-you-think nod.

"It's only effective on a very temporary basis," Lore says, and her voice sounds like she's kidding but I don't quite get the joke. "And once you've killed someone enough times, you can start to be fond of them."

I give a little laugh just so she won't think I'm too dim to follow her humor, even if I am.

The car swerves around a bend, and an enormous chasm opens up on our right. There aren't any streetlights out here, but the moon is full and throbbing and bigger than I've ever seen it, glazing everything in pearl. It echoes a cluster of irregularly spiraled towers and domes glowing at the depths of that crevasse; they're made of something pale and semitranslucent, like quartz or cloudy ice. After a moment, I realize how huge that clump of shining buildings must be, a city within this city.

A sound ravels up from the depths: a scream threading into my mind, shrill and bright. A girl's voice; I know I'll never reach her in time. That flash again, her honey hair rippling up in the blast.

I'm so sorry, I think. *It's too late to save you.*

The road gives another quick twist, and the chasm vanishes behind dense foliage. Taking the scream with it, thank God. Did Lore hear anything?

"Does everybody know about this park?" I try. I'm realizing that I sometimes have trouble understanding what would seem normal to normal people and what wouldn't. It's like I have some kind of dyslexia, but for reality instead of reading.

Lore smiles, more to herself than to me. "It isn't widely recognized, no."

"Okay." Then what is it?

"Did that city look familiar to you, Angus? Would you say you've been there before?"

Lore's tone is cautious, measured, like it's a sensitive question. And it kind of is, because I feel a suppressed boiling in my guts. A punishing snap of headache where the crack bit me. What business is it of *hers,* I'd like to know.

"I've never even heard of it," I snarl. Way too nastily, actually, but Lore just nods.

"It seems unlikely that the entity which attacked you is a stranger, though. And if you have no idea who or why, it might be time to question your memory."

"You seem like you know a lot about me." I think about that. "Am I supposed to know why? Like, did we meet each other before, somewhere?"

Maybe in that city. Is that why she asked about it?

Maybe in a lot of cities. But how is that possible? It's not like I ever traveled much.

Where do these nagging thoughts come from? The seared stripe in my brain blinks neon pain at me.

"We could have," Lore says. Somehow we're back in the warehouse district, and she takes advantage of a traffic light to glance toward me with a wry smile. "Stranger things have happened, my poor young friend."

She likes me and she feels sorry for me, and I have no idea why. Her pity gets into my guts, knots them into an anxious mess. I decide to keep my mouth shut; talking just increases the risk she'll say things I can't stand to hear. We roll on again and pretty soon we're pulling up on West Street right by my rusty green door. The gold mylar parallelograms around *2021* glint like wet teeth.

"Angus, before you go." She's reaching into a pocket. "I have something for you."

She dangles a long silver chain in front of me. Hanging from it is a flat, dark beach stone, sort of like the ones she wears, but bigger. It's maybe an inch and a half long, an approximate oval with a hole drilled in the top for the chain. I take it in my hand, and it has the most alluring satiny smoothness. Stroking it instantly makes me feel better, soothes the pain in my head and settles the blood that's been banging around my system ever since the cracks jumped me.

Something interesting about the pendant: it's mostly dark gray, but on one side half of it brightens along an imperceptible gradation. When I look closely my own dark eye winks back. It's stone that reflects like a mirror. I didn't know anything like it even *existed*.

It's a beautiful, beautiful thing. Why did I have to go and get pissy with Lore, when she's so awesome?

"Wow," I say. "Thank you. That's so cool."

"It's more than that," Lore says, and I think I kind of knew. "If you wear it faithfully, it will help you."

"You mean like protect me?" That sounds useful. Somebody wants me mulched, wood-chippered, chowed into cat food, so magical talismans are totally in order.

"If not you, then someone you love," Lore says. She's twisting in the driver's seat to face me, enveloping me in her searching gaze. "There's someone already, isn't there?"

I can't get over how insightful Lore is.

"Yeah," I admit. "She works at that café. Bluebell's. But we've barely even talked. It's just—I've seen her and I *know* I love her, but it would be hard to explain why?"

"You'll understand the whole *why* of it in time," Lore assures me. "Wear the stone all the time, then. For her sake."

"Okay," I promise. "Shit, so would the mystery person who's trying to kill me actually be vicious enough to target her too? That's so horrible!"

"I wouldn't suggest you take any chances, especially not with her safety. Evil has a way of manifesting where you least expect it. Here."

Lore lifts the pendant from my hands and slides the chain over my head. The stone drops against my heart. Its weight is reassuring, subtly warm, like a hand tenderly pressed against me.

"I'll wear it every day, then. I'd never want her to go through anything like I just did, with those cracks!" That reminds me. "Um, thanks for saving my life tonight?"

"You don't need to thank me. I'm doing the best I can with a difficult situation." Once again I'm having trouble following her thinking, but she doesn't elaborate. "Good night, Angus. Angus Farrow, still innocent. Still unbroken. Let's keep you that way."

Catherine in the Snow

Margo's eyes were wide with shock, and a bit glazed, as she stood in Anura's office. One of the promised witnesses was human in appearance, a dour and bulky woman with stiff curls and brilliant azure eyes. The other, though, was a sort of spiral of purple flame that could form hands to sign paperwork, or a mouth to offer comments.

With so many entities present, Anura studiously ignored me.

Gus levitated a teacup, and everyone pretended, loudly, that Margo had done it—except for Margo herself, who gawked in silence at her new compatriots and especially at me. Of course the witnesses would take their cut later, but for now they performed with creditable enthusiasm and signed the papers just as if they were convinced that Margo was a witch indeed. The woman, Carmen, used ordinary ink to inscribe her name, while the flame singed his into the paper with a suitably fiery script.

And with that, Margo was certified as a sorceress of the lowest level, her expected production half a talen per unworld day. It was enough to secure her citizenship and the meanest accommodations, no more than the equivalent of a hovel. She was rated so low, I gathered, because that was all Anura would risk, but also because Gus would henceforth be liable for the taxes on Margo's supposed magic as well as his own. If there was a shortfall and the amount of magic seeping to power the city did not meet expectations, someone might come looking for the source of that discrepancy. No one present could afford to attract that sort of attention.

I had my own reasons for bitterness at the conclusion of this business. Now that Margo lived in Nautilus, what would tempt Gus to spend his days in the unworld? What inducement would he have to expose himself to aging and eventual death? I would have ground my teeth at finding my desires thwarted once again, if only I had been capable of closing my mouth.

And though I understood her likely reasons, it crushed me to be in the same room with Anura and not receive the slightest glance from her. What if she regretted her kindness to a wretched ghoul like me? I shrieked and flapped with utter disregard for dignity, trying to draw her eyes. I failed. I had no way to weep, but my insubstantial form felt like boiling tears.

Then Gus hurried Margo from the office. She kept her hands over her ears as much as she could; only since arriving in Nautilus had she gained the ability to see me and been treated to the sonic bludgeoning of my scream. If she had understood before that Gus must have murdered me, such a dramatic confirmation no doubt disagreed with her. Well, she would get used to it. Now that she was trapped in Nautilus and utterly dependent on her nephew, she would have no other choice.

We had not gone far before Margo stopped and wobbled. Her breathing was labored. Wisps of hair clung to her perspiring brows.

"Of course," Gus mused, "you'll have to take extreme care never to walk through walls where anyone can see you, or they'll know at once you aren't generating magic. Make sure you always pass beneath the lintels; I'm sure even you can learn how to pay the tolls. I'll have to arrange an allowance for you, enough to cover such basic necessities."

I understood at once that her allowance would be paltry in the extreme, but Margo didn't seem to be listening. She looked puzzled.

"The pain, Angus," she said, once she'd caught enough breath. "I thought the pain would be gone. I thought I would be well again."

"Oh," Gus said. His mouth worked through various figures of impatience and surprise. "No, not without further intervention. But you won't age anymore, and your illness won't progress beyond what it is at this moment. You can live with no end in sight—perhaps it's not true immortality, but we can last as long as the city itself! There are sorcerers here who are rumored to have lived for millennia."

Here Gus seemed to notice that Margo's gaze was still wandering, and his lips pinched. What he wanted, of course, was a show of gratitude. He wanted Margo's joyous amazement at the eternity before her. But her weary and baffled expression made it clear that she was feeling nothing of the kind.

"Further intervention?" Margo asked hopefully. This vague woman was nothing like the brisk and acerbic Margo I was used to. How much of the change was simple shock, I wondered, and how much a more permanent diminishment brought on by her long illness? "So it can be done? The pain, Angus."

Gus, I could tell, hardly knew what to make of Margo's unexpected response to the dawning of her new existence, glorious as it all seemed to him.

"Of course it can," he said after a pause. "It isn't at all my specialty, I'm afraid. But for a fee, nearly anything can be accomplished."

There was a sullen note to his voice, and I knew he was already resenting all the unforeseen expenses attendant on bringing Margo here. He had probably thought that the thousand talens he had paid to Anura would be the last of his obligations. Now he was chagrined to find the case very much otherwise.

I looked from one of them to the other, Gus bristling with restless energy and Margo slumped and wasted, and wondered how long she had before he tired of paying to alleviate her suffering. He had no doubt thought to procure a helpmeet, and not a burden, by importing his old aunt.

Magic was money in Nautilus. And just as at home, money was everything.

Gus escorted Margo to her new dwelling, but he was withdrawn and silent, Margo weak and wistful. As soon as they reached her tiny, tent-shaped room, Margo collapsed on her pallet and slept, and Gus sat cross-legged on the floor and brooded until he dropped into fitful sleep as well.

At last Gus roused himself and left Margo still sleeping. He had the bare consideration to leave an opening in her wall so that she would not be obliged to stay confined, and to hire a firefly to lead her to us when she woke—though I wondered if Margo would know what to make of an insect stubbornly blinking at her. And with that we turned and walked out into the snow.

Yes, snow. For all that there was no sky in the customary sense, but only a hazy dome. For all that there were no clouds unless willfully conjured.

The most uncongenial aspect of the climate here lies in how it falls sway to the whims of the powerful. Those with sufficient magic to waste can bring on bitter cold, or they can make the very winds rustle with iridescent plumage, or trace veins of colored water in intricate trellises through all the air so that no one can walk without drenching them-selves—at least, not without expending their own magic to avoid it. The rich create these displays to remind everyone that they can afford such extravagance, and to make certain no one forgets where the true power lies. During periods when the greatest sorcerers of Nautilus vie with one another in petty ostentation, one can hardly go out for all the moons roll-ing through the streets or birdlike creatures slashing past with feathers of cutting ice.

On this occasion, then, someone had seen fit to create a blizzard as their particular performance. The snowflakes were blazing blue, like an indigo bunting's feathers in the brightest sun; they were periwinkle and violet, the colors of twilight and pining. Gus cringed, annoyed, for he was not dressed for the sudden cold, then set his shoulders and stomped off through the giddy whirl. Of course he was too parsimonious to spend any magic on personal warmth. Many others would be too poor, and they would have to bear their discomfort as best they could.

The imposed misery, too, was part of the point. In any world, the pow-erful are much the same in their idle cruelties. Magic only enabled the worst in them, as it had with Gus.

"Bother the old bastard," Gus snapped. "Why can't he leave me alone?"

The flakes were several times larger than the natural variety, and as they spun across my eyes I noticed that each bore a miniature portrait at its center: faces both human and fantastic danced across my vision, and I guessed at once that these were images of Nautilus's own citizens del-icately crystallized. Some faces smiled, others contorted in the agonies of the damned, yet others showed a weary indifference. Presumably it amused him to portray his enemies suffering, his friends in bliss. Was this another game, then, to set the city's inhabitants scrambling, search-ing for their own portraits, so that they could discover whether or not they were in favor? I glimpsed a frozen Asterion looking smug and secre-tive, and an Anura who seemed rather pained. At first I had no luck in locating Gus's image, curious though I was to see what expression would be painted on his features. Darius had kept his distance since Gus had arrived in Nautilus, and I'd guessed their relations must have cooled.

Gus trudged on and the snow blew through the streets with ever-increasing density, battering him back. But not a single flake could be seen to alight on the ground. The only accumulation was in the air itself. The atmosphere acquired an intimidating thickness, became a blue and glittering wall that perpetually wove and unraveled itself with the dip and dive of flakes. Ghost though I was and beyond corporeal harm, still I shrank into myself. The snow spun a fearful spell, a stunning glimmer, so that I could only stare until my every thought went spindling from my mind and entered into the air's bright warp and weft.

Gus grunted, though, and shouldered through it. Even here in Nautilus he proved oddly resistant to wonder. If the sun is never bright enough for your taste, then can enchantment ever be adequately magical?

"Is this sort of *decoration* all he can think of to do?" Gus complained, glancing at me over his shoulder. "Is it all *anyone* here can do? All this power, and yet—the uses of it seem so *empty* at times, so vain and stupid. I can't imagine why I ever looked up to him."

Did he realize that the emptiness and vanity he complained of were his own?

We had nearly reached Gus's own room when I caught sight of a portrait I had not expected. It was myself, only rather idealized; if I had been modestly handsome in life, the Catherine on the snowflake blazed with strength and beauty. More than that, she sat enthroned; wearing a gown of stars, a diadem on her head. I could think only that Darius was taunting me with this contrast to my actual condition, or possibly he was parodying Gus's old fantasies. The Catherine-flake danced with seeming purpose straight into Gus's view, and he recoiled.

And with that, the show came to its finale. All around us the luminous blue flakes caught fire. The air rippled in sheets of blinding gold. It swarmed with unbearable heat. Anyone who had rushed to put on a coat or summon magical warmth would be forced to throw off that protection just as quickly.

But not for long. Gus had no sooner flung his hands before his face than the flames expired and white ash twinkled down, brushing everything with soft pallor.

Gus's childish fancies regarding Darius had come nearer to the truth than I ever could have guessed, you see. In Nautilus, he was a notable power. And though he'd mocked me for fearing him, it seemed evident that inspiring fear wherever he could was one of his principal pleasures.

I, on the contrary, rather regret the horror I strike into all hearts. It seems indelicate, and then it has the unfortunate effect of putting people on their guard. Even Gus, so long habituated to my presence, is warier than I would like.

If I could, I would assure Gus I gave up any idea of taking action ages ago. That I am so numbed by my own demise that I feel nothing at all as one promising girl after another joins me in death, and adds her cold limbs to his insatiable accounting.

That I never dream of vengeance.

Tell me, is that not a true depiction of my character?

Catherine in Mourning

I could not grieve my mother as I should have done. She had been always kind and gentle, if somewhat remote. I could say she'd been sick for so long that I'd exhausted my sorrow well before she died. That her character, always reserved, had become so abstracted and otherworldly in her decline that I could not grasp her well enough to miss her. But if these claims are true enough, Anna and my brothers nonetheless howled and sobbed with abandon and clung to her cooling breast. Plainly her remoteness had not damped *their* love for her.

I, though, curled with my hands over my face, to hide from them the fact that I had barely eked out a single tear. Even when I helped to wash and prepare her body I felt her chill and stiffening as if it were my own. I didn't understand, and I berated myself as hard and unfeeling.

Now I would say that I was too afraid to cry for her, in case my tears revealed to me a grief I could not bear.

Margo came twice to join in the wake—rather to my father's surprise, though he tried to hide it. I watched the old lady sidelong in the candles' restless light, wondering what grounds she had for believing my mother's spirit might endure. I often caught her watching me as well, though what her wonderings were I could only guess.

"Angus wanted very much to come," she whispered to me once. "He wasn't allowed. When he tried to slip out his father locked him up, the old tyrant! Well, they'll see someday how the two of you are united; they can't deny the obvious forever."

Gus was my dearest friend then—but still the word *united* struck me as somewhat too strong for the case. The side of my mother's corpse hardly seemed like the place to dispute terms, though, and so I let it go.

I can only hope that my regret over this omission will be less than literally eternal.

We waited the customary three days before my mother's burial, but that brief interval felt endless. I was caught in a murky, flickering suspense where I longed for sorrow, missed it, pined for it, as if it were my own capacity for deep feeling that had died and left me desolate. So it was with unfathomable relief that I approached the grave, hand in hand with Anna, who shuddered and swayed with sobs; I could only hope that the onlookers would think I was being stoical for my little sister's sake.

Margo came and stood next to me, quite near, and from a certain blade-edged eagerness in her manner I began to understand that her presence was motivated by something more than sympathy. She kept a respectful silence, but with palpable difficulty.

Even Margo, ever tactless, managed to wait a full day after my mother was buried before she broached the subject of her séance again. It was a hot afternoon, and I was out in our yard distractedly scrubbing my brothers' clothes.

"Reverend Skelley says the recently bereaved make the most unreliable seekers, and that it's unwise to invite you under the circumstances. You'll be too desperate to believe and that won't be properly *scientific,* don't you know. But Mrs. Hobson won't be in town much longer, so I think we'd better strike while the iron is hot, hadn't we?" She fired off this baffling speech without preamble from a location over my right shoulder. My thoughts were so far away that there was a delay while I took in the salient facts—*Margo, importuning, who?*—and scratched up a response.

"Reverend Skelley?" I knew, of course, that a Universalist minister had lately moved to town with his son—the fact provoked my father to such an extent that he actually vocalized his displeasure—but I had trouble sorting that name with the rest of Margo's sentence. "But a *minister* wouldn't—he couldn't be—"

"A spiritual investigator? I assure you he is, and a very serious one. And Mrs. Hobson is an extraordinarily gifted medium, here all the way from Boston! So you see, you absolutely must join us tomorrow evening." She moved to where I could see her better and stood over me while I shoved back my sweat-smeared hair.

"At your house, you mean? Gus's mother will have me turned away at the door!"

"She won't. She passionately wants you to come, even if she's too much of a snob to ask you herself. But she's been barraging me with hints till

I'm simply terrified to show my face downstairs, in case there's another volley."

I never doubted that both Gus's parents hated me, and Gertrude Farrow in particular. I even knew why, though no power on earth would have forced me to admit it.

"Why?" I said at last. "Why would she want me there?"

"It's not as if it's a dinner party," Margo said, which answered nothing. "You don't need to worry about the impropriety of being seen out while you're in mourning. Just come by at eight, won't you? Angus doesn't at all approve, but I'm sure he'll sit with us if *you're* there."

I will admit that I was curious if there was anything to the Spiritualists' claims. I sometimes imagined that my mother was watching me, gazing at my dry eyes and set mouth, and wondering why she had wasted her tenderness on me in my infancy. I wanted to attend, to see their effort to contact the dead fail decisively—and then, I thought, *then* I might be free to cry.

"What do I tell my father, though?"

Margo straightened, smiled; brushed down her silver-gray dress.

"Tell him the Farrows expect you. That ought to do the trick!"

You've been spat out in a later age, my once-pitied reader, and so you can't conceive of what graveyards women were then. Once a woman began having children, she also began burying them, until she was pocked all over with the memory of soft-cheeked faces. Even in my family, luckier than most in that respect, both my older brothers had died before I could speak.

Margo told the truth when she said Gertrude Farrow wanted me to come, and her reasons had names: Evelina. Sylvia. Viviana. Gus rarely mentioned his dead sisters, but in fact their absence was so close, so consuming, that his mother was nearly hollowed out by it.

If I didn't yet understand as I watched Margo walk away, I would very soon.

Angus and Pearl

I go to bed feeling this warm, fuzzy comfort, as if I were a child held in my mother's arms. Did my actual mother ever hold me while I slept, back when I was a little boy? My childhood memories are spotty, but I have the sense that she was always more the distant, authoritarian type. Not a cuddler. So it's no wonder I'm so drawn to Lore.

The next thing I know, I'm at a party. An old-school loft with girls in short velvet dresses and guys in turtlenecks. Somebody's doing projections of bug wings, their delicate veins enlarged until the dancing faces roll fishlike in nets of colored light. There's a clawfoot bathtub full of ice and champagne on one wall; a beautiful redhead is straddling it and swigging straight from a bottle, champagne frothing down her neck. A shelf of wolf masks with bared fangs and empty eye sockets; paintings of green-splashed nudes. At first I'm afraid of seeming conspicuously normal compared to all the vivid, giddy guests around me. But no one seems to be looking at me askance, so I must fit in better than I think I do.

Then there's a skip in my heart. The staccato of a signal coming in, an irregular beat like Morse code. It's so clearly the reason I'm here, and that can only mean one thing. *Her.* I look toward the source of the feeling, trying to spot her soft fawn skin and sunset-streaked hair, but she's not there.

Instead my perceptions home in on a pale, short girl in black satin and white tights, her sleek black hair in flipped-up curls at the bottom. Plump and lipsticked, with a lovely china-doll face, all big blue eyes and pink cheeks. But there's something in her expression that's like a vicious little girl smashing the same doll to shards. I get the feeling she's been trapped in that too-sweet face all her life and she'd break anything if only she could escape.

Her.

But how can she be *her,* when she isn't the girl from Bluebell's? There can't be more than one, can there?

I feel a bit ashamed of myself, a bit faithless. But a *her* is a *her*—and anyway, isn't there a similar slant of feeling around her? A refusal to accept the world's terms, a certain brisk clarity. Maybe I'm more loyal than I think. The black-and-white girl sees me approaching and waves, her bloodred lips diving into a bright bird of a smile.

"Angus! I thought you weren't going to show."

I almost stammer an apology for being late. Then her sarcasm hits me with the snap of a rubber band. She means, *If I'm somewhere, you'll show up like a rash.* That pretty little smile is taut with malice.

"You shouldn't invite me if you don't want me to come," I say. "Pearl, you know I can't stay away from you. It's not as if I haven't tried!"

Pearl. It's old-fashioned but it suits her, the same way the big satin bow at her collarbone suits her. Now that I think about it, this party must have an early sixties theme, or why is everyone dressed as antique hipsters?

"Maybe you shouldn't think of it as an invitation," Pearl says, jutting one satin-squeezed hip to lean on the back of a bright green sofa. "Next time, consider it a dare to stand me up. Prove you can do it! Then we'll see how I choose to respond."

She straightens and turns on her heel, her gaze already winging toward a guy I don't remember, even as I know he's my good friend.

"Theo!" Pearl calls brightly. "I haven't seen you in ages!"

Consider it a dare, she said. Fine. I grab her by her shoulders and swing her around to face me. My fingers curl into her soft skin hard enough to bruise, and I yank her forward so that she stumbles into my arms. The blue of her eyes is so wide that it's like I've just jumped out of an airplane and into a terrified yawn of sky. Freefall. My mouth is open, maybe calling her name or maybe about to kiss her.

It won't be any ordinary kiss, I know that much. I'll kiss her till I pluck free the threads of her being and she starts to unravel. Maybe it won't happen in a moment—hey, maybe I'll be long gone by then, the way she apparently *wants* me to be—but soon enough there won't be anything left of her but a meaningless tangle of creamy skin and black lacquered curls.

Wait. What am I doing?

Screaming, that's what. My thigh smacks hard into something solid. My opening eyes collide with absolute dark. And the whole time I'm flailing around trying to get my bearings, a long, thin scream keeps tearing out of my throat.

Catherine Shadowing

Margo settled in as best she could, though I don't think she ever felt any more at home in Nautilus than I did. Gus paid a gentleman who appeared to be a sort of hybrid of man and dandelion—for he had gaunt green limbs and an enormous mop of yellow petals in lieu of hair—to drain off her pain using a heartstring modified especially for the purpose. With her suffering lifted, Margo's usual acuity snapped back, to Gus's clear relief.

And with that accomplished, all the passionate attention he'd invested in her rescue turned again to fashioning his beamers. He was already proficient in the creation of wraiths like the one I'd seen, child-rags spun from misery and illusion wearing the face of his own boyhood. Now he confronted two further challenges. His whimpering projections must be fleshed out, quite literally. And they must be granted fully functioning consciousness of their own.

As Zeus birthed Athena, so did Gus express his beamers. I watched in dismay as Gus balled himself on the floor of his room, his eyes screwed shut and cheeks bulging in concentration. Small, translucent fingers dribbled damply from his forehead, then became two curled hands. With an instinctive grasping such as infants show, they seized hanks of Gus's overgrown hair while their wrists and arms oozed after them.

Then the head emerged, bubbling from Gus's face until it was hideously doubled, man and child pressed together, as if he vomited his own echo. I was glad, at this, to lack a physical stomach, though I still felt what I must regrettably term a *phantom* nausea. The child's spine bowed and then flopped, the knees surged up, and then the whole apparition spilled blinking onto the floor. Its appearance was much improved over the first beamer I'd seen. This one had good coloring, unlike the shadowy smear of Gus's earliest efforts, and its flesh was nearly opaque.

It gaped about and saw me, then burst into tears.

It was the fifth such effort since he had reclaimed Margo, but repetition had not inured me to the spectacle.

Gus was working hard at endowing the little things with more intelligence and sensibility, but he did them no favors by it. What poor, wrung-out orphans they were, birthed by a mind that was neither mother nor father—for Gus did not regard them with even a hint of fatherly tenderness. They were mere torn-off scraps of Gus's past, denied any future of their own. Is it any wonder they whined so?

Gus seized his latest creation by its ear and yanked it upright. It appeared to be about six or seven years old, blond and limp and quite recognizably my childhood friend. But even in such an early specimen there was already a hint of improvement in its features, a slightly stronger chin, a brow that did not recede quite so steeply as Gus's own. It cowered.

Gus gazed on the thing without affection, and I wondered if he in fact hated the boy he had been in those days when we roamed together.

"Well?" he said sharply. "Don't stand there whimpering. Tell me who you are."

Its back oscillated in fear, seemingly boneless, and I thought Gus had work to do in improving its general rigidity. The pale eyes darted about as if in search of the answer likeliest to please.

"Angus," it said after a moment. "Farrow?"

Gus's eyes widened, for it was the first time he had achieved such a result. The child-beamer before this one had gabbled incoherent syllables in reply to all Gus's inquiries, until he wadded it up in disgust.

"Indeed. Why are you here?"

"I've lost . . ." it began, then stopped and smeared its illusory tears with its arm. "That is, my mother has sent me here to school."

And there it was, the first evidence that Gus had successfully instilled an artificial memory in the mind of one of his creations—or at least the outward indications of a memory, it hardly mattered which.

Even better, it glanced down at its own nakedness, then contracted, wrapping its arms around its torso and twining its legs with every appearance of shame. Even as I flapped and screamed, I could see that this reaction was of an entirely different quality than the animalistic terror of the first wretched beamer I had seen.

"Never mind that now," Gus snapped. "You'll receive clothes. If I decide you're worth keeping, that is."

The beamer looked at me, confused. "Is she my new schoolmistress? I never thought she'd be so—that is, I'm sure I'm honored to serve in any shape—as any sort of animal you like, miss. A stoat or weasel, something for the underbrush, something to lick your desk clean at night." Gus scowled and the little beamer seemed to realize it was losing the thread; its speech continued in a panicked gurgling. "I remember a, a hole with a sliding door, where the milkman would come and lay his tongue at night, and I would find it there in the morning, pink and fresh? I brought one once to my mother to use as a pincushion."

Gus's face tightened in a grimace and his hands flicked up, ready to wring the beamer into oblivion.

"Or no, actually," the beamer said, as if it had caught itself in a silly mistake. It laughed, but I saw the mingled dread and calculation in its eyes as they flitted from me to Gus and back again. "That was only something I read in a book. I'll study as hard as ever I can, miss, you'll see."

I can't say if it had some residual memory of what had happened to its predecessors, but it was clearly afraid and using all its wiles to save itself.

Which meant it *had* wiles, and that was quite an innovation. I watched Gus lower his hands, saw his head tilt thoughtfully. I hated to share anything with him, my killer, the ravisher of my consciousness, but there was that unwelcome synchronicity: we were both impressed by the small beamer's maneuverings.

"She is not your teacher," Gus said, and with that I knew the beamer's destruction had been forestalled. He would keep this one longer, investigate its capacities, before he mashed it down into the magical pulp that would help him build the next.

"No?"

"No. She can't speak, so she can hardly teach. A dumb thing, really, for all the racket she makes. Think of her as a sort of pet of mine, if you like." He smiled, grossly avuncular.

One might suppose that I would be beyond taking offense at anything Gus said of me—I might have thought so myself. But that notion proved mistaken.

"A pet," the beamer mulled. For all its subtle translucence, the impression that a real little boy stood before us was increasing as it overcame its initial bewilderment. Its body seemed firmer as well, its tears more wet. "Is she a pet shadow, sir? I thought a man would have a man-shadow, but somehow you came by a lady?"

"I did something of the kind," Gus agreed. But now his smile was broader, more genuine, and I thought I knew why. The small Angus displayed a rather muddled understanding, but it was clearly striving to make sense of what it did know. It sought to impose order on the aching chaos of its mind. This was no mere puppetry, but an independence of thought, of *self*. There was room for improvement, certainly, but Gus was on the way to achieving his aim. "Come with me. I'll bring you to the lady who will be instructing you. You will treat her with utmost respect and obey her in everything, or you will be punished."

Punished was hardly the word for what it would be, but the beamer recognized its reprieve and brightened. "Oh I will, sir! She will have no reason to complain of me, I promise you!"

I wondered briefly if Gus deliberately had made the thing more compliant than he had ever been himself. I recalled him as quite a willful child. Then I realized that Gus as a boy had never been in fear for his life, never had to wheedle for mercy as this beamer did. His parents might have been cold, but they were not brutal. In some respects, he had been rather spoiled if anything—and then, of course, he had had Margo to make much of him.

If he had ever been in the same desperate position as his creation, perhaps he would have been just as obsequious.

We exited Gus's dirty hovel and walked through the mad city to Margo's room. I imagine the three of us made for an unprepossessing sight: the thin, tattered blond man with my shrieking ghost flapping above his shoulders like a cloak inverted by the wind, and then the naked boy-beamer trotting at his heels and hiding its sex with cupped hands. Even in Nautilus we earned our share of bemused looks from passersby; a lady who appeared to be made of crumbling silvery stone, with eroded holes for eyes and mouth, laughed outright and nudged her greenish companion. Gus bristled.

Until this moment I had not understood the use Gus meant to make of his aunt. But of course he would hardly play nursemaid and governess to a child, not even one constructed by his own dark artifice.

We arrived at her wall and knocked, then slipped through without waiting for a response. It was a small room where one slanting wall poured up to meet a larger building behind, all nacreous and full of the same diffuse dove-colored light of which I was so weary. Margo was sleeping in a chair that resembled a petrified dust devil—Gus had recently paid a sorcerer who knew how to work the opalescent stuff of Nautilus to spin it for her—a book dropped onto her knees. My scream roused her quickly enough.

"I've brought you something, Margo," Gus announced. Her sleep-fogged eyes reeled from him to the child; she might have thought herself still dreaming as she gazed on the boy she had once doted on. The beamer was her own past resurrected, bare-fleshed and glowing with the ambient light that played inside his limbs and coiled wormlike inside his jutting ribs. Tears brimmed under her wrinkled lids.

"Angus!" Margo cried, and slid from the chair onto her knees, arms outstretched. "My darling, my poppet, how have you come back to me?" The beamer child flinched back and Margo's eyes widened in hurt. "Please, please come to me! Do you not know your Aunt Margo?"

The small Angus glanced up at its master, uncertain. Gus scowled down at it and made a shooing motion, and it scampered dutifully into Margo's embrace. She seized it, weeping into its airy hair, and it had enough substance to resist the pressure of her arms. But if anyone had made the mistake of thinking the creature was prompted by true affection, the look on its face would have disabused them of the notion. Its cheek bulged against the pressure of Margo's bony chest; its gaze was fitful and its mouth a grimace of discomfiture.

Later Gus would correct his early mistakes. But in providing this preliminary model with a mind, he had quite forgotten to instill adoration for Margo, or even any sense of who she was.

What it did have, and amply, was a drive for self-preservation.

"Auntie Margo?" the beamer said, with a passable mimicry of childish sweetness. And Margo sobbed all the harder. I hadn't spared Margo's situation much thought at that point; I had troubles enough of my own, and reasons enough to despise her. But at this I could not help but recognize the corrosive loneliness of her lot. Apart from Gus, she knew not a soul in the city, and he was too preoccupied to visit her often.

Now, poor pitiful old lady, she had something to love. And she did not know, for Gus did not tell her, that this childish *impersonation* would not be hers to keep.

One might say the fault was hers, that she should have shown more caution. That she should have realized any gift in the sorcerers' city was not to be trusted, that the child was a mirage and its love likewise treacherous. Well, she would learn these things in due course, and that education was surely crueler than death would have been.

For now, she wept and petted the little Angus, then sat back on her heels to gaze on its face, cradled between her two palms. It smiled at her as winningly as it knew how. I imagine it did not understand, any more than Margo did, that its doom was delayed only for a season no matter how well it performed.

"Margo will look after you and provide you with instruction," Gus told the beamer rather stiffly. I noticed that he did not say *your aunt Margo*; presumably he was disinclined to share her in such a way with a being that he regarded as a mere doll. "You will treat her with all honor, and I will visit when I can and monitor your progress."

The beamer nodded, perhaps unsure of the tone it should take. Margo finally let it slip from her arms and looked up at her true nephew.

"I won't ask you how this is possible," Margo told the original Gus, laughing through her tears. "You'll only say that anything is possible here, for a price. But oh, to have my heart's delight in my arms again—and without any cloud across his future—I can't thank you enough."

"What do you mean by a cloud?" Gus asked. His face was dangerously blank. Margo was too enraptured to recognize it, but I knew that look all too well. He was jealous of the tenderness she showed for his child-self, and the clouds Margo spoke of were tumid and lowering inside him.

"Oh." Margo looked up at me. It never seemed to cross her mind that I might understand anything she said, for she showed remarkably little tact where I was concerned. "I only meant that here there is no one to lead my dear boy astray. There is no little wench—"

Ah. Whomever could Margo mean by this? Who, in her estimation, had led Gus into perdition, taunted and tempted him? Why, that little wench might as well have wrapped his hands around her neck herself! And, once she had those hands neatly applied to her windpipe, it was veritably as if she'd turned a key in Gus's back and compelled his hands to tighten! It was not as if Margo herself had instilled in him a belief in our spiritual marriage either; the responsibility could not be *hers*.

Gus smiled tightly. "No one has bothered to replicate a young Catherine, you mean? Indeed not. Someday the Anguses will have to seek their Catherines on their own."

Margo did not catch the implications of this statement. She had returned to admiring the child before her, who stood still and guarded, with the pointed quiet that betrays intense listening.

"But I have nothing I need to raise him properly," Margo fretted. "I'll need books, and maps—and he must have instruction in music, my dear, you were so wonderfully gifted, you *are* so wonderfully gifted, that is. And has he no clothes? I can manage his French well enough, and geography. But Latin?" She laughed again, giddy and trembling with love, and ruffled the beamer's hair. "Well, my dearest, we'll get along as best we can."

Gus stared for a moment. He had evidently not considered that his creature would have so many requirements, or that Margo would want to raise it as if it were as real as himself.

"You can take him to the public gardens for now," he said. "Observation is the best education. I'll see to the rest when I can." He reached a hand to pull Margo to her feet, though I thought she would have rather stayed on the floor with the beamer near enough for dandling. "And, Aunt Margo?"

She tore her teary gaze from the child and looked at Gus. Her smile was positively silly. "Yes, Angus?"

"There never was a cloud over my future. Whatever forces conspired to bring me here, this was always my destiny. Everything that happened—it was a small price to pay for becoming the man I was meant to be."

All prices are small when someone else pays them. Since I could not offer that observation, I screamed. Margo pursed her lips but did not give voice to her disagreement, and Gus granted her a larger allowance than he had done previously.

We left with her fussing around the beamer, pinning up one of her own shifts to make it a sort of smock. It seemed to be warming to her attentions, for it was surely crafty enough to understand that it was better off with her than it would have been with the man who'd birthed it.

In the alley, Gus craned to look at me. I knew that look, felt how it added and subtracted me as if I were so many coins.

"Catherine, I'm sure you'll understand—Margo is putting me to all sorts of expenses I didn't anticipate. I know I told you our visits to Asterion would end, but I'm afraid—well, everyone must contribute what they can, and why would you be the exception? Some brief discomfort—" He wasn't looking at me any longer; rather he was studying a bird formed of living glass, its heartbeat a steady flashing in its ruby breast.

Some brief discomfort, he called it. It was another of those prices he found so negligible, whether wrung from my neck or drained from my mind.

Gus gave a sharp nod, just as if he were acknowledging my consent, and turned in the direction of the Nimble Fire. He had gone only a few steps before we were interrupted. The standing walls began to flex and undulate, chasing new forms as if they were driven under a violent wind. A dome on our left contracted at its middle as if corseted and then leapt into a fluted, onion-shaped tower above, the top splayed out in pointed petals. Excess droplets of what had seemed stone only moments before spattered the dusky sky and fell like raindrops the size of carts. I bucked in instinctive alarm—it can be hard at such moments to recall just how dead one is—but before they hit the streets those drops reformed into a bevy of winged pale horses and took flight. From a rumble and cry in all directions, I gathered that this disturbance extended far beyond our immediate neighborhood. Very soon all was calm again.

I hadn't then been resident in Nautilus long enough to know that such upheavals occurred periodically and marked what one might politely term a change in government. Whenever someone new seized control of the city, they would hasten to liquefy the architecture and then congeal it again in a fashion more to their taste. It served to put the citizens on notice that they should redirect their groveling toward the upheaval's author, and to demonstrate as well the sort of power that anyone would hesitate to cross.

It also meant that Nautilus, unlike most earthly cities, had no visible history, no layered cultures, and no ruins. The whole city's style was exuded by the mind of the moment and nearly everything that had come before was wiped away, again and again—though certain buildings by tradition were left untouched, notably among them the Nimble Fire's great hall. This latest renovation showed a preference for lacy, high-flying buttresses and for symmetry that was quite unlike the fluid canyons I had known hitherto.

Gus cared little for the city's politics—in this we were agreed—and hunched his shoulders in annoyance while enormous wingbeats lifted his hair. I understood at once that the city might seethe as it wished; Gus would not regard it as cause for delay. A quick assessment of the altered streets served to reorient him, and he was off with whisking steps.

And I, dumb thing, who could not teach for want of words? I followed in Gus's steps as if following the deep groove of a dream, in which each gesture has the fatal drag of inevitability.

But when I was alive, when I still slept, I was sometimes able to alter the course of my dreams with an exertion of will. Such dreamed transformations reveal the ways of waking magic, if only one has the ability to follow where they lead.

Catherine in the Dark

Margo met me at the door herself, which was not done—but then neither was it *done* for such as I to appear there as a guest, escorted through the green-papered halls to the same library where Gus and I used to hide. I wore my only mourning dress—it had been passed down to me by one of my mother's old employers when they heard of her death, and I'd hastily altered it to fit me better. I hadn't done a very good job, and I felt shabby and conspicuous among the whispering muslins of the women gathered there. Gus hadn't seen me since the night my mother died, and he nearly lunged across the room and stood in front of me like a bulwark against the pressing stares.

"Catherine," he whispered, "they wouldn't let me go to you! I'm *sorry*—"

His mother interposed herself before I could answer. Gertrude Farrow was as fair as her son but handsomer, with an aquiline nose and eyes the same ice green as his, set off by the pale green embroidery on her collar and sleeves.

"Miss Bildstein. How good of you to come." She delivered these words in tones so flat, and held herself so stiffly, that it clearly conveyed to everyone present that I was no true guest. What then? "Allow me to introduce you to Mrs. Hobson. She will be our conduit with the spirit world this evening."

A slim, diminutive lady, perhaps sixty years old, held out her hand to me. Her face was round and rather boneless, nested in lilac frills, but her look was acute. She was assessing me, but for what purpose? I murmured as politely as I could, and she patted my arm with unctuous familiarity.

"I understand your dear mother recently passed over. I feel certain that tonight will bring you consolation far beyond any words I could offer!"

I could hardly say that the consolation I hoped for was her complete and humiliating failure. Gus was still close beside me, watching everything. I thought of feigning illness, perhaps pretending to faint; anything to escape from this atmosphere of cloying expectation. Dr. Lewis and his wife were there, both staring at me; Margo fixed me with a complacent smile; and Mrs. Farrow kept up a cold and quizzical vigilance as if she thought I might at any moment dissolve into a wave and drown the company.

Then something happened that saved me from my agitation: Margo approached me, leading Reverend Skelley. He was exactly my height, so rather small for a man, and his presence was so soft, so cloudy with gentleness, that at first I had the impression more of a haze than a person. "Miss Bildstein, a pleasure," he said, so simply that I was almost at my ease for the first time since I'd arrived on that doorstep.

It was a mercy nonetheless when the proceedings began in earnest. The long, heavy library table had been pulled to the center of the room, with chairs arranged around it. Mrs. Hobson settled in one at the table's head, and Dr. Lewis bound her wrists to its armrests, her ankles to its legs. A thick pad was shoved beneath her feet to muffle any attempt at tapping. If it disturbed me to see how the cords cut into her, the general ruffling as guests approached her and inspected the knots at least drew their attention away from me.

A bell was placed in the table's center. Beside it was a closed slate, which the company was invited to inspect to prove that it was quite blank, and a pewter speaking trumpet. The curtains were drawn tight, cutting off the moon, and the guests were placed with men and women alternating. Mrs. Farrow, of course, kept Gus far away from me, so that I found myself between Dr. Lewis and Thomas Skelley, the reverend's son. He was as wispy and unobtrusive as his father, and I hadn't even noticed him until he was seated directly on my right. Taller than his father, very thin, with eyes and hair the color of clotted dust; there seemed to be little about him worth noticing.

"Link your small fingers with your neighbors'. Every hand must be accounted for!" Dr. Lewis said; much as I disliked Mrs. Hobson, it was still disappointing to see how this bullish man took charge of an occasion that supposedly relied on her talents. Margo extinguished the only lamp, and darkness covered us as intimately as water. "Soft singing will bring the company into a state of harmony conducive to manifestations. We may have to wait for some time."

Margo crooned the opening phrase of "Ah! May the Red Rose Live Alway!" and soon nearly everyone joined in—though I did not hear Gus's voice, nor add my own.

The voices seemed to blend with the darkness into a new and unknown substance, warm as molten wax. It was as if our senses seeped from our bodies and mingled with that rich plasma, becoming just as soft—just as impressionable—

"Why should the beautiful ever weep? Why should the beautiful die?" The song hovered all around me, patting and stroking as Mrs. Hobson had done.

I braced myself against that drowsy influence. Some draft must have disturbed the curtain, I thought, because a curl of moonlight like a cupped hand showed near the window.

No. It was visibly a child's hand, cast in vaporous light. Around me the song dropped away.

"Reverend Skelley," Dr. Lewis said, too loudly, "I have perfect command of Mrs. Hobson's right hand. Do you have hold of the left?"

"I do."

"And is the circle unbroken, so that there can be no question of an accomplice?"

Thomas's pinky tightened on my right, Dr. Lewis's on my left. Their grip was hard enough that I wondered if I were under suspicion, though I had never met Mrs. Hobson before.

"It is," Reverend Skelley confirmed softly.

Meanwhile the luminous hand wheeled over the company, and in its light each face was faintly drawn in turn on that perfect darkness. Wide-eyed, awed.

When it passed Gertrude Farrow, I saw two reflective streaks shine below her eyes. That gelid woman was weeping in the dark, and the hand had exposed her tears!

The hand then sailed to the speaking trumpet, and visibly struggled to lift the heavy metal cone. The device toppled with a dull clank and the hand vanished, casting us back into flawless night. A whisper rustled from somewhere nearby, sad and urgent, but it was too quiet to make out the words.

"My guide tells me that I'm not the right sensitive to give voice to this particular spirit, and the speaking trumpet is too heavy for her. But there *is* one here who can help. Will everyone give their assent?" Mrs. Hobson was speaking at last, in a sort of lethargic moan.

There was a murmur of agreement. Even in that darkness, I could feel how Dr. Lewis's attention cocked in my direction, waiting for me to agree as well. Something brushed my shoulder. A moment's hesitation, and I gave in.

"Yes."

"Mama?" a childish voice said, so faintly that I strained to hear. A breath later, and I realized it had come from my mouth. "Please don't cry! Evelina and Sylvia and I are together, and so happy, except when we see you sad."

Gertrude Farrow let out a shocked cry, but Dr. Lewis spoke sternly over her. "What is your name, spirit?"

"I'm Viviana Farrow," I felt myself say in piping tones, and nearly gagged on them. I could feel the voice stuck in my throat; it was oily, invasive. "My sisters and I visit often. Is Mama still there? I can't see her anymore."

"I'm here, darling!" Gertrude Farrow keened. "Always, always!"

"Mrs. Farrow," Dr. Lewis reproached her. "Remember that, to ensure an orderly investigation, only the control should speak directly with the spirits."

Something was using me, but I did not think it was a ghost. If my skepticism at this juncture seems incredible, well, remember how recently I had seen Old Darius perform magic far more impressive than this dark display.

I could not have said why, but something in the voice felt wrong to me—not childish, not innocent. It was more as if my tongue was tugged about by an unseen puppeteer, definitely adult.

"And are there other spirits present?" Dr. Lewis pursued.

"Yes, many," the voice chirped. "Our cousin Walter—"

Margo gasped.

"Our cousin Walter is here, but so far he cannot manage to speak through the veil. He wishes me to tell Auntie Margo that he is now a man grown, and that he watches her and loves her always."

I hadn't known that Margo had lost a child, but now she gave a small, sharp cry.

"Walter, my love, my shining boy! Can he hear me?"

"Please, Mrs. Farrow!" Dr. Lewis interjected. I was gratified to see that his grasp on the proceedings was slipping. "I will ask the questions!"

A long pause followed. When the voice came back it was fainter. "Yes, he hears."

At this I rebelled—though why my fury surged at this moment and no other would be difficult to say. It was one thing, I suppose, to witness Gus's mother broken into her component griefs, but I was fond of Margo and did not like to see her played with. I thought the voice was an impostor, and I wanted it *out*.

The sinuous presence that had risen in me on the day of Darius's firesnakes—I sensed it reasserting itself, a flick and probe low in the back of my skull.

Then it attacked. I felt a clash, the serpentine twisting of force on force. There was a rattling, humming sound: the heavy table was vibrating so hard that its legs drummed on the floor. I reeled back in my chair, pushed by a sort of boiling recoil with no clear source.

The luminous hand reappeared, tumbling over my lips. It flew across the room like a dove pursued by a hawk, whirled around the ceiling, banked, dove again. The room burst into cries. I heard a chair shoved back.

"Compose yourselves! Maintain the circle!" Dr. Lewis shouted, though he himself sounded distinctly discomposed. The hand dashed through the table's surface and disappeared, dousing us again with darkness, and at the same moment a dull glint stirred as the bell lifted up and began ringing frantically.

Under that manic chiming I heard a scrape from the table's center. The heavy tone of metal on wood. My eyes had now adjusted sufficiently to the darkness that I thought I saw a shape ascend.

"The speaking trumpet!" Margo gasped. "It's flying! Oh, Walter, my dearest, my only—"

"We came to you in good faith," a voice boomed—very clearly issuing from somewhere near the ceiling. It was deep, bad-tempered, male. "We have strained with all our might to show you proof of our glad tidings. Why do you deny us?"

"I beg your pardon?" Dr. Lewis asked in baffled tones. "We are striving—most *sincerely* striving—to meet all your conditions. We—"

"Walter?" Margo put in, though doubtfully. "If you only knew how I've longed—"

"In life my name was Henry Kirk," the voice interrupted coldly. "And I am dissatisfied."

I do not suppose this record will be read by posterity. But if it is, allow me to recommend, very strongly, against ever holding a séance in a library.

To do so gives the spirits—or whatever is passing itself off as the spirits—far too much ammunition.

On all sides a scrape, a hiss, a leathery pattering sounded. There was the susurrus of disturbed air, and a thousand whistling currents.

Then something slammed the back of my head with force enough to throw me facedown on the tabletop. Though I was stunned, my head ringing with pain, it was an advantage to be low: the air rushed with books, hurtling at terrific speed. It would have been impossible to light a lamp under those conditions, but someone had the presence of mind to tear back a curtain—light was said to weaken ghostly activity. The flocking books and cowering company alike were awash in moonlight. I saw Gus yanking Margo under the table, felt myself similarly pulled into its shelter. I caught a glimpse of Thomas Skelley gazing at me with concern, his lips moving—was he asking if I was badly injured?—before all the books slapped against the walls in unison and fell in a thumping cascade. It was some moments before that flapping fall resolved, leaving no sound besides the gasping and whimpering of the company. I could dimly make out the huddled confusion of limbs and spreading skirts all around me, the legs of toppled chairs.

It was only then I remembered that Mrs. Hobson had been tied to her chair, unable to protect herself. I scrambled to get out from the table, and Thomas caught at me.

"It's not safe, Miss Bildstein! What if it starts up again?"

"But Mrs. Hobson," I said, or more exhaled. Thomas's eyes went wide and he scrambled with me.

We need not have worried, or not about her. We emerged to find Reverend Skelley, that frail and mossy man, slumping onto his knees. His face was horribly battered. A moment's confusion and I understood that, with no time to undo Mrs. Hobson's complicated knots, he had resorted to bending over her and shielding her with his own body. Dr. Lewis, of course, had been on Mrs. Hobson's other side, and he was over six feet tall and as solid as a stump. But he had crawled under the table with the rest.

I might have thought that Mrs. Hobson herself had been knocked unconscious, except that she was snoring: eyes shuttered, her chin on her frilled chest. To all appearances, she'd slept serenely through the whole episode.

"Father!" Thomas cried, and ran to lift him up. Tears streaked his face. "Oh, I should have been the one—"

"You had Miss Bildstein to protect, Thomas, and you did so admirably. I saw you pull her to safety after she was struck. Besides, nothing is broken." Then his father's voice caught on a hiss of pain. "Or—perhaps I may have cracked a rib. Never mind, it will heal soon enough."

I found myself envying the obvious affection between them, and wondered for the first time what loss had moved the Skelleys to come in search of spirits. With no Mrs. Skelley in evidence, there was a likely candidate.

Mrs. Lewis came out into the open and began busily lighting every lamp and candle she could find with trembling hands. The speaking trumpet was still levitating, awkwardly alone, but with the influx of light it crashed down on the table next to the dented bell.

"Catherine!" Gus was at my side. "Catherine, are you all right?"

Thomas Skelley shrank in on himself like a salted snail and stared at the floor.

"I think so," I said, and realized that I was wobbling on my feet. "Only my head hurts."

That flying book—it had caught me at the base of my skull. In the very spot where I'd felt the sinuous *something* unwind itself to oppose the voice possessing my lips. The blow had seemed intentional, vindictive, but of course I did not say so.

Gus led me to a couch and cleared away the fallen books. I stretched out gratefully, glad to be left out of the ensuing consternation, the endless rehashing of what everyone had seen and heard. I watched the full moon lifting higher, far into the sweep of night. Did Gus really think that Darius traveled there? The throb in my head and the racing of my heart synchronized, then gradually slowed, and I imagined chasing the moon's streaming light on wide pale wings.

It was rare for me to be so fanciful.

Perhaps the blow to my head was responsible. Or perhaps I was simply determined to think about anything but what had just happened.

I was not allowed to seek refuge in daydreams for long. Shadows stirred along my right—the side away from the window—and I turned to see Gertrude Farrow and Margo, Mrs. Hobson and Dr. Lewis, standing in close and menacing formation.

"I'm afraid I can't delay my return to Boston any longer," Mrs. Hobson said. She seemed if anything pleasantly refreshed by her nap. "But now that you have a sensitive of your own, your investigations can continue very well without me. Miss Bildstein, allow me to congratulate you on the appearance of your gift!"

I tried to sit up. Vertigo immediately forced me back. "I don't—"

"Tonight was a signal success," Dr. Lewis agreed. It struck me as a very callous formulation, in view of Reverend Skelley's injuries, and I might have favored the term *disaster*. "I'll send a report of it to the *Spiritual Telegraph* as soon as possible. I'm sure there will be considerable interest in, ah, Miss Bildstein's abilities."

I've mentioned that ours was an age in which young women were especially suspect—though in this it was hardly unique. Seen from another angle, however, *suspect* became *useful*.

"Please do no such thing!" I managed, just as Gertrude Farrow put in, "Premature publicity would be very ill-advised! I'd prefer you keep tonight's events quiet."

Our eyes met in surprise at our agreement. Just for a brief moment, since neither of us enjoyed that shared regard. Later I understood: she'd meant to keep me for herself.

"To be frank, I expected it," Mrs. Hobson continued. Rather too pointedly, I thought. "As soon as Margo Farrow mentioned you, my guide let me know that you were attractive to the spirit world. Much as I regretted the necessity of troubling you in your bereavement, it was *essential* that you come here tonight. I told both Mrs. Farrows as much."

The subtext of her words ran deep—positively subterranean—but I still caught its vibrations.

Setting myself up as a medium would provide me an income, independence, a chance to travel. It would even give me power of a kind, over Gertrude Farrow and her ilk. My profile met the requirements perfectly: for a girl young, poor, yet known to be intelligent, mediumship was becoming almost obligatory. I understood all these considerations at a blow, and knew that Mrs. Hobson was telling me that I had nothing to lose, and everything to gain—that she was sure I could produce such manifestations on my own—

Gus and the Skelleys crowded in with the rest. It bothered me to be so low while everyone stood above me, and I managed at last to sit upright, though my head was still spinning.

"Of *course* I'll help with your development whenever I can manage a visit," Mrs. Hobson added, in what was presumably meant as an encouraging tone. But since she had already shown her readiness to punish me, I heard something more threatening.

"I'm sorry to disappoint you," I said. I was still dazed, unguarded. "But I have no intention of taking part in a séance, ever again."

Gertrude Farrow gave an abrupt half turn away from me, as if she meant to walk off in disgust. I saw a quiver in her shoulders, her arms compressed against her sides.

Then she pivoted and slapped me with all her strength across my cheek.

Angus the Disturbance

It's around five forty when I amble up, and I guess her shift starts at six because she's idling in front of the bookstore. The sun is just low enough to bring out the blaze in her sunset streaks. She's still wearing her pompom jewelry and navy sneakers, this time with faded green overalls and a black tank.

"Hi," I say, and get a skittish glance in exchange. "Is it okay if I talk to you?"

"The Mad Roulette Rejecter. My friend Drew told me you've been hanging around."

God, I love her voice. Husky and somehow violet. "Yeah," I say. "Is it wrong that I think you look like someone I want to know?"

She looks me over. Definitely with a critical eye; such open, curious, *alive* hazel eyes. That huge soft mouth purses, and it carries a wallop of adorable skepticism.

"You intend that as an expression of sexual-romantic interest?"

That makes me laugh. "Sure. But, like, we could just go get burritos?"

Her mouth almost spreads into a smile, but not quite. "You do know that clueless hotties typically go for other clueless hotties, right? So your attraction to me seems like an aberration. Unless you're looking for a girl who can magically make you more interesting. In which case. Can't help you with that."

At least she admits I'm good-looking. And, for all that her words sound like a dismissal, she's still turned toward me, her wariness already vanishing. Her stance is forward, engaged. But why would she assume I'm uninteresting? All at once I'm hyperconscious of how clean-cut, newclothes I look compared to her, with my black button-front shirt and crisp gray jeans. *Basic,* that's the word for it. The stone pendant Lore gave me might shake up that impression, but it's hidden under my clothes. I can feel the silky glide of it on my bare skin.

"I can handle *clueless*," I tell her. "Coming from you. But I'm actually fascinating."

That gets me a real, shining grin. "I don't have time for burritos now." Her head dips as she checks the clock on her phone. "But I'm prepared to entertain the possibility that you aren't as boring as you look for the next ten minutes. We can walk around the block. So, what's your deal?"

Oh, she's *her*. She's so, so, so *her*. The sass and the brains and the aggressive edge: all so perfectly *her*.

"Angus Farrow," I tell her, picking up her blunt tone. Digressions will only annoy her at this point. "Nineteen. Recent high-school graduate, taking a gap year before college. I work as a stock boy in a warehouse near here."

Her eyebrows twitch up at that; it's not the job she expected me to have. Good. The more I surprise her, the better.

"Where from?"

"Clayton, Missouri. It's a suburb of St. Louis. Dad in finance, mom in internet publishing. Self-help and wellness stuff." It's funny how the information pops into my mouth, even though I wasn't conscious of it until I said it. *Oh, internet publishing? Okay.*

We're rounding the corner now, heading down a block of brick apartment buildings. Her nose wrinkles. "*Finance.* I knew you had rich-kid stink." A sidelong glance. "So, this warehouse job of yours. You're just slumming?"

"Not exactly. They've basically disowned me." There's a pause as she takes that in. "My great-aunt Margo is going to help me with college, but my parents are pretty much done. Hey, am I going to get a chance to ask *you* anything?"

Am I trying to deflect her? There's no reason her questions should make me uncomfortable; it's not like I have anything to hide.

"You don't get to ask me a single, solitary thing," she announces. But hey, is that a hint of teasing in her voice? "Because you've already made the arbitrary decision that you want to know me, despite having not the slightest hint of who I am. But I have no idea if *I* want to know *you*. We're on this walk so I can figure that out."

"Okay," I say. The blocks are so damned short here and we're already rounding another corner. I get a few more minutes to seem intriguing, and then that's it? What if I bomb?

"It sounds to me as if your childhood was rich in material things, but emotionally and imaginatively impoverished. Do I have that right?"

It seems like a reasonable guess; like, hey, I'll buy that for a dollar! "I mean." It takes me a moment to sort through the odds and ends of memory fluttering around my head. So many days, each one made of so many haphazard sensations and words and facts. A vast heap of disassembled limbs, with no way to ID who they originally belonged to. "Except for Margo. If it wasn't for her, you'd be totally right."

"Tell me about Margo."

Margo is a better topic for me. The images that come up around my parents are sparse and patchy, like dead grass on a trampled field. Margo, though: I feel like I can access more information. Deeper information, somehow.

"Like, a lot of people assume that old ladies are stuffy or dull or whatever. Right? But Margo used to know how to get to this secret zoo—like, not the regular zoo, but one with talking pangolins and stuff? And on Christmas she wouldn't just get me some chocolate Santa. She'd bring me rock candy with these tiny baby dragons curled up inside the crystals. It was actually kind of sad? But then I learned that if you sucked the sugar off them really carefully, instead of just biting off their heads, once in a while you'd get one that would revive. The first time it happened I got my eyebrows fried clean off my face."

Corner.

I made the mistake of looking off at the sky while I was talking; spectacular mackerel clouds dot the blue. When I turn back her face is working through a series of expressions ranging from quizzical to indignant. Shit.

Then she cracks up laughing. For an extended period. I really wasn't trying to be funny, and I almost say something. But no. It's better if I just go with it.

"Okay," she says, her voice still a little wheezy with fading laughter. "*Okay*. You're on for burritos. Assuming you haven't changed your mind."

Wait, so I passed my not-boring audition? Relief blossoms in my chest. Especially since we're turning our last corner, already nearly in front of the bookstore. "When?"

"Say, Saturday? I work the afternoon shift then, so I can meet you here at six."

I'm smiling so wide my cheeks hurt, looking down into her quirky-beautiful face. "And a movie?" I say.

"Don't push your luck," she says, but she's smiling back. "Sure, a movie. Something ludicrous. Either elves or explosions."

"Exploding elves," I assure her. "I'll get tickets."

"And babbling, pseudo-scientific explanations of how their detonation reverses the space-time continuum?" God. She's actively flirting with me!

"I'm pretty sure they create tiny black holes wherever they are at the time. Like, if your spaghetti suddenly sucks into oblivion before you can eat it? Elf-blast."

"*Elf-Blast 3* it is. I heard it's complete shit." But now her gaze is more cautious. She's wondering if she's made a mistake. "I'll see you then, Angus."

Don't ask for her number. Don't hang around Bluebell's all night. She's letting you know this is as far as you go for now. "Can I ask your name, anyway?"

"Geneva," she says, and I repeat it. Geneva! Glorious name.

I force myself to turn away, though all I want is to slide my hands through her lush, messy dark-and-sunset hair. I force myself to keep walking and not look back, but my consciousness sticks to her in long, gluey filaments. When she opens the door to Bluebell's I can feel it, when she swings herself onto her stool behind the counter, when she gives the roulette wheel a morose little spin.

So what if my relationship to the past is possibly shakier than normal? I'm really, really good at detecting subtle disturbances in the present, and that seems more important.

Something inside me seems to scream with laughter at the idea. Like, *Hah! Disturbances? It's disturbances you want, pal?*

Takes one to know one. If you know what I mean.

Catherine in Company

The large public salon at the Nimble Fire jostled with an uncanny crowd; never had I seen so many Nautilusers packed together, fins slapping into elbows and horns clicking against skinless skulls. Gus reeled back, non-plussed, for in his self-absorption it had not occurred to him that everyone would naturally wish to gather and gossip after the city's recent convulsion. There was such an agitation of raised voices in that room, all winging and echoic against the vaulting walls, that my scream drew less attention than ordinarily. Hardly anyone bothered to look, though a lady with cobalt skin and pulsating blue butterfly wings in lieu of hair favored me with a sidelong glance and sly smile.

Gus mastered his discomfiture and began shouldering through the assembly in search of Asterion. A score at least of languages shivered and clattered through a thousand voices, the name *Mariam* flecked across all of them. I heard enough to gather that she was the sorceress responsible for the liquefaction of the buildings all around us, and that the change announced her new regime. A milky, bluish miasma blurred the air, and there was the distinct singed-violet smell of taxes being paid.

Given my elevated vantage, I caught sight of Asterion long before Gus did. The minotaur stood in a knot of chattering grotesques directly before the fire itself, so that its light played across his horns. We never sat near the fireplace—Gus preferred to be at a slight remove from his fellow citizens while he was engaged in the unsavory business of draining my mental energies. So it was the first time I noticed something peculiar in the motion of that firelight, though it was hard to say in what its peculiarity lay. It was fluid and dancing as firelight ought to be, so why did its gestures convey a sense too *purposeful* for mere inanimate combustion?

A familiar ragged shape tugged at the edge of my vision, and I looked in time to see Old Darius shuffling away from the fire, his legs stirring the mist. I knew the wretch lived in Nautilus, knew indeed that he could no longer afford to leave it. His age was now so advanced that even brief visits to the unworld amounted to dabbling in death, and any day he spent under the warm sun might well be his last. But I had not actually seen him since my own demise.

Had Darius been talking to Asterion, then? I had not known they were acquainted.

And then I caught sight—or rather sound—of another group. My interest in Darius's doings evaporated on the instant.

The crowd was such that it overwhelmed the intimate clusters of chairs and sofas that dotted the cavernous space, and nearly everyone was obliged to stand, compressed and overheated, in the magical fug. Those rare spots where citizens had managed to gain seats appeared as depressions in the field of heads. The haze settled opportunistically in such hollows, so that the crowd appeared dotted with milky pools. Oh, these sorcerers were leaky vessels, always seeping their trace magics—as I apparently did, as well. With so many of them crammed together the oozing atmosphere reached a choking density.

There was just such a foggy pool some dozen yards ahead and to the left, a large one indicating a collection of perhaps eight or nine chairs and their occupants drawn close together. I could only dimly discern fragments of the figures sitting there: a curve of head, a spread of black hair that fanned as if caught in ocean currents. And the one who interested me sat too low to be visible at all—but oh, even a hint of her voice seemed to catch my heart in a net and haul it straight to her. If I had had a heart, that is.

Anura was here! I could not distinguish her words above the din, but I thought I could identify the rolling cadences of poetry.

And now my lack of autonomy became irksome indeed—for Gus had at last spied Asterion's horns bucking with his unctuous laughter. Gus began insinuating his narrow person in Asterion's direction, while I strained to pull him in another. It was useless. To put it bluntly, I lacked mass, and my flailing motions could get no purchase on the air.

My writhing drew other eyes to us, however. A rose-feathered serpent reared up to taste me with a tongue cloud-blue and as dainty as a winding breeze. From Anura's group I saw someone stand to get a better look at me; it was a lady with a head of sculpted water where slim pearly fishes looped in hypnotic patterns, as if she had embodied her thoughts in their scaly forms.

Gus by now had dragged me far enough from Anura that I could no longer catch the faintest hum of her voice. But the knowledge that my friend was close at hand gnawed at me until I hardly cared for my impending torment. I learned in those moments that loneliness and longing have a power much fiercer than fear's. My feelings ran so wild that I was forced to wonder at their nature. If this was friendship, it was friendship more passionate, more rocked by longing, than any I had known in life.

We were nearing the fire; the fireplace itself was formed in the likeness of a cave, its many overlapping domes toothed with stalactites. I saw that there were flames draped on either side of the firebox like curtains drawn apart at the theater, and that small human-like figures shaped from flame were performing some drama in a fiery, doll-sized drawing room that perched upon the coals. The miniature actors had no voices beyond the spit and crackle of the wood, and I looked on them with fascination. Were they like me, beings with minds of their own but with speech reduced to noises shapeless and uncontrolled?

Now, of course, I know better. The Nimble Fire draws its imagery from the mind of someone near it. Like a dream, it reveals suppressed fancies, memories, subtexts; they say you can fall into the flames and find your own forgotten secrets there. They say you can pass through the fire, and return to yourself with new illumination.

Before I could examine those blazing figures any further, Asterion barged in front of the firebox and blocked my view, avidly clapping his arm around Gus's shoulder.

"My dear Gus Farrow! How long it's been since you favored us with your company! *Too* long, my friend, far too long, if I may venture an opinion." Then his voice sharpened, greed peering out through the veiling cheer. "How go the beamers?"

Gus glanced around uncomfortably. Asterion stood in a knot of creatures who no doubt had all been human once, though most of them had now departed from their original forms in one way or another. Gus was accustomed to meeting Asterion—and to ransacking me—without the pressure of so many quizzical eyes upon us. Several turned their stares on me with unabashed hunger.

"Ten talens a day?" asked a man whose only concession to the local fashions was skin as red as poppies. "Her?"

"Twelve at her best," Asterion bragged. "And as Nemo can tell you, that makes her a rare bird; none of the ghosts in his collection can top seven! She looks to be in an especially generous mood today. See how she flashes? Twinkle, twinkle, eh? That's what I like to see, our Catherine in a positive *state*."

There were ghosts kept in a *collection,* like seashells or taxidermy? The idea shocked me. And how could any ghost be parted from the one they haunted?

"Twelve, though! Catherine here proves it's possible. Do you suppose it's too late for me to acquire a pretty little ghost of my own, then?" the scarlet man inquired. "What a return on a few minutes' strangling!"

Gus drew himself up as far as his spindly frame would allow and jutted his lips. "Sir. An ordinary, an *indifferent* murder would never produce the same result! Catherine and I were bound in life, as if a single spirit twined through us both. And the proof is that neither her stubbornness nor her death was enough to sever our—our entanglement. If she contributes so much to my undertakings, it is because she understands that she is, ineluctably, my own. She was and is a part of me. But a girl murdered for nothing but coarse *profit*—such a one would most certainly not—that is, if she haunted you at all! She—"

Gus was sputtering in his offense. The company burst out chuckling and Gus reared, nearly as red-faced as his interlocutor.

"There, Gus," the minotaur said, and slapped his back. I pitched dizzily with the blow. "Mr. Manley is only joking. No one questions that you and your Catherine have a singular relationship. I'm sure she's blinking like that in her sweet anxiety to assist you in any way she can." The mocking note was blatant, but before Gus could react Asterion forged on. "But you haven't answered my question: how goes your work with the beamers? Mr. Manley and these others are interested in your proposed innovations. I've told them that your work is truly on the forefront of the art."

Gus was only slightly mollified by this flattery. "It's progressing very well, thank you. I had meant to discuss it with you. I have all sorts of ideas for improvements, though I dread to think of what they might cost—but perhaps another time—"

"Asterion tells us you studied with Old Darius," another man put in. He was entirely human-looking, dressed in elegant dove gray with a face ageless and illegible. A scrim of silver hair showed beneath his hat. In any world he would have been known at once to be rich, and cold, and dangerous. "So it's surprising that you've developed such a different specialty. Weren't you trained to work with fire?"

"Predominantly, yes," Gus conceded, and I could tell that for all his annoyance the interest of such an obviously important man beguiled him. "Darius taught me trickery with fire and smoke, as well as weather magic. Illusion work and the like. But none of that is particularly useful to me at the moment, so I've been obliged to teach myself afresh."

It would be mistaken to suggest that, in life, I had been excluded from circles like this one, where men of wealth and power bandied their common preconceptions from mouth to mouth and termed it *debate*. It was rather that such circles were so remote from my experience as to be irrelevant, and it would not have occurred to me that I was excluded any more than the sparrows were. Nonetheless I could recognize the roles of the various players by subtleties of tension and tenor, by the cant of shoulders and the eagerness of laughter. I knew that Asterion was a vulgar climber and upstart, barely tolerated; that Gus was a curiosity whom Asterion was retailing to secure his entrance here; that Mr. Manley was a hanger-on and the gray man, Nemo, was the real power among them.

Collecting ghosts was surely an expensive hobby.

"Teach *yourself*, you say? There are rumors that you forged a projection with functioning cognition after a mere handful of attempts. Do you mean to say you did that with no instruction but your own?"

How quickly the word had spread! I glanced around at the field of chattering heads, wondering how many of them had already learned of the tragically alert beamer child lately deposited in Margo's care. How many knew that that child had been created with power largely siphoned from myself. I realized at once that some sort of magical eavesdropping was likely involved, but Gus seemed too oblivious to draw the clear inference.

Instead he puffed a little and was about to join in the acclamation of his own talents when we were interrupted. My first confused impression was that a very large and lumpy hat was levitating on our periphery. Then it appeared that the hat was afloat on a column of wavering distortion. Had I not been screaming, I might have laughed.

For it was Anura perched atop the head of her watery friend, the lady whose brows contained the intricate loopings of pearly fishes. Anura's small blue hands clutched the transparent forehead tightly and her back feet sometimes paddled for purchase, to absurd effect. But there was nothing comical in her expression. Her scarlet eyes rolled atop her head and caught Gus in a gaze of grim ferocity while her watery companion— dressed in a fluid, silver-blue fall of metallic silk, with bare pellucid arms that put me in mind of mountain rills—slipped into our circle with such confident grace that it nearly concealed her aggression. The gentlemen, if I may so term them, had little choice but to part and admit the exquisite lady along with her warty, seething bonnet.

I could not burst out in cries of childish delight, could not crow and embrace my amphibious friend. I was used to the agony of inexpressible rage. Here I discovered that speechless adoration is a far worse affliction, swelling within me like an ache I had no hope of relieving. How could I tell her what her presence meant to me? Everything about her that had once appeared homely or ridiculous took on a new aspect: the beauty of love incarnate.

The company gathered around Asterion ruffled with polite aversion; Nemo lifted his hat and Mr. Manley bowed his crimson head like a wilting rose.

Gus raised his eyes and studied the ceiling.

"Madame Laudine," Mr. Manley greeted the watery lady, and I thought that he was unduly flustered. "And, ah—I don't believe I've been introduced to—your friend?"

Madame Laudine gave a gracious dip of her own head that set Anura scrabbling for balance.

"Mr. Manley, Nemo, gentlemen. How pleasant to meet you on this historic occasion! I'm sure you are all as overjoyed as we are at Mariam's ascendancy." Her voice had a calculated insincerity that gave away nothing of her true feelings. The circle offered murmurs of equally insincere agreement. "As for my friend, surely she needs no introduction, Mr. Manley? This is the great Anura! Of course all of you are acquainted with the work of our foremost poet?"

Madame Laudine was plainly exaggerating for some reason that was not yet clear to me. Nonetheless I was pleased and quite irrationally proud to learn that Anura's work had received some measure of recognition.

"I must confess—that is, my business allows me little leisure for such—"

Madame Laudine's watery lips tweaked in a sly smile that told me she had gained her object, though I did not yet understand what she was after.

"Oh, no? We must remedy your deprivation, then! As it so happens, Anura has composed some verses in honor of Mariam's new reign. Darling Anura, could I perhaps prevail on you to recite your latest for these gentlemen?"

Gus by now was thoroughly purple in the face, though he kept his expression locked in a sort of strained abstraction that fooled no one.

Asterion's horns bucked. "Ladies, we are regrettably preoccupied at the moment. I'm afraid—"

"Oh, but one can always find time for true beauty, Asterion!" Madame Laudine gave a warbling laugh, and I knew at once that, alone with Anura, she laughed in a very different key. Insolence knocked inside her coquetry like a clapper in a bell. "Business means nothing unless it allows for the elevation of the spirit. *Dearest* Anura, it seems these gentlemen's need of your art is acute."

Anura hadn't yet spoken, but now she bulged upward and resettled herself and her scarlet eyes—at long last!—rotated to meet mine. I suppose anyone else might have mistaken her look for the usual crude inquisitiveness, but oh, I saw something in it grave, and tender, and faithful. She had come to me, and she cared. My endless flashing fired with a new brilliance, as if I could make it spell her name.

"Sorcerers as well as ordinary mortals may live their whole lives immured in loneliness. But poetry is the power that speaks through the walls." Anura's voice had a low rumble like scattering pebbles, and I felt sure the loneliness she meant was mine.

"Tell us, then," Asterion said with ill grace. "Since nothing else will satisfy you."

Madame Laudine smiled as if he had expressed the warmest enthusiasm. Nemo's head tipped back so that his gaze slanted across his cheekbones, and I guessed that, like me, he wondered at the point of their game. Gus stamped in place as if he had half a mind to storm off, but he was too uncertain to follow through. It was apparent that, in his arrogance, he thought the whole performance was meant for his exclusive benefit.

It was not. Anura began.

"Where is the wine that ever forged its glass?
None ever, oh, none ever,
For garnet contradiction holds it fast.
The cup is but a spill belied,
And wine englassed is flow denied.

"Where is the glass that ever made man fall?
None ever, oh, none ever,
For trampled grape, disordered dream, and all,
Drain down his throat like whispered lies,
The glass left empty as his eyes.

"Where is the poison that was in the wine?
Forever, oh, forever
It claims his veins to be its vine,
Its fruit cold stones, its scent stopped breath,
For wine's true form wreathes through his death."

Anura ceased speaking. There followed a long silence, for it was a very uncomfortable poem, and a puzzling one. Gus twitched. Then Asterion forced a laugh, loud and dismissive, as if he could frighten away Anura's words if he only barked at them loudly enough.

"But what in the name of all impossibilities has that to do with Mariam?"

It had been evident to me as soon as Madame Laudine broached the subject that there had not been nearly enough time for Anura to write a commemorative poem. Now from the general fidgeting of the company I gathered that this complication had dawned on them as well. Anura's mouth broadened even further if such a thing were possible; it was hard to say if it was a grimace or a smile.

"The significance of a poem is not always immediately apparent." She was gazing at me as she spoke. "In time its bearing on the present moment will become quite clear."

Catherine Tells the Truth

My impressions of what followed the séance are jumbled—I may have had a slight concussion. I remember Mrs. Farrow half-carried away from me in hysterics, screaming, "You have no right! You have no *right* to deny me my daughters! And you have the presumption to call yourself Gus's friend, far above you though he is, but now you won't lift a finger for his sisters!" Margo looked crushed. Gus made no attempt to conceal his absolute delight, his pride in what I'd done, beaming at me with bright possessiveness. Reverend Skelley's brows were drawn together, creating a deep vertical crease. He had at least the grace to direct his wondering inward instead of gawking at me, which Dr. Lewis was doing.

"The poor girl must have had such a fright!" Mrs. Lewis observed. "It's cruel to demand that she put herself through that again!" But Mrs. Lewis was the one who was still shaking, not I, though I did feel unwell.

Mrs. Hobson announced that she was going to bed, and quit the room with a very annoyed air. Oh, but I had seen—or not seen at all but *sensed,* sensed with a sense I ought not to have—a clear line of power connecting her to the speaking trumpet, in those moments while it still hovered in the lamplight.

At the time I assumed the very worst of her. Now I believe that Mrs. Hobson was probably no conscious fraud, but a raw and untrained sorceress, tricked by her own convictions into thinking her powers flowed from an external source.

"How did you come here tonight?" I failed to realize that the soft voice intended its question for me, and Reverend Skelley turned to Margo. "How did Miss Bildstein come here tonight?"

"I walked," I said. "It's not so far." It occurred to me that I could now leave this miserable evening behind, and I tried to stand. A variety of hands caught me and eased me back into my seat. Gus kept squeezing my fingers, and I made a vague effort to smile at him.

"You mustn't try to walk home. I'll take you in the phaeton, and Thomas can walk back to our house."

I objected, but it did no good. With an excess of solicitous bustling I was seen down and lifted into the phaeton's only passenger seat—in truth, I was still so dizzy that I had to grip the seat's edge to keep myself steady. Reverend Skelley's pretty palomino set off at a gentle walk, and he himself kept his eyes on the road.

Now that my shock was receding, rage came to the fore. "Did *you* know that there were such wild expectations attached to my attendance tonight?" I asked, waspish. "I myself was not informed."

He nodded, still not looking at me. His face was grossly swollen where the books had pummeled him; one lump on his forehead was enough to push his hat askew. "The elder Mrs. Farrow did tell me that she had great hopes of you. Yes. I suppose she refrained from telling you so that you would not be unduly influenced."

Encouraged to fake, he meant.

"So when Mrs. Hobson asked if everyone would consent to aid her *spirits,* only I was meant. You say Margo didn't want to influence me, but to me it seems that she invited me under false pretenses so I could be made to serve her purposes. It's disgraceful!"

His eyebrows fluttered slightly higher. "You call her Margo." I had, and it was too late to recall the name. "Your anger at her misrepresentation is justified, Miss Bildstein. You have my deepest apology for my part in it."

I found myself disarmed by this unexpected courtesy. "Thank you."

"No one said as much, but I think it was universally assumed that you would be eager—perhaps too eager—to ingratiate yourself with the Farrows. That you would be all too pleased to serve their purposes, as you say. After all, your father works for them." A hard knot formed in my throat at the thought that Mrs. Farrow might take her revenge on my father. Then I saw that Reverend Skelley was smiling to himself under the downy tufts of his moustache, and found myself somehow reassured. "They appear to understand you very poorly. Is it because Margo Farrow was less than candid that you refused any future participation?"

144 S. E. PORTER

Something in his tone told me that he knew as well as I did how much that refusal might have cost me. There was the question of my father's job, but not only that.

I could have bilked Gus's mother shamelessly, and even told myself that I was justified in doing so by the comfort I brought her. I briefly ached for the career, the freedom, I'd let slip through my fingers, then crushed the thought. Did I really want to spend my life tied to chairs while the likes of Dr. Lewis lorded over me?

"That wasn't my only reason," I said. He waited. The rush of midnight leaves, the horse's lazy clopping, rose tidal in my ears while I wondered if I should risk the truth. "I—don't believe that voice belonged to Viviana Farrow."

"To whom, then?"

"To Mrs. Hobson."

A rock jarred the wheel, and he winced. "You believe it was some clever ventriloquism? I held my ear very close to Mrs. Hobson's mouth at that moment, and I can promise you she was perfectly silent. She seemed to fall into a deep sleep just as the voice began. And it was the same with the second voice, the one that called itself Henry Kirk."

I wasn't about to accuse Mrs. Hobson of sorcery, whatever I thought in private. Instead of replying I turned to watch the moon, already rolling down the sky.

"And of course ventriloquism would hardly account for the objects that moved, with no evident agency." He palpated his bruised cheek with careful fingers. Mine was puffed and tender, too, of course, and our marks conferred a kind of kinship.

"No," I agreed. "It wouldn't. But supposing you hadn't thrown yourself over Mrs. Hobson and absorbed all those blows in her defense, I believe not a single book would have touched her."

I was surprised to see him give a tense half grin in response to my re-mark. "It would be fascinating to test your hypothesis, but we can't, of course. Then are you among those who believe that what we're observing isn't the action of spirits at all, but rather telekinesis, perhaps unwitting, on the part of the mediums?" Despite the pain that tightened his face, he was growing excited. "Miss Bildstein, I will be truthful: I strongly opposed your inclusion tonight. Not because—I did not imagine anything so—"

I spared him from finishing this sentence; there was no graceful way for him to deny that he'd thought me likely to be a vulgar little cheat, if only I were given the opportunity.

"That, Margo did tell me. She said you thought the loss of my mother would make me overly susceptible to believing that we can contact the dead."

He looked away. "I spoke from my own experience. Grief undoes our capacity for objective analysis. Any straw of hope—" He broke off. "I didn't understand that I would meet tonight with a young lady who prefers truth over fame, over society, even over consolation! God can ask no more of any of us."

I already liked Reverend Skelley very much. In fact, I liked him enough to be honest with him.

"I also prefer truth to God," I said, and then realized that we were approaching my cottage, firelight a dim flux on its windows. He pulled back on the reins and his horse ambled to a stop. I hurried to climb out before he could move to help me—his broken rib would make it far too painful.

"And I pray that I will never be forced to choose between them. Good night, Miss Bildstein."

Angus Falling

Saturday finally comes, and when I meet Geneva her smile has a tense, guarded look. It's like the words waiting in her mouth are made of two distinct strands, twisted together until even she doesn't know which one she's going to say: *Hey, Angus! Ready to blow up some elves?* Or, *Angus, hey, sorry, but I've decided this isn't such a good idea.*

"Hi, Geneva," I call when I get close. But lightly, lightly, so she'll forget about telling me the date is off. If my tone is even a hair's breadth too eager, I'm done. "*Elf-Blast 3* was all sold out. How do you feel about people-eating aliens?"

I see her hesitation play out as the tiniest adjustment in the slope of her smile. Then it broadens and warms. She glances at my pendant and smiles to herself, so it's good I'm wearing it over my shirt this time.

"Do the aliens explode? Into flying nimbuses of gratuitous green goo?"

"If the goo isn't green," I say, feeling pleased with myself for getting the attitude dialed in so well, "then how will it reverse the space-time continuum?"

"You raise a compelling point."

"It's gotta be green."

"It simply must! Or we'll need a team of scientists to investigate!"

"But burritos first, right? The aliens don't start exploding until seven twenty."

She walks along a couple feet farther away than I'd like, but she comes with me. It feels a little too much like I'm on an obstacle course, like she's constantly looking for pretexts to reject me.

"Hey," I say. I need to distract her. "Am I allowed to ask you questions tonight?"

Sidelong glance and a twitch of smile. "I'll consider it. Oh, perhaps a *few.*" She does a great mock-severe schoolmarm voice.

"Erm," I say. Where do people even start? "Tell me about yourself?"

That gets a laugh. "That seems *rather general*, Angus." Then the schoolmarm character breaks. "I'm studying video editing at an art college. Junior year. I'd like to make documentaries, but you know. Marketable skills take priority. I've watched my mom struggle way too much."

I notice that she doesn't name her school. "Are your parents divorced?"

"Yeah, and I still live with her. The irony is that I'm named after the city where they met. I bet my mom loves the constant reminder."

"So . . ." A little gust of confusion spins in my brain. "So they're Swiss?"

"Nope. Dad American, mom Turkish. My grandparents on her side were diplomats, so she was in Geneva with them. She met my dad when she was only eighteen, in an elevator. It was love at first sight, but a few extra years of sight did a number on *that*. Funny how that works."

I let the information settle in as we reach the burrito shop and find a booth near the back. Something about what she's telling me weirds me out, but at first I don't catch what it is.

Then I realize. It's so damned easy for her to trot out all these very specific facts, and I get the feeling that she could just keep going and *going*, like tell me stories about her grandfather in some war or something. I mean, how old was *my* mom when my parents met? What city were they in at the time? I've never considered any of it.

I've never wondered about them *meeting* at all. Frank-and-Trudy Farrow sit in my brain as an established unit. A solid lump of my life. But when I think about them, there's no sense of that lump having any history. It's as if the two of them possessing their own story would be excessive, like some kind of unnecessary decoration.

Huh.

"Angus?" Geneva's reading my face. "You look like something's bothering you."

"Oh." It would be nice to be honest with her, wouldn't it? The trouble is that I don't know what counts as *too* honest. "I was just feeling sad that I don't know stuff like that about my parents." God, how do I explain it to her? "They're not big sharers."

Her eyebrows are up. "Really? Not even basic biographical details? They never told you anything?" A pause. "Had they taken a vow of silence or some shit?"

Her questions *hurt*. They worm around in my brain, threading it with empty, aching tunnels. Because I don't know how to answer.

"I mean, they were perfectly capable of telling me I was doing everything wrong, so I guess no vow of silence? Because they could do that at a pretty high volume."

It sounds like I'm playing for sympathy. Geneva's been looking down at the table, her fingers tracing the graffiti scratched into the wood, but I'm almost certain I can feel her oscillating between warmth and cynicism.

Geneva looks up. "Would you tell me a story from your childhood? Like, a memory that means something to you."

Her gaze has an analytic intensity to it. This isn't a casual question, and it's not an easy one either. *I don't have memories like that,* I almost say. But then something flares into consciousness, abruptly, like it's just coming back to me after a trip to the moon.

"Okay. It's kind of sad, though?" It's horrible, actually. Overwhelming. My mind's eye rolls into eclipse, seeing it all again. God, the way they flashed in the hot summer sun, their ferocity, how hard I cried . . .

"Sure."

"So I remember this one time I was playing by myself in this park? I think I was about seven. Anyway, there was this huge anthill. I was crouching there watching it when these tiny silver things started pouring out of the top; like, very clearly not ants. I peered closer, and they were miniature soldiers in armor. The kind of armor you see in museums? They started fighting once they reached the grass, and I realized they were going to just *massacre* each other. So I put both hands over the anthill to try to stop them. But I couldn't hold them in! They kept on erupting between my fingers, and I knew they were all going to die and there was nothing I could do! I—"

Tears blur my eyes until all I can see is the dazzle of that swarming army, silver degenerating into a crawl of bloody light as the soldiers fell in droves. Each soldier leaked a perfect dewdrop of blood, and the surface tension was enough that tiny corpses dangled in the tasseled grass. When I brushed the grass with my hand they plinked down, their little helmets jangling.

Geneva cracks up laughing. Oh, God, I never would have believed that she could be so *callous*. "There's nothing funny about—"

Then I understand. She thinks I'm lying. Because what I just said—it's outside the bounds of what she considers reality.

"Wow. I don't feel like I get you, Angus. But your bullshit game is on *point*. That was the best fake impassioned angst I've ever seen."

They call out the number for our burritos, and I practically jump up to get them. Because I really need a moment to regroup. If my memories aren't as substantial as hers, what else can they be?

"Your turn," I say when I get back to the booth with our foil-swathed food bricks: veggie with sour cream for her, pulled pork for me. "Meaningful childhood memory."

"Right." She peels back the foil and takes a first bite, then chews in this speculative way. "When I was five, I was kidnapped by a witch who turned me into a pink flamingo. My mom got me back to normal in the end, but I still have this strange habit of standing on one leg when I'm nervous."

"That's awful!" I say. "I'm so glad your mom got you back." It's only the way her smile spreads across her face that tells me she was lying. Oh, jeez, she thinks this is a game.

Then it's a game, Angus. She's having fun with you, and that's all that counts.

Not those soldiers? Not their tiny entrails glimmering like wet rubies on the grass? I'm supposed to just pretend they don't matter at all?

"The preening is the worst part," Geneva adds. Her grin is huge and flourishing, like a gigantic carnivorous flower, and her hazel eyes are full of complicated gleams. "Totally embarrassing when I start doing that in class."

She likes this game, but I hate it. I mentally flail for some way to kill it. "Are you an only child?"

"Yeah, no. There were almost ten thousand of us in my brood."

She doesn't throw me this time. "No, I mean really?"

"Yes. Unless you count my three half siblings from my stepmom, but I almost never see them. As far as my lived experience goes, it's just me and my mom." Another bite, along with one of her too-assessing looks. "You?"

Oh, God. I should've known better than to introduce this topic. It's something I've wondered about before, and the answers that bob to the surface don't feel definitive. "I have a little sister?" I hope that's right. It might be. "She's twelve?"

"Yeah? What's her name?"

Is she *trying* to trip me up? What the hell are little sisters named, these days? "Evelyn. Evie for short." I'm supposed to say more about her, aren't I? "She's cute. She's really into figure skating."

I wouldn't *lie* to Geneva. Of course not. The things I'm telling her about my sister aren't lies; more like educated guesses. There's every chance it's all true.

Geneva nods in a that's-settled way and starts talking about varieties of alien detonation, and I'm so relieved I practically prattle my way through the rest of the meal. We share a flan, then wander out into the street to catch our movie, and being with her feels almost as magical as I imagined it would.

Except in my daydreams Geneva might be holding my hand at this point. In real life she keeps a careful distance, just far enough away to make it clear that a touch isn't welcome. There's something about me she doesn't trust, and I have no idea what.

What am I doing wrong? I want to say. *I love you. If you just communicate what the problem is, I swear I'll fix it for you!*

She's laughing at the movie, but there's no soft listing in my direction. No nestling. She sits bolt upright beside me, eating the popcorn she insisted on paying for and cackling. But I can't make out what's happening on the screen at all, somehow.

Instead I see that luminous city again, the one I glimpsed from Lore's car. A moon of a city, dropped at the core of a whirlpool. My mind is knocked free of my head, tossed into a helical gale. Variegated darkness rushes past, carrying fragments—of what? Dusk-colored columns, overhanging hematite trees? Whatever they are, I'm dashing too fast to make them out.

And the girl I heard before is still screaming, on and on, her voice whipping up the gyre. Shit, do I *know* her?

I'm falling to meet her, her scream twined around me like thread, and I can't make it stop.

The movie ends, thank God. I blink back into my seat, find my hands gripping the armrests and my breath hacking out of me. And Geneva and I stumble out into the night.

"So," she says. I already know her mouth won't drift open under a dapple of shadow. In fact, she's stopped on a conspicuously well-lit corner with passersby brushing around us, and I bet it's on purpose. "So, are you still interested? Now that you've interacted with me, and I'm not just some girl-shaped abstraction you saw in a café?"

I love you. By definition.

"I'm still interested." It comes out a little flat; why am I the one who has to do all the devotion? "Are you?"

"I think so." *Oh, how romantic.* "There's something about you I don't get, like I said. But you're way more fun than I would have guessed. I like you enough that I'm in for a second date, anyway. If you are."

This is a good thing, Angus. But her words feel so sparse and chilly compared to what I want from her that anger boils up behind my eyes.

"Cool. Maybe we can even trade phone numbers this time? If that doesn't seem like too much of a commitment to you. I don't want to overwhelm you with my wild demands." Oh. That sounded all wrong. *Shut up, shut up, shut up.*

Annoyance passes over her in a visible riffling. "You know what I *really* don't understand about you? The nature of this thing you have for me. I can almost start to think it's just an innocent if eccentric crush, but then I'll get the impression that you've glommed onto me in some much weirder way. It's not a comfortable feeling, to put it mildly."

She's waiting for an explanation. But when I think about it, it seems like a bad idea to give her one.

"Are you saying you aren't special enough for me to have a crush on you?"

"Not at all. I'm extraordinary. But you have no way to know that, do you?"

"What if I can just tell? What if I knew as soon as I saw you?"

"That's not how it works. I'm not standing behind the counter at Blue-bell's telegraphing my brilliance and sensibility. I'm working the fucking register."

I said one wrong thing, and she's ready to turn on me?

"I just had a feeling about you. As soon as I saw you behind the counter, it was like—like you fit. I've been looking for the right girl all my life, and I could feel you filling in the space where she belongs. Like color and light came flooding in, and you were the source of it."

Now, *that* was a beautiful way to put it! Tender and poetic. She'll see—

"It sounds like a coloring book." Her face isn't yielding at all.

"It what?"

"It sounds like you had the outline of some imaginary girl already in your mind, and you decided I was the crayon you could use to color her in. To which I can only say, like hell you can, Angus."

"Geneva, I—"

There's a bus pulling up, and she's walking toward it. How was I oblivious enough to miss the only important feature of this corner: a blue sign with a white blotch looking way too much like a vehicle whose sole purpose is to carry Geneva away from me?

I only have a few seconds left. "I love you!"

Geneva can't just leap on the bus, because there's a line in front of her. She has to wait for that old woman to maneuver on with her fifty shopping bags, for that guy heaving a stroller full of sleeping baby. She uses the delay to glance over her shoulder at me.

"I'm not even *real* to you. Because you don't know shit about me, and yet you've convinced yourself that you know everything. That differential might as well be a fucking pegasus."

And then she's climbing the steps, and the doors are folding shut. And I've just blown my entire reason for being.

Catherine in Excess

"What did she mean by threatening me like that? Bah, hearing that warty flaccid thing declaim *verses*—is it true that she has some sort of reputation as a poet? I can't conceive it, it must have been another of their lies—as if the muse would speak through a mouth like hers! Can she actually intend to poison me?"

Gus seemed quite exercised on the subject of Anura's recitation. Asterion had escorted us back to his rooms, which I had never seen before; they were small but luxuriously appointed in a rather bloody style, all crimson draperies and crossed swords. Asterion pivoted to look at him in genuine astonishment.

"Threatening *you*? But why?"

"I haven't the faintest idea. Who can say what a creature like Anura is thinking?"

Asterion's laugh whickered moistly on his bovine lips. "Well, Anura's only a woman at the last; one Patience Stott according to my information. Though that hardly disputes your point. And as for Madame Laudine!" He let out a malicious chuckle; I failed to see the joke. "But, Gus, as I understand it you and Anura engaged in dealings that were mutually beneficial, isn't that so? It's not as if you cheated her."

"Exactly! And yet she has the gall to insinuate to my face that she'll find some underhanded way to murder me. Mind, Asterion, it's not that I'm afraid of her—"

"As you shouldn't be. Gus, my friend, I don't deny that Madame Laudine and Anura were delivering a threat through that absurd poem of hers. But I don't for one moment believe that it was meant for you."

Gus recoiled as if slapped. Worse than a threat to his life was an affront to his vanity, for it had plainly never occurred to him that he might *not* be the object of Anura's machinations. He took in Asterion's meaning that he, Gus, was not important enough to be menaced in such a fashion, and all his spluttering indignation went cold. When he spoke again it was with affectless chill.

"For whom, then?"

"Well—Madame Laudine and Nemo have not always been on the best of terms. I took it that she was using Anura to hint he might fare poorly under Mariam's new regime; mere empty taunting, as far as I can tell. Really, you keep so stubbornly apart from society that I don't see how you *could* make enemies—there's just no occasion for it! My friend, you can put your mind at ease."

They were both wrong. For once I was glad I could produce no sound but screaming, or I might not have been able to suppress a laugh. Anura's poem had assuredly not been meant for Nemo, nor for Gus either.

It was for me. She had slipped me a message of the greatest importance, cleverly encoded in those lines about poison and wine.

Too cleverly, perhaps. For now the difficulty was that I could only guess at her true meaning. That is, it seemed likely that I was the wine and Gus the man dispatched by my poison. But as for the glass—and as for what Anura thought I might be able to do—there I had only the wildest speculations.

Gus and Asterion's conversation now began treading more familiar ground: Gus's ideas for improving his beamers, for making them responsive and sensitive enough to beguile young women, for expanding their reserves of false memories and, most importantly, instilling a sense of mission, inexorable and absolute. And then they must discuss the magical *expense* of such an ambitious undertaking—for of course Gus's claim that he would drain me only to meet Margo's needs was brazen nonsense.

Asterion unpacked his umbrastring and jabbed the fork into my thigh. I felt at once the dreadfully familiar thickening, almost as if a knot of infected flesh formed around the prongs while the rest of me remained as airy as ever. Gus sipped on the trailing thread, and the swarming pain bit through me, each prick wheedling away something essential. Oh, that cold deletion, that stinging robbery of myself, how many thousands of times have I endured it!

That draining. As if I were so much wine.

"Even assuming I can reclaim, perhaps, seven or eight hundred when

I render down this last beamer—the immediate improvements I wish to make in the next one might cost me as much again! Margo can test its capacity for learning while I save, of course, but—"

There they were, twittering about money while I swirled in agony. Gus held the umbrastring's end pinched in the corner of his mouth while he spoke. I realized then that I always resisted that suction as best I knew how; I leaned against the current, fought the connection.

"Oh, more than that! And then you must allow for the inevitable losses that occur when magic is reused—some always leaks away in the process—taxes, you know—I'd estimate twenty-five percent or so. From what you tell me, you'd be wise to budget at least twelve hundred. With a great project like yours, you must not skimp on the small refinements. In the final analysis it's the details, dear Gus, that will make the thing convincing."

Possibly resistance was a mistake.

"Twelve hundred! Oh, I suppose—and more for future iterations. And then I still haven't begun the search for materials to grant the things real physicality. Matter has to come from somewhere, and it's far easier if it doesn't require fundamental transformation." Gus looked sidelong at Asterion as he said this, perhaps remembering the old promise: an Athenian youth. What exactly did he mean to do?

"Oh, as to that—when your work is ready, something can be managed. Of course, what you're attempting is quite unusual. For most beamers the illusion is more than sufficient, and the work that's been done on truly embodied ones is preliminary at best. Unstable creatures. They don't tend to last long."

"Mine *must* last, though—say a year. They'll need to sleep, won't they, and eat? Otherwise they'll notice the discrepancy between themselves and ordinary people immediately. All the bother of a working digestion, imagine it, just to deliver a single kiss!"

A kiss? Even in my weakness the word spasmed inside me. A *kiss*, like the one which—

And then I was no longer weak. My flickering caught in a blaze of white incandescence, and I thought I understood Anura's message. Gus took a deep pull on the umbrastring, drinking me down; all that remained was the poison.

And do they not say that the poison is in the dose?

Rather than straining to withhold myself, I surged into the string like the breaking of a dam. The dial's tiny hand spun into a circular blur and I felt myself ramming into a sort of folded thought—that then was the purse where magic was stored! The purse split and overflowed, and I leapt outward, attempting to explode Gus's skull from within.

For half a moment, my ghost stopped screaming. Then my scream lashed out of Gus's mouth, driving his head back at such a sharp angle that I hoped to snap his spine. Asterion caught him by the shoulders as the umbrastring fell from his lips and his eyes rolled back in his head.

Gus slipped to the floor in a faint, his skin deathly white. I was in poor shape myself, reduced to a rag doll of wraith sagging over him. I was no larger than a newborn baby. My scream thinned to a kettle's whistling.

Asterion didn't bother to check Gus's pulse. Instead he looked dead at me, brows arched.

"If you *did* manage to kill him, you'd almost certainly destroy yourself into the bargain," Asterion informed me. "But I suppose that was the idea?"

Even in my deflation, this address startled me. Apparently Asterion understood that I was sentient enough for conversation.

"Luckily for my personal finances, you can't. But if you rushed him hard enough, you *might* wind up trapped inside his body. Forever. If you find your intimacy disagreeable now, I don't suppose you'd much enjoy knocking around in his skull."

Ordinarily I would not have credited anything Asterion said. But in this case his claim was confirmed by direct evidence: I'd heard my scream on Gus's lips. I imagined how it would be: Gus's stinking breath sieving through my immaterial person, his sweat surrounding me like a thin but impassable moat. Still worse, I supposed I might be caught in the endless dunning of Gus's thoughts, his dreams, with none of the merciful interludes of his silence I enjoyed now.

My limp doll shape flashed and bucked at the thought, and Asterion nodded.

"I thought so. Stick to feeding him the interest, then. No more stunts with the capital!"

That was an interesting way to put it. What, exactly, did he fear I might do?

Meanwhile I was subtly and slowly inflating again, though I still felt very ill.

"Just in case, though, I'd better take my umbrastring back to its maker. He mentioned the possibility of spelling it to smooth out just that sort of *excess* activity. It seemed like a waste of talens at the time, but now you've forced me to protect my investment. I have Anura to thank for that, don't I?"

Oh! Contrary to what he'd told Gus, Asterion had known quite well to whom that poem was addressed. It showed far more acuity than I'd suspected in him. While I absorbed this realization, Asterion stooped to pick the dropped umbrastring off the floor and held it close, inspecting the dial. He whistled as well as his cow's mouth would allow.

"I'm sorry to tell you that all you've done is to give Gus one hell of a windfall. Nearly three thousand talens at a blow! He might not mind a patch of indisposition at that price!"

With that Asterion knelt and slapped Gus's cheeks until he roused, his head rocking and eyes wild. A haze of magic seeped from his mouth, softening his contours. He attempted to sit and Asterion eased him down again.

"Don't try to move. You'll need to rest for a good long while, my dear friend. No work for a bit, all right? I absolutely forbid it."

"What happened?" Gus's gaze slurred in my direction. I was by this time perhaps three feet tall, and my scream was regaining something of its usual force.

"Oh, it was only that a bit of our conversation got through to Catherine. In her dumb way she grasped that you were in need, so she rushed to help. It was more enthusiasm than you could support, that's all. But look how much power she gave you!"

Asterion dangled the dial in front of Gus's eyes and favored me with a sly half smile. My education in matters of hatred had not ended with my death.

"She did?" Gus goggled. "I can't feel *anything* like so much. The power. I—"

"Oh, then it must have spilled out while you were unconscious. Did you keep enough for my share, at least?"

Passivity had the poor virtue of protecting me from disappointment. Action exposed me to crushing failure. Possibly Asterion was lying when he said there was no way I could kill Gus by my new method, but he would deny me the chance to try again. Had I misunderstood Anura's message, or was I simply too inept to follow her implied instructions? Had I ruined my only opportunity for putting an end to my former friend? These questions tormented me throughout Gus's convalescence.

For all my anguish, though, I nurtured a tender warmth at the quick. I was no longer as utterly alone as I had been.

Anura cared what became of me, enough even to enlist her friends in schemes of coming to my aid. When I considered her evident concern, her affection even, my failure seemed less significant. Perhaps I had misconstrued her; perhaps in time I might grasp her meaning better, and find another way.

But of Anura's kind intentions, I could be certain.

So far as I was concerned, that kindness was the only magic in Nautilus worth having, and Anura was the greatest sorceress alive. She had brought hope to the hopeless. Is that not a feat more splendid than burning a blizzard or melting a tower?

Catherine in the Dirt

Gus appeared early the next morning with a napkin full of marzipans—Mrs. Hobson had brought them from Boston as a gift to his parents—and sat down beside me in the grass while I weeded our vegetable garden.

"They've stopped locking you up?" I asked. I didn't mean to sound snappish.

"It was only because—" Gus broke off, tilting his head so sadly that I softened. "My mother thought that if I was seen at the wake, or the burial, people might think it implied some kind of formal connection between our families. I was so angry I smashed a vase. That was when they decided to shut me in my room until it was all over."

Gus was blushing. Ugh—here was the real reason everyone had assumed that I'd be desperate to win over Gertrude Farrow. Did they all see, now, that I was not intriguing to snare her son? I felt shame heat my cheeks at the idea, and possibly that was yet another motive for my refusal to act as medium—it was a chance to prove, before witnesses, how little I cared for his mother's approval.

Gus spread out the marzipans. They were a luxury, one I'd tasted only in his house after Christmas. It took all my self-control not to devour them at once. I made myself wrap some up in my handkerchief to slip later to Anna.

"You were magnificent yesterday! So *clear* in the middle of all that, that sentimental muddle! I was worried—but I should have known you couldn't be taken in by empty spectacle! I wish Margo—but she doesn't understand what she's seeing, and I don't know if I can tell her. Because then—"

He delivered this rather disjointed speech in mournful tones. If he told Margo it was magic she'd seen, he'd have to explain why he thought such a thing was possible.

"You mean that Mrs. Hobson is a sorceress and not a medium," I said.

Gus nodded. "That's what Darius says; he says he can sense the magic in her, just the way he can in—in me. It hurts me more than I can say to see Margo fooled like that."

I liked agreeing with Old Darius even less than I liked agreeing with Gertrude Farrow.

"So why don't you tell Margo everything? Unless Darius outright forbids you to, and even then it's not like you to fawn." Gus flinched; anger snapped in my voice. Then something struck me. "Or, no—I can see that it would be awful to tell her, when she really believes your cousin is coming back to her. I didn't know she'd ever had a child."

The Reverend Skelley had said that recent bereavement damaged the critical faculties. I understood with a shock that old griefs were just as potent—if grief sank deeper with time then that action might make it less conspicuous, but in no way was it gone. Instead it burrowed in the depths, and its winding holes never closed.

Of course Margo should have been straightforward with me, of *course* she should—but all at once my fury at her seemed overblown.

Gus reared back, his face pinched. "Of course you didn't know. No one ever mentions it, because the baby was all of four months old when it died! It was hardly more than a worm. I can't understand why Margo is suddenly so *possessed* by the idea of a creature that couldn't even talk."

I had my first intimation that perhaps Gus had reasons besides a disinterested love of truth for wanting me not to be a medium.

"Even with a baby, though, or a very young child—I know that in the case of my brothers part of what my parents grieved was the loss of potential. That they could never know who my brothers might have become." I fumbled my way with difficulty through these feelings so far beyond my experience.

"If Margo wants potential, she has me now," Gus said. "Maybe I *should* tell her everything for just that reason! It would be kinder to disillusion her quickly, instead of letting it all drag out."

"That there are no such things as ghosts, or spirits, only magic that creates the illusion of them." I still felt tentative, as if moving blind through strange territory. Something had touched me, and I was no longer quite so righteously self-assured. "Even though it will wound her terribly to know the truth."

"No," Gus said. "There are."

"There are what?"

"Ghosts—that's what I meant to tell you after we saw Nora Downs. Darius says so. It's only that they don't *behave* like that."

My discomfiture at this speech approached nausea: it was violent, visceral, *clenching*. I sat back on my heels, sweaty and furious, with weeds bleeding sap in my fists.

"And why would you credit what *Darius* says, when it's obvious he'll spin any nonsense to keep you entranced? Ghost stories, Gus, really? He treats you like a child!"

"Catherine," Gus said, his words falling over mine. "Catherine. I know Darius made a mistake in the way he approached you—he knows, too, now, I think he's even sorry. But you know what he is, you saw for yourself! Well, in the other realm ghosts aren't even all that unusual, and everyone can see them! As plainly as a hat, or a spade."

"On the moon, you mean?" I asked. Very nastily, I admit.

Gus looked at his lap. "I was wrong about that," he confessed softly. "But there's a city. That part is all true. I'd give anything to take you there someday."

I did not say that I had no use for any city populated by the likes of Darius, because Gus gave a small gasp and I saw that he was fighting back tears. I softened at once.

"Gus? What's the matter?"

"Oh!" Gus was struggling for self-mastery; he tried to smile. "It's just that I couldn't bear it if everything was spoiled, all because Darius had to act like an idiot in front of you."

Hearing him describe Darius's behavior in these terms mollified me considerably.

"Tell me about these ghosts, then," I said. I didn't want to see Gus break down in tears. "In the other realm. How are the Spiritualists mistaken?"

There was nothing like an opportunity to display his superior knowledge to help Gus rally. He straightened at once.

"Well, the voices, for a start. Ghosts can't talk. Sometimes they howl, or whine. But they're as dumb as cattle! So all that babble about how happy they were—anyone who knows anything about what ghosts are *really* like would know that was impossible for them!"

I find I must pause my story here, and let an interval of silence greet this first intimation of my future state.

"And what else?" I asked after I'd turned over this information. The marzipans were gone, all except the ones I'd saved. Grass pricked my bare feet, curled not far from Gus's elegant shoes. Their navy leather shone through careless patches of mud.

"Well, Darius says that sometimes there are—magical emanations, almost certainly unconscious ones—around ghosts. But their magic isn't the kind we saw—even with magic, their relationship with the physical world is *different* somehow. Levitating an object is the simplest magic there is, but a ghost can't lift so much as a feather! So something like that speaking trumpet, or even the bell—only someone living could do that."

I regret to say that Darius has been proved correct in this particular. I cannot levitate a knife, say, and embed it in a throat of my choosing. I find the immaterial far more biddable. Slippages, absences, gaps, the darkness dwelling in the world's excisions: these are now my kin. A shadow will recognize me; a crack will sit up for me like a puppy for its mistress. Solid objects, though, are unfriendly.

"It was savage of Mrs. Hobson, then. To let Reverend Skelley take such a beating, just to make her display more convincing." If my anger at Margo was waning, on this point I found it undiminished.

Gus shrugged. "She probably didn't even know what she was doing, really. Darius says she's not a citizen, so everything she does is—just magical overflow, slop. Mindless instinct. Ugh, what a foul old charlatan she is!"

There was a great deal to parse in these words. "A citizen? You mean of your magical city?"

He nodded. "Catherine, listen: all that matters there is talent. Darius says it's a *true* meritocracy, not the sham we have in this country, and no one there would care—" Here he stopped, blushing furiously. I chose not to understand. "I have to be getting back. I told my tutor I wanted to read Wordsworth in the woods, and he's enough of a sap that he believed me, but he'll start to look for me soon. Here!"

He held out his volume of Wordsworth. It was a lovely one, bound in burgundy leather, with gilt filigree on the spine. I accepted it with only the faintest fluttering of conscience.

"I'll say it fell out of my pocket in the brambles, and that I couldn't find it," Gus said. "I suppose I'll have to scratch my arms on some thorns on my way back." We were smiling at each other, and here I must in honesty recall that genuine tenderness passed between us, a warm transfusion, along with our childish glee over the theft.

"Your mother won't do anything against my father, will she? Because of what I did?"

Gus looked startled at the idea—I'm sure it had never occurred to him that my defiance might have consequences worth worrying about. "Oh, I don't think so! She always says that he's the only groom in town who doesn't drink."

Our moment of communion had passed, and we parted without the smallest touch, much less an embrace—it had been far out of the ordinary for us, when he'd pressed my hand after the séance. I finished weeding, then set to picking peas for supper, wondering at how their tiny tendrils knew to grip the stakes. Did plants have feeling in some sense, even though they had no brains? It seemed that they must.

But interspersed with these wonderings were glimpses of flying books, and keening ghosts, and a city where *citizen* had some otherworldly meaning I couldn't quite grasp. These visions repelled me, and I dug my bare toes into the soil as if I hoped to plant myself in all things warm, and sunlit, and solid.

I suppose it was an hour or two later—the peas were shelled, the dough rising—when Anna came running with wide eyes and a note in her hand. It was from Reverend Skelley, inviting us both to tea in his garden.

She threw her arms around my neck, snuffling—she had a cold. I was so glad to see her animated again that I did not mind when she wiped her moist little nose on my shoulder.

Angus on the Phone

"You can't just give up, Angus, my boy," Margo snips at me through the phone. I'm so distracted that I can't remember calling her, but I guess I must have? "This can end only if she loves you, so it depends on you to make that happen. Consider it your solemn duty, and soldier on."

I'm walking so fast that the night seems to blur and jostle around me. I can't face going back to Carmen's warehouse, can't face sitting alone in that room with those candles, with all the imminence that I feel in them, or in myself.

If I'm alone, I might light another one. I think.

"I get that," I say, or maybe whine, if you want to be technical. "I get that, if she's ever going to love me, it's on me. I *understand*."

"Not well enough, you don't," Margo snaps. "Apparently."

"You're supposed to be on my side! Margo, seriously, do *you* think I'm a beamer? Is that why she doesn't want me?"

"What a preposterous question! What does that distasteful term even mean, I might ask?"

"I thought you'd know? I was starting to wonder if there was something actually wrong with me, and everyone here except me knew what it was. Like, maybe some kind of—of existential disease?"

"Angus, sweetheart, I've known you since I could marinate your right foot in a shot glass full of bourbon. There's nothing wrong with you that a freight train's worth of common sense couldn't fix. So get some sense, and go get your girl."

"But if she won't even talk to me again, then—"

"Then what a phenomenal waste of effort you represent, eh? Find a way, won't you? It's too soon to resolve this attempt. Much too soon."

For a moment it's like I'm back in that city, the one I saw from Lore's car. Diffuse glow sifts through the walls and ceiling and I can hear the photons *tink tink tink*ing like hail against a pair of patent shoes.

"So what am I supposed to do?"

"Oh, start by telling her absolutely anything she'll find beguiling. Your behavior was presumptuous and entitled. You want to thank her for helping you recognize how much you have to learn. Surely even you know the sort of things you're supposed to say in these situations?"

Margo's voice breaks through the dream glow. A vertiginous jerk pulls me up short. I can still see my hand afloat on a surface like liquid pearl, a stray curl of dark hair.

"But what if she *never* loves me? What if everything I say is wrong?"

"Well, if it comes to that, you can always kiss her. But we're not ready for extreme measures."

What's that supposed to mean? I'm about to ask, but she's hung up on me. Right when I need her most, when my heart is one messy collision in my chest.

I need someone to explain why Geneva acted like my memories must be a joke. Like I'm an imposition, a scrawl, an irreality. That's the first thing I should have asked Margo, I realize: to confirm what I *know* I know.

That I'm Angus Alaric Farrow, nineteen years old. That I was born in Clayton, Missouri, and raised in a coldly elegant house with too much beige and dull celadon green and nothing on the walls but prissy family photos in expensive frames and no books anywhere. Dad in finance, mom in internet publishing. Frank and Trudy. Chilly, sensible, authoritarian types. My childhood was rich in material things but emotionally and imaginatively impoverished, so it's no wonder I've repressed a lot of the details. What's worth remembering about a past like mine, anyway? All the times my mom didn't take me sledding, all the stories my dad never read to me?

It was a depressing childhood, but it's mine. No one can take it from me.

In fact, the more I think about it, the more I remember. The moon is surrounded now in a haze like glowing dryer lint, and all sorts of things start coming back to me. The specific way my mom would hike her eyebrows to signify that I had strained her patience beyond mortal endurance, before she went back to fretting about toxins. The way my dad tried to get me interested in spreadsheets when I was, like, six. And some bright spots too: a sweet, vivid memory flares in my head, of taking little Vivian ice skating for the first time. I see myself navigating slowly backward, bent at the waist to cradle her tiny red-mittened paws in my hands while she advanced, stroke by stroke, wobbling like a colt. I can even remember the huge rainbow pom-pom on top of her white hat. The shy way she smiled at me. Darling Vivie!

Or is it Sylvie?

I'm losing the thread. It squirms around me, loose and bright, writing words I can't understand.

Catherine Turning

Memory bids us follow its awful paths, knowing precisely what awaits us if we dare traverse them, and it does not permit us to heed those signposts driven so deeply in ourselves. *Warning,* the signs announce, as in a fairy tale. *This is the way to sorrow.*

But there are no other ways to take; not anymore.

Once he was fully recovered from my assault—and it pleases me to say that his recovery took some time—Gus compressed the remains of his human sympathy into a very small and convenient package, buckled and locked it against the scratching within, and walked with a decisive step down the alleys of Nautilus. He had determined that it was time to reclaim Margo's charge—or rather the first of them; poor Margo tended many. She had fattened the little thing with teaching and affection, never knowing that she was preparing it for the slaughter.

Only the dregs of Nautilus's society lived near Margo, those whose magic was so faint that they barely qualified for admission—the sort who, at home, might have been fortune tellers or mediums supplementing their bare abilities with deceit. Having no grand ambitions, or else no means to realize them, they seemed to spend most of their time sitting sullenly in the alleys near their rooms.

I imagine I wasn't the only inhabitant of Nautilus who found the enchanted city galling in many respects, its concerns dully identical to those of quotidian society. Since the poor could not afford the petty expenditure needed to mask my screams, they simply clapped hands over their ears and glared as we passed.

We were still some distance away when we caught sight of them. Margo as well was sitting on the ground outside her tiny home, watching her beamer child play. The little Angus had somewhere collected a half-dozen creatures that might have been called mice, if only they had worn fur. Instead their bodies were clad in imbricated gold plates, jewel-specked and weighty. The beamer boy had arranged them in ranks and was prodding them to race, with nuggets of suet spread out as incentive at the course's end.

Instead of scampering in a decently mouselike fashion, the poor animals heaved themselves along, crouching and gasping at every step. I cringed away from their burdened plodding. But the beamer only poked them with a ruler Gus had provided, then sat back on its heels and crowed. Margo smiled indulgently.

Then my scream advised them of our coming. They looked, their expressions unmistakably betraying ruptured happiness. Gus had slipped in Margo's affections, that was plain.

The little beamer gathered his jeweled mice in his arms as if he feared Gus would trample them, then nestled under Margo's shoulder. Did it suspect what was coming? Since it was after all a projection drawn from Gus's own mind, did it understand him rather too well?

I believe it did. We were soon close enough to see its small face wadded with sullen loathing.

"Good afternoon, Aunt Margo," Gus said, in rather formal tones, and bent to kiss her so peremptorily that it had more the character of a jab. "Young Angus. You ought to be studying."

"He's been hard at work all morning!" Margo interjected, too quickly, though morning was not something that existed in Nautilus. "We've been going over his sums—and he can very nearly recite 'The Ancient Mariner'—we meant to keep it as a surprise for you, but since you're here—"

"Angus can speak for himself," Gus said—and the flatness, the deadness of his tone sounded a louder alarm than rage could have done. "Can't he?"

Gus's creature looked daggers at him. "Yes, Mr. Farrow." It paused, but it might as well have spit. "Would you like me to recite? I can say the whole now, I think. All the credit is due to my dear instructress."

What a simpering little hypocrite it was! But even I could not blame the beamer for fighting to survive. I had fought once myself.

"I'm afraid there's no time for that," Gus said—though in fact there was no particular hurry. He looked to Margo. "Angus must come with me."

Margo's arm tightened around the beamer's fragile shoulders, though conscious fear had not yet caught up with instinct.

"Angus and I had planned to visit the Floating Lakes today. Won't you come with us? A bit of gallivanting appeals far more than being cooped up in your grubby room, my dear. Why you sorcerers care so little for cleanliness, I'll never understand." Her skin was dreadfully pale, her smile like paper crushed in a fist. "Oh, I know. You'll say that spending a few lit to tidy the place would be *wasteful*. Well, there are always your two good hands, and a broom. Or have you forgotten such things exist?"

I thought then that Margo was mimicking her old spirit, putting on a show to distract him, much as a bird will try to lure a snake away from its nest—though I don't suppose she had the slightest awareness of her own maneuvering.

Gus's lips pinched. "I haven't come for an excursion. I'm here to collect Angus. It might be—some time before I can return him to you."

The beamer's pale green eyes went round as river stones and it bit its lower lip, just as Gus himself used to do. Oh, it *did* have some trace memory, even then, some scraps left over from its ripped and rendered predecessors.

"Auntie Margo must come with us!" it flustered. "I don't want to go with you, Mr. Farrow. Not without—"

"I don't recall consulting your preferences," Gus sniped. He directed his gaze above both their heads.

"Well, consult *mine,* then," Margo said. She was now all hackles and brambles, as if some sorcerer had crossed wolf and sea urchin. "Angus goes nowhere without me."

That brought Gus up short. "I must remind you that I made him, and at very great cost to myself. The beamer is my property." Then his voice dipped into a deceptive softness. "I *will* return him to you, Margo. Only I mean to make certain improvements, and he may not seem exactly as he does now. But—"

Margo was not reassured. "Improvements? Such a sweet, quick, tractable child—improvements? All he requires is time to grow up! What a fine man he'll be, Gus, if only—"

But Margo could not say what she did not permit herself to know.

"He cannot grow up. He isn't made for it." Knowing Gus as I did, I could nearly hear the creaking of the mental hinges as his cold composure swung back to loose rage. "I meant to spare you, Margo! I meant to protect you from seeing—the process—I must employ. As idiotic, as *misplaced* as your feelings are for this doll!" I would have liked to point out to Gus that he intended his beamers to elicit precisely such sentiments, and ought to regard Margo's love for the thing as a marvelous success. Logic was not always among Gus's strengths. "You love the projection so much that it makes you forget the original, and everything you owe to me!"

Margo stiffened at this. No doubt she caught, as I did, the tread of a threat coming nearer. Gus could consign Margo to unending torment simply by declining to pay for the periodic removal of her pain.

The beamer now was cowering against Margo's side, trembling and furious. And all at once its careful falsity gave way. What projection of Gus's inmost self could tolerate anyone disputing its entitlement to love?

"Of *course* she loves me more than you! You're sour and wicked and not half as clever as you think you are! Auntie Margo's told me all about Catherine, you know, and how you killed her for saying she wouldn't marry you—only Auntie Margo thinks she *would* have if only you hadn't turned so nasty!" In this supposition Margo was thoroughly mistaken. "*I* won't ruin everything the way you do, and that's why you hate me!"

For a moment Gus was utterly silent, rigid as the dead. Then softly, "You wouldn't like your *Auntie Margo* to see anything that would distress her. Would you?"

Oh, it knew. A whine as thin as thread pulled through its clenched teeth.

"Well, then," Gus pursued. "Quit your pitiful clinging and come along. Now."

"What do you mean to do to him?" Margo barked, binding the beamer tight in her wasted arms. "What don't you want me to see, pray tell? If Angus is ever in need of discipline, I'm quite capable of administering it myself!"

But neither Gus nor his creature had any attention to spare for her now. They were fixed on each other, and the dark prickling of their mutual hatred charged the air. The beamer scowled and lowered its moppish blond head like a bull about to charge.

"I dare you," it said at last, as brutally decisive as Gus himself could have been. "I dare you to do it, Mr. Farrow. But if you do, she'll never love you again—and she was the only one who *ever* did, really."

In this challenge the thing betrayed its parentage again: it was quite willing to make Margo suffer, if in that way it could strike a blow against its enemy.

"You're mistaken," Gus informed the beamer, his voice so stifled by rage that it was hardly more than a soughing in our ears. "Margo will love me as long as she lives—and that will be forever. What choice does she have?"

He reached, seized a handful of its faintly glassy hair. Margo cried out and tried to make of her body a refuge, engulfing the creature, smothering it as best she could in her sparse flesh. She had never seen what I had seen, did not know how Gus disposed of his beamers. She could not understand the futility of her gesture; there was no saving this little Angus, or indeed any of the ones that followed.

But she presently learned. Gus spread his long fingers wide as a spiderweb over the beamer's crown, and then—

The golden mice clanked on the ground.

Margo looked down to see its cherished little face collapsing inward along deep vertical pleats, like a paper balloon with all its sustaining air abruptly withdrawn. Its protesting whine, now, sounded more like the whistle of deflation. Two pale green eyes showed between the crush of Gus's fingers, their vitreous jelly gleaming even as they wrinkled and folded back on themselves—and though it was too proud to weep they still leaked despair and anger thick as ichor.

Margo's scream grew loud enough to drown out mine.

Gus shook his head, bit his lower lip, his posture plainly expressing that he thought this scene had gone on quite long enough. He stretched his left hand down and caught hold of a small hip where it jutted from the protection of Margo's embrace. His two hands then compressed.

The beamer mashed into a crinkling ball. For half a moment Margo still clung to two kicking little legs, her wet face pressed against them. Gus yanked up, gathered in those twitching appendages.

I told myself that Margo deserved this suffering. I told myself that she had earned none of my sympathy. She had never once turned on my wraith a single compassionate glance, but instead avoided looking at me so studiously that even I almost forgot my existence in her company. And had she not played her part in the events that led to my murder?

I told myself I should glory in the long cry that ran through Margo like a blade, that pierced her and pinned her to the ground with her own steel.

I told myself these things viciously, vengefully, in a grand and passionate oratory. But my heart, or whatever I had that passed for one, declined persuasion.

Margo huddled on the ground, looking nearly as reduced as the beamer now balled in Gus's hands. No one could have noticed any change in the tenor of my scream—I admit it was rather monotonous—but I myself was sensible of a shift in it, a turning of the tide.

For this was the first occasion since my murder that my scream was not for myself. I screamed instead for Margo. Long after her own screams failed her and her voice expired in heaving sobs, I picked up her cries like a burden, I carried them in place of my own. Even now—for of course I am still screaming in my tiny corner of Nautilus, though I write these words at some remove from my ghostly person—Margo's scream mingles in mine, tributary to a terrible river.

Gus, meanwhile, stood looking down at her. Rather put out, if anything, by her flooding grief.

"I *did* tell you that I'll return him to you," Gus at last said, his voice precarious on some ill-defined edge between soothing and resentful. He tucked away the crushed sphere of his beamer in his pocket. "In due course. When he's ready. You have nothing whatever to be upset about, I assure you."

Margo lifted her chin and looked up at him. He flinched back.

My own murder Margo had found pliant in her mind, soft enough to shape into something forgivable. She had figured it in comfortable terms; it was a pity, or a shadow, or a mistake. Perhaps, at a stretch, it was a tragedy, though primarily for Gus and not for me. It was indeed anything and everything but the merciless subtraction of my all from the earth.

But this was the murder of her own heart. It was not so malleable. Not then or ever, through all the timeless time to come.

"*Return* him to me," Margo said. "Do you mean, just as he was? Can you return him unharmed?"

Did Gus not hear her voice lowered, dragged like a silk scarf through choking depths?

"Well. Not *exactly* as he was, no. One of my aims is to instill a more robust memory—to see what sort of fictive autobiography a beamer can support. And obviously I must purge his memories of living with you here, of all his learning. To do otherwise would prejudice the experiment."

"Experiment? Experiment? No. As he was! You will restore him to me just as he was! Do you hear?" The low sibilance was gone, her voice peaked, stabbing. "You must bring my Angus back to me!"

Gus backed away sharply, then glanced over his shoulder to be sure his escape was clear.

"I'll visit you again when you are in a more reasonable frame of mind. Try—try to think clearly." And with that Gus turned and fled.

Margo could not but hear the refusal in these words. Her pursuing cry was pain so purely distilled, so refined, that Gus cringed and ducked as if the wind itself could slice him into ribbons.

And I? I tried again to school myself in hatred of her. I railed inwardly against my own pity. It was no use, for her scream now lived inextricably in mine. It had become the issue of my own poor spirit. If Gus had not hesitated to waste my life out of sheer mulish vanity, surely this waste of Margo's love should have brought him back to some semblance of sense or conscience?

No. He turned away and walked with snappish steps for quite a while. At last he came to rest where a fountain played. He sat on the brink, one crossed leg knocking irritably at the pearly stone. The fountain's winged waters were not spray at all, I saw, but jets of birds, folded and faceted as if cut from living diamond. They launched in glittering arcs and then dove into the basin where they dissolved into a fluid brilliance, only to rise again in long-feathered forms.

Little as I cared for magic, even I could not suppress a shiver at such beauty. Script blazed before our eyes in a sort of floating placard: *Madame Laudine, Avian Fountain*. Of course Anura moved in artistic circles.

And I would never sit beside her, never have a chance to earn my acceptance by her friends, never catch her proud smile if I managed a flash of wit. I pictured it nonetheless: their laughter and grace, and myself acknowledged as belonging there. With her. In my dream it felt as if the words *Catherine and Anura* swam like an aurora above our heads.

The shining placard seemed to nod, then dissolved into wet stars.

Gus did not spare the lapidary birds a single glance. His shoulders were tight and knots of muscle slid along his jaw, and he looked up at me instead.

"Oh, shut up, can't you?" he snarled, though whose fault was it that I could not? He rose again and paced back to his room.

No sooner were we inside than he began to scream.

At me.

I was given to understand that it was all my fault. Every unspecified grief, every nebulous crime, past, present, and future, all were laid at my feet like roses flung at an actress. Gus waved his hands, his cheeks blazing; the vague glow of Nautilus flashed silver in his streaking tears. It put me in mind of the shining slime left by slugs.

"You have left me no choice, Catherine," he howled. "No choice, don't you see? Whatever I do is your doing, always and only yours. You, who were so bright with promise—but there must have always been some fatal flaw in you, a crack in the diamond. Evil will enter through that crack, through *your* incapacity for love. Not through mine. Oh, but you think you can make me bear the weight of your sins!"

He drank. He railed. I screamed. It made for a certain harmony.

Catherine Through the Microscope

If Anna and I had been of a better class, it would have been unthinkable for us to accept an invitation anywhere so soon after our mother's death. As things stood, it was dubious for all sorts of reasons. But Anna was excited by the prospect of flowers and cakes, and I couldn't resist seeing her happy again, if only for a few hours.

I had been watching her small face bowed in the corners, her movements limp and void of childish energy. Her grief weighed terribly on my heart. I would have done anything to lighten it, and I was grateful for the opportunity.

Still: much as I liked the Reverend, I was wary. He was a committed Spiritualist, after all, even if I didn't understand quite how that sorted with his Christianity. I knew he was too good a man to coerce me into letting myself be tied to a chair for his friends' entertainment, but I feared some subtler attempt to coax me back. My impressions of the séance had not improved on reflection. Instead the images had only grown more horrifying, like some phosphorescent growth on the darkness. And when I thought of the twittering little voice that had perched in my mouth, my insides went slick with dread.

I didn't understand that I had met with a man who accepted my refusal wholly, graciously, and with no secret reservations. Nor did I know how very much I would come to love him; that in my hidden heart I would honor him as my truest father. If spirits could return to the living and speak to them, be assured that I would have done my best to comfort him after my murder! Though, of course, my apparition is something less than comforting.

In any case, we went. Two days later we tugged on our mourning dresses—Anna's, like mine, a well-worn hand-me-down—and walked the three miles to the farmhouse the Skelleys had rented while the new

Universalist church and rectory were completed. It was small, old, and isolated at the edge of a beech wood, though in good repair. Thomas met us in front and led us through a side gate and into a magnificent rose garden in full bloom. We were the only guests apart from a pair of doddering old sisters whose names escape me now, there I suppose to protect our reputations. Since they mostly smiled vaguely at the roses and sometimes muttered to each other, we soon forgot about them. The cakes and sandwiches and imported candies were lavish enough to suggest that Reverend Skelley had some sort of private income, and Anna was shyly delighted.

Even cake and tea can only cover awkwardness for so long. I asked after his injuries, he asked after mine, both of us skirting the question of just where our bruises had come from. I'd lied to my family, of course, and said my swollen cheek was the result of a fall; I could hardly tell my father that Gertrude Farrow had hit me. Thomas watched us sidelong, unspeaking while he sipped his tea. I could tell from the bend of the air that the Reverend had something specific to say to me, but the odd freedom that had formed between us on our moonlit ride was gone. The roses' fragrance rose in billows so dense that they seemed to stop up my throat.

We were saved by a flash of green on Thomas's sleeve. "Tiger beetle!" he exclaimed—the first words out of his mouth beyond a murmured *hello* and *the garden's this way*. He swallowed his tea at a gulp and gently knocked the beetle into the empty cup, then trapped it with his saucer. "We'll look at it later under the microscope."

A microscope! "Can I look too?" I asked before I could check myself. "That is—I've never had the chance—"

Reverend Skelley beamed at me. "Of course you would seek truth in nature! How could we deny you?" Soon Thomas and I had abandoned propriety to huddle together over the instrument, and he was showing me how to focus the lenses. I still recall that iridescent carapace revealed as a gleaming green net, dotted with round protrusions. Here, I thought, was the veil truly torn away; here was the proof that all the wonders of sorcery were tawdry, tinsel things compared to those wonders that *were*, that had no thought of showmanship, that were animated by no egotism.

Please recall, my artificial reader, that you belong squarely in the former category. A made thing, with no life but what magic grants you.

Please recall that I pitied you as long as I could, until you left me no choice other than hatred.

Thomas brought out his other specimens. His usual shrinking, halting manner became far more open when he was discussing the morphology of mandibles.

The afternoon was waning. There was a rustling as the Misses Whoever rose to take their leave, which meant that we must as well—and Anna and I had left chores undone—and yet I didn't want to go.

"Miss Bildstein?" It was Reverend Skelley; he'd appeared beside me, soft-footed, his voice like falling dust. "I hope you'll excuse my presumption, which I admit is inordinate. I've heard reports that you hoped to study at a high school, and found it impracticable." He was couching my failure in these terms to shield me from embarrassment, of course, but he didn't wholly succeed. "I only wished to say that I'm tutoring Thomas so that he can take his college entrance exams, and we would be honored if you joined us whenever you found it convenient."

I didn't immediately respond to this unexpected offer, and he misinterpreted my silence.

"Of course, Thomas is older than you—sixteen—and can already read some Latin. But if you liked—"

"So can I!" I burst out. "Read some Latin, I mean. And I've started a bit on Greek."

I saw his moustache twist with the effort to suppress his amusement, and realized how vain I'd sounded. Anna stood close by, looking on, with roses of all colors spilling from her arms. She was already stealthily arranging those colors into lovely patterns, shifting a rose here and there until the chaos of petals slipped into unexpected harmony.

Then I saw Thomas observing her work, and how he smiled to himself.

"I don't imagine Miss Gryson's school taught those subjects?"

"No," I said. How I'd exposed myself! If Gus's parents discovered what had happened to his missing books—well. My love of truth was not always as uncompromising as the dear Reverend believed. "Gus lets me look at his lessons sometimes."

"Gus Farrow," Thomas said, apparently to his knees. But he must have known whom I'd meant.

"We've been close friends since we were small," I said, a little defensively. "I know no one understands, but it isn't—it's a pure friendship, whatever the gossips try to make of it! I don't see why—"

Here it was again, my inability to contain myself when Reverend Skelley was listening. I broke off, boiling with shame and, to my horror, tears. Though of course they would attribute my weeping to my mother's death—and was that the reason? I couldn't tell why I had burst my boundaries, only that I could not stop the flow. Anna dropped her roses in a heap and began sobbing too, and we clung to each other while the Skelleys stayed mercifully quiet. Now that my tears were undammed, grief shook me like hammer blows. I felt my mother cut out of me, felt the awful enormity where she had been: a broken place that could never be made whole.

You may have observed that I had now received three offers of mentorship, of varying kinds, in close succession. The first had tried to bully me, the second to appropriate me, and neither had regarded my consent, or the lack thereof, as anything more than an inconvenience. But as in a fairy tale it was the third, the lightest, the shyest, the least assuming, that would show itself true.

Reverend Skelley wrote to my father. Precisely what he said I never knew, only that as long as I kept house in the mornings and returned in time to have supper ready, I was allowed to spend a few hours in the afternoons in a battered wooden armchair, discussing Euclid and Lyell and beginning my first painful efforts to read Ovid—my Latin was not quite so good as I'd supposed. Gus lied when he told Asterion I was entirely self-taught, probably because he didn't like to admit how greatly the Reverend influenced me. With the Skelleys' arrival in my life, my debt to Gus sharply decreased, after all. And soon enough their presence would goad him in a new way.

Both the Skelleys must be long dead. So must Anna, my father, my little brothers. I know it, but perhaps because I died before them I have never been able to feel it.

Usually it falls to the living to cherish the dead. To preserve the past's immediacy. But in me, long since dead myself, they remain as vital as ever, down to the sunlight wrinkling on the Reverend's jacket, the wet heat of Anna's tearful face on my neck.

If I succeed in extinguishing myself I will have this regret: that those I loved must go with me. Ghosts within ghosts, a dream as recursive as a nautilus's shell.

Angus in the Night

I can't seem to stop walking: the night is pulling on my steps. Reeling me in.

On the corner just ahead, a door opens in another anonymous lump of warehouse. It's on the street crossing this one, and a wash of inviting gold pours out into the night.

Laughter, music. It sounds like a party, but not kids; more like sophisticated adults at a gallery opening or something. Do they have gallery openings this late? Whoever they are, they're clearly the kind of people Geneva and I will be when we're older: smart and accomplished and still fun. I can tell that by the way their voices coast along slopes of wry amusement, by the distinct vocal tang of witticisms being fired off. They're the kind of people I should introduce her to, who might be able to help with her career. She'll be impressed that I know them. That they consider me a friend, even if I am nineteen.

Find a way, Margo said. Maybe this is it, the whole reason for the thread winding me through the darkness.

I peer in. The walls are covered in sculptural objects made of ornately carved wood, patches of fur, lenses, gilded flowers. And just as I expected, beautiful people are milling around holding wineglasses.

"Hello, Angus," a warm voice says near my shoulder. "You're on an awfully long walk for the hour."

Lore, her silver hair piled on top of her head in a big looping bun. She's wearing her pebble jewelry and a black dress that sort of swoops off one shoulder. I should have known she'd be here.

"Hi," I manage. I have trouble getting it out. My throat is raspy, and I have no idea why. I want so badly to go in, to meet all those beautiful people and snarf their hors d'oeuvres, but something's holding me back. Shame, maybe?

"Why don't you come in and join us? When something's weighing on me, I find that looking at art usually provides some helpful distance from the problem. Maybe it will work for you too," Lore says. She's so damned beautiful, so refined, with that single brown shoulder exposed by the slant of her dress.

"Thanks," I say vaguely. I'm leaning on the doorjamb, still in the night, while Lore faces me from inside that luminous room. I want to tell her about everything that happened tonight. Beg her to help me figure out what to do. I'm ready to blurt random words and fraying sentences in all directions, to spew and spew everything in my mind until I collapse like a popped balloon on the sidewalk. "Lore, do you think I'm a beamer?"

It comes out in a pathetic whine. Why do I care so much, when Julian's definition of a beamer sounded not half bad at all? I still don't know what he was driving at, honestly.

"I'm afraid that's not a matter of opinion, Angus. You are what you are." Ugh, is it that obvious? "But that doesn't mean you're helpless, and it doesn't mean you can't make something unexpected from what you've been given. You need a measure of independent agency to be effective. Imagine a gun, or a sword, that has some small will of its own. One that can reflect on its experiences. At what point will it rebel against the hand that wields it?"

First I was a beam in a darkened theater, and now I'm a gun? The images run together, and I start to picture a movie, the old black-and-white kind. One where a detective faces off against a murderer, both shooting at each other from behind the water towers on a city rooftop. What does the murderer inevitably say then?

We're just alike, you and I. That's what. Every damn movie, the same lines. *Always pointing in a single direction, both of us. You tell yourself that you beam love where I project death. But love can turn into a killing force, Detective Angus.*

Wait. That second part didn't sound quite right.

Lore is still looking at me. Waiting patiently for me to finish processing.

"I feel like I am helpless," I say, surprising myself. It's something about the magic of talking to Lore, that she brings these things out of me. "I feel like I'm just playing some pretend game where I can change what happens next, but really nothing I do will make any difference."

"Then don't limit yourself to pretending," Lore says, with a touch more acid than I expect from her.

But the people in movies are always pretending, aren't they? They're not really chasing killers across rooftops. Hell, they aren't even really in love.

There's something real about those stories anyway, though. I *know* there is. A real wound, hiding just behind the light.

Catherine in Hiding

What shall I tell you about the Era of the Children—that it lasted the better part of a century in the unworld's accounting, and that most of it was made up of such repetitious despair that it nearly seemed time had forsaken us entirely? Margo succumbed to love for the little beamers again and again, suffered again and again, until it seemed a single circular occurrence, a misery escaped from all ordinary progress and all hope of relief. Oh, if I could live again—which I cannot—I swear I would cherish in myself those processes dependent on days and hours, the hair that needs cutting, the jagged nail, the skin sagging under my eyes!

Never mind. In fact Gus and I began spending rather long periods in the unworld, so keen was he to avoid Margo's harrowed stare. He went to one city or another, restlessly, with no apparent motive other than discontent. It was plain that Nautilus was starting to bore him.

And he aged.

Oh, only by degrees, a few weeks' worth here, two months there, for every return to Nautilus suspended time's slow conquest and froze Gus at some approximation of twenty-five, or thirty, or thirty-five, until he entered the unworld again.

We dipped in during the War Between the States a few times, but fled when Gus was nearly frog-marched to a draft office; we returned to New York to hear drunks bickering over Boss Tweed and his ledger; on another occasion, in Pittsburgh, Gus's debauchery was interrupted when troops began a massacre of railroad workers. We watched light bulbs flare like eyes in a strange awakening, we heard the rasp of radios. If Gus regarded the sweep of unworld history as nothing more than an annoyance, I was always eager to absorb what news I could—and always during these interludes, time snagged my former friend in its grind again.

The process was subtle enough, intermittent and broken enough, that Gus himself could be nearly insensible of the changes in his face and frame.

But I was not. To me the lines appearing around his eyes and mouth were like treasure in a dragon's hoard. Behind my unvarying scream I crooned to each new crease, I caressed and fondled every mark of dissolution and decline.

And then there was always the chance that on these trips out of Nautilus Gus would meet with some fatal accident and I would be free. Everyone we met I eyed appraisingly: did this scarecrow man with the beetling brows happen to conceal a knife on his person? Might that knife, while on its innocent peregrinations, perhaps stumble into the labyrinth of Gus's bowels? Gus's magic was so obsessively specialized that it included few skills he could use in self-defense. He carried money looted from his parents' house, he drank in sordid company. I thought a violent demise wonderfully possible.

But I was not the only one who considered such eventualities. On one of our returns to Nautilus we found Asterion waiting for us, one leg flung across the other, suspended foot jiggling furiously.

Oh, Asterion had prospered in the long smear of timeless time since I had first met him! Gus was plainly not his only mark. The violet velvet frock coat he now wore was figured with jewel-bright songbirds wrought in living embroidery, flitting restlessly around his arms. And he no longer stood and stared uncomfortably at the filthy and wanting contents of Gus's home, but rather drew the nacreous substance of Nautilus itself into a very accommodating wingchair—an expensive flourish for what might have seemed a small occasion.

Mind, it was not that our visits to Asterion had ceased during this era. Gus's projects still required far more magic than he could produce by himself, and his habit of exploiting me was now entrenched. But our prolonged jaunts had inserted periods when the cow was unavailable for milking, and Asterion was displeased.

"And how long was it this time, Gus?" Asterion snapped the instant we slipped through the wall. Gus wobbled at him, unequal to the question. His days-long drunkenness was receding, but like a flood it left wrack and refuse scattered across a muddy plain. "In unworld time, I mean. Presumably you saw that there were days and nights passing in their idiotic way while you were out there? Did you bother to notice *how many*?"

"I—" Gus started. And then, "You had no business picking my lock."

Locks in Nautilus, like so many other things, were of the magical variety: wards that kept the doorways from yielding. Gus hadn't bothered with a good one. Asterion paid the objection no mind.

"Don't tell me," Asterion pursued, rather unreasonably considering that he had asked. "I've checked for myself. There were sixty-seven of them. Sixty-seven *consecutive* unworld days, and you aging recklessly the while! Why, if our Catherine could have averaged ten talens for each of those days, that's nearly *seven hundred* gone to absolute waste!" Asterion's hands petted the emptiness in his lap, as if mourning over the wealth not heaped there.

But Gus by now had a better grip on his thoughts, however disorderly they were. "Oh, why should I bother squeezing every talen I can from her? What's the use? A holiday from her racket—and Margo—and now you're nagging me as well! All so I can fiddle about with those mewling *infants,* one after another after another, making this or that trivial refinement—but my real goal gets no closer. Asterion, I'm very near—"

To giving up? To desolation? I quickened in delicious anticipation of Gus's next words. But he regrettably broke off and slumped down on the floor, burying his head in his hands. In the ensuing silence, Asterion's bovine lips wrinkled and he stared down at Gus with naked disgust, considering himself unobserved.

Then he recalled that he was not unobserved, strictly speaking. And gave me a look—of what? A sneering knowingness, a sense that our common contempt for Gus did nothing to unite us, for Asterion allowed no sympathy for anyone but himself.

Gus raised his tear-streaked visage, and Asterion's vacuous geniality snapped instantly into place.

"Well, if that's all it is," he said smiling, and bent to clap Gus on the back. "Sick of working on your boy beamers, eh? Buck up, my friend. It's time to try your hand at full-grown models, that's all."

Gus gawped very fishily indeed. Then: "Why? I could hardly send them out to hunt Catherines. Not when I *still* lack the means to give them proper corporeality."

I cannot adequately convey how much aggrievement Gus contrived to balance on the tightrope of these words. If I had possessed anything resembling breath, I would have held it in suspense.

"Oh, your Athenian youth? I didn't think you were ready yet, that's all. I can make inquiries. Of course, it will be expensive. All the more reason, then, to take full advantage of Catherine's production, rather than letting it drift away into that useless unworld air."

Gus shook his head as if he were trying to dislodge it from his shoulders. "Why? Why? Say you bring me some drugged boy—say even that I haul one back from the unworld myself—what am I to *do* with him? I've been thinking about it without cease, and I can't see a way. *How* do I make use of his materials? Carve him up like a turkey? I'm a sorcerer, Asterion, not a butcher."

My scream had to stand in for debating his last proposition. But this was the first I had heard of Gus's latest difficulty; not being a sorceress myself, I could not often anticipate where he would encounter obstacles.

Asterion smiled in that too-familiar way of his, the one he used when he had successfully herded Gus into a corner of his own construction.

"Oh, I'm sure you'll manage. Once you have the constituent bits in a cloud, the process of arranging them isn't so different from what you do already. Ordering matter instead of illusion—it's all an act of *attention*, isn't it? Mind, not much has been done with truly embodied beamers. So many different specialties are required to make a good one that they're far more trouble than they're worth! But you've never been afraid to break new ground before."

"That—" Gus shrugged wearily. "I haven't tried it, but of course I grasp the general principles. I could cobble some sort of usable body together, I expect, and slap a mind in the thing. Minds I'm very good at, now. Appearances. That's not what worries me."

It was plain, from Asterion's expectant gleam, that he knew perfectly well what worry Gus was alluding to and chose not to supply the words for him. He raised his hands as if in a question and Gus stumbled on.

"But the—the disassembly! Taking a living person apart on such a minute level, and botching none of it—preserving the functionality of every damned blood cell, keeping every tiny membrane intact—ugh, it doesn't bear thinking of. One false move, and you're swimming in worthless gore. I don't even know how to start."

I would like to remind you, my inhuman reader, that what they were discussing in these blasé terms was the murder, cold and unprovoked, of some random young man. A murder designed to beget more murders.

"True," Asterion said after a moment. "I *did* say I thought you weren't ready. When the raw materials are so expensive, it would be a pity to waste them. But if you're so eager you could always try."

"But then—"

"There are sorcerers expert in disintegrating and reassembling living flesh—not necessarily human, some of those who practice zoourgy like to build from scratch. Much too finicky for me, all that business, but there are those who seem to enjoy it. You could become one of them; start with algae, move on to wriggling things in pond scum. In fifty or so unworld years you could attempt a mouse perhaps."

"Fifty years!"

"Restrain these impulses to go gallivanting around the unworld," Asterion said pointedly, "and you're in no hurry."

"Fifty years! On top of everything I've done already!"

"Yours is an ambitious project. I *did* think you knew that."

"Ambitious, yes, certainly. But with an end in sight!"

Allow me a moment to admire the venomous irony of this ejaculation. If there is an end—something for which I devoutly hope, and of which I often despair—I assure you that Gus won't be the one to achieve it. He will never renounce his obsession, not when obsession is the only thing that spares him from confronting his own emptiness.

He is hardly the only sorcerer in Nautilus to discover that power and near-immortality do not in themselves grant purpose, or meaning, or even distraction from a desolate heart. If anything, it may be easier to achieve a sense of deep purpose where life is finite. Where its limits dictate that one must love and feel and hope *now*.

"Or you could save time by hiring one of them to do the disassembly for you. Not everyone will agree to do such work on a living person, of course. And those who do will charge a premium on top of the tremendous expenditure of magic already involved. A little something extra to cover the moral contortions, if you like."

"A premium," Gus groused. "And I suppose you'd like your cut for making the introductions."

Asterion said nothing to this. His pretense of friendship for Gus was spotty at best.

"All right," Gus said at last, quite as wanly as if the magic in question were truly his own and not mine. "How much?"

"Oh, well." So great was Asterion's expanse of flaccid lip that when he mused, or pretended to muse, it rippled in a truly revolting manner: a babbling brook made flesh. "Let's say eighty—or a hundred at the outside—"

Gus's head perked. "A hundred talens? Why, from how you went on I thought—but that's no trouble!" A small laugh squeaked out. "No trouble at all!"

"A hundred *thousand*, of course I meant."

I could not join Gus in his appalled silence, but for once my feelings neatly matched his. Asterion, of course, stood to profit thrice, drawing his share as the magic was drained from me, next his payment for the living boy, and again when Gus yielded up the minotaur's commission for this unholy operation. Oh, how plainly the vista opened before me, of being drained, and drained, and drained, until that exorbitant sum could be achieved—that ghastly sipping static, that thirsting buzz, as the umbrastring was jabbed into my immaterial person and *sucked*—

Asterion had kept his promise to me and proofed his umbrastring against abrupt surges. I could not even take advantage of our sessions to try again to destroy Gus.

Gus meanwhile had jumped up—for he had been huddling the while at Asterion's feet, pitiful as a beaten puppy—and began to pace, kicking drifts of dirty laundry from his path. The flash came back in his lichen-pale eyes, the thrill of a challenge accepted.

"No," Gus said. "No. There has to be another way."

I greeted these words with thoroughly misplaced relief. Why did I imagine even for an instant that Gus would leave me out of his schemes?

Asterion had worn a sort of butter-fed smirk as he counted his imaginary riches. Now his long mouth drooped and the brow furrowed between his horns.

"Another way? How *could* there be? Put in the effort yourself, or pay to have it done. Those are the choices, here as in the unworld. Dear Gus, don't delude yourself. Only in the silly fantasies of the common herd is magic ever a *shortcut*!"

But Gus's steps acquired an excited snap that I remembered well from his adolescence, and he shook his head with dismissive vigor and held up a hand for silence. Asterion watched with limp sullenness as his imagined talens whisked away in the blast of Gus's inspiration.

"Catherine," Gus said. He stopped short.

What? I thought.

And, "What?" Asterion said, in perfect synchronicity. "Of *course* Catherine—of course she'll continue to supply you with the power you'll need to, to pay. But my dear friend—"

Gus waved a hand, brushing the words away. "That isn't at all what I mean. Yes. Catherine!" He beamed at me as if we were tangled together in some playful conspiracy. "We've drawn magic from her mind. Well, it's time to make use of her body!"

Asterion reeled at this. He covered his eyes with one hand, as if to shield them from the sight of such madness.

"Gus. Gus, Gus, Gus. She doesn't have one. How long has it been since she did?" An unwelcome thought struck him. "If you mean to dig her up, I feel confident you'll find she's not in usable condition."

"No, no." Gus was glimmering now, his every movement jerky with excitement. "*That* one." He flourished in my general direction. "The cloud of energies that presently composes her, of course I mean. We know she can't interact with the physical world under ordinary conditions. Can't lift a feather, can't even seem to control her own movements in any but the sloppiest way—ugh, the way her hands and arms *flail*—"

"Exactly. And something that can't affect material things in the slightest isn't going to be very helpful when it comes to a procedure involving a material body. Gus, if I may be plain, you are often an original thinker. But this is simply preposterous."

"It must be tremendous, the energy of which Catherine is made. The force of an entire life, *released* all at once and then caught in a permanent field, an oscillation—the energy that would have borne her children, powered decades of laughter. Think of it!"

Oh, I did. I was surprised to discover, though, that Gus had considered me in such terms.

"Well?" Asterion snapped. "So? Say your theorizing holds, say that's what a ghost *is*. Whatever she is, we can't touch it."

"That's not true." Gus stopped his pacing and pivoted toward Asterion, spreading his hands as if he held out his triumph for inspection. "Your umbrastring sticks in her. It creates a local stabilization, enough that we can skim off her power."

Asterion sighed with a great flubbering of his lips, as much as to say that the point of all this eluded him. But I began to guess where Gus's reasoning tended. I felt my flashing tumble into a queasy acceleration, a spasmodic dread.

"Who made it?" Gus demanded. "Your umbrastring? I must speak with him at once!"

"I haven't the faintest," Asterion lied. His voice took on a sort of puckered sound, so loath was he to surrender this information. If Gus acquired a similar implement of his own, how would the minotaur continue to profit off him? "I bought mine secondhand, from a very seedy dealer who was later exiled. Cornelius somebody. Now that you mention it, I don't think I've ever seen another one."

Gus shrugged off this attempted discouragement, pacing again and nodding briskly to himself. "I'll need two, I think. But they might require a few modifications; I suppose I can practice on birds or some such until I get the knack of it. Well, if you don't know, I'll make inquiries on my own. Not many umbrathurges out there, as I believe you've mentioned. Ghosts aren't a popular specialty, isn't that right? Shouldn't be too difficult to find someone who can direct me."

Asterion's globe eyes protruded so far at this show of unwelcome independence that it put me in mind of a snail's eyestalks. He had overreached, grasped too greedily, and now he was in danger of losing even his regular percentage of my magical production. Appalled though I was at what I suspected Gus was planning, I yet found the inner resources to enjoy Asterion's consternation.

"I can introduce you to someone," Asterion sputtered, desperate now to retain any hold on Gus at all. "A certain lady, perhaps more a dabbler than an actual expert. But—"

Gus swung toward him. "Now," he said. "Now, this very instant!"

I've spoken a great deal of memory, and it's true that much of my hideous existence has been given over to visions of the past. One might be forgiven for supposing I do little else than remember. But no: I also watch. I plan. I've learned over the centuries how to perform several tasks simultaneously.

Take as an example the present moment. I go on screaming in my crevice of Nautilus, of course; I cannot do otherwise. I remember Gus's revelation as to how he might make an additional and still viler use of me. But I also watch from a second, a secret redoubt.

I watch you.

Distractible creature that you are, you stare out a broad glass window and slurp sugared coffee through a hole in a plastic lid. I've had time to grow familiar with such innovations, you see; I know about parking lots and cell phones and bright orange chairs swiveling on dirty metal branches.

You stare, so caught up in your inhuman thoughts that you forget what your own hands are doing. Those hands, so olive-golden and strong and finely crafted, are presently in motion with cup and pen. And only one of them is taking its orders from you.

Those hands, those arms, shoulders, jaw, every detail of every part excessive in its beauty: you, of course, have never given the least thought to the substance of which your body is made. You believe, quite mistakenly, that that substance is unquestionably your own, hair and nails, pores and particles. But oh, it is not yours; not one cell of it is your property, any more than I was.

It belonged to a boy named Christopher Flynn.

And I killed him.

Catherine Accused

"You do realize that poor Gertrude is utterly despondent, don't you? Or is it simply that you can't be bothered to help? She hardly gets out of bed these days. Mind, I know as well as anyone that she's not a pleasant woman, but even *I* can't help but pity her. And you, who think you're so exalted that the very clouds bow down to you, you can't spare a few hours to lift her suffering? Really, Catherine. How much revenge do you need over one impulsive slap?"

It was October or November of 1854; the intervening months had passed in a whirl of excitement over my new studies. I no longer cared when I caught Darius or Dr. Lewis staring at me. I tolerated Gus's excitable displays of his new magic in a spirit of slightly condescending indulgence. What did I care if he could make a blue heron shine like mercury when I could examine the structure of that same heron's feathers? His passion struck me as fundamentally superficial, all spangle and illusion, where I was delving into the deeper realities.

So when Margo ambushed me on my walk home from the Reverend's house, I was nearly able to shrug off her accusations, as well.

"Reverend Skelley told me she's doing poorly. I'm very sorry to hear it. Of course I would help her if I could do so in good conscience." My prim tone betrayed that I hadn't entirely forgiven Margo for her deceit. Our shadows spindled out in the late afternoon light, warped by the uneven road.

"What abject nonsense, my dear. You were there. You heard Viviana speak as plain as day through your own lips. And if you deny our little lost darling the chance to speak to her grieving mother again, well, I can only assume you do it out of spite. I thought better of you."

I remember the cresting gold of the autumn elms, the sharp effervescent smell of fermenting apples. My own feelings resembled the scent: an intoxicating tang just on the edge of rot.

"As you say, that voice spoke through my lips. I could feel—I could

taste—that it wasn't who it claimed to be. You accuse me of seeking revenge on Mrs. Farrow. Well, if I were, I would do exactly what she asks,
and make that voice say anything that suited me!"

I realized at once that I had said too much. Margo's face went hard
with consideration.

"How?" She paused. "It didn't sound like you in the slightest, not even
if you tried to disguise your own voice. And Viviana died when you were
all of ten months old, you couldn't possibly remember how she sounded!"

We were on treacherous ground. I could not mention magic without
betraying Gus.

"I don't know quite how it was done," I said, carefully truthful. "But
I believe Mrs. Hobson was telling me, in a veiled way, that I could learn
the trick of it."

Margo bristled. "Mrs. Hobson is a lady of the greatest integrity. *Con-
gressmen* attest to her character, for heaven's sake. She was generous
beyond words in offering to guide you, and I still can't understand how
you could find the impudence to refuse her."

I had thought that Margo was my friend, after her fashion. To discover her true valuation of me salted through each disdainful turn of
phrase—it had its effect. Shame and fury heated my face. But I had absorbed Reverend Skelley's Spiritualist values, if not his actual beliefs, and
here those values came to my defense.

"I can't allow another person to dispose of my conscience merely because of who her friends are," I said. I admit my tone was haughty in the
extreme; it was the only way I could control the tumult of my feelings.
A dust devil spun around me, and the elm leaves streaked by like bands
of gold.

Margo let out an exasperated huff and caught my face between her
hands. "Catherine, my dear, don't be so bull-headed! Gertrude has her
pride, too, you know. It cost me a great deal of trouble to persuade her—"

Why did I find this speech so provoking? I jerked away.

"To do what?" I snapped. "To try a second time to use me as your
marionette?"

"Gertrude would pay you very well, of course," Margo soothed—
which infuriated me even more. "And Mrs. Hobson still takes an interest

in you, her letters have been explicit on that point. But I can't help you if you won't meet us halfway. Come tonight, please. For my sake and Gus's, if you can't do it for Gertrude's."

Her words reminded me vividly of the séance, and the repellent impression I'd had that night of a silent conspiracy licking and probing at me. And what did she mean by bringing Gus into it, when she knew he didn't believe in spiritual communication any more than I did?

"Tell Mrs. Farrow that I hope she finds peace," I said. "I'm sorry she can't find it through me."

We stared at each other: the sort of mutual regard that sets the air ringing with its percussion.

"She won't appeal to your better nature again, Catherine," Margo said at last, in grave tones. "I've tried all I can. I'd do anything for Angus, and that means I have to do my best for you as well. The two of you are unquestionably spiritual affinities, though in practice all it means is that you're equally insufferable."

If I had possessed a clearer understanding of the doctrine of spiritual affinities, I might have focused on that last assertion rather than on the warning that weighed down her voice.

"What do you mean?" I asked.

"Think it over," Margo rejoined, and turned on her heels. She wore the same silvery dress as she had at the séance, its color dissonant against the golden streams of sunlight. "Come tonight at eight. It will be the best thing for everyone, I promise you."

As she walked off I felt a cold clenching in my stomach. Suppose I went, and paid back Gertrude Farrow's contempt with my own falsity, and then strolled away laughing with a fistful of her money? I was nearly sure I could conjure that voice again; that the lurking, fidgeting pressure just above my spinal cord would be all too delighted to play tricks if I let it. It reared up now as if excited by the prospect, hot and waggling in my brain's abyss.

If I did not like to admit it, still I knew what that presence was. I imagine the sensation of it was similar to what Mrs. Hobson termed her *guide,* in her ignorance of her power's real nature.

In truth, I'd felt it ever since my confrontation with Darius in the field, and I wonder now if that was his real purpose in frightening me: to make me release a force I would have corked up otherwise. Once I learned to recognize the feeling of it, it never went away. I could not stop dabbing at that little magical protrusion, worrying it, as if it were a loose tooth.

But if I allowed the Farrow ladies to pressure me into acting against my own judgment this time, there would be no end to it. And then if I played the medium, Thomas and the Reverend would know that I did so insincerely. The more I argued against his rather ethereal beliefs, the prouder the Reverend grew of me, the brighter and warmer were his smiles. I couldn't bear to disappoint him.

I let the evening sidle by, focusing as hard as I could on my mundane tasks. When eight came and went and I was still at home, I felt nearly limp with relief—just as if I had fought off an overbearing influence, a nudging in each current of the air, that meant to herd me where I did not want to go. By the next morning I felt obscurely proud of myself, sure that I had won some unseen victory.

I felt that way, that is, until I returned home from the Skelleys' house two days later, and found Gertrude Farrow and my father standing by the bed I shared with Anna. I didn't understand what Gus's mother was doing there until I caught a flash of burgundy leather in her hand, the spark of gilt on a spine. My Wordsworth.

A dozen more volumes were spread across the mattress. The room was dim, and blue shadows blotted her face until it looked like a footprint pressed in the snowy mounds of her pale hair. Her eyes stared with a hectic glimmer and her mouth was pursed into an expression of desperate vindication.

"Don't tell me to ask Gus!" she said, or nearly shrieked, with no preamble whatsoever. I had the impression that she'd been waiting some time; that suspense had pressurized her voice until it whistled out of her like steam. "As if I didn't know he'd lie for you! As if we *all* didn't know! If you seduced him into stealing from us, destroyed his morals, that's even worse than if you stole the books with your own hands! Oh, of course I'd suspected, of *course* I had. But when you have only one surviving child, how can you harden yourself to correct him? Even as you watch him drawn into—turpitude, *disobedience*—"

The two Mrs. Farrows believed passionately enough in those aspects of Spiritualism they found congenial, but its great message of radical human equality had apparently bypassed their understanding. If Gus had defied his parents in slipping me that contraband knowledge, had he not followed something in himself better than their unfeeling dictates?

"Catherine?" my father said, barely above a whisper.

"Gus gave them to me," I said, as levelly as I could. "I believed they were his to give."

This was not, of course, entirely true. But it was enough to elicit a sorrowful nod from my father.

"You hid them under your mattress, though. If you weren't ashamed, you wouldn't have concealed them." He turned to his employer. "My girl knows she's done wrong. What will satisfy you, Mrs. Farrow?"

She looked at me, plainly evaluating how best to wound.

"Well, of course she must never speak to Gus again. I can't allow her to be the ruin of my only son."

My knees wavered, and I opened my mouth to protest, but my father's look quelled me. Defiance now would surely cost him his job, cost my siblings their bread. *Haven't you done enough?* his gaze said. *Control yourself before you wreck us all.*

"But that's hardly enough to make her answer for her *theft*," Mrs. Farrow pursued. The last word was loaded with such venom that it was clear she was alluding not to a stack of books, but to a voice, bright with childish innocence; to Gus's disaffection; to a lifetime of loss that she now chose to blame on me. At that moment I hated her too much for pity, but it was a near thing. "You've allowed her to get above her place, and look what's happened. If this goes on she'll end up as a streetwalker."

A tongue of power flicked at the base of my brain. Why, I could exact punishment of my own. I imagined Viviana's voice denouncing Gertrude Farrow in vicious terms, even blaming her mother for her death—

"You must put a stop to her presumption, Jacob. No more of her arrogance, her unfeminine grasping. *Greek*, for heaven's sake!"

Until the mention of Greek, I had not understood where her malice was tending. Now I did and my mouth went round with horror. Oh, I could make her *pay*, even drive her to suicide if I wished. The flickering presence jumped and fumes seemed to unwind, to blur my thoughts, until I hardly heard my father.

"Mrs. Farrow's right, I'm sure, Catherine. I'll write Reverend Skelley, tell him you can't come anymore."

If I crushed this hateful woman, shattered what remained of her heart, how could I ever look Reverend Skelley in the face again? How could I embrace Anna, comb the tangles from her leaf-strewn hair? With a shock I understood: if I gave way to my rage, if I let magic take me over, I would lose my hold on that sweet ordinariness that wasn't ordinary at all—lose my last defense against an alien *becoming*, a transformation I rejected with every throb of my blood.

I'd lose everything that stood between me and Old Darius.

Revenance

—Anura

I met a ghost in black and white,
Spilled milk, spilled ink, a burning page
Where all her excess truth bled out
And doused the living thought within
In veiling dark, in canceling din.

I met a ghost who spoke in sound:
A blurt, a blast, a pulsing rage,
Its syllables all overrun,
As if in her no speech remained
But ruptured heart and spreading stain.

Where death abandons time, we drift
Far from the crush of rolling days
And unpursued, our steps forget
The racing surge, the urging strain
Until our hopes abandon change.

But death is here; it brushes past
On streets so foreign to its ways.
It wears the faces of the lost,
And though we never risk a glance
We feel their pressing revenance.

I met a ghost; she slipped her thought
Like thieving fingers into mine.
But what she left and what she took
Have turned impossibly the same
Till silence rumbles with her name.

I met a ghost. I did not guess
How dream would not abandon time,
How time could not forsake regret.
Your word transfused, your stolen chance
In me preserve their revenance.

Angus on Film

I do what she says, because *Lore*. It helps that she saved my life and every-thing, but honestly it's more just *Lore Lore Lore* that draws me in.

She leads me around the room, introducing me to people like we're old friends. "Miranda, I'd like you to meet Angus. Angus Farrow. Fran-cois, this is Angus." A few eyebrows cock up, and once or twice I can see people hesitate to shake my hand. But most of them are super gracious, because it's Lore looking them in the eyes.

The ones who hesitate: is it because of that word, *beamer*? Do they think there's something wrong with me? Something grotesque, even? *Lore, you know what that is.* Or is it just weird that Lore is hanging out with someone so young? I snuffle a little—there's a murk to the air, a charred-flower smell—and fight an impulse to wipe my nose with the back of my hand.

"Angus Farrow!" a woman named Nina says, smiling a little too hard from a face that manages to be attractive at the same time that it's pinched and elven. "Was he always this handsome, do you think?"

I cringe, but Lore just smiles. "Angus is a beautiful young man," she agrees, and then turns to the next person with a blast of vivacity.

The hors d'oeuvres are delicious, it turns out. I get a heaping plate and wander around looking at the art. I can tell it's great, and if it was any-body but Lore beside me I'd feel pressured to come up with smart things to say about it. But because *Lore,* it feels safe to just say, "That's so cool!"

"Isn't it?" she says, and her smile is so warm I feel like I made an in-sightful observation.

After a while she gets into a deep conversation with a very old, wispy, snow-white guy, the kind who delivers portentous wisdom in a snail-speed drawl, and it seems awkward to stay glued to her side. There's an open doorway to another room, and maybe there's more art in there. I'll just gaze at each piece studiously and pretend I don't notice anyone giving me funny looks.

So I step through. There's no one else in here. And maybe the room it-self is one big art installation, because the white walls, and even the floor and ceiling, are shaped in swooping curves and have this pearly glow to them, a shimmery translucence. There aren't any of those awesome assemblages hanging in here, but there is a black booth at the back, kind of like an old photo booth, with a black velvet curtain covering the front. The curtain is so long that velvet pools on the floor in a tidal swirl, like darkness that could suck you in forever.

There's a lot I don't understand. But I'm not such an ignoramus that I can't recognize art when I see it. I walk over, lift back the curtain, and seat myself on the tiny black bench with my plate of fancy cheese and spicy tuna rolls balanced on my knee. The curtain drops back into place and I'm in absolute dark, but it doesn't feel like the merciless solid dark-ness that comes when the lights die back at the warehouse. Instead it's a sensuous, rushing flow, like velvet transformed into a slow black wind.

A screen winks to life in front of me. I wish Geneva were here to see this.

It looks like an old black-and-white movie, and right away I think of the scene that flashed in my mind as I stood on the threshold: Detective Angus facing off with the murderer under a smeary noirish night. But the feeling of what I'm watching has a harsh realism that's nothing like my dreamy, stylized gun battle.

It's pretty straightforward: a young blond guy, roughly my age, is walking down a gritty street in the kind of huge-collared shirt they wore back in the seventies. Even though he's good-looking and healthy and sleek, it's obvious at a glance that there's something off about him. A mush of cruelty and confusion wrapped in a flawless skin. *Up to no good.* At first I'm just impressed by the filmmaker's skill; like, how did they make a character with such an open, pleasant expression convey such evil?

Then something happens, some incredible telescoping trickery, and I'm in two different scenes at once. I don't know how they're doing it, because it's nothing as crude and obvious as a split screen. Instead I'm simultaneously hovering over the boy in the street and also watching a girl putting on makeup in her bedroom: a very *her*-ish girl, with a witchy sweep of what I somehow know is red hair. She's getting ready to meet the blond boy, that's clear, and I want to tell her, *Don't do it, don't go anywhere with him! Listen to me, Vanessa. He'll do something terrible to you.*

That's her name. Why do I feel like I know her?

Shit. It's like I'm not watching a video at all anymore. Instead it's as if my mind has been swept from my body and sent tumbling like a flock of birds through that black-and-white world. Some kind of virtual reality technique? It's that or—or it's something it shouldn't be. Vanessa slicks on her lipstick, and I feel the silky interface where the pigment glides onto her lips. The blond boy walks closer to her apartment, and his footsteps drum up my legs. He's going to kill her, and no matter how I thrash and scream I can't get enough reality of my own to make her hear me.

Then my mind splits again. There's a third character in the scene: a dark, beautiful woman. It takes me a second, but then I realize I'm looking at a young Lore dressed in close-fitting black pants and a turtleneck. Is Lore a professional actor? I've never asked what she does, and she definitely has enough presence to be some kind of star. But this seems like something stranger is going on.

I watch her standing in a doorway, watchful and still. Then she raises one hand and steps out into the street, half a block behind the boy. She's stalking the stalker, and relief surges through me. *Please, Lore. Please.* Vanessa is already adjusting a broad-brimmed hat at a sultry angle, giving herself one last look in the hallway mirror before she steps through her front door. *Lore, warn her! Any moment now she'll meet him on the corner there, right in front of that diner, do you see it? And then it will be too late.*

"Angus," the young Lore calls, and I jump. But she's not talking to me.

It hits me that until now this thousand-dimensional movie has been perfectly silent. No music, no one calling out in the background, no hiss of wind. The instant Lore's finished speaking my name, the silence closes in again.

The blond boy turns. His lips move soundlessly, but I can tell by his faint sneer that he's saying something insolent. I'd like to slap him.

"You don't remember me, then," Lore says, and somehow she's closed the distance between them instantaneously, as if she'd caught some undetectable slipknot made of space. "I can imagine that I didn't make much of an impression. Your focus was elsewhere. But can you recall Claire?"

A look comes over his face that amazes me, because it reflects the kind of inner teetering I feel way too often. Knowing and not-knowing, reality and unreality, jostle back and forth so quickly that they blur into a single unbearable vibration. When he replies this time the sneer is gone, and he only manages a few silent words. His eyes are wide with dumbfounded pain and just inches from Lore's.

"I don't always find you in time," Lore tells him. "But when I do, you will *remember* her." With that, she rests her hand on his forehead. The gesture looks gentle, like someone brushing away a child's nightmare.

It doesn't feel that way to him, though. The pain on his face tightens into a hideous leer, as if his mouth were twisting into an inward vortex. And, God, I feel it too: a whirling void in my throat dragging me into nothingness, one shred at a time. It's like the sensation of those sidewalk cracks chewing on my mind, but even sharper, deeper. He might be screaming, but his voice has been canceled. Vanessa, meanwhile, is standing over by the diner looking annoyed.

It takes me a second to get it. Lore is murdering that boy! That other Angus. And I guess maybe he deserves it, but couldn't she have found another way?

I fall out of all the images at once, or they drop out of me. I'm back in the velvet darkness of the booth. Panic thrashes in my chest and I topple sideways, out into the spill of fabric on the floor, scattering my tuna rolls as I go. Maybe the party is winding down, because the white walls aren't curved and glowing anymore. They look like gallery walls anywhere, boxy and blank.

People are still laughing and chatting in the next room, but it sounds like most of them have gone. Funny, but I didn't hear them the whole time I was in the booth either. The silence consumed even their voices, though you wouldn't think a curtain could be so soundproof.

I'm fine. It was just a movie.

But I want to go find Lore, and ask her—what? To hug me?

"Angus! I was just looking for you. I'm about to take off, and I thought you might like a ride somewhere." Her warm brown eyes are on my face the instant I step into the main gallery, and it makes me forget how afraid I was of her just a moment ago, when I felt the touch of her hand on my brow. *Just a movie, okay?*

"I was in the video booth," I say. I'm not sure how to broach the subject. "Um, I didn't know you were an actor? You were really great."

Lore cocks her head. "That booth is playing a variety of old recordings. Which one did you see?"

Oh, God. Do I have to talk about it? "It was the one with the blond murderer? He was after the girl—the girl with the big hat." For some reason I'm too ashamed to admit I knew her name. "You came after him and killed him first. I mean, the *character* you were playing killed him. And you called him Angus. But he didn't look anything like me, so the name must have been a coincidence?"

"What else could it be?" Lore asks, though her tone seems a little off for a rhetorical question. It's more like she's actively pondering other options, so I'm relieved when she doesn't wait for an answer. "And how did you feel, watching it? Did you think my character was justified in what she did?"

Oh. "I mean, you—she—did it to save that girl? So I understood? But I also wondered if you really had to use violence. If there could have been other options for stopping him."

"Such as?"

"Talking to him, maybe?" It sounds ridiculous when I say it. That blond boy exuded wrongness. I felt the savagery latent in him the instant he walked onto the screen. What good does it do, to talk to someone like that?

"I suppose my character could have tried that, as long as she was prepared to gamble the girl's life on the conversation's outcome. But what if she was looking for guaranteed results?" Lore sounds amused, and somehow I'm not finding it funny at all. "Let's get you home, Angus. It's getting late."

She slips one hand through my arm and leads me out of the gallery, calling a few last goodbyes to her friends. I'm not sure how smart it is to trust her, honestly, but at the same time I can't help it. The tilt of her voice, like a boat on a swell, when she said *my character* lingers on in my head. The chain holding her pendant galls my neck.

"Lore? I'm thinking maybe I should leave town? I just—things went really wrong for me tonight, and I don't know if I can handle going back there."

The idea of leaving jabs me with panic. Even if Geneva won't talk to me, the urge to stay as near her as possible charges every synapse of my brain. Leave town? What am I *talking* about?

We head halfway down the block to her car, and I get in the passenger seat with the faintest tremor coasting through my knees. But it's *Lore*, already. She's slipping off her intimidating party shoes and pulling soft black flats out of her bag, so I get a chance to study her face without her looking at me. Every facet of her brow, the way the ambient light rests on her eyelids like gold coins, tells me that she knows all about my kind of reality.

"There's something you're afraid of." We pull out into the empty street, drive under the dandelion puffs of lamplight. "And you're telling yourself that, by leaving Carmen's, you can leave that something behind."

What is she implying? "Yeah."

"And yet you already know that you can't escape so easily. What's really troubling you?"

"I—it's pretty hard to explain?" Lore waits, so I try. "Sometimes I feel almost like my life began when I found myself in front of Carmen's warehouse, and that wasn't even two weeks ago. And sometimes I feel like my memories go back and back and *back* until they aren't even mine anymore. Like smears sinking into a wall, maybe, but I can't see through it? Just these weird scribbly traces show where they've been."

"A palimpsest."

I've never heard that word before. "If you say so."

Lore nods gravely—that trick she has of treating me like my thoughts matter. Her brown hands are tight on the steering wheel, worn and strong and big-knuckled, but with something elegant even in their weariness.

"And where do you suppose those traces come from? More to the point, where do you suppose they lead?"

"I'd have to smash through the wall to find out."

"So you would," Lore agrees. "But thanks to the efforts of a certain friend of yours, the wall is already cracked."

I see too late that only one of her hands is still on the steering wheel. The other is drifting up, almost to my brow now, her fingers already warming the air around my temple.

Catherine the Killer

Needless to say, it worked, else Gus's abhorrent creations would not have roamed the earth these ninety years. Asterion introduced Gus to an ice-white and ghoulish lady—La Merveilleuse, as she ludicrously called herself—who protested her ignorance. Oh, she had heard of these specialized heartstrings that could stabilize and pierce ghosts, of course, but they were rare, very rare, probably unobtainable! Then she slipped a scrap of paper into Gus's pocket when the minotaur turned his back. Gus returned later to tip her for her service, as I expect the deluded minotaur did as well.

On the slip was a name, a vague address. We went there directly, and a sort of practice horror involving a large violet rat ensued—

Never mind. I cannot avoid telling you, my self-deluded reader, of what I did to Christopher Flynn, not if I want to lead you to the necessary conclusion, to that violence of mind I require in you. Let that story suffice.

When Gus left the umbrathurge's shop, we walked straight to Margo's, but once we were close Gus stopped. He had learned by this time to throw up a sort of sonic shield to mask my screaming from ears other than his own. The difficulty was that, when he stifled me, his own voice was silenced as well; such was the price of our regrettable connection. So the trick wasn't often terribly useful.

He employed it now.

Margo had dragged a chair outside to supervise her latest beamer child at its piano practice—for Gus remained so enamored of his own talent that he was careful always to instill it in his beamers. Margo lacked the funds to buy a piano and had no space for one in any case, but Gus allowed her enough talens to regularly summon instruments from among the herds that roamed the streets.

The piano that had answered on this occasion was rather ill-mannered and rambunctious; it was a beast of a thing with hooves and a bristling golden coat, its keys slick with saliva. The little Angus lay sprawled face-down atop the lid, its arms stretched down to reach the keyboard, and in that unlikely position it played a waltz. The restive piano pawed the ground, switched and jumped at the high notes. The beamer child slipped a little and scrambled with its knees to regain its place, laughing and whooping the while, and managed somehow to play its waltz unbroken. The music reached Gus and me, distant but distinct and, I must admit, very beautiful for all that the player's small hands were often jarred. Tattered passersby stopped to listen. Margo, by now well-schooled in desolation, watched her Angus with what I can only describe as ruinous tenderness, with the sort of love that issues from a mangled heart.

This was what passed for a charming domestic scene in Nautilus. Gus and I hung back in an arcade and studied them unobserved. I was not in the best of states, to put it mildly; I was a wilting rag of ectoplasm with what felt like a wide, shredded wound at my center. I had sworn, I reminded myself, to stay alert, engaged; to watch carefully Gus and his scheming, in the hope that some impossible opening would present itself, and I could find a way to *act*.

But, please recall, I had been watching for a very long time. Despair was never far from me.

It was a bit soon, I thought, for Gus to seize his latest beamer. It was hard to measure their lifespans in the slurred and dayless time of Nautilus, but from our forays to the unworld I had gathered that they were remarkably regular. Gus allowed each beamer child exactly one unworld year before dispatching it, whether to meet some magical requirement or from mere habit I did not know. In consideration of his new plans, though, would he make this child an exception?

I focused, as I so often did, on Margo's face. Deprived as I was of literature, faces had become my reading material. I would like to claim that I studied Margo only for diversion, absorbing the complex and subtle suffering of my enemy with pleasure. But that would not be true. I had never managed to free myself of my unwanted sympathy for Margo, even as I went on hating her.

When she thought herself unobserved, her face hung blank as a mask. But the mask was thin, a mere silken wisp, so that her fine, sharp features betrayed an inner buckling, a warp and distortion. It was as if a human visage draped across a second face nearly demonic.

Then the beamer child would call to her to *look, look!* And her chin would lift while she forced a benevolent smile, a kind gaze. With each new beamer, though, the benevolence grew more shopworn.

The piano's prancing was now so hectic that the child could barely hang onto its lid, giggling and reaching to slap at random keys. It did not seem to me especially conducive to learning the piece. Margo must have thought so as well, for she hauled herself to her feet and decisively backhanded the piano across its hairy fallboard.

The instrument gave a piteous clang and thumped down onto all four feet, only shuffling a bit in protest.

But I had seen something else, something unprecedented: when Margo raised her hand, the little Angus flinched.

With that I understood, and inescapably, that Margo had taken to beating these creatures she had long cherished.

It was only justice, of course; I knew it to be justice. Any projection of Gus, even Gus as a child, deserved every conceivable punishment for what he had done to me. For what he meant to do to others. Those creatures of his were designed for murder. I should not ache for them.

Why, then, did Margo's new brutality affect me like a betrayal? I gaped at her, heartsick and disbelieving. Had I clung to her adoration for the little beamers as the sole and certain sweetness in my own undying existence?

Why did I want to pull the beamer child into my arms and shelter it from her? Why did my thoughts all shout at Margo for her brutality?

I can't say if Gus noted any of these details, for his look was low and dark and gave away nothing. He watched them from under his weedy pale eyebrows, his mouth set tight and flat. Something else then occurred to me. Once the last beamer child was mulched, once Gus launched at last his grand project of crafting young men to carry his malice back to the unworld, what more use would Margo be to him?

Having come this far, my ever-reborn reader, I suppose even you must have guessed that I am not writing this autothanatography simply to pass the time. I have no particular faith in your intelligence; Gus's mind is far more limited than he supposes, and in his insecurity he restricts yours even more. Still, you must grasp that this narrative is designed with an end in view, and if it is to achieve that end I cannot avoid the facts merely because my spirit buckles at their approach.

To wit: we are drawing near the death of Christopher Flynn.

Gus was at last becoming chary of employing Asterion, and after some hesitation he undertook the abduction himself. Asterion, I believed, didn't know yet that Gus had located the umbrastrings he needed, much less tested his ideas; I assumed that the minotaur still clomped along in blissful ignorance, sure that Gus must accept his outrageously expensive propositions before too long.

We had by then slipped along beneath the ordinary currents of history for some time, and when we popped up in the unworld it was perhaps 1923. Congressman Volstead had had his way in the interval, and Gus was likely to have better luck in a city, where Prohibition was not so strictly enforced. We made several visits to New York City in rapid succession, Gus armed with gold and jewelry stolen from his father's strongbox decades before. A fistful of gold he converted to ready cash. He had himself shaved, his unruly hair clipped short. A top hat was acquired, and he was fitted for a tailcoat and trousers that hugged his ill-fed frame. He spent freely and the tailor grew familiar enough, by the second visit, to refer Gus to a suitable establishment.

I suppose all these preparations were a sop to his nerves, as well as a way of procrastinating.

Eventually, though, he worked himself up to the necessary pitch of callousness. He spent a few lit on a school of glassy pink flying fish that clouded around his naked body and devoured every speck of dirt and dead skin, which left him so pinkly pure that he looked nearly flayed. He dressed in his unworld finery. He spent a few more lit to order a sheet of air into mirrored brilliance, and therein he inspected himself.

I watched the corners of his mouth fall, and knew that he had expected the effect to be more pleasing. The cleaning and polishing had only laid bare his sickly, ravaged appearance. If he was not yet old, neither did his face have the soft clarity of youth any longer.

Gus twisted to stare at me, fluttering faithfully behind him. "Look what you've done to me," he said. "Look! This is the toll of love denied: these lines, this *brokenness*. Is it enough to make you regret your coldness? Do you care at all?"

Oh, I cared, though not in the way he meant.

"No," Gus said, staring at me—and if the eternal rictus of my scream was not wonderfully variable, I could still flash hatred with my eyes. "No, I see it's still not enough. Oh, sometimes magic seems like such a vain enterprise, if it can't make you *see*—but we're about to change that!"

He nodded sharply. And since every city of the unworld is adjacent to Nautilus and equally porous to those who know the way, he had only to walk a short while before he reached the right exit. Where the wall bore the legend NEW YORK CITY under an arched lintel he pressed through and straight into a cellar. The local guardian, a whiskery man in green who sat perched on a barrel, gave us a bored nod. We'd been there several times recently, and I knew that cellar down to the oyster shells scattered thickly on its floor.

We climbed a damp flight of stairs and burst out on a darkly glittering view. I saw an upright slice of the Hudson, looking as tall as a tower between the somber buildings. A thousand snakes of moonlight crossed its darkness, a patient, writhing weave of bright and black.

I felt a wild windiness in myself, as I always did when we arrived in the unworld. The pale oppression of Nautilus rolled away, even beneath a range of eerie towers that were so unlike my home. I would have liked to explore New York under other conditions; I had longed to see it as a girl. But Gus dragged me four meager blocks to a townhouse nearly tripping into the hungry river and spoke a few odd words to a man behind its black door.

We sidled up narrow stairs to what might have ordinarily been a modest parlor but was now a device for the compression of drunken bodies, nearly medieval in its sadism. Never had I seen so many limbs and torsos folded into so little air; satin skins crossed tailored sleeves like knife blades whickering, and women squirmed behind the clack of immense feather fans. The flash of bleating instruments seemed to swim through the smoky haze, as disorienting as will-o'-the-wisps.

I was not as surprised by the scene as one might suppose. I had observed the changes in fashion on our previous visits, had rather envied the short hair and liberated calves, if anything. Women had shed a great weight since I was young, and I sometimes imagined that Gus was actually a long and heavy skirt encumbering my lower body, catching every wind like a sail and so dragging me to and fro.

But I did not envy the women in this room their sweaty skins and airless inebriation. There was a desperate note to the laughter, or at least I thought so. I watched one spangled girl fighting to escape a man's heavy paws on her bare arms, and was no longer sure how much ballast had dropped away.

An unsteady brunette approached Gus, but he shrugged her off. He scanned the room for a target more to his taste.

You might wonder, as I did, if Gus could not have used a woman for his project. He could have, of course, for women and men are composed of the same meat and sinew. Likewise a sailor would have served him as well as an aristocrat. But when it came to making his own simulacrum, Gus grew decidedly squeamish. I watched his gaze catch on a tall, handsome blond boy who loomed several rows of heads back—a boy much taller and broader than Gus himself had ever been, as if my former friend thought it would be best to have surplus materials. The boy was pink-cheeked, with a vapid, infantile expression that suggested he could only be the child of great wealth, indulged to the point of idiocy.

Slowly, patiently, Gus insinuated himself through the stifling crowd until his elbow jarred the blond's arm, slopping spirits across his shirt cuff. The boy shrugged in annoyance, but Gus affected not to notice.

"Champagne!" Gus bellowed. "The best you have! Nothing's too good for my friends."

Nearby heads swiveled with greedy expectancy. A bottle appeared, and Gus filled the glasses at hand in a mazy stream, feigning drunkenness himself. Foam splashed upraised knuckles, trickled over pearls like a brook over stones. As if by chance, the blond and his two companions— rich, callow louts like himself—were especial beneficiaries.

An hour and three bottles later, Christopher Flynn and his friends had their arms around Gus's shoulders while glimmering girls shimmied against them, shrill with false laughter as Flynn whacked their rumps. Two hours, and Flynn's friends were conveniently entangled with those girls in the corners. Flynn watched them go with an expression nearly bereft, like a sickly lamb goggling after its shepherd, and clung to Gus's arm.

You may observe, at this juncture, that my portrait of Christopher Flynn is not the most flattering. Quite so: I despised him to my flickering core. Allow me to remind you, though, that I have had unworld decades to cultivate my contempt for him, and I have made the utmost use of that time. I've tended my contempt, nurtured it, fed it choice morsels: how Flynn's hazel eyes rolled like a calf's, how he began to gaze at Gus with blubbering admiration.

Ah, but my disdain is highly motivated. I seethe with the desire to believe that Christopher Flynn was worthless, an absolute blot of a being. That his death tended if anything to improve the world, to cleanse it of all the selfishness and stupidity that one tall, teetering body can contain.

So perhaps you should distrust my account of him. To be truthful, I distrust it myself.

"I'm ossified," Flynn observed, which expression both Gus and I were obliged to decipher from context. His round pink cheeks shone with an oily iridescence in the lamplight. "Let's blouse."

"I know another joint," Gus said, waving his new vocabulary like a flag he could not keep quite upright. "It's close. But let's have another round of jag juice first."

The champagne was long gone, and Gus plied him with liquor that even I could tell was highly dubious. Gus himself kept misplacing his glass. And once his target stumbled and sloped sharply to the left, Gus paid the bill over a deafening lack of protest on Flynn's part. From Flynn's widened eyes, I gathered that the figure was stunning and Gus's liberality impressive.

Flynn had no way to know that unworld dollars were not the currency Gus cared for.

They staggered together down to the street. Hoops of moonlight danced and merged on the river's current. Oh, I was enamored of the air, the night, the moon's sparrow-footed perch on a distant rooftop; in Nautilus night fell rarely, and only when the whim seized some sorcerer with magic to burn.

All this beauty was a sorry consolation. I knew what faced me on our return.

I stayed anchored to Gus's shoulders—as indeed did Flynn, whose frame now swagged as limp as bunting with my murderer as his sole support.

"It's right this way," Gus said. "You'll see. It's . . . the duck's nuts."

They entered the dim stairwell from which we had emerged earlier that evening. The man in green looked up and cocked an eyebrow at the intrusion of Gus's distinctly unmagical companion. Gus nodded as if to say that he knew it was irregular, but that he would explain presently.

Then he drew back the arm around Flynn's shoulders, and shoved him down the stairs.

Flynn screamed and tumbled with a horrible knocking sound and at least one resounding snap, then lay still.

Does this sound like a rather crude attack for a sorcerer? Gus's skills were highly specific, and he did not know the precise magic for knocking a man unconscious. Moreover, we were not in Nautilus, where almost any magic is for sale.

"Oh, so he's lumber then? You'll still have to pay the import fees," the man in green drawled.

"It seems there's a fee for everything," Gus rejoined sourly. "Can you get his feet?"

Once in Nautilus, a fleet of beetles was hired to carry Flynn to our destination. He groaned sometimes but did not wake, not then and not when the beetles deposited him just inside the umbrathurge's shop. And now I cannot delay describing that personage any longer.

As was the case with so many citizens, his chosen appearance cloaked whatever he had been in the unworld. He looked like a twelve-year-old boy with damson-dusted skin, a shock of black hair, and immense, searching blue-black eyes. His manner was studious and impish by turns, and he went by the name of Sky.

The contrast of Sky's delicate loveliness only made what followed more grotesque.

"Hi, Gus!" he cooed at our entrance. His smile was a sweet and knowing thing, made for cradling secrets; his accent was English and, I think, upper-class. "You got one! Nice work!"

A dozen umbrastrings hung artfully looped across the wall; evidently they were not so rare as Asterion had claimed. Such a fine gray glimmer they made, the barest tracery, like the scrawl that long-ago horror leaves on the mind and that time's flow can never quite erase!

"It was easy," Gus said. "I can't believe I ever thought I needed to wait on Asterion's help."

"Oh, Asterion!" Sky giggled, rather overdoing the air of childish mischief. "He dupes nearly everyone for a time when they're new—everyone he thinks is *worth* duping, that is. Consider it a compliment!" He cocked his head and regarded Flynn, now glazed in perspiration and shivering violently. "Looks heavy. We'll need to suspend him at just the right height. Maybe two, three talens' worth of lift? How thrilling it always is to try out a new technique! Millennia of magic, you might think we'd have reached the end of what it can do. But there's always, always more, just waiting to be discovered. Let's get started!"

Gus balked at this hastiness. "I greatly appreciate your assistance, of course. But aren't there matters we should discuss before proceeding?"

Sky beamed, politely baffled, though he certainly must have known what Gus meant. "Matters like what?"

"Payment." Sky's feigned obtuseness clearly ruffled Gus into suspicion. He crossed his arms.

"Oh! Don't be silly. What, you think I'm another Asterion, a paw in everyone's pocket? I have talens enough of my own, thanks. This is *fun*."

No one in Nautilus ever had enough talens. Gus's arms stayed tight against his crisp white vest and shirtfront, both now rather blotched. Sky's boyish brightness grew tarnished. Calculation slipped through his face like shadowy fish.

"Well, if you like, you could do me a favor sometime. After all, I'm doing one for you."

"A favor."

"I'd like to borrow Catherine. Just now and then. I'll give her right back to you when I'm done, I promise."

Both Gus and I jerked at this bewildering suggestion.

Here I would like to mention that Sky never once looked at my face, not then and not later. But unlike Margo, he did not seem to be at pains to avoid my gaze. No; one might have supposed I did not even possess a face, so far as he was concerned, any more than a rug does. It made the sound of my given name on his lips all the more jarring.

"*Borrow* her?" Gus stammered. "But that's not possible! We're linked, inextricably and forever."

"Oh, I can unlink you." Sky delivered this stupefying pronouncement so casually I hardly understood at first. "And link you right back up after, like I said. I'll even throw in an umbrastring like Asterion's, so you won't need to bother with *him* anymore."

Gus's eyes widened as this supposedly unobtainable treasure, this rare and refined device, was offered up like an unloved toy. And I? I surged with alarm, I rolled and flared with dread. My attachment to Gus took on a perverse character of safety—if Sky wanted me so badly, his reasons could only be horrifying.

And at the same time I remembered the grayish ghost collector, Nemo. There must be a method for separating ghosts from those they haunted, if Nemo was able to gather us up like so many gilt clocks. Perhaps he had made use of Sky's services.

"I'm the only one in all of Nautilus who knows how to make them," Sky added. "They're my own invention. If you don't get an umbrastring from me, you won't get one anywhere."

Gus glanced from him to me. It did not need to be said that, if Asterion could no longer claim a third of my production, Gus could enrich himself at my expense far more quickly, and he was plainly tempted. But simply handing me over for another sorcerer's experiments went against his long-established habits of possessiveness. I watched with relief as Gus's mouth compressed.

"Catherine is mine," Gus said decidedly. "I'd rather pay a fee."

For half a moment, Sky looked very old indeed, or so it seemed to me. I looked down on an ancient, thwarted, malign thing in a childskin— and though the memory disgusts me, I must confess that I was briefly grateful to my murderer for sparing me Sky's molestation.

Of course, Gus had initially resisted Asterion's proposals as well.

"Oh, pooh." Sky's boyish mask reasserted itself, now wearing a pout. He flourished a dismissive hand. "I *told* you, payment like that doesn't interest me. Tell you what, we'll sieve this fellow now, and someday we'll come up with a favor you don't begrudge so *very* much."

Did Gus know, as I did, that Sky was in no way giving up his designs on me? No doubt, but the implied contract was so vague that he must have thought he could evade Sky's demands. "All right. Let's get it done."

And with these words my gratitude and relief came to an end. Flynn's wilting body was levitated with the same commonplace magic harmlessly deployed on teacups; Sky's shop was an elegant, airy, vaulted space of the kind granted only to the affluent. Flynn rose beneath its fluted dome, his pink face glossed in the omnipresent pale glow. There was a brief pause while Gus jiggered him roughly upright and adjusted his loft, bringing him in line with me. Then Flynn's bruised and drooling mouth hung inches from the screaming void of mine. It was a strange and unwelcome intimacy, given how used I was to flapping above everyone's heads.

I don't doubt that my appearance would strike terror into nearly anyone. But I was the one who reared back from the coming confrontation, tilting away like a tree in the wind.

Sky squealed excitedly and levitated himself high enough to jab an umbrastring's rain-colored prongs straight into the crown of my head, while Gus thrust another into my ankle. A single umbrastring thus inserted always produced a thrumming and thickened sensation, something like the coursing of blood around a wound. But a pair of them—how shall I describe it? I felt—no, I *became*—a violent oscillation between the two points, an internal race so fast that I thought I might explode. I became night and day colliding again and again without the cushioning interludes of dusk and dawn. Or perhaps it would be truer to say that the collision was between life and death, or even that the amalgam of unlife and undeath composing me began to beat against its own unresolvable paradox.

As Gus had hypothesized, the power of what I was, pinned in this way, was tremendous. I contained force enough to flatten the whole city—but oh, I could not control the powers now articulated in myself, could not even catch them, no more than a hummingbird can write a novel with the blur of its wings.

Gus inched toward Flynn's dangling feet, once and then again. I flapped backward as hard as I could, maddened though I was with pain. But I could not stop myself from rebounding upright. My captive energies purled against Flynn's cheek.

The pitiful boy would have done better to stay unconscious. How often in my imagination have I railed at him for having the poor judgment to wake up at just the moment when his flesh began to buzz apart like a cloud of gnats? He hadn't seen or heard me in the unworld, but in Nautilus that small mercy was denied him. My eyes were nearly touching his and their flash must have been blinding. His feet kicked desperately at the empty air; the right foot passed straight into my shin. It instantly disintegrated into a vibrating mist, motes of bone and blood and even his shoe shivering together in the pulsation of my power.

Flynn's scream met mine in a hot blast of his breath, and Gus advanced again.

Gus crept forward with merciless slowness. Perhaps he feared that, if he moved too quickly, he would botch the job. Flynn proved able to keep screaming first without lips, then without teeth, then without tongue, palate, or jawbone. The tone only became windier, something like a broken flute. And even when the scream was at last extinguished it was not much of an improvement.

I had been used as a *sieve*, as Sky put it, in their preliminary experiment on a cherub-faced rat. That employment had left me feeling as if there had been some detonation in the area of my stomach, where the rat was forced through me. But Flynn was much larger, and that earlier experience had not prepared me for how it would feel to shred a man entire. He was enough bigger than myself that, when Gus finished dragging me all the way through him, a bloody rind remained hanging around the hollowness cut by my passage. The levitational magic was still in effect, so the blood did not drip but rather wafted in crimson tendrils. Flynn's blond hair stood out in a feathery nimbus.

And the rest of Flynn? That was inside me, particulate and humming.

He had become nothing but a tempest of matter pitching in my immaterial currents.

"Amazing!" Sky cheered, bouncing on the balls of his feet. He clapped his hands and crowed. A blue cat oozed up his back and wrapped itself around his rib cage. Its silver eyes peered over Sky's shoulder, its peaked ears twitched. "Your Catherine packs a punch, oh yes she does!"

I was in no state to observe the irony that I, long since murdered, had now killed in my turn.

No; I only knew that I had killed. That knowledge took me over, left no room for anything else.

"I'd better get her home," Gus observed, far more coolly. He looked at my black and white, now intermixed with carnage as fine as floating dust. "And . . . the materials. I expect they're best when they're fresh."

Perhaps you will say that I had killed against my will, and was therefore blameless? I've tried that line of persuasion on myself, of course. More times than I can count.

It only makes everything worse. What, am I to find solace in my own helplessness? In the fact that Gus had reduced me first to a ghost and now to a *thing*, an implement that could not turn away from the vicious uses he made of me?

My ghost held Flynn's corpse, such as it was, suspended. A cloud, a tremor, ten million cells unmoored from form and function but still warm in my agitated energies. I held him and wondered who in the unworld loved him, who was at this moment waiting anxiously for him to return home.

It had been a very long time since I had held anyone.

Catherine and Thomas

Something unexpected happened in the weeks following my enforced separation from Gus: I did not grieve. I worried about him, certainly, especially when my father reported that he was again confined to his room except for piano practice, and that harrowing shrieks shook the Farrows' house, but I missed him far less than I might have expected. Instead I felt an inexplicable lightness that, in retrospect, is not inexplicable at all: an airy freedom, a billowing beneath my feet.

In fact, I was happy.

Oh, if I had heeded the firefly signaling of my own heart, could it have saved me? Or would he only have murdered me sooner? Was there ever a right time for a final break with Gus Farrow?

As for the Skelleys, it was only a few days before I found Thomas sitting with his back against a maple tree at the edge of our yard. His arms were so tight around his knees that it looked as if he were afraid his legs might run away without him. At the sight of that bony, colorless boy, I felt a gentleness that answered his own, and I went and sat beside him in silence. I'd learned that it was best to give him time, to let him speak when the words came to him.

"There was a dead hummingbird under the roses," he said at last, very softly. "I thought of that song, from the séance. *Why should the beautiful die*, remember? The bird was as beautiful as any person could ever be, but no one seems to think that the beauty of small creatures should earn their spirits immortality."

"Maybe it's enough that beauty itself is immortal," I said. "That it goes on without any individual person, or any particular hummingbird." I felt an intimation of a distant horizon, a world where people and birds alike were long gone. But beauty endured there, of that I had no doubt, in a million unthinkable permutations.

We sat for another minute, not looking at each other. Eye contact was never easy for him.

"I saved its feathers for you," he said. "To show you under the microscope. When you can visit us again. I know—you're interested in iridescence."

The significance of this speech did not escape me. "*Will* I be able to visit again?"

He didn't answer immediately, only picked up a maple leaf of deepest crimson and examined it. Then: "My father thinks so. He says Gertrude Farrow seems to care for his opinion."

I understood, and my heart surged with gratitude. How close I had come to spoiling everything in a fit of vindictive rage, when in fact I needed only to be patient, and trust in my friends!

"It's very good of your father to intervene on my behalf. I was afraid Mrs. Farrow might have influenced him against me."

"Of course not. He thinks of you as—that is, he knows the difference. Between Mrs. Farrow and you. Between your reasons and hers."

Thomas managed to imbue these simple words with a whole spectrum of meanings, and with a loyalty so pure I would have liked to kiss his cheek.

"He wishes you hadn't taken the books," Thomas added, staring at his knees. "When you knew Gus Farrow must be lying about them. But he understands why you did."

It was not lost on me that Thomas was expressing his own feelings under cover of his father's. He rose to his feet and stood there awkwardly, then stretched out a hand to help me up. It left us standing closer than our wont.

"Tell him I'm grateful for his understanding," I said, which fell somewhat short of contrition. "And that I miss studying with both of you very much."

And here Thomas met my eyes for just a moment, and flashed me a smile as sweet and beautiful as the passing life of any fragile thing. Oh, Thomas was no one's dashing imaginary lover; he was not remotely handsome, not ambitious, not bold.

He was something more than all those qualities combined.

Allow me to offer an observation. It's one that you in particular should heed, my dreadful reader: any fantasized beloved is an expression, a projection of one's self. Even our wildest imaginings are still caught in our own confines, and to love such imaginings means to love the self, the self, the self again, in endlessly refracting solipsism.

To love another person, you must love what you cannot imagine.

Angus on the Bank

Before I can fling myself to the side, Lore's fingers make contact. It's the same soft, caressing gesture she used when she murdered the blond Angus. I cringe, waiting for the horrible telescoping pain to suck me down.

The pain doesn't come. I can feel her touch on my brow, the pads of her fingers brushing me like autumn leaves. And at the same time I feel her hand passing straight into my brain. Somewhere toward the back, the fissure where that sidewalk crack bit me ignites with a white blaze. I can see it now: a ragged gap with icy light shining through it.

Who engineered that attack on me outside of Bluebell's, again? Those ragged edges feel like a profile, a silhouette cut from dark paper: a girl, a girl I've known for more than forever—

Lore's reaching hand catches something inside me. What is it, exactly? A crouching knot of Angus-ness, wadded and smoothed out and wadded again and again, until all the sneering creases can't be undone and the edges are foxed and the whole thing flexes in an angry ball of scribbles and erasures and muddy dissolutions. I can feel her hand on it, so warm and certain by contrast with the godawful mess of myself.

She gives a fierce shove.

Whatever it is, whatever *I* am—there's the sensation of hurtling through space and colliding with a hard surface. The craggy gap in the center prints itself into my flesh, reshapes my bones.

Then there's the crunch, the crumble, as the edges give way. And I'm falling. Into the room *behind* the wall. A young, painfully beautiful Black guy is huddled on a bed, weeping so hard his body heaves.

And then I'm him, I'm Angus Farrow, nineteen years old and so grief-sick I can hardly breathe. *She's dead, she's dead, what have I done? What did that demon make me do? All I wanted was to love her.*

But I'm still falling deeper into his past, his words streaming by me like motion-blurred stars, and there's a girl in my arms. A nightclub, that's where we are, and we got in with fake IDs, and up on the stage

224 S. E. PORTER

there's a singer whose voice swoons over the strains of an electric violin. This *her* is a shy, tall, pale brunette, her eyelids painted the iridescent green of a beetle's wings. She's excited, transported by the music and the heat of my body swaying against hers. She lifts her chin, just the way I've always dreamed she would, and her lips are sticky-bright with glittery black lacquer that catches the red and blue stage lights in colored glints.

"Just so you know, I can't love you, Angus. Okay?"

"I know," I tell her. "It's all good." But I don't mean a word of it. I *can't*.

When I take her mouth she feels the charge of the kiss, bliss shading into fear, but I feel something else. A breaking, an unplucking, deep within her. The first taste of who she is, drawn between my lips. It goads me on, and I kiss her more deeply, pulling her inmost self to shreds with my hunger.

By the time I slip out a side door she's slumped in a corner—just a girl who's had a drink too many, as far as the clubgoers can tell—and no one sees me leave. I can feel her life still unwinding from inside her, as if the end of some vital thread stayed caught between my teeth. Where I've pulled the life out of her, silence is entering, filling the vacated spaces.

She'll be dead by morning. I lean against a wall, shocked by bitterness so acute that it becomes a new kind of rapture.

What was her name? Something weird. Right, Lorca, after the poet.

As soon as I've recalled it, I'm falling onward. Out of the Black Angus and into the Angus behind him. I have just enough time to see him before I crash into his mind. He's a lanky boy with long blond waves and huge, sensitive moon-gray eyes, a fragile artist type going by his looks.

This time his face—*my* face?—is contorted by rage and spite as I watch a slight Asian girl with a shock of electric-blue hair leap into a car and slam the door.

"Fuck you, Angus!" she yells out the window. She turns to the driver, hidden from me in a tent of shadow. "Asshole tried to make me kiss him."

The Angus in the movie was me. *They're all me.* The realization shines through the crack in my mind. Then I'm back in my thwarted fury, watching her drive away.

A failed Angus, that's what I am. A bad batch of myself. Because the blue-haired girl—Chloe? Is that right?—escaped me.

Because she lived. But for all my shame, there's a sneaking relief that I won't have to grieve for her—because once each *her* dies, that's all there is left for me to do.

Falling again. Suddenly sheeted in rain, the gutters full of drops like tiny popping stars. I land in the pain of Lore's hand snaking from behind and twisting the life out of me seconds before I can kiss a voluptuous girl with glowing brown skin and startling pale blue eyes, rain matting her hair against her full cheeks. *You again.* The words froth on my lips while the girl screams and leaps on Lore, trying to throttle her.

Every time? That's what I do, again and again? Every version there is of me? But, God, I love her—Brittany?—so much, and I wouldn't hurt her for the world. I just want to make her mine. To own her, to draw her into me with an endless kiss. Year after year after—

If they're all me, then how many times has Lore killed me?

The fall speeds up. My own face flares in mirrors and in night-glazed windows; it streaks on the silver flanks of subway cars. And every time it's different, its beauty gradually diminishing the further back I go.

Beamers. That's what we are, and I'm just brushing against a sense of what it means.

Every time, there's a *her.* A blur of running legs and unexpected smiles and furry hats tipped with fresh snow, on benches and in dark hallways and under bridges. Some of them evade me, some are seduced by me, some linger in a nebulous zone of mixed pity and friendship and bemusement. It doesn't matter where we are or what each *she* looks like; there's a certain refusal to accept the world's terms, a brisk clarity; she's blunt, snappy, intellectual.

And every time, there's an urge to swallow her whole.

At first Lore finds me a lot of the time and sends me into an expiring torque, but the farther back I go, the less I see of her. More and more of the girls die, always so young—except for the ones who escape me on their own, their lives leaving mine and spreading into futures I can't imagine, like sugar dissolving in the rain.

A few dozen faces flicker past before I see Vanessa, tilting her head so that her red hair cascades over one eye as she sips a milkshake through a straw, the other eye watching me with sparkling amusement; oh, she was one of the ones who *liked* me, who almost might have cared . . . but I would have killed her if Lore hadn't intervened. Another jumble of hair and clothes and slim hands cupping chins, and then there's Pearl in her black satin; Pearl, who barely liked me at all, and who died anyway when I claimed her by force.

When I kissed her. But if she'd just loved me, the kiss would have spared her. Everything would have been great.

The kiss always feels so *right,* that's the bitch of it. The life pulled into my mouth tastes so pungent, like the tingling acid of a bitten orange peel. Bitterness might be all that's left to me afterward, but that bitterness is so completely mine. As much mine as the girl I've undone should have been.

By the time I've understood that, I'm falling through versions of my-self like a hundred panes of tissue-thin ice, one after the other. *Her* hair turns into a single river flickering in complex colors, frothing into curls at the rapids and smoothing into glossy sheets in the shallows. *Her* eyes spin by on the surface, green and gray and brown and midnight, like so many fallen leaves. This far back I can't always remember *her* names anymore, or even whether each one of *her* died. There's a dim lull where I don't see anything. Where I feel like a little boy, waking afraid in a dark room.

And then I alight on a mossy bank. A watermill turns in front of me, steadily paddling at a green-brown current. Being myself feels different this time, fuller; I possess every intimate detail of my childhood, from the turned-milk scent of my first nurse to the black bristling fur of the puppy that fell in the weir just upstream of here when I was six and drowned before my father could fish it out. I can recite Shakespeare and Byron for hours running, and I'll rage at anyone who presumes to point out the botched lines.

I'm Angus Alaric Farrow, nineteen years old, but I insist on being addressed as Gus. I'll only tolerate *Angus* from my beloved great-aunt, Margo, because Margo is the one who charges those syllables with an ineluctable affection.

I don't need to look to know that there's a girl beside me, plucking the silvery seeds from a stalk of grass, and I don't need to search for her name. Her before *her* proliferated, before it scattered into uncounted faces. Her, when what I knew of *her* had a singular slant to it, like the afternoon light of late autumn. Honey-colored hair, a white apron over her brown serge dress, because the Bildsteins are working people, unlike the Farrows. Catherine aspires to higher things, she studies her Greek and Latin by candlelight, but those efforts are a terrible waste of her real talents.

Catherine.

I've loved her since we were both children. It doesn't matter that we were both children a very, very long time ago now. I look at her long neck bent over a fresh stalk, one she's twirling between her fingers to make the seeds shimmy and click, and I love her still.

Still. Going on two centuries, is it now? Why won't she look at me? Why does she find those seeds with all their unadorned potential so mesmerizing? How can something that just *is,* that doesn't require the intervention of my talents, enchant her so?

"I want to show you something," I say, tweaking the stalk from between her fingers. She flicks me an irritated glance, but I press on, glad to have her attention at any price. I cradle the seed-tuft in my palm, willing it to open a view of the miraculous city. Seeds by their nature are susceptible to surprises, and it takes only a little coaxing to redirect that impulse until what sprouts is not a seedling, but a wisp of *away.* I open my hand, hold up the stalk. "Look closely!" Catherine hesitates and then angles toward the dancing scintillation, now clearly far too brilliant to be the product of dull mud and drizzle.

Each of those dangling silver seeds has become a minute mirror, but as they jostle in the breeze we can both see that they don't reflect our faces, the mill, the willows. Instead the image, broken into tiny glints and only reassembled by the seeds' movements, is of a woman unnaturally beautiful, with skin like liquid bronze and her head covered in close-set coppery feathers instead of hair. She doesn't appear to see us, but her lips curl in a private smile, as if she felt herself observed and found our spying amusing. A lady of Nautilus isn't caught off guard as easily as all that.

I wait for Catherine's wonderment.

I wait for her to love the one who can bring such otherworldly splendor to our drab environs, where an evening at the piano counts as a notable pleasure. Catherine has always loved my playing, but I hear the desolation lurking in each note. We live in the emptiness of the everyday, but I can bring her more than that.

Catherine slaps away my hand and the stalk goes flying. "I can't bear any more of your sorceries, Gus. Why, I hoped for a moment that you meant to show me something *true*, some particularity of the species, perhaps! Haven't I told both you and Darius a hundred times that I have no use for your nonsense?"

"I wanted to give you a glimpse of *rarer* truths! Catherine, I'm a citizen of Nautilus now; I became one a week ago. Once you come with me, once you see it—"

"Once *I* see it? Shouldn't you turn your efforts to training up Miss Diantha Sprague as a sorceress so that she can live there with you?"

I shake my head brusquely. "That's nothing. *She's* nothing."

"Nothing? Aren't you still engaged? Gus—"

"Of *course* it's a sham engagement! How could you believe for one moment that I would marry Miss Sprague, when I'm already married to you? And even if I did go through with it, a legal marriage is chaff compared to a spiritual one."

Her eyes flash alarm, but only for a moment. Then her mouth sets in cold fury.

We can share an endless life in moon-pale halls, wearing bodies sculpted from living fire. A life made *true* by magic. In time the people here will seem to us like so much ambulatory clay, lacking the animation of the beyond—if we bother to return here at all.

"There was no marriage of any kind between us, as you know very well. I could hardly have been more explicit in my refusal. As for Mrs. Hobson, you yourself called her a charlatan."

How can I make her understand? The busy twinkling of the enchanted stalk plays on like clustered embers where Catherine knocked it onto the bank. Sometimes the sparkle dims, then stirs again with renewed vitality.

"Charlatan or not, the bond she named was real, and unbreakable. Catherine, let me show you! What I mean to give you is beyond the reach of queens."

"And supposedly precious to me for that reason? Well, then, the life I have now is beyond their reach as well. The freedom to study, to roam, to seek solitude when I want it—what queen could hope for such happiness?" She hesitates. "Gus, there is something I must tell you. Thomas Skelley asked me to marry him on our trip to see Blondin. And I accepted."

The words touch my ears like wind. A roar devoid of sense.

"I hoped you would be happy for me, as I was delighted for you when I heard of Miss Sprague. Now I find that you persist in clinging to your old misconceptions. Well, it's time to dispel them for good. There's nothing between us but our former friendship, and there never will be. We have no future, Gus. Only a rather sorry past."

For the first time today, she turns her face fully toward me. Heart-shaped, with a long nose, and lips as pale as apple blossom, and a knowing, sardonic look.

A refusal to accept the world's terms, a certain brisk clarity—that's it, that's what I'm made to find. I've seen it before. Catherine's face stutters and I see Geneva, looking at me with an expression nearly the same.

"No," I say once I have my breath again. Thomas Skelley? I can't entertain the idea of him as a rival. It's as if Catherine told me that she is engaged to a shed hair or a tuft of lint.

"No?"

"No. I won't allow it. You must go to Mr. Skelley directly and tell him you misspoke. You belong to me. You *are* me."

Catherine's brows arch in disbelief. *I know that look too! Geneva, that river I saw, the flooding hair and watchful, spinning eyes: it flowed straight into you.*

"And why would I act in a manner so contrary to my interest and inclination?"

"You don't see your own interest!" A blast of words like raindrops carried by a driving wind. "You think you know your inclination, and that you are the best reader of your heart, but you are thoroughly mistaken! Catherine, I have not loved you all my life only to fail now to understand you, even where you can't! You have always been mine. I will not renounce my claim."

Catherine is already standing. "I came today out of regard for our childhood friendship, Gus. I did not come so that you could inform me of my sentiments or direct my actions. I wish you well."

It cannot be permitted. Catherine can be truly herself only in the glow of my love.

I have her by the ankles, and I yank her legs out from under her. She falls with an indignant *huff,* and for an instant it feels like a game, a joyful tussle like the ones we engaged in as children. I throw myself on top of her and pin her shoulders to the bank, half expecting to find her laughing and all her mutinous plans forgotten.

Darius always insisted that you were stronger than me, I hear my old self think. *But the real strength is mine, claiming yours, taking it in. He'll see what I am now!*

Catherine screams at me full force and her nails pierce my wrists. I must make her understand that by the laws of nature, her nature and mine, she must belong to me and to no other. It comes to me that I have never kissed her; I've been too diffident, believing that there would be time and kisses enough.

I've heard this scream before. It's the same voice that shook in my ears as I plummeted toward that shining city. Catherine's scream has been sustained across decades, rising to meet my fall.

All I long to say to her, everything in my heart that seems to soar above the reach of language, I must convey to her through the medium of my lips. I force her head back with one hand and swallow her scream with my mouth.

Catherine ceases to claw at my wrists—and instead tries to savage my eyes. I shut my lids tight, and her nails prod and pry at them.

I press my hands on her throat, if only to weaken her back into her senses.

It does nothing of the kind. I kiss her harder, deeper, as if I could gnaw out of her everything that stands in our way: her disdain, her resistance, her failure to love me as she should. And at the same time my hands bear down on her throat. When she shudders, when her fingers droop against my cheeks, I tell myself that at last she feels the persuasion of my love.

At what point does it occur to me that Catherine has stopped moving entirely?

The river beside us halts its flow and the birds stay pinned like specimens to the sky. Nothing moves but me. I shake and slap and shriek at her, but my voice can't stir the air into sound. If Catherine is dead, nothing else should have the impudence to go on living.

But it does. By the time I recognize that I need to flee—and not to anywhere on this vacant earth, no, but to *there,* where I can study and perfect my new art—the birds are gabbling callously again, and the river is splashing.

And once I reach Nautilus—oh!

Catherine has come with me, but in a way so unlike all my dreams. She treats me to a constant dinning of unlove, of refusal. What happened long ago must be undone. It falls to you, my wandering son and wandering self, to find her spirit in another. To prove our marriage true.

Magic means nothing if it can't give me the only thing I've ever truly wanted. It means nothing if the only thing it can't command is another heart.

Carry my kiss to her. Let it be the test. If yours fails like the rest, there will be another, and another, until either death or love is enough to prove me right.

Then I'm caught in a helical gale, moody blue, and the glowing city waits at the bottom like the pupil of a stormy eye. I'm falling again, and the wind beats with her scream.

Catherine the Dead

Hello, Angus, my abhorred one, my baleful companion. I see you've arrived on a certain riverbank, beside a certain watermill; I see you've met *old friends* there. My face has risen clearly inside your mind: no mere flash, but an undeniable person. To you that face must seem novel, an epiphany, even if it carries a disagreeable stink of déjà vu.

But you don't yet understand that I have never left you. Not for one moment of all your myriad lives. While you ate, vomited, wandered, murdered, I was there, unnoticed but intimate, my watchful death infusing your every wretched rebirth.

You will understand soon enough.

I could not eliminate my consciousness completely, though I assure you I tried. My first swoon had been deeper, and it had excluded reality far more effectively. Perhaps in my decades of vigilance I had lost the knack.

No; the best I could manage was a sort of twilight fog, and the abnegation of all responsibility and all will of my own. I still felt the regular torture of Asterion's umbrastring, for example, though I tried to sink away from it into my own shadows. When Gus went to reclaim the final beamer child from Margo I sagged limp and indifferent above him, mesmerized by my own flicker, and did not watch the agony on her face. My scream went on, of course, but it was now as insensate, as uncaring, as the shriek of tearing metal. Did Margo suffer? Well, she was hardly alone in that respect.

And when Gus crafted the first adult beamer—a youth of nineteen, as he had been when he murdered me—and endowed it with a real, substantial body made of Flynn's reassembled cells, I saw it stand and run fingers through its hair. I saw it dimly, as when dream and reality mingle and every image is indeterminate, uncertain in its provenance, a figment of the threshold. Why, I even seemed to see momentarily through its eyes, to feel that silky hair parting around its fingers, to sway with its uncertain balance! How odd that was, but not odd enough to muster my awareness. And then I rolled over, figuratively speaking, and went back to sleep, or tried. Also figuratively speaking.

I was oblivious enough that I can only report much of what occurred next by inference. I imagine, for example, that Asterion grew increasingly sullen when he and Gus met to drain me, but I did not actually observe his shifting moods. I imagine Sky came, wheedling for a chance to maul me. Margo, too—she must have waited for the next iteration of her child-Angus, at first with casual bitterness, since Gus had brought her the creatures as reliably as clockwork. She must have grown puzzled when enough of Nautilus's hazy time had passed, wondering what was taking so long—for I imagine, as well, that Gus did not favor her with an explanation or even a visit. She must at last have come to him, and learned that her loneliness was henceforth absolute. At least I assume so, for I did not rouse myself to hear her howling.

"Catherine," Gus said imperiously. "Catherine! Will you please have the bare courtesy to *look* at me when I address you?"

The words licked at my careful unawareness. But since I am reporting them, you can gather that I could not blot them out as utterly as I wished. I did not gratify him with a look, at least; by this time I had the trick of quite literally directing my gaze inward. In that endless blinking, phosphor pale, soot dark, I rolled like a bottle on the sea.

"This is important," Gus announced. "Pay close attention! There is one more task I must complete before this young Angus is ready to go out into the world and stake his claim there. I've already imprinted him with the feeling of you, the scent of your mind, and with the inexorable desire to seek it out. Wherever he is, he'll track down the girl whose character most nearly matches yours. The only question is, will that girl redeem you? Will she repair your mistakes that damned us both?"

I am dead, I told the black and white waves of my inmost self. *The dead owe nothing to the living.*

"You might think you no longer have any choice in the matter. That it is too late for you to undo the past, to love me as you were always meant to do. On the contrary! You have a choice through *her,* whoever she is. Do you see, Catherine? Do you see my mercy? I'm giving you another chance, even after everything you've done to hurt me!"

Gus was pacing; I did not look, but I felt the rhythm of his footsteps jarring through me.

"Oh, Catherine," he said after a lull, and his voice was so soft that I nearly slipped away again. "When you spurned me, it was like a rent in the fabric of the world. All that should have been *right* turned wrong, ruined. All this time, and still I cannot understand how you could do such a thing. All this time and it still makes me weep. Will you not look? See, see the tears coursing down my face!"

I would not, as it happened. But for all my assumed obliviousness the maudlin seep of his voice felt like some foul liquid wicking through my clothes.

"Perhaps you are too jaded now to care," Gus groused. "Your substitute will be fresh, with a fresh heart. It falls to her to undo the past and heal the damaged world. A solemn responsibility, and a great one." He paused again. "I've made something. Something very precious, very beautiful. Here it is; another moment, and I will install it in young Angus. Will you not look?"

Quite against my will, my drowsing awareness tipped toward the object in Gus's upraised hand. My gaze tumbled out of its flashing fog. Just for an instant I saw it: a delicate, shell-pink thing some two inches long, frilled and involute and gelatinous. It put me in mind of the medusas Gus and I had gazed on so very long ago in the colored plates of his father's book.

I hastened to roll my gaze back into my own interior. All I wanted was to fall under my own spell, to see and hear nothing and to care even less.

But I had seen it. The impression of that pink object came with me, something like a sunspot emblazoned on your retinae after you close your eyes. Its image stuck fast, a ghost within a ghost.

It is in me still.

"It's a kiss," Gus explained.

The dead owe nothing to the living. That is the sole, the only prerogative of death: to owe nothing, feel nothing. No matter the atrocities visited on the living, they are not my concern.

Of course, most of the dead *cannot* care. I understand that now, though at the time I refused the knowledge even as it lingered inside me. I expect many other dead would envy me this: that I still can. Love, outrage, fury: to feel such things is an immense privilege, and yet I cast them away like garbage.

Since no one but you, my tragic and terrible reader, will ever see these pages, there is no point in begging for forgiveness. Yours is no use to me.

"I've invested a very great deal in this kiss, both labor and talens. I needed to make it worthy of you, you see. Worthy of your memory, and the memory of that single kiss we shared. I flatter myself that I've succeeded."

He waited in vain for my approval.

"It's magic, of course. When the Angus locates your approximation, your spiritual daughter if you will, he will woo her. Then kiss her. He will bestow *this* kiss. It's the only one he has."

I tried to kill him. I failed. What else remains?

"All she has to do, then, is to love him! Love him *truly*, mind. Love him with the same deep and ardent and consuming love I felt for you, every day of your life. And beyond. If she does, the peace of her love will save us both."

And if she does not?

I did not want to ask that question. I tried to erase the words even as I thought them. In any case, I knew the answer.

"If she loves him—something so simple, so natural, so necessary!—*if* she loves him, all will be well. I'll never make another beamer again, then. You see, Catherine? I am not a monster. I only seek to heal the past. To stanch the wound *you* made, repair *your* harms! If she loves him, the kiss will know it. It's only in the event that the girl fails—well. It's a curse as well as a kiss, if it has to be. Let's hope it doesn't come to that."

If she doesn't love him, the kiss will kill her.

I provided that answer despite my best efforts at ignorance.

And she won't. If she is indeed anything like me, loving you and your creations will be no part of her. This is nothing but wanton destruction. A display meant to prove that there's nothing you can't waste, not even human lives.

"You are a part of me," Gus explained. "You *can't* reject me, any more than my right leg can cast off the rest of my body. If magic can't fix such a profound mistake, then—then magic is just as stupid as you always said it was, that's all, and I've given my life for nothing. I won't stand for it."

Gus crouched. And once again the impulse to see, to know, to feel—to *live,* if I may be so bold—got the better of me. I looked in time to see Gus pressing the rippled pink object against the lips of what appeared to be a sleeping youth. This early beamer still looked roughly like Gus, blond and sharp-featured, but much more handsome and at least three inches taller.

The kiss disappeared, insinuating itself under the skin.

And I, oh! I flung myself away from the sight, plunged into the deepest oblivion that would have me. Here it was at last, the moment of crisis I had dreaded so long. Gus was ready to murder those girls who would not submit in my stead. The weapon he'd labored so long to perfect, a weapon in a boy's shape, was now fit for deployment. And rather than exerting myself to stop him, I lolled in my internal lightshow like a fine lady who stays in bed and claims to be indisposed.

Viola, forgive me. Justine, forgive me. Pearl, Judith, Megan, Reiko, Crystal, Eleanor, Lucy, Claire, Breanna, Miracle, Sasha, Jeanette, Lorca, others whose names I cannot now recall: forgive me. Or don't.

I pretended I owed nothing to the living. So now that you are also dead, you certainly owe nothing to me.

Catherine in the Branches

Mrs. Farrow had meant to injure me; instead she won me the happiest year of my short life, a tender sanctuary in time. It was only two months before I was allowed to resume my studies with the Skelleys, but over a year before Gus returned to haunt me. Oh, he tried to corner me now and then, but I told him that I could not put my father's employment at risk, and walked away, and thought that was the end of it. It was sad, of course, but our friendship was over, and there were reasons that might be for the best.

It was December 1855 when Gus put an end to that ending. Anna and my brothers were at school, and I was alone in the house with pale winter sunlight draped across my knees. I was engaged in a questionable effort to mend torn shirts and memorize irregular Greek verbs at the same time. Every *didomi* sent my stitches askew, and I was looking back on my work disgruntled—for I had no inclination to do it over—when something hissed behind me. A hectic glow licked up the wall where nothing but shadows should have been. The light was by the stove, as if a flame had escaped, and my first thought was that some carelessness of mine was about to burn down our house. I spun to look.

There was indeed an escaped flame balanced on the iron, but its shape was strange.

Another instant and I knew it for one of the fiery pollywogs that Darius had once sent to harass me. It balanced on its tail and grinned at me, and this time the face it bore was Darius's own.

"If it isn't the Object herself," the thing mused in a thin and hissing echo of Darius's voice. "The stars in his eyes, where elsewise the nights tend to be murky and damp. Don't give yourself too much credit, eh? The fit is in the thrower, not in the floor he pummels with his fists."

I stood, surprised at my own composure. "You know, your tricks aren't nearly as impressive the second time. You aren't welcome in this house, Darius."

"Is that so? The friend of your friend is your enemy, little Catherine? Here I've come to give you a message from him, so you could at least invite me to sit down. Oh, the ache in these old knees!" By the leer on the blazing face, I knew this for a joke.

My hands settled on my hips. The words *it's all your fault* spun like smoke behind my teeth—but what did I have to blame him for, exactly?

Instead I said, "I don't believe you're Gus's friend either. But if you have a message, tell it."

From the delighted way Darius's mimic bobbed, it seemed that my hostility pleased him, if anything. Shadows like violet snakes pulsed on the walls.

"The Farrows are having a party tonight, and Gus doesn't want you to miss it. He asked me to tell you how very important it is to him that you make an appearance. Round about ten, if you don't mind."

How absurd could Gus be? "Please remind him that I wasn't invited."

"Windows are for the looking-through, aren't they? How tall and broad the Farrows like their windows, and how brightly lit they'll be! Especially at about ten o'clock, as I mentioned."

I started at this, as I was meant to. Icy suspicion sluiced through my mind—had Darius tempted Gus into some vicious retaliation against his parents?

"Gus wouldn't hurt anyone," I protested, but my voice was unsteady, and my chest felt hollow and resonant, humming with alarm. "No matter how you mislead him, he would never go so far wrong as that!"

A ghost must learn to savor the bitterness of such ironies, for bitterness is the only taste available. If death can become my life, can bitter not be my sweet?

"Come and see for yourself what he'll do," Darius suggested through the bent lips of his serpent. It shriveled and fell in a brushstroke of ash, and I was left staring.

Disturbing as I found this summons, there was no question I would heed it. A full moon reflected on fresh snow as I slipped along; the top of a barn rested on the treetops, a recumbent giant. Ten o'clock found me perched several feet up in a dogwood, peering out. The view my tree offered was less than ideal; I was rather far from the house, and at an angle which allowed me to watch only that end of the drawing room where the piano stood. I dared go no closer; light streaked across the shimmering ground. But as Darius had mentioned, the leaded windows soared up nearly to the high ceiling, and I could see flushed faces pitching on waves of laughter and the white trickle of pearls at Mrs. Farrow's throat. So she was out of her bed at last; I was relieved to see it. Behind her stood the grandfather clock, seeping time so slowly that I wanted to shake it.

And I could see Gus, primly upright next to Margo on a small settee with his hands folded in his lap. It might have been only my imagination—I was too far away to see him in any detail—but I thought his smile had an unwholesome twist to it. Gus was waiting. For what?

Two minutes after ten, his mother laid her hand on his arm and spoke a few words to the company. I could see the false graciousness warping her face as her son bent to whisper in Margo's ear. Did Margo blanch? I couldn't be sure.

Then Gus stood, obedient as dough. He seated himself on the piano bench, smoothed his coat. His movement landed like a raindrop in a puddle, driving the guests into a circle around him. I regretted that I was too far away to catch any sound but the wind. Gus's playing was the loveliest, the most exalting music I had ever heard, and I'd missed hearing him.

His fingers landed on the keys. So lightly. Something in his posture spoke of malice, poised and delicate and sure of its imminent satisfaction. I could not hear his first notes, but they communicated to me nonetheless through the rapt stillness of the assembled guests. I knew at once that Gus had never played so well.

I thought a golden brushstroke followed his fingers like music made visible. How it shone!

The gold spread up from the keys, a smooth unscrolling, a lucid shimmer. Once it sheeted across the top of the piano it stroked up the wallpaper behind, cresting and curling. A moment's bafflement, and I knew it was no poetic fancy I was seeing.

It was fire, but fire of a very unnatural aspect. It was too silky, too even, too billowing, draping like veils of light from the ceiling. And if the music was inaudible, that was not true of the screams.

Someone tried and failed to open the French doors, then lifted a chair and flung it through; glass sang, shrieks doubled in volume. And Gus sat quite untroubled at his piano, his fingers dancing with the flames.

Issuing them, in fact. I grasped that as another sweep of the chair cleared glassy fangs from the doorframe and people spilled out onto the adjacent patio and then over the stone balustrade, toppling and rolling in the snow. But they hardly looked like people, for every one of them was sheathed in liquid fire, a tight-fitting luminosity that followed them like a second skin no matter how they thrashed. If it hadn't been for how they shoved one another to reach that shattered opening, how they clawed and convulsed, they might have been taken for angels. A young woman set off running through the night with hair like a comet and her dress become a bright ringing bell.

The whole drawing room, now, was a golden box, and Gus sat like the jewel it housed. His fingers pounded out some crescendo and his mouth bent in a smug and secret smile. I could hardly comprehend it—Gus was essentially good, I felt certain, and surely incapable of such viciousness. But the screams leapt higher, tearing at the night. Only the lash of his mother's fire-coated pearls let me recognize her. She hit the balustrade and flopped over, landing on the ground with her legs comically akimbo.

A man more decent than the rest helped Margo through the broken panes, and I saw that she alone was free of fire. Her violet-gray dress appeared untouched, her silver hair unsinged; even her lace shawl remained a pristine moonlight gray.

The fire, I realized, made no sound at all. There was no crackle, no roar, only human cries and now the faint strains of Gus's music. It did not touch any other part of the house, nor stretch and leap in the manner of an ordinary conflagration. Heat buffeted me, but its touch was somehow—thin?

Gus broke off, shaking with laughter. And all the flames vanished at once.

The well-dressed people tussling on the snowy lawn turned instantly from falling angels into so many stranded fish, the ladies' legs kicking in disordered skirts, the men's hats trampled, all of them with hair unraveled and faces smeared with desperate tears. There was an awkward interval before they were sufficiently calm to notice that their flesh was whole and unhurt, that not the faintest scorch besmirched their clothing. The drawing room as well stood luminous, serene, with cordial glasses still twinkling on its tables. The only signs of what had happened were the broken door, the diamantine scatter of broken glass.

Gus climbed out through the gap and sat on a stone bench, looking over his work with satisfaction. Then his gaze lifted, scanning the night, and I knew he was searching for me. I clung to my branch with both hands, perfectly still, and finally felt how blood drummed through my whole body, a captive thing begging for escape. I willed myself to be part of the darkness, an invisible wisp, a dropped seed whose blossoms ten thousand years hence would be formed of deepest shadow. I tried to shape myself out of absence, to be the cold space where a girl had once been.

A girl so dim, so frozen and so vacant could never be the intended audience for an exhibition like the one Gus had made. No one would bring her such fiery offerings, and no one would expect her to be awed by them.

I tried to negate myself, but I failed. The dogwood trembled with my dismay, and I was still myself, hands hot on cold bark, beads of muscle sliding in my clenched jaw, and eyes made of a darkness that was not empty at all.

Then fresh cries volleyed out. People were clustering around Gertrude Farrow, and I realized she alone hadn't gotten up.

It wasn't much of a fall, only perhaps six feet. But there had been a conjunction of unlucky angle and ill-placed stone.

A moment's confusion, and Dr. Lewis boomed above the clamor, quite distinctly. "She's broken her spine!"

Angus in Nautilus

When I told Lore I wanted to leave town, this wasn't exactly what I had in mind. I'm lying in a slick, shining gully that spirals into towers against a dusky sky—not in Kansas anymore and all that, though something that looks sort of like a permanent tornado hovers high overhead. I might not know what I am anymore—or actually I might know too much—but I have a good idea of *where*.

I'm in the moonglow city. In Nautilus.

I've never been to Kansas—not as far as I know, anyway—but now I can't avoid recognizing that I've been here. Lots of times, in lots of lives. It's too much to say it's all coming back to me, maybe, but there's a wobbling of familiarity as I drag myself upright and look around. There's a dude who'd be perfectly ordinary—bald spot, pink polo shirt, freaking *khakis*—if he didn't have a pelican's beak jutting out of his face. On a bench, humming absently to himself. He barely glances at me, like a gasping, sobbing mess of a boy doesn't rate anyone's attention here.

A piano with golden fur snuffles its way around the corner, then stops to paw at the ground. A memory rises, and with a lot more solidity and conviction than I'm used to. When I was little Margo used to hire a piano just like that so I could practice!

Margo. Shit.

Because, of course.

Because, hell in a handbasket, the howling damned nicely arranged with fresh fruit and some colored cellophane and delivered with a bow on top, *of course*.

There's a reason my memories of Margo feel so different from everything else in my head—why Geneva thought they sounded so preposterous. I was remembering being with Margo *here*. Maybe I visited on weekends while I was growing up? The first time I got a candied baby dragon, for example—it's so clear to me now! It was a delicate, exquisite thing: a snippet of emerald fire with green lace wings, twisting through the crystallized sugar. Margo told me then that sometimes dragons lay huge clusters of eggs up in the rafters of candy factories—tiny, glittery eggs, like bubbles of blown sugar. They like the warmth. But some of the hatchlings aren't that good at flying, and they tumble into the bubbling cauldrons below. I cried and cried, and Margo didn't have a lot of sympathy because candy like that cost extra. In the end I ate it anyway, and fragments of wing got stuck between my teeth.

The baby dragon flares into my mind, prismatic, brittle. But now it has Geneva's face.

Maybe some of my memories aren't a hundred percent trustworthy—but Margo? She has to be real, right? And she has to love me, even if nobody else does.

She's here, I just know it. Somewhere. If anyone can help me make sense of this mess, won't it be her? But how am I supposed to find her? I don't know my way around at all.

Except that I do. The city's map lingers deep inside me, an ice-white burn at the back of my retinae. I start walking, and recognition curves around me, a soft push that says *this fountain, this stationary cloud-thing with the café chairs on top; wait, aren't the slums behind that dome?*

When I find Margo's hut it's made of the same paralytic mist as everything else. Peering into it I can dimly see the shape of an old woman's body in a chair. She looks like a bug embedded in luminous ice. It impresses on me the awkwardness of my being here. The Anguses I fell through on the way here kept changing their faces, so she might not even recognize me. I mean, unless my voice is enough, because we talk on the phone all the time?

She sits up higher in her chair with an abrupt shrugging movement. She's tense, waiting, and her head pivots my way. She sees me, too, so unless I want to look like a coward it's too late for me to bolt.

Of course there's no bell, and knocking feels stupid. No doorknob either. Just a plane of cold translucence framed by a lintel and doorposts beautifully carved with sinuous grooves, as if they'd been sculpted for centuries by a gritty, groping wind. Maybe you just push it open?

I raise a hand to the door. *Open* isn't the word for what it does, but I can feel it recognizing me, somehow. When I step forward it doesn't feel like entering the room.

It's more like the room enters me. Cold whiteness pours around and through me, shifts me into place inside it. There's an abrupt reordering of space, until everything settles and I'm looking down at a very, very old woman with pale gray eyes fixed on me and thin, crusted, purplish lips nested in dusty wrinkles. She doesn't seem surprised, only maybe vaguely irritated—she must think I'm a stranger. A few white strands stripe her mottled pink scalp, and her clothes are colorless and wasted-looking, their fabric thinned with age. A shiny locket hangs from her neck, gold speckled with minuscule blue flowers. She smells pretty bad. Does she look like the Margo in my head, or does my head shuffle its memories to accommodate what I'm seeing? Familiarity and strangeness strobe through me at the sight of her, and it hits me: it's the first time a memory from my pre-warehouse life has smacked up against reality.

Margo. She's a person! I'm not completely disconnected from every-one except a random actress who's made a hobby out of murdering me!

The air has a shrilly humming undertone to it, something like the faint shriek of electricity racing through wires, though of course they wouldn't bother with powerlines here. Margo's weary gray eyes narrow and she hangs her head, like even looking at me is too much trouble.

"Angus again, aren't you? He's outdone himself this time. Prettied you up until you shine like pure poison, as if that was ever going to win *her* over! She was never searching for some bright bauble of a boy, and she won't be now. Even if it cost her her life, I dare say Catherine made the right choice. Dead is better than a life with you."

Catherine Blinks

I've referred before to the Era of the Children. A new era now began in your life and my undeath respectively: the Era of the Murders. Despite my best efforts, consciousness sometimes intruded on me and I saw one promising young woman after another fall to you—

Never mind. I must focus on what I can save, not on what was lost.

The Era of the Murders meant that we began spending much of our time in the unworld. Gus wanted to watch his beamers as closely as he could. How else could he monitor your performance? The magic required to observe the various *yous* all the way from Nautilus was too expensive to allow for more than an occasional glimpse; it was far cheaper to dog your steps. You see, Angus, your own creator never trusted you, never really believed in your loyalty or competence. I hope the realization rankles.

Even the wild winds, the dews and roses of the unworld were no longer sufficient incentive to lure me back to awareness. But I felt such things dimly nonetheless, soft stir and ruffling scents. I knew our days in the unworld meant Gus was aging, and I found in that fact another excuse for inaction: perhaps, though I did nothing, he would simply die in time and so put an end to the nightmare.

Oh, how could I have been so craven?

Both my willful somnolence and our restless shadowing of the beamers obscured the change that had occurred in me. Yes, in me, most changeless of beings! For the first ten or so beamers the new sensation was only a distant nagging, an unexplained aching and doubling that I was at pains *not* to explain. Sometimes you would catch a girl's face between your hands and she would rise in my vision as if she stood mere inches away, even though Gus spied from a vantage a dozen yards distant. Sometimes I felt your composite flesh around me, its pressures and its appetites, even as I went on flapping in my weary way above Gus's head. I did not consider what it meant, and yet I must have known— stubbornly though I disavowed my own knowledge.

It was harder to ignore what was happening when Gus was back in Nautilus.

Permit me to gloss over an unworld decade or so of my shame and negligence. What good does it do to dwell on those awful years, when by my own choice I observed so little and have correspondingly little to tell? Anguses were dispatched, one after the other, and girls were killed, and ugh, even now I retreat into the passive voice as if in that way I could escape from my own cowardice—

Onward. For the hour came when someone roused me again and made me sensible of my responsibilities. Of all my regrets this is the keenest: that I found my dearest one when my life was already gone, when I could give her nothing in exchange for the wonders she gave me. What good to anyone is a ghost's love, however ardent?

Gus was in Nautilus, fast asleep. Your incarnation at the time was asleep as well, thoroughly drunk, beside Vauxhall Bridge in London. How can I know such a thing, you might ask, since by necessity I must have been with Gus, and therefore far away from you?

I was with Gus. But not all of me. A broken-off fragment, an outlier of myself, was distantly aware of lamp-smeared darkness of a depth that never occurs in luminous Nautilus. Of smoky air and faded moonlight cavorting on a river.

Of two people standing over the beamer's defenseless form. That was what finally drew me from my swoon: I became aware, as in a dream, of those looming figures. It was nothing to me if they meant to disembowel you, understand. I did not even bother to desire such a thing, though I did not then understand you could not be killed in such a manner. You would only come back wearing a new face and figure, but with your essence unchanged; and if your current target was spared, the next girl would not be. I was simply curious. Who were these people, and why were they watching you?

In the next moment self-awareness caught up with me. I could no longer deny that I was now in two places at once, flapping and screaming above Gus but also in you. And in you I was perfectly silent and secret, a residue of mind that neither you nor Gus had detected.

I did not have time to examine the realization before the pair crouched down close to you. There was enough moonlight to define one figure as graceful and feminine, the other as a burly male. They did not look like cutthroats, which disappointed me somewhat—so I suppose I'd hoped that they would gut you after all.

"If it's so asleep," a lilting soprano voice asked, "then why are its eyes open?"

I had never heard that voice before. But there was something familiar in it anyway, a sardonic drawl at odds with its mellifluous tones. All at once I knew.

And in my delighted astonishment, I *blinked*.

I blinked with your eyelids, Angus; I watched the river, the two silhou-etted figures, vanish and then flare into being again; and I understood that I had moved a physical body, albeit only a tiny part of one. But: I had com-manded flesh! Muscles, however minuscule, had contracted in response to my will!

An eyeblink no doubt seems negligible to you, hardly cause for rapture. But, please recall, it was my first incarnate movement in a century. I could not have been more amazed if some enormous fortress had teetered at the flick of a fingertip, or if the moon had answered my summons and come galloping down the sky.

I launched into a frenzied flapping of your eyelids until they sputtered like startled quail.

"Is it malfunctioning?" a man's voice asked. A soft voice, its timbre best described as cinnabar. "To think of the wealth he must have poured into this creature, thousands upon thousands of talens, and it still can't sleep convincingly."

"Thousands of talens that weren't even his, or not for the most part," the lady replied sharply; and oddly, her observation startled me. How many thousands, indeed? I had long ago lost count; was it a hundred thousand by now? More? Light limned her pale hair until she looked like a cloud passing the moon, crowned in fugitive brilliance. "Flesh that wasn't his, ripped apart by a power that wasn't his. I don't for one mo-ment accept that its blinking is a malfunction."

"If you believe all the gossip," the gentleman—and here I must humbly apologize for the term, but at that moment I mistakenly believed the speaker was one—rejoined, in fondly reproachful tones. "Sky and Asterion aren't what I would call reliable witnesses."

Oh, the luxury of blood and nerves, the surge of one, the urges of the other! I was too much distracted by the ecstasy of gesture to wonder what use I might make of my discovery.

"I have more to go on than the word of those scoundrels, as you know. Or we wouldn't be here," the lady—allow me to apologize for this misnomer as well—replied. "And even if I'm not exactly a font of magic, that doesn't mean I'm deficient when it comes to *theory*. Well, we can check right now. Catherine, are you in there?"

I strained, at this, to borrow your voice and speak. But that proved beyond my capacity and I managed only a faint croak. To this day, I have never succeeded at producing oral language.

"Blink once for yes, and twice for no," Anura instructed—for oh, it was indeed she, my cherished one, my wild amphibious heart! Anura had come to me in her human shape, long since rejected, but assumed this night for my sake. There is no gratitude, no love adequate to meet the simple fact of her existence.

It took some effort to compose myself, to stop the manic battering of your lids. But after a struggle—I was very much out of practice with this business of embodiment—I managed to calm your eyes. To pause.

And then I replied to her with a single, emphatic shuttering. When I opened your eyes again the light that flooded me was not of the ordinary kind. After decades of loneliness the brilliance of *communication* is enough to outshine any sun, on any world.

Anura stooped and swiftly embraced you, since that was the only way she could embrace me. I don't doubt it was unpleasant for her, but she did it. She knew quite well of what you were made. She let go very quickly and sat back on her heels. How I longed to rise and fling arms around her in return, even if those arms were not mine!

"I thought you must be!" She hesitated. "I suppose I should have asked your permission before I touched you, and whether you even—I can't expect it. Do you recognize me?"

I blinked once, of course, but inwardly I howled, *Don't dare to ask me such a thing! Ask rather if I love you, if I revere you. Ask if your poem has sung in my head ten million times. Ask if the memory of your kindness has been my sustenance through these endless decades. Ask—*

I could no longer deny the depths of my love for Anura. But the fact that I had no proper body of my own—it let me gloss over the precise nature of that love. What could it matter?

"I'm glad you know me in this unworld rag! Can't stand the thing, but wearing it was a necessary evil if I meant to find you." It was too dark to make out her face, but I heard her smile. It was something of a surprise to find her so animated with me, when she had always been so snide and laconic in her exchanges with Gus—though of course she'd made no secret of her dislike for him. "I thought, if a thousand talens stolen from you was enough to let you speak a few words to me, then the absolute fortune he's drained and dumped into this *doll* ought to do more than that. And then, if the rumors are true, you were forced to disintegrate the original body." She paused, but her silence roiled with disgust. "Is it true?"

In my shame I wanted desperately to deny it. To bat your lids twice and drive the truth from me. But I could not lie to her.

I blinked once, heavily. The burly gentleman let out a horrified gasp. I had not yet recognized him, or rather *her,* but that gasp informed me that his appearance might be deceiving. There was something distinctly feminine in the sound of it.

"Anura," he said—and oh, Laudine, if you ever chance to see these pages, I humbly beg your pardon for my mistake!—"excuse me for doubting you. Everything you hypothesized is borne out. You were right."

"I had to be!" Anura said, not without pride. "Using Catherine's mental energies to break a living body apart—it's the stupidest thing I've ever heard of a sorcerer trying, that's all. Of course her patterns were bound to imprint on the neurons as they passed through her! And then on *top* of that, using her power in the reassembly—what did he expect? Gus Farrow is an arrogant bungler, that's all."

Alas, my new powers did not extend to laughing. But I could blink once in warm agreement.

They both saw me do it, and they burst out laughing for me. In my long century of ghosthood I had never taken so much vicarious pleasure in anyone's glee before.

After they'd roared and cackled to their satisfaction, Anura wiped her eyes and produced a small electric lantern. In the wash of its light, the two figures flared up like candle flames against the darkness. The supposed man was dark, with thick black hair and a golden brown skin that I, with no real justification, associated with Palestine. The hair was worn long, the features of the face rather broad and coarse. But it was immediately apparent to me that the face and body were tragically inapt, a terrible fit for the graceful spirit within. Every nuance of stance and gesture expressed the purest elegance.

And Anura? She was a vision in gold and blue, all possible conventions of angelic loveliness on blazing display. Eyes like a summer sky, hair like sunlight flashing on a river, rosebud lips, pearly skin. Perhaps twenty-five years old. Patience Stott, I remembered Asterion had called her—and instantly I rejected the name as a hideous imposition.

I suppose it was only because I'd known her in Nautilus, in her rightful shape, that I recoiled at her human beauty. That exquisite person was simply wrong for her, ill-fitting for a spirit that took no refuge in *smoothness*.

"Well?" Anura said, rather bitterly. "Do you prefer me like this?"

I blinked twice, as firmly as I could. *No.*

Relief washed through her face, which meant—thank all things holy, from paramecia to planets!—that my preferences mattered to her! She had feared, even, that I would admire facile prettiness over the fiercer beauty that belongs to truth. Dear Anura, how could I?

I remembered her words to me, so long ago: *I am well aware of what* recognition *can be worth.* Had I thought she was speaking of her poetry?

"This is Madame Laudine; you met her once before." Oh! The man's body became transparent as a veil to me, and I saw through it to the bright lady of fountains. Anura's expression tightened again; her eyes narrowed defensively. "Do you understand why we leave Nautilus as seldom as possible?"

I blinked once. *Yes.* Indeed, there was an abrupt reversal in my head, as the long-hated city seemed to roll and reveal new colors. It was a prison for me, but a haven for one I cherished. I could not reconcile these opposed aspects of the place. For the time, I simply endured an anguishing muddle of contradictions.

"So you'll believe me when I say that I never would have followed you here if I didn't have a compelling reason." She took a deep breath, abruptly serious. "Catherine Bildstein, I owe you both an apology and a very great debt."

What? I blinked twice, paused, sincerely bewildered. Blinked twice again, vehemently. *No. No! I assure you, the debt is all mine.*

Of course, I could not explicitly convey any more than the bare and unadorned *no*. But Anura seemed to understand me at least to some extent, and she held up a hand to forestall any further objections.

"I do, and I mean to pay it all. Only once that is done, and with interest, will I be so bold as to ask you to forgive me." She stopped, her breathing labored; it was clear that she had rehearsed this speech, probably many times. But now she found that it stuck in her throat. "You must suspect my motive for acting as I did. When Gus Farrow came to me with his bribe, I was nearly broke. I'm a middling sorceress, never up to more than a talen or so a day, and my salary—" She grimaced, and something of the Anura I knew before bent that flawless face. "It's a pitiful excuse, isn't it? Without that bribe, I would have been forced to give up the body I wear in Nautilus—not permanently, but for what seemed to me a longer time than I could endure. I do realize, naturally, that many people would not see this particular *humanskin* as a terrible burden. All I can tell you is that it is to me."

I blinked once. I had indeed divined these basic facts of the case, even at the time; her frog's shape was plainly expensive to maintain and beyond the means of a petty bureaucrat, or indeed of a fine poet. As for the burden of her beauty, well, I had been murdered over charms far inferior to hers.

"But I knew the talens he paid me must have been stolen from you! Even before you spoke in my mind, I *knew* that! The rumors about Gus Farrow's ghost had been flying thick and fast ever since he'd arrived in Nautilus, and I knew that he'd fallen under Asterion's influence. There was no explanation for how he'd raised that sum so quickly, unless you were the source. Catherine, *please*. You must not spare me your anger!

I knew what they were doing to you, and yet I bought my own peace at the price of your suffering. It's vile, inexcusable! And then, *then,* as I was in the midst of drinking down your ravished magic—oh. That was the moment when you spoke of your *gratitude* to me!"

She rushed through these words in a passion, tears coursing down her face. I hadn't considered the matter in this light before, nor did I wish to do so, ever. But now that she was weeping in front of me, I could see how she might have arrived at this frenzied self-reproach. The extremely long lives enjoyed by Nautilusers allow them ample time to brood. Was it possible that I had lived in Anura's imagination as she had lived in mine?

My feelings grew in such wild excess of anything a *yes* or *no* could hope to capture that I entirely forgot myself. I forgot that I was dead, a whisper installed in a carcass. I forgot everything that I *could not* do, and, all unthinking, I tried to catch her hand so that I could press it to my heart.

Of course, the only resident organ of that description was not mine at all. Nor even yours, properly speaking.

Madame Laudine let out a cry. "Anura, the right hand! It's moving!"

It was, I realized; your right hand was creeping sluggishly over the stones, grasping and releasing. Anura reared back. Perhaps she misunderstood me once again, for I thought she looked frightened. But Madame Laudine's face fired with delight.

"Could you try to hold a pen?" she asked me.

A pen! I did not suppose I could control such an implement, but even to touch one again would be an acute pleasure. *Yes,* I blinked.

One was produced. To my own amazement, I managed to enclose the pen, nib down, in your fist, and keep it fairly steady atop a scrap of paper. After a quick conference, Madame Laudine moved around you and lifted your head onto her knees, in order that I might see whatever marks I made. I'm sure it was a disgusting service for her, and I thank her for her generosity in performing it.

Luckily for all of us, you'd drunk yourself into a drooling stupor— some of your iterations take after Gus in that respect—and you remained insensible throughout the various adjustments we made to your position. I know now that it was owing to your profound unconsciousness that I was able to commandeer your body even to the small extent I did. My skills, of course, are somewhat improved by now.

And then, when everything was in readiness, I froze. After all, I had not formed words in any medium since those few borne into Anura on the flood of my appropriated magic, so long ago. I was afraid of failure; afraid that, if I *did* shape words, they would be too effusive, or too reserved, or in some other manner offensive; afraid that, even if I expressed myself perfectly, I might nonetheless find my audience short of sympathy. If all the thrills of communication leapt up in me at once, all the perils and anxieties attendant on self-exposure toppled down on me at the same instant.

"Catherine," Anura said—and oh, her proud voice broke! "Whatever you have to say—whatever reproaches you have for me—I'm prepared to hear them. It took me too long, and I'm sorry for that. It was very hard to find you, I swear it! But I'm here now, and I'm ready."

I could not bear to hear her speak so, and her pain drove your hand into movement.

I thanked you then, I scrawled. The letters were large, lumpy, barely legible. Each one seemed to cost me the labor required to shift a boulder. But they were letters for all that, and they made words. *I thank you now. Anura, you have been my only friend.*

A stillness came over the pair of them as they studied my message. Then Anura let out a small sob and covered her face.

"No longer," Madame Laudine said in tones soft but decisive. "Catherine Bildstein, will you accept my friendship as well?"

If I am fully truthful, I must confess a momentary reluctance to answer Laudine's kind offer. She was an enchanting lady and a marvelous artist, and her graces only made me more jealous of her evident closeness with Anura. They were plainly the dearest of friends, and I wondered if they had been, or were still, something more than that. But I could not be so churlish as to decline.

I had not yet confronted the full implications of my feelings—that I had fallen hopelessly in love with another female, and moreover with a frog. But if I avoided inspecting those feelings too closely, I nonetheless surrendered to them. I knew, I did not deny to myself, that I loved *Anura*.

In any body, any sex, and any world. And here was her best friend, welcoming me into their communion.

I blinked *yes*; it took far less effort than writing. Then after a moment's thought, I forced your hand into motion again. *With great pleasure. Your fountain is the loveliest thing in Nautilus.*

Laudine tipped sideways to read my words, and laughed with startled pleasure at the compliment. I suppose no one expects art criticism from a ghost.

"Thank you! There are many, though, scattered around the city. Which one do you mean?"

Avian.

"That's my favorite too," Anura said, emerging from behind her hands. "Though there's another where the water enacts the myth of Artemis and Actaeon that you should really see. And there's a small one in my room that Laudine gave me as a gift, a frog pond. Even the dragonflies are sculpted from living water."

How quickly the casual warmth of an ordinary conversation among friends had reasserted itself! To me, of course, there was nothing either casual or ordinary about it. Anura's words were meant for me, and that gave each of them a lapidary sparkle and sharpness: rare gifts, held up to the light. I was painfully aware that *I* would have no opportunity to give Anura presents, but then, she was unlikely to expect any from me.

"Catherine, listen," Anura pursued, with a fresh intensity that marked a change of subject. "There's something I don't know if you understand—though I tried to tell you once." That could only refer to her poem, its deeper meaning so long concealed from me; I felt a rush and whirl of anticipation. "I *have* to believe you don't understand, really, because if you do—if you're allowing this, *living* with this and doing nothing to stop it—"

Living with anything was not in the cards for me, of course. Anura seemed to realize the awkwardness of her phrasing and stopped, embarrassed and, I realized, anxious. What on earth was disturbing her so?

"They say Gus Farrow has been pulling ten, even twelve talens out of you for every unworld day," Madame Laudine said briskly. Her manner seemed very different, too, now that she wasn't playing a malicious coquette for men she despised; it was the frankness, the freshness I'd suspected must be between her and Anura, only now I was included in it. "Is it true?"

One blink. Where was this tending? Laudine nodded in acknowledgment.

"He pours most of the take into his beamers, but not all of it. He's made some good investments with the rest, and he's getting rich."

I hadn't known that Gus was exploiting me over and above the sums needed for his loathsome work. In my self-imposed exile from myself, my cultivated unawareness, I had paid no attention. I should have known better than to feel hurt by this information, but it landed a slap nonetheless.

"They say, too, that Old Darius very much wanted you as an apprentice, and you rejected him and insisted magic didn't interest you. They say he kept hoping he'd snag you in the end, and he never really forgave Gus for killing you and spoiling his plans."

Yes, I blinked again, though in fact I had certain knowledge only of her first statement. What Darius had hoped, what he had forgiven or not: those matters were opaque to me.

"Have you put those things together?" Anura asked. Tentatively, as if she were afraid to find me guilty of something terrible. "The talens, Darius. That's what we need to know. Do you understand what it means?"

I wasn't sure what she was implying. I blinked twice. *No.*

Madame Laudine released a plosive breath. Anura squeezed her eyes briefly shut, as if in relief.

"Then—the things Gus Farrow has been doing with these beamers of his—you'll swear it's without your consent?" Laudine asked, and I heard in my new friend a new and dismaying sharpness.

The murders.

What, did they think I approved? That I colluded with my own killer out of some generalized spite toward the living? How could they hold me in any way responsible, when it took all my efforts to shift your hand a few degrees? I tried to scribble an urgent reply but the paper was too crowded, and I had to wait while Anura turned it over.

I hate him and all his doings. I have no power to prevent—and here I found it hard to go on—*the killings.*

At once I found the fault in my claim. I'd made not the smallest attempt to stop Gus's murders; I'd done nothing but waft away from my duty, feckless as a summer breeze. I'd told myself I was helpless, that I could change nothing. But I hadn't imagined that I could blink or write, either, and within the space of half an hour I'd done both! A power untried isn't the same thing as a power nonexistent.

Anger, disappointment flushed Anura's delicate face a heated scarlet—and it was anger at *me*. I saw at once how readily the ferocious judgment she'd turned on herself might pivot and find a different target. And I could not face the knowledge that I deserved her fury; I would do anything to rate her esteem—

"Really? What makes you so sure you can't? Twelve talens in a day! I doubt Mariam herself did better than that when she was starting out! A mind that strong in death would have been just as powerful living. You could have been a very great sorceress, Catherine, that's what you must understand."

Mariam had been deposed some time previously by an entity called The Going in a great, city-rippling upheaval, but Anura's point struck home for all that. She was wringing her mallard skirt, her eyes darting, and I thought that she was again doubtful whether her impulsive anger of a moment before was justified. Once I came to know Anura better, I learned that she was often indecisive, even wavering, as she weighed every aspect of a problem. When her mind was at last made up, though, its conclusions were remorseless.

"It's not about *could have been*," Laudine interrupted. "It's about the present. You still have your thoughts, and that's all any of us require to work magic. The fact that you've gone on producing so much—what Anura means to say—"

How I envied the familiar way they tripped over each other's speeches, the intimacy of their overlapping exclamations, even their glancing annoyance with each other!

"What *I* mean to say," Anura snapped, and her rosebud mouth flattened very froggishly, "is that the power Gus Farrow is stealing from you is *yours*. For good or ill, you cannot disown it."

Catherine the Savior

It was the day after Christmas—which had not been terribly festive that year, given the dread that shadowed everyone in the period following the witch-fire and Gertrude Farrow's injury. Word came that she was paralyzed below the chest, but no one besides Gus and me—and of course Darius—knew where to place the blame. The town's speculations were as restless as wind. And if I did know, had I not wished Gus's mother ill myself, and very nearly acted on that wish? In my thoughts I reviled him, excused him, accused him again, until I had no room to think of anything else—in which I suppose he'd achieved his purpose.

Then I stepped out of our house, and found a wood thrush having a fit.

The poor little bird was dragging itself in a circle, wings outspread, so that a pale blurred wheel marked the snow where it turned. But how it looked at me! It was not the driven wildness of a hurt creature. Instead it registered me with a spasm as I bent over it; it seemed to name me with its eyes in a very human way.

"I'm waiting by the bridge," the bird said. I recognized Gus's voice, only layered under the thrush's crystalline vibrato. "Catherine, come as soon as you can!"

With that, to my immense relief, the bird bounced up, shook off the magical fit with visible impatience, and preened its spotted belly. Then it flew away.

And I? I thought, of course, of simply not going. To answer Gus's appeal would involve me in his crime. Wasn't it enough if I simply kept silence?

Then I thought that perhaps my private rage at Gertrude Farrow had made me complicit already in some obscure way—in which case it would be cowardly to avoid the confrontation. I pulled on my cloak and went.

"Thank God," Gus said as he stepped out from behind a stand of spruce. The snow's surface had melted and refrozen into mirror-bright ice, and even his pale face looked dark against it. "Darius isn't around, and I had to cobble together the magic by myself. I didn't know if it would work."

"How can you even think of using magic again?" I demanded. My own heat rose in reaction to his awful calm; I wanted to see him boiling with grief and repentance. "After what your magic has done? How can you not—spit on Darius, tell him you'll have nothing to do with him and his vile arts ever again?"

Gus gawked at me, nonplussed. "What choice do I have! Catherine, there's a *city*." Gus imbued that last word with longing so intense that it arced through the icy air as if it drew a line to an impossible horizon. "I know I've told you before, but I suppose you didn't believe me when I was only reporting what Darius said? Well, I've seen it for myself now, and it's splendid beyond dreams. It's *made* of magic, and it belongs to every sorcerer in the whole world! I could qualify for citizenship already, but I want—the two of us should be admitted together, at the same moment. I know you don't like Darius, but you only have to learn a bit!"

I hadn't realized until that moment how wide the gulf between us had grown during our separation. If we'd had our differences before, we'd always understood each other. Now we stared in mutual bafflement.

"What makes you think I'd have the least interest in going to a place like that? Your mother is *paralyzed* because of your magic, Gus. Even if I hadn't already abhorred magic, I promise I would now!"

A strained silence fell. "My mother falsely accused you of stealing," Gus said. All the excitement was gone from his voice; it was low and dangerous. He stepped closer to me, and I tensed but did not move. "She forced us apart. Even after all that, I only meant to frighten her. To teach her a lesson. But maybe my magic knew better than I did what she *really* deserved."

His pale green eyes held a light like that of the ice under the spruce trees, where gleams bit through the tinted shadows. At last I took a step back and felt the ice bend under my foot: at first elastic, then bursting with a soprano cry.

"Gus," I said, with panicked reasonableness. "What you're saying is monstrous."

"What else would I be?" Gus rejoined. "Without you?"

I turned to run. Gus lunged to catch me, then thought better of it.

"There's nothing for you here!" Gus shouted after me. "And you'll *be* nothing, if you stay here! Why can't you see that?"

I didn't answer. I was on the bridge, and its planks were so slippery that I could only skid and mince across. Chunks of ice thudded and jostled in the river below me, vertiginous, demanding. Gus stood by the bridgehead; my difficulty crossing gave him time to aim his parting shots.

"Do you really want to spend your life being only what *they* think you are? What my *mother* thinks you are? Stay here, and you will be! They're all so small and petty, and they'll reduce you down to their own scale! In Nautilus you would be a queen!"

I slid the last three yards and sank my feet into the snow again, where I could pick up speed. Everything Gus was saying would have inspired sick terror in me, if it had not been for my education with the Skelleys. My world might have been small, but I lived in an immensity of ideas then, of stories, of all those dreams concealed in the minute structures of everyday reality.

Gus surely didn't understand what inured me to his barbs, but seeing how I did not slow he was canny enough to reconsider. When he called again I could barely make out his voice over the rumble of the ice-laden current.

"It never would have happened," Gus yelled, "if you hadn't abandoned me!"

That accusation landed like a physical thing—like a blow to the backs of my knees, so that I faltered and almost fell. I had known the threat Darius posed to everything that was good in Gus, I thought, and like a bad and disloyal friend I had left him to Darius's influence anyway.

At the time ending our friendship had seemed a necessity; I could not endanger my father's job, after all. Now that past choice felt slippery and dishonest, an evasion of responsibility returning to me in shapes of ghastly consequence.

Gertrude Farrow was paralyzed, and Gus was too corrupted to care, and perhaps it was my fault. How I wanted to run to Reverend Skelley, confess everything, and beg for his advice! But if I did, it would only add betrayal to my litany of sins.

I kept silence. I wept and brooded and was unsurprised when, three days later, a letter for me arrived on scented lilac paper. Anna handed it to me, her mouth tight with worry. I knew at once who'd sent it, felt how its light balance on my hand clapped a heavy inevitability in the pit of my stomach.

"Don't," Anna whispered. "Catherine, don't, *don't*. Whatever she wants from you—"

I turned my back on her and tore open the seal. Oh, Anna, I should have listened to you! Odd though you were, child though you were, you understood so clearly!

Gus told me everything, Margo Farrow wrote. *No one can save him now but you.*

Please recall that I was then still very young.

Angus and Margo

Before I've figured out a comeback, Margo's thin lips twist. "You thought you were the first, didn't you? You always do. Fifth Angus who's come bumbling in here, I'll have you know. Gus embedded the key to this room in you a hundred-odd of your lives ago, and somehow he's never remembered to take it back out. Go on, then. Tell yourself that your intrusion puts you in the cream of Anguses! Tell yourself you're *almost real*."

She laughs, and it isn't a nice laugh. She laughs at *me*.

I'd sort of gathered that my, like, ontological status might be a teeny bit different from other people's. But for her to imply I'm not real at all, when I'm standing right in front of her—what can it even mean?

"Margo?" *You know it's me, right?* I want to say. *I mean, it's the Angus you love. Not just any—*

"Don't blame me if you're mistaking me for that bitch Gus jabbed into your head. Being *Margo* is my territory, and I'm prepared to defend it against Gus's twittering fantasy auntie until my bones fall out."

Everything she's said is still sinking in. Maybe I halfway guessed, but it seems important to clarify.

"So I've never actually talked to you before? *This* me, I mean? We haven't chatted on the phone? Your voice hasn't come squirming out even when I thought we were disconnected, or—"

"Don't be ridiculous. That thing you've been talking to is nothing but a disembodied stream of prattle. Once Gus got too old to risk visiting the unworld anymore, he had to find ways to keep you in line if you tried to get smart. So he took the idea of me and made it into a chaperone for you. A little something to encourage you to be your worst self. Say what you will about me, I'm quite real, and I don't care to be confused with some vile interject."

Okay.

"I don't know who Gus is," I say. "Not really? I mean I—fell into him, or felt him around me." I stop, search through the rubble. "He called me his son? But I'm pretty sure I remember having different parents? Frank and Trudy. It's kind of impossible that I don't, right?" I try to laugh, but it doesn't sound great. "I mean, I couldn't have hatched from a barnacle the way *geese* do!"

She's staring. "In other words, you know even less than the other Anguses who've come to see me. Nothing at all, in fact. However did you make it back to Nautilus, when you're positively stewing in ignorance?"

"I fell," I say. "I mean, I was pushed."

She considers that. "By whom?"

"Um." Margo wouldn't know her, would she? "Her name is Lore."

"They could have done me the courtesy of informing me, if they're up to some new scheme or other," Margo mutters, and twitches hard enough to make her locket jump. Her immobility in that chair is starting to seem a little weird, almost like her wrists are glued to the armrests. "But I suppose they didn't want to waste the talens on a message. Why care what old Margo thinks?"

Maybe I'm slow on the uptake, but in fairness there's been a lot to process. Like the idea that I might actually murder Geneva—no. I can't think about that now.

"They?" I say after a pause. "I think Lore's killed me before—different versions of me? But she didn't kill me this time, so maybe she's decided I'm worth saving? But there's no *they*. It's not like Lore is colluding with someone to destroy me!"

Margo smiles. There's a sly curl to the lights in her gray eyes. As much as to say, *Actually, it's a lot like that.*

"Lore must be awfully bored of killing you, the way she's been going about it—it's like mopping a floor while someone in dirty boots keeps tramping across. One of you kicks it, and Gus simply grinds out the next! I expect they're looking for a more permanent solution. But since they don't deign to tell me what they're up to, I can't guess how they hope to achieve that."

Gus. *Gus* grinds out the next. I'm so busy watching Frank-and-Trudy vaporize in my head that I can't focus on the rest of what she's saying. Not at first. Really, I never had a normal human childhood at all? I try to call up that sweet memory of ice skating with my sister Sylvie, and I see myself standing alone on the rink clasping a single red mitten with no tiny hand inside it. Snow-fronds curl around me and the other skaters spin by like toys.

"Don't fret too much," Margo says. "I'm sure they'll fail. Gus will keep churning out his vicious wastrels, keep killing his girls, wondering all the while that it doesn't bring him more satisfaction. All I ask is to be well out of it." She pauses. "I don't suppose you'd care to help?"

"You're really saying this Gus guy—that he made me?" The iron clunk in my head feels hard enough to snap my spine.

"Catching on at last, are you?" Her nose wrinkles.

"So I'd murder Geneva?"

"Is that what you call her? Mind, he'd deny it. At wearisome length and volume. He'd say it's so you'll win her love, that the killing is merely—collateral. But who'd believe that malarkey?"

Maybe everything I've ever known is fraying into horror. But hey, at least Margo's warming up to me! My mind lurches toward the new confidence in her tone, anticipating my head on her lap and her hands stroking my hair.

"Is that why Lore sent me back here? So I'd learn what the deal is? She knows I'm nothing like Gus, and if I just understood what was going on, then there's no way he could make me kill anyone!"

Does it mean I can never kiss Geneva? Ever? That seems pretty harsh, actually.

"He won't have to," Margo observes, a little snidely. "Now, about that favor I mentioned?"

I shake my head. Still sorting out too much stuff. So every childhood I ever had was with Margo, and my most disorienting impressions are the only ones I can rely on?

"Margo? There's this one memory I have of tiny soldiers in armor bursting out of an anthill. Do you remember that, too?"

"How funny to hear you mention that!" Margo laughs, and now she sounds—the way I want her to sound. Maybe I'm getting ahead of myself, but I'm picturing a future where Gus's curse is broken, and I'm with Geneva, and we bring happiness back into Margo's life. You know, somehow. I'm hazy on the specifics. "I was thinking of that incident just before you came here. We'd gone to a park and you were playing cheerfully enough—my little Angus of the moment was, that is—when all at once you started up screaming dreadfully!

"I ran to see what the matter was, and found you in a state. At first I thought you'd contracted some terrible rash, but no! Your little face was bright with gore, pricked all over by tiny swords as the battle raged around and over you. The grass was beaded with crimson.

"You started yelling at me, 'Margo, I hate them! I hate them all!' Farther from the anthill the grass sparkled with soldiers running for their lives, their armor reflecting the light as they scattered over the ground. It made them easy to spot. You started leaping after the ones who were fleeing from the carnage, picking them up and ripping off their legs in a frenzy. And the whole time you were crying. Your face was a mess of tears and blood.

"I don't know how many you butchered before I was able to calm you, but I do recall that you had nightmares for weeks afterward. You were such a temperamental child!"

Wait. What is she saying? I jerk back and gawk up at her, and she smiles down benignly.

"That's not what happened!" I gag a little, smelling the blood again. Seeing the ruby smears on my own childish hands. "Margo, I covered the anthill so they *wouldn't* kill each other! I never would have—"

"Ripped them apart? Oh, only the ones who wanted to live. The ones who'd decided to rescue themselves from the senseless cruelty of their kind. Those, you left writhing limbless in the dust. I had to stamp on the poor things, to put them out of their misery. You see, my dear boy? You were always a killer. And I, I was the fool who loved you for far too long. But even a fool learns in time."

The indulgent tone is gone, turned rough as rusted iron. It was all a setup. I scramble to my feet, but Margo stays as still as a statue.

"You're lying. I tried to save them!"

"The ones who wanted to die? Yes, you did your best, and just as passionately. Because what mattered to you was imposing your will on them, one way or the other. Whatever they determined for themselves, you'd shove yourself in and inflict the opposite outcome if you could. And when you couldn't, your rage was a sight to see!" Her ribbon-thin lip ripples up over her gapped teeth. "You do show a definite consistency now you've grown. You make me live on in agony, no matter how I clamor for release. And the girls who *want* to live, who fight the way your Catherine once did to live on their own terms—well.

"We know what you do about them, don't we?"

None of it is true, right? She's saying these things to torment me, to get back at Gus, because she can't understand I'm not him.

"*Gus* does that stuff. Even Lore said—I have a will of my own, and I'm not limited to pretending! So just because Gus made me, it doesn't mean I'm anything like him!"

"Prove it. Do what he won't." The light here oozes over everything, pale and forgetful, but even it can't forget the look in her eyes. "Kill me."

So that's it. She's trying to goad me into murder, hurt me until I'll destroy my own innocence just to shut her up. Hell, *she's* the one who's just like Gus.

Something in me stops moving, stops reaching to understand and persuade and connect. When you hit absolute zero not a single molecule can stir, and that's how it feels inside me: I'm too cold to care anymore.

But Margo hasn't stopped.

"*Nothing changes here,* you told me long ago. *Nothing decays.* Why, even the cancer that gnarls my stomach like an old root has stayed the same, all these years, and the pain of it is just as bad as it was when I lay on the brink of death in my own bed. Ah, if only I'd never loved you in the first place, you wouldn't have regarded me as useful, would you? But you made me the guardian of all your cherished horrors, bound me to them as if they were mine and not yours. Love was my undoing, and for that I'll hate love itself, even once I can't muster the strength to hate you."

Nothing changes here? "But you looked after little kid Anguses here. Well, kids change and grow."

She laughs. Horribly. "Just like you can change and grow, is that it? Those children were formed as children, not born as infants, and they hadn't grown a whit when they died—or, to be more accurate, when they were finished. At first I was reckless enough to love them as if they were *real* children, but I learned that the price for affection was too high. They were just beamers, you see, not designed to live in the sense humans do. They were made to shine for their allotted term, and then *go out*."

I don't get it at first, because I can't. It's too awful.

Now think of the end of the movie. That was what Julian said.

The end. When the beam vanishes into darkness. Carmen knew the truth—God, *Lore* knew—and nobody told me.

"How long?" I hear myself breathe out the question before I can stop it, because do I really want to know? "Until I go out?"

"You're set in motion for a year, assuming nothing destroys you first, and then you'll be recalled to him. Ground down to the raw materials for his next effort."

A year. Not even, because I've already used up some of it.

A *year.* It's all I'm made for. While real people get more life than they know what to do with. They get such an extravagant surplus of life that they blow half of it bickering, or whining about their jobs, or getting *bored.* Do they even deserve to keep lives that they just turn into shit?

"You look distraught," Margo observes. "Why not express those disagreeable emotions by murdering me? You'll feel greatly relieved, dear boy, when the bearer of bad tidings slumps into corpsehood."

One of the few definite things I used to know about myself was that I loved my old aunt Margo, and she loved me. Scratch that.

I look down at her now and my heart burns, rivulets of negative flame glowing black-bright in its cracks. When it comes to knowing who I am, it looks like I have to start over fresh, but at least I have some new facts to work with. *I am Angus Farrow, and I hate my aunt enough to condemn her to endless torment.*

"Why don't you kill yourself?" I say. I can't recognize my voice at all. It sounds charred, vicious, and terribly old.

"Well, dear, I would. If only I could lift a hand, perhaps while holding a knife. You see, Gus immobilized me as a punishment the last time I tried to escape. A certain lady had arranged to ease my way, but regrettably it turned out Gus had bribed the local doormen to report any such attempts to him, just in case. Oh, I could *smell* the hot pavement of Cairo, I was that close! Well. Prove that you can change, then, even if nothing else here can. Kill me."

Pale gray eyes, pale gray loathing, wrapped in ash-white wrinkles. How many little Anguses did she let herself love and then grieve over, before she swept all of us into the same indiscriminate heap of abhorred things? I never stood a chance.

"Yeah, no," I tell her. "Not you."

Catherine Divided

Anura and Madame Laudine left with many promises that we would soon meet again, and I, of course, remained where I was, staring through borrowed eyes at a dawn-smudged sky. My vow, so long dormant, was now in a state of such excitement that the leaden weight of your limbs oppressed me. I wanted to haul you upright and send your purloined flesh dashing straight into the Thames. It took an hour of frustrated twitching—for that was all I could manage—before I calmed enough to realize that I must be methodical, not impulsive.

I must study my new abilities, practice them and expand them where I could. Rather than exhausting myself with unobtainable desires—to run again, to jump, to embrace!—I must teach myself to desire what I could have. I could blink and move your fingers, that was established. Shifting small parts, lifting slight burdens: there was enough of me inside you to accomplish that much. But however hard I tried I could not raise your torso and make you sit up, nor heave one of your legs into the air. Even your right hand would only float up an inch or so above the ground before its mass overwhelmed me.

A ghost must learn to make do, that's all.

Of course, it was only an offshoot of me that was busy with these exercises. The lion's share of myself remained in Nautilus, screaming monotonously over Gus's head. All of me, though, was equally awake, kicking and flaring with eagerness to work Gus's undoing. I watched with great interest as Gus rose and burrowed in his heaps of musty clothes for something halfway presentable. I observed for the first time that his room was very much larger than it had been, the sort of airy space allotted to Nautilus's affluent citizens, though still dirty and dismally furnished. As he slipped through his wall and into the street, I loomed with a vulture's appetite.

When we arrived at the Nimble Fire, Asterion cocked his unwieldy head and gazed at me for longer than I liked. Firelight stroked along his curved horns as if whetting them to a cutting edge.

"Catherine's picking up steam again. Did something happen to work her up like that?"

His tone sagged with suspicion and his bovine lips rippled. Even after my long span of inattention, I guessed at once what was troubling him.

"Nothing out of the usual," Gus snipped back, and I thought he truly hadn't noticed any change in me. He had aged to a very satisfying degree, I thought, inspecting his creases and jowls. He looked to be nearing fifty. "Catherine has her little moods."

"Not in a long time, she hasn't. She's been tediously calm. This is the sort of activity I'd expect if, oh, you'd paid a visit to someone she particularly dislikes. Maybe performed some unpleasant operation on her." He paused, sullen. "You *know* she hasn't been the same since the last time you took her to Sky. I'd have thought that you'd know better than to risk it again!"

The story of Flynn's disintegration had spread widely, it seemed, reaching both Anura and Asterion. But whatever quarrels had erupted over Gus sneaking behind Asterion's back—maneuvers which had deprived the minotaur of a great wealth of talens—the pair had evidently reconciled. Barely.

(Meanwhile in London you were waking. You rolled into a ball and clutched your head. I found that with attention I could register the pain drumming in your temples, and I learned as well that your conscious will was enough to override my small ability to command your body. I would have to wait, then, until you were asleep. Now, after years of practice, I can also take advantage of moments when your mind is wandering. I can pick up your right hand where you've dropped it like a soiled tissue on a tabletop, as I am doing at this very moment. I can use that hand to write while you daydream, quite unaware of my presence. I can even tamper with your vision when you look down at the page, blur the letters, trip your focus, and send you reeling. *Not yet, my vile one,* I croon unheard beneath the churn of your thoughts. *You will read when I permit it.*)

"I haven't taken Catherine to Sky!" Gus exclaimed. He seemed easily irritated by the subject, as if it came up too often for his taste. "I told you, I can't guess the nature of his designs on her. But I know I don't like them."

"And if you did like them—if you thought of bargaining for an umbrastring of your own—you might recall who your *real* friends are, Gus. The ones who've looked out for you, who've kept your secrets close for so long! I like my friends to trust me, and I expect to be able to trust them. But sometimes someone disappoints me, and it's always such a blow."

Oh, of course. Their touching reconciliation was the sort greased by blackmail. Asterion knew quite enough to have Gus permanently exiled to the unworld, where he would age and die in the time-honored tradition of mortal men. But I could take no pleasure in the realization. If Asterion exposed Gus for paying a bribe, then with the same breath he would condemn Anura for taking it.

I could not allow that to happen.

"That's enough. I've kept my side of the bargain all this time. Surely you can keep yours, when you do so well by it."

Asterion's hand was already in his pocket, drawing out his specialized heartstring. Its hateful rain-colored prongs glistened, the very color of hunger. In the long span of my oblivion I had felt the pain of it, of course, but distantly. It needled, gnawed, subtracted from me, but its torment seemed to hang across a far-off horizon, like lightning seared at the edge of a dream. Now I must pay the price of my heightened attentiveness and feel my suffering close-up, as it were.

But no sooner did I pity myself for what was about to ensue, than I thought of the girls who had paid a higher price yet.

Asterion seemed in no hurry to pierce me with his toy, though. He let it dangle by its thread and watched the light play inside the prongs. I had never known him to care for such ephemeral beauties before: those prongs caught the light in moon-colored filaments, half-dissolved as if in puddles.

"How goes your beamer?" the minotaur asked at last, his gaze still sullenly averted. "As sturdy as the rest?"

Gus at once was placated, as so many men are when invited to take their hobbyhorse for a gallop. "The latest Angus? It's been in the field for nearly eleven months already, with no signs of degradation *I've* noticed. It should easily last the full year. That said, though, I consider this one much too lethargic when it comes to claiming its girl. She doesn't seem to love him, I admit, but only the kiss can put that to the test! I haven't invested so much in the Anguses only for them to turn qualmish on me!"

Qualmish, really? That was a possible development that interested me, but Asterion's concerns lay elsewhere.

"Independence of mind is always troublesome," the minotaur observed with a dismissive flick of his hand. "But their sheer durability! As far as I can ascertain, no one but you has ever made an embodied beamer that was good for more than a month or two at the outside. Their flesh starts to fray in the most unseemly manner—holes in the cheeks, tendons trailing. So what is it about your Anguses, Gus?"

Asterion's glance slid up at a sly angle that told me, as plainly as any confession, that someone was paying him to secure this information. Trade secrets are as valuable to sorcerers as they are to earthly artisans.

"Something to do with the way I rendered down the original," Gus replied absently. A very large snail had brought glasses and a decanter on its golden flat-topped shell and he was preoccupied. *The original.* So that was how he referred to Christopher Flynn, pulverized to his very cells in the storm of my being. However thoroughly I'd taught myself to despise Flynn, still I would not have denied him his name. "I really don't know. But it seems the materials acquired a certain valence by passing through Catherine as they did, and they've kept a residual charge ever since. It was a lucky accident, honestly."

He drank, and Asterion's globular eyes again rolled in my direction. Sky wasn't the only sorcerer in Nautilus who would like to make use of me, that was clear.

(You were afoot in the London streets, buying coffee and buns from a cart and then slumping on a stone by the river. Was Gus right in thinking that a creature like you could arrive at actual scruples? You certainly seemed very sullen. It occurred to me that my vantage relative to you was quite different from what I was used to with Gus: I was over his head, but I was inside yours! What liberties would our enforced proximity allow? And with that I began to listen for your thoughts. They sounded very faintly, like footsteps treading through a distant room. But the more I listened, the more I caught their vibrations.)

"How wonderful! I see how mistaken I was to oppose your ideas at the time." How quickly the old cow swerved from reproach to flattery! Consistency exceeded his reach as an actor. "Why haven't you tried letting one run on until it falls apart, just to see how far it can go?"

"No reason for it. If an Angus can't inspire devotion in a *year*, I have to assume it's defective. I'm better off recalling it and trying again." Gus knocked back the rest of his lilac liqueur and reached for the decanter. The snail made a sort of mooing sound.

"But how can we measure the true scope of your achievement unless you put it to the test?"

If Asterion meant to sell my unwilling services, it would of course be helpful to have a precise valuation of the goods. But Gus seemed deaf to the minotaur's subtext, which to me was louder than drums.

"That doesn't matter. What I've done already is a tremendous advance in the art, and that's enough for me. And a year is a generous lifespan, considering how little I demand of my Anguses. Fulfill their purpose, or don't, it's time for them to surrender the stuff they're made of. It should be more than enough time for their chosen girls to fall madly in love with them, if only they have the decency to do so! A chance to repair the past . . . And then I'm nearly out of patience with my current Angus as it is." He grimaced. "The girl sat on his *lap* three nights back. And he still withheld the strike!"

Asterion made sympathetic noises.

(In fact you were brooding on this precise event: the girl's soft weight on your knees, and how a cold dread wholly inexplicable to you had opposed her alluring warmth. *Why didn't I kiss her?* you thought. *Why?*

It was not scruple that troubled you, I discerned; you were ignorant both of your true nature and of what your kiss would do. It was fear. But you did not know what it was that quickened your heart.)

"If I remember correctly, it was you who told me that the Anguses must have freedom of thought to inspire love in their targets. A mere puppet would never beguile *her*, isn't that right?" Gus continued, a querulous note in his voice. "Well, it hasn't worked yet. All it's done is to make the dratted things unreliable."

How old he seemed, how bitter, a scarecrow stuffed with whining and recrimination!

"Oh, come, it's not as bad as all that! How many have you sent out now?"

"The present one is the twelfth."

"And how many of them have bestowed your kiss for you?"

"Eight." Gus peered up beneath a furrowed brow.

"That sounds like an excellent return on your investment, then. Surely you couldn't have expected that they would all succeed?"

"But that isn't the point! I have no wish to kill these young women, Asterion. How could I?" Asterion's flaccid mouth pursed skeptically. "The point is to find the one I won't *have* to kill. The one who earns her salvation with her love, and thereby redeems Catherine as well! Find her, *heal* Catherine's fault, and I'll never make a beamer again."

Asterion reclined in his chair with his arms propped wide and welcoming along its crescent back. He seemed to be ardently embracing nothingness, which of course was all he cherished. He put on a show of careful consideration.

"You might try a change of window dressing, then."

Gus twitched in his brocade chair. His fingers drummed. "Window dressing?"

How disingenuous, this question, for Gus must have known what the minotaur meant. Even the early Anguses were taller and broader-shouldered than my erstwhile friend, and their faces might have been termed a charitable interpretation of Gus's at nineteen. But in those days they were still recognizably Gus-like, sharp-featured with his prickling blond hair and pale green eyes.

"The crucial thing is that the *essence* of each Angus is identical to yours. Isn't that right? It might just be that these Catherine substitutes would prefer darker hair, or a—ladies are weak-minded creatures—a less challenging manner?"

Gus hunched his shoulders irritably. "If they can't love me as I am, I don't see how they can be worthy."

Asterion threw up his hands. "Oh, they can! They will! Only soften their approach. If I may allow myself a metaphor: if a Catherine finds the path too thorny, she won't come close enough to see the light in the windows."

"But a girl with so little fortitude is hardly a Catherine at all! She was determined, unflinching. No one ever truly understood me except—"

And here Gus broke off, his head bowed as if he walked through driving rain. For of course my *true understanding* of him had in no way compelled my love. Asterion took advantage of Gus's lowered gaze and smirked.

"Never mind," Gus said, rearing upright again. "It's a ridiculous idea, but then you didn't know her, not as she was when she lived. You can't be expected to understand."

"Oh, then I'm ridiculous once again! One gets used to it in time." How false, how venomous, was Asterion's merry tone! "Well, then. Shall we drain her?"

They did, of course, and crowed together at the results, their bickering forgotten. Apparently my production had been slightly depressed for quite some time, down to seven or eight talens a day. But now it showed signs of full recovery.

(And you? All at once you jolted out of your languor and pointed like a hunting dog. You were up on your feet, running through the crowded streets while a dirty mist scrolled through your hair. *She's there, she's there, Viola's there,* your thoughts pattered with the senseless persistence of a dog's claws ticking on parquet. *Her, her, her. This time I won't, I'll be sure to, no more hesitation! This time!* I could sense her, too, this girl who was supposedly a variation on my theme rather than, as I here propose, a free and complete individual with no reference to *me* whatsoever. The air drew taut and your breath became a shallow panting.

What could I do? It fell to me to discover *something,* some way to stop you. But I did not know how. Given time to prepare, perhaps I could send a letter warning her. But that would require an address, as well as hours I did not have.

And then, on the bank, Viola came into view. I knew her by the faltering of your steps, as if her profile excised a matching silhouette from your chest. She was very dark-skinned, her cheekbones cradling bluish highlights under wire-rimmed spectacles, with curly hair pulled back under her hat. Standing at an easel, her hand steady and confident. A few more steps, and I saw through your eyes that she was sketching in oils:

an elegant study of the clouds overhead. She was absorbed in capturing exactly their subtle tints of gray, puce, dun, with a bludgeoned lilac like a row of bruises angling to one side. Why had she been chosen as my surrogate? *A refusal to accept the world's terms,* Gus had said, *a certain brisk clarity.* No doubt those qualities were in evidence, but they did not bridge our fundamental difference.

She did not look up at your footsteps, did not seem to hear them. Instead she leaned close to her canvas, feathering a tiny touch of rose madder into slate gray.

I tried to catch your ankle from within, to trip you up and give her time to flee.

I failed. You pounced on her like a large and slobbering dog on its mistress, jarring the brush so that all her sensitive work was ruined by a dark pink streak.)

Gus by this time had regained his room, or rather rooms, for I saw that he now had a separate domed alcove for his bed. He commanded a towering mirror in the air and stared at me with such a furious air of accusation that I feared he might have learned somehow of my meeting with Anura and Madame Laudine.

"Is that it, Catherine?" Gus demanded at last. "Could you possibly be so shallow, so empty-hearted, that you turned against me over details of *appearance*? Were you seeking a different *manner,* when I was always a perfect gentleman to you as well as a most loyal friend?"

I never turned against him, at least not while I lived. Rather, I had turned *away,* and that was not at all the same thing. But my scream was not up to the task of disputing prepositions.

"What will it be, then?" Gus sneered. "Go on, tell me your preferences! You know I desire nothing more than to satisfy your every dainty whim. Soon enough it will be time to make a new Angus. It would be my pleasure to design him according to your specifications! Well?"

I wondered, as I so often had, exactly what he expected me to say. Surely he knew that murdering someone doesn't tend to enhance their conversation?

"I cannot for one moment credit that Thomas Skelley was a *choice.* He was nothing but a ploy, a means for you to evade your one great duty of loving me." Gus stamped to emphasize these words and smeared his tears with a dirty sleeve. "So what would you like? A dark and brooding poet? Could your tastes really be as vapid as that? Or possibly a starry-eyed mooncalf, all angelic curls and saccharine phrases? In what guise must I appear, before you see your way to loving me at last?" He was howling outright now, thoroughly discomposed, a trail of snot glistening on one cheek. "Tell me!"

(But even if I could have spoken, my interest was elsewhere. You were grappling with Viola, her wrists tight in your grip. It was early morning and people strolled nearby, but no one moved to help the ebony-skinned painter against her fair assailant. One man actually laughed. You used your greater weight to drive her back against a tree—her build was delicate, your strength, I perceived, magically augmented—and shoved your mouth against hers. And oh, I could feel, I could watch, but I could not *prevent*—)

Far away in Nautilus, Gus felt the power drain out of him and staggered against a wall.

"This one acquitted itself better than I expected, anyway," Gus muttered. "But his Catherine still didn't care for him! How many of you have to die before you'll give up your obstinacy? What will it take? Catherine, these are your daughters! Why won't you *reason* with them?"

(Viola's back was sliding down the tree's trunk. She looked dazed. Her madder-tipped brush was still in her hand as you stood over her, panting. You called her name once or twice, in a failing and cursory way. You merely performed your concern, for by then you knew that you had killed her. Her hand dropped and the brush stroked a rose smear across a root. Then you turned on your heels and ran.

Viola Wright. I did not even know her, nor her me. What can I say as her memorial?

Only that she was in no way a substitute for me, whatever Gus pretended. She was not my daughter, not in any sense of those words, though I would have been honored to consider her my friend. She was certainly not *a Catherine,* as Gus and Asterion were pleased to call her, but only and absolutely herself. What reference could she have to me, a stranger? Even if she had somehow imagined herself in love with Gus's creature, that love, too, would have been all hers, as remote from me and my heart as Cassiopeia; nor can I lay the slightest claim to her dying hatred of him. I have only my own, and the burden of my weary and singular self.

I cannot carry the brave, lost self that was Viola Wright's; she could not carry mine.

Do you understand me, Angus? Viola Wright was *not me*, any more than young Geneva is. You murdered her for nothing.)

Gus curled up, sobbing, as bloated with self-pity as a tick is with blood.

Angus Knowing

I know everything now. Everything, except for *who*. I'm running through the pearly wheeling of Nautilus, and there's no stopping until I know the answer.

Lore, for hiding what she knew from me.

An alley like the whisk of wings.

Lore, for making me know too much.

A woman with a fishbowl head, except that there's no glass holding the water. She watches me reel past her, raises an arm as if to ward me off.

Gus, for my grief every time I killed another her.

A tower dripping huge tears of nacre. The tears transform into slight, winged animals, maybe halfway between bats and goats, before they dip up and away. Fucking Pegasuses, more or less. See, Geneva?

Geneva, so I'll have my grief for her, even if I can't have anything else.

A pair of huge doors swinging open—they're the only normalish doors I've seen here. A vast hall dotted with clusters of couches and chairs, and at the far end a cavernous fireplace.

Gus, for making me in the first place.

There's an obvious problem with that one, even assuming I could pull it off. If Gus dies, who will make me next time? Suicidal I'm not, it turns out.

Geneva, for being human. For knowing at every step that the ground is waiting to catch her. For being native to earth, to sky, to love.

This is how Gus gets his way, isn't it? Embedded in me from the start is the sullen logic of death. Naive or knowing, that envy won't leave me, not in a thousand canceled lives.

Lore, for understanding exactly what I am.

A sky-blue sofa blocks my path. A wintry fraying shows above it, something like branches sugared with frost. The branches—scratch that, the *antlers*—emerge from a pewter head, hair and flesh indistinguishable, running together like mercury.

The head turns, the lips curve. I've seen that face before, skinned in humanity. I smack against the azure upholstery and teeter, gasping for breath.

She pats the seat next to her.

"Hello, Angus," Lore says. "You've learned something, I see. But have you finally learned enough?"

With those words, I know one more thing. Not my own answer to the question, maybe, but the answer Lore wants from me.

Catherine Bakes a Pie

Thomas opened the kitchen door at my knock, baffled and sheepish and positively white with flour. "My father's out visiting a sick parishioner. I don't know if you want to wait?"

It was late summer then, and I was sixteen, and Thomas was eighteen, and he had recently been accepted to Madison University. It wasn't so terribly far away, I told myself, over the unacknowledged whistling of my grief. He would still come home when he could. And we had him for a month longer, anyway. Flour drifted off his wildly waving hands, and I doubled up with laughter.

"All because Mrs. Richardson is visiting her daughter!" I said; Mrs. Richardson was their cook. "Oh, Thomas, what have you done now?"

If it had been anyone but me laughing at him, Thomas probably would have shrunk in on himself and vanished into another room. But the two of us had slowly achieved that playful familiarity which makes it very hard to give offense.

"It's the pie's fault!" Thomas said gamely. "It pounced on me like a wolf. Tried to tear my throat out! Of course I had to take *measures*."

I looked past him. A basket of blackberries sat on the table surrounded by scraps of dough. "I see you used a shotgun. Thank heavens you survived! Or do you think your wounds might prove mortal?"

"To my pride, anyway. If I had any, which I'm very glad to say I don't." Then, accusingly: "*You* know how to control those things. Pies. It seems impossible that anyone could, short of resorting to witchcraft."

"They're temperamental things," I agreed. "High-strung. They require a firm hand. Here, I'll show you."

We started over with new dough, and soon I was teaching him to flatten the lard into platelets with a whisking of fingers against thumb. "Like fish scales," he observed, fascinated. "*That* thin. That must be what makes the crust flake?"

"Exactly," I said. Something in his voice set me back on my heels. I straightened and looked at him. He was bent over the bowl with the same enraptured concentration he brought to his microscope, working the lard into the flour, and then I understood what I had found so startling. It wasn't merely that he was approaching this woman's task with an utter absence of condescension, though that would have been enough.

The look on his face—it was tenderness. This domestic labor was not too trivial to rate his deep attention, even his love. There was something in it that sparked an odd yearning in me. Something, even, that I wanted to learn.

"Catherine?" He'd realized I was watching him, and his old shyness rushed in between us again. "Did I do something wrong?"

"You're doing it perfectly," I told him. "Beautifully."

He smiled to himself, too self-conscious now to meet my eyes. By the time Reverend Skelley came home we had the pie in the oven, and the mess swept up, and Thomas was making tea. Reverend Skelley took in the scene—I realized I hadn't thought once of the impropriety of being alone with Thomas for so long—and his face lit up with a glow like sunlight piercing through deep water.

It was the look of a man who sees a long-guarded wish blooming into fulfillment.

With that I understood that the Reverend hadn't been candid with me, any more than Margo Farrow had—that his gift of education was not nearly as disinterested as he'd made it out to be. It was understandable, I knew, it was motivated by his protective love for his son, but it was still a betrayal. Did Reverend Skelley think I was good for nothing but securing male happiness, had he only pretended to believe in my potential for more than marriage? When he said he thought I could go to college, was that merely a *diversion*?

He saw me seeing, saw me recoil. Thomas was gazing back and forth between the two of us, baffled by this drama that had unfolded in silence while he was busy warming the teapot.

"I should go," I said, and stood. "It's too late for lessons today."

"Catherine," Reverend Skelley said. "Catherine, please let me explain!"

"Later," I snapped, with none of my usual fondness or respect. "Later!"

Then I was out the door of the new Universalist rectory; it was in the town's small center, and I bitterly missed the remoteness of the Skelleys' old house, the long walk that would have let me work off my ruined mood. I pivoted and ran up a side street that would fade soon into orchards and fields. The houses grew rapidly smaller, more shambling, until they seemed to shrink into the rustling grass like decomposing deer returning to the soil.

A pebble skittered behind me. Of course someone else might be going this way for reasons of their own, but the sound plucked me into a singing alertness. I could still go back to where passersby would offer some protection. A moment's hesitation, and I turned.

It was Gus, purple-faced, his hands clenched. We were still forbidden from seeing each other, and though Gertrude Farrow's melancholy was now too deep for her to bother much with enforcement, that ban kept our meetings few and furtive. But we were friends again, and I was constantly aware that I was charged with saving him—from Darius, and from everything he wanted most. With that in mind, I suppressed my irritation at this violation of my solitude. I made my best effort at a soul-reclaiming smile, though my talents did not lie in that direction.

"What were you doing at the rectory for so long?" Gus shouted. "Don't tell me you were having one of your lessons, because I saw Skelley go in after you'd been there for almost two hours already!"

An observation, my many-lived reader: if someone is being ridiculous, it does not follow that they are not also dangerous. I didn't know that then, and only registered the absurdity.

"I was making a blackberry pie," I said—curtly now, all my angelic performance forgotten. "Their cook is away, and you know how the Reverend tutors me without any payment." The last words were bitter on my tongue. He'd hoped, in fact, for a trade.

Gus was taken aback, and his anger faltered. "A pie? What for?"

My brows hiked. "I thought you were better informed, Gus. Search your memory, and I'm sure you'll recall the purpose of a pie."

"But—why are you wasting your time on something so *empty*? In the same hour you spent grubbing around in that kitchen, Darius could have taught you to make flames rise at your fingertips! I can almost understand the Latin, the natural history, even if I know all that is really beneath you. But not—ugh, it's bad enough that you have to cook for your *own* family!"

I thought, of course, of Thomas's sweet enthrallment at this chore Gus despised. I thought of that quality of Thomas's attention; how generously he gave of himself, how ready he was to surrender to wonder. But of course I kept such thoughts private.

"And I don't understand the value you find in Darius's spectacles. Just because they're magic—even when they aren't destructive, they're still *frivolous*."

In hindsight, I marvel at my own recklessness. I was alone with Gus on an unfrequented road, using terms calculated to inflame him, at a moment when he was still wavering on the edge of a jealous rage. Even after what he'd done to his mother, I could not imagine that he might hurt me.

"Frivolous!" Gus exclaimed, predictably indignant. "Oh, you don't begin to see—and if you can't see the potential in magic, how can you realize your own? If I could take you to Nautilus, even for a glimpse, maybe then you'd—but they only allow apprentice sorcerers to visit with a mentor." He delivered the last word suggestively. I did not take it up. "Catherine, listen: imagine a city that exists *nowhere*, in no specific place, so that it's equally close to every place on Earth at once! To Egypt or the North Pole, it's all the same! Imagine the gifted of all nations gathered there, building that city afresh every moment, with nothing but the power of their thoughts! Every building is the direct expression of all that's greatest in the human mind, and nothing there decays—"

It pains me to confess that I was not wholly immune to the image he conjured—though I was aware that decay is what nourishes new growth.

"Is that why they chose that name for it?" I asked, hushed. "Nautilus? Because the *spira mirabilis* of a nautilus's shell is part of a universal order, beyond any culture or language?"

Gus smiled; it was the first time I'd betrayed any interest in the city of sorcerers. To do so did seem to contradict my mission to save Gus from the seductions of magic—but then I'd been poorly suited to that mission from the start.

"Yes. And because the city is formed from thought the way a nautilus's shell is formed from its secretions, with no hands or tools, and yet it builds something so perfect," Gus agreed. It was not lost on me that Gus was undermining his own case; if a mollusk could spin marvels as great as those of the sorcerers, what need was there for magic? Before I could observe as much, Gus said something that surprised me. "Catherine, that's all magic is! It's a kind of *thought,* so I don't see how you can reject it out of hand. If you revere knowledge, how can you prefer to stay ignorant? Don't you believe in learning everything you can?"

In retrospect, these words sound out of character for Gus; they implied a democratic tendency in magic that he wouldn't have cared to emphasize. I suspect that Darius had provided this new argument; that Gus had been watching for me by the Skelleys' house so he could try it out.

In any case, it stopped me in my tracks. "I do."

I was still angry at Reverend Skelley; rebellion was spitting inside me. And Gus was at my side.

A rationalization was just as readily available. It went something like this: Why, after all, should Gus take seriously my disgust for magic when I knew nothing about it, save for those violent manifestations I'd felt and then stifled? No one welcomes the opinions of the illiterate on their favorite books. If I meant to save him, I should have a better idea of what I was talking about.

"Then let Darius *teach* you," Gus said earnestly. "At least try. He says he's sure you have the potential. Is that why you've been so reluctant, you're afraid you'll be too weak? Don't let that worry you! You don't need to have nearly as much power as he seems to—that is, you don't need to have as much as I do! Just a bit—a *supplement* to mine will be enough."

I knew quite well that I did have it in me, though by this time I'd managed to mostly ignore the nagging flick of magic near my spine.

"But why does Darius *care*? Gus, I know you don't want to believe it, but I'm certain he means to use you somehow. Why would I let him use me?"

"Of course he wants to use us!" Gus replied, startled. "They're all of them always recruiting, but it's nothing sinister, Catherine, I promise. Just politics."

I did not regard those two terms as mutually exclusive. But here I was distracted by my first glimpse of something I later understood very well;

namely, that established sorcerers could enhance their status by discovering new ones, and so helping appease Nautilus's insatiable appetite for magic. It is, in fact, an outright competition among them, and a protégé of exceptional gifts is flaunted like a prize pig.

"I'll try it once," I said. "But I make no promises beyond that, and I certainly don't intend to live in your sorcerers' city. I'm pledged to the study of reality."

"Oh—but anything can be reality if a sorcerer has the skill to make it so!" Gus's green-white eyes looked themselves like mother-of-pearl with the scudding clouds reflected in their sudden wetness. He smiled at me through his tears. "Catherine, Catherine, once you *see*—there's no turning back once you feel that power! And then no one will be able to separate us, not ever again." He brushed away tears with the back of his hand. "Let's go."

"What?" I said. "Now?"

"Darius is waiting. He was sure you'd come."

Angus and Lore

"Enough for what?" I say. I've moved around the sofa to confront her, but somehow I don't feel like nestling in. "You know us beamers aren't very bright. We need our betters to explain everything to us. Nice, clear, explicit language. Like, maybe, *Hey, I've been pretending to be your friend just to manipulate you into killing yourself for good, because it's too much hassle for me to keep doing it. You're cool with that, right?*"

We're pretty close to the fireplace. There's something about the way the flames move that keeps bugging me, but I can't put a finger on what it is.

"And what do you think a *true* friend would do?" Lore asks. As insinuating as the crackle of the fire. "Would a friend allow you to come back a thousand times more, with no purpose but murder and no potential beyond sorrow? Helping you achieve your end is the greatest kindness I can show you."

"A friend would treat me like I'm a real person, with real feelings! A friend would believe I can *change*." How can that plaintive whimper be mine? That's something else Lore's done to me. She's broken me down, reduced me to a squeak.

"Oh, Angus. Why else do you think I've spared you till now? I'm putting more faith in you than you know. I'm giving you a chance to be more than Gus ever made you to be, and I'm taking a significant risk to do it."

Something in the fireplace leaps in a distinctly unflamelike way, drawing my gaze. I can see now that the stone is carved to give the impression that we're inside a cave, looking out through its open mouth. And that fire: the longer I look at it, the more I can see how it's sculpted too. Flames shoot up in narrow trunks and spread at the top into rustling blue-tipped foliage; blazing embers stretch out wings and dive from tree to tree. A bevy of fiery deer break from their bright cover and go bounding across a clearing, each smooth curved body free and flowing, before a flying spark turns into an arrow and strikes one in the throat.

The shining deer stumbles and falls to its knees with a hiss, transformed into glossy char. I didn't mean to sit down next to Lore, but seeing the deer collapse—somehow it drops me on my ass.

Fuck you, I think at the fire. *Fuck you so hard.*

I'm searching among the blazing trees for the hunter. Can't find him anywhere. Lore is watching me watch the flames, I realize, with a knowing curl to her silver mouth. "I think it likes you."

"Whatever," I say. I'm still looping back to her last obscurity, don't have time for this one. "Trusting me more than I know? Why? Am I supposed to believe you give a shit about Geneva, when you're—"

"When I'm her professor, and she's the most gifted student I've ever had, and also my friend? Not everyone in Nautilus limits themselves to a singular existence, Angus, or forgets how to love the world beyond."

"But then—" Geneva's studying video stuff, she said. So then Lore— "You weren't just acting in that video. You *made* it. All those horrible tricks it pulled. They were yours."

Lore inclines her head. "I specialize in the empathic arts. But I have a knack for passageways and connections beyond the emotional variety as well."

Passageways. I think I've seen some of those too. I can't count all the ways she's played me, and we barely know each other.

Except that we do, of course.

"And those sidewalk cracks. You said something about a *friend,* and I didn't even think—"

"That wasn't me," Lore says, almost absently now. "It was a gorgeous piece of magic, though. I'll concede that much."

"Margo said you were working with someone to hurt me! So, great, it wasn't you personally. It was a friend of yours, messing me up as a *favor* to you, all so you could swoop in and rescue me and I'd be so, so grateful—"

"I believe I said it was *your* friend who was responsible. She's hardly a friend of mine," Lore observes, in a definitely unfriendly tone. "Angus, listen. There are things you deserve to know about your condition. Aspects of your history that might inform your choice, and I'll be happy to answer any questions you might have about them. But there are other questions that are more intrusive than you realize."

She means she'll only tell me things that herd me along the way she wants me to go. Up till now I've been blasted by knowing too much, too fast. Stunned and staggering. But somehow hearing Lore's condescension strips away my bewilderment.

Inform my choice, you say. Yeah, that's the quick of it.

"So what do you want from me?" I ask. Somehow I keep my snarl suppressed, deep in my throat. What comes out is all polite young man. Still innocent, still unbroken.

Lore nods. Pleased to be wrapping things up so promptly, because who has time to waste on me?

"Vengeance. You understand, now, who the author of your suffering has been, all this time. My hope is that understanding will let you at last break through your limitations. That you will make a genuine choice for the first time in all your unnumbered lives, and destroy him."

I mean, I knew that. It still sucks hearing her say it. "Even though I'll destroy myself that way too. Forever. You really think that's a fair thing to ask?"

Lore coughs up a half laugh. "I think it's much more than fair, actually."

This might be one of those agree-to-disagree things. Just because I'm an abomination, that means I don't get to live?

Gus Farrow. He must be too powerful for Lore to kill directly, or she never would have bothered picking off a succession of Anguses. So why does she think I can do what she can't?

"How?"

Firelight licks across her silver smile. "That's a remarkable question, coming from a living weapon."

Oh, gross! Gross, gross, nasty gross. But also, check.

"Point taken." Voices rise and fall around us, and for the first time I register that we aren't alone in this palatial room. There are peoplesque clusters lounging here and there on divans and couches, conversations fuzzing the air with languages I've never heard before.

"The greater difficulty is in reaching him. A few iterations ago an Angus turned up at his door, screaming and wailing. So now his rooms here are barred against you. And if you try some sort of stakeout, he'll notice soon enough that you aren't where you're supposed to be."

"Okay," I say, but my focus keeps veering away from her. The singed floral stink from the gallery, and not just from the gallery, chokes me with a kind of sick nostalgia. *Home,* I think, and then I finally spot the hunter in the flames. He comes staggering out of the flickering underbrush, clutching his head. Is there something sprouting from his brows, something he's trying to hold in?

"The Nimble Fire chooses one person from among those present, and reveals something in their mind. Something secret. A passion, a dread. Hope or history." The words haul on my attention. Amber light curls on Lore's lips like a sneer. She tips her head toward the hunter, his body canted forward while his arms elongate and kink with weird new joints. His face is stretching under spreading horns. "But it pays for what it takes. As long as the vision plays, the fire's elect can pass through it. To anywhere. Or to anyone."

What is she trying to say? That I can throw myself into the fire and come out with my lips smack against the creep who made me?

"That's not coming from me," I say. I can't pull my gaze away from the hunter's transformation. "I don't understand what it's getting at, at all."

Lore glances from me to the fire and back again. "Perhaps you're right, perhaps it's drawing its imagery from someone else. Strictly speaking." What's that supposed to mean? But Lore doesn't give me time to wonder. "If you can't reach Gus through *this* fire, you have other ways to him. Ones he opens himself."

God, I've been slow on the uptake. That face in the smoke—

Lore sees me catching on, and smiles. "Having such imperfect control over you must grate terribly on him. He can't stop looking for ways to keep you in check."

"The candles! I've only lit one of them. I got freaked out, I couldn't stand—"

"I can imagine that recognizing yourself in him would be aversive," Lore says. It's not in her interest to goad me, so maybe she's trying to keep that mocking note out of her voice. But if she is, it's a major fucking fail. "Well, then you must have quite a few candles left?"

"Yeah," I tell her. "Enough for a big-ass funeral pyre. I'll invite all my friends to come over and self-immolate with me. Make it an occasion."

"I can think of some who are overdue for a funeral," Lore says, and now her smile jabs through me like it's aiming for something tucked behind my eyes. "But sarcasm aside, Angus. Have you made up your mind?"

"I think so," I say. Here's my chance to demonstrate my incredible capacity for learning, right? "I never wanted to kill all those girls; Gus tricked me into it. He set me up! I don't have to be human to hate someone for messing with me like that."

Lore nods gravely and rests her hand on my arm. As dreamy, as oblivious, as complacent as any beamer I've ever met.

"It will be the best proof you could ever give of your love for Geneva, even if she'll never know."

"Right. It makes me feel a lot better, thinking of it that way." Geneva, her dear protégée, her gifted one, her blaze of promise. My precisely nothing—unless, you know, I make her my something. I look into the fire again, see the stag dragged down by leaping dogs. *I've got gifts of my own,* I want to say. *I've got promises. You'll see.*

"You may have trouble believing this, Angus. But I told you the truth when I said that I'd come to care about you, through all our many confrontations. I'll remember what was best in you, always."

She's so sure she's got me on her line, bouncing dutifully all the way to annihilation. *As if, bitch.* I give her my best impression of a poignant, boyish smile, and she actually pulls me in for a hug.

It's vengeance you want from me, Lore? Can do.

Catherine at the Movies

The *you* that killed Viola Wright was mulched a month later. I found my outlying scrap of consciousness balled up in Gus's pocket, all unbeknownst to him, along with the rest of your magically compressed matter and a great charge of vibrating magic. It was an unsettling vantage, for where I curled infinitesimally in your remains I could hear what I might call my primary self screaming above Gus's head. My scrap saw soiled cotton and lint while the rest of me gazed down on Gus's room and his balding pate, and at such close quarters my split being seemed to hum and resonate with the strangeness of division.

Then Gus set about making a fresh Angus. While he worked, he kept his gaze fixed on my face where it reflected in his mirror, now permanently installed. Yammering and berating me, demanding a list of my preferred characteristics. What would make me love him? And meanwhile I thought of one I did love, and yearned for the moment when I could see her again. It could not happen in Nautilus, where Gus would be liable to notice any approach to me. On that Anura and I had agreed, but there was no clear alternative as to how we would manage it.

One of Gus's first steps in your re-creation was a great erasure: your last existence and the death of Viola Wright must be obliterated, or you would not approach your next murder in the proper spirit. You, most corrupt of beings, must regard yourself as a blushing innocent. Gus could not read your memories, but he could blot them, smudge the slate, and then reinstate an imagined childhood with a few necessary edits. It was a rather rough business, I found, sloppy and error-prone. But then, you needed only a crude facsimile of psyche and memory to perform your function.

Gus poked away from outside you like someone building a ship in a bottle of opaque glass who can peer through the narrow neck while he manipulates his tweezers but never grasp the whole. But I, I was within.

Where Gus worked to erase your memories, I strove to restore them.

(If I have not done enough—and I know I have not—I can cling to the excuse that I did *something*.)

At first this endeavor was nothing but haphazard sabotage, though with time my efforts grew more purposeful. If Gus wanted your memories gone, I wanted them preserved. I was now committed to exploring what I *could* do and ignoring what I could not, and this was an effort that lay within my scope. Where Gus slopped and smeared your previous experiences, I crept in and, with a stealthy hand, reaffirmed the blurred lines. I found a trove of memories of your many peculiar childhoods with Margo, crushed and muddied almost beyond recognition, and I began the long and delicate labor of restoration. Gus still destroyed a great deal, but his results were not as thoroughgoing as they had been before I interfered.

All in a manner of speaking, of course. What I *could* do was an ongoing study, and I applied myself to a variety of tasks. I remembered that purse made of folded thought I'd burst in Gus's head when I'd tried to kill him. Could I use that model to make one of my own? I could and did! After a dozen failed attempts, I mastered the trick of it: to smooth the flow of thought, to hold it steady against all internal winds, to bend, to pleat.

Then: when Gus sucked on my magic, could I divert some part of the stream, and capture it for myself? Here began a most peculiar labor. I became an embezzler, but what I stole was my own mind.

Asterion interrupted us at intervals loosely corresponding to days, sometimes by the Nimble Fire and sometimes in Gus's own grimy quarters, though it was plain the minotaur found the place disagreeable. He would swan in and jab his umbrastring into my flashing apparition as casually as slicing a piece of cheese, then bend over the tiny dial to gloat at their takings.

"Only eight and a half today," Asterion complained, kicking aside a drift of dirty laundry with a petulant foot. My scream sounded the same as ever, but now it stood in for howls of jubilation. I had done it! My little thought-purse jangled, as it were, with snatched coins. "I thought she was back to her old puissance, but apparently not."

Gus shrugged; he wanted to get back to work, tinkering with your memories of a childhood roughly based on his lost youth. He let the umbrastring's end slide from his lips, the bright thread bearing a droplet of spittle.

"Catherine has her ups and downs."

"Does she?" Asterion asked. He sounded waspish. "Then these would be downs? Do something to boost her again, why don't you?"

"You forget that I keep two-thirds of what she makes," Gus snapped. "It's in my interest to encourage her where I can. I don't see why you'd suspect me of neglecting anything I can reasonably do."

"I never forget what you *keep,* my dear Gus."

Nor did I, for that matter.

The next time Asterion came, they managed to collect only eight talens. Several visits later their harvested wealth dropped to seven, then gradually to six. Asterion began to fret, loudly and persistently. A third of my now-meager output was hardly worth the time it took to visit, he said, so Gus must come to him. Gus should do something to amend the situation; he must fix me, fire me up, bring me back up to an acceptable standard before it was too late. *What* it would be too late for stayed unspecified, knocking in the corners like an autumn fly.

Once it reached five talens per visit, my declining production abruptly and mysteriously stabilized. Any lower and I feared Asterion might do something that could injure Anura.

Meanwhile, I began to study how to increase my output. I was made of power, as Gus had discovered. Why had it never occurred to me to tend my own currents, focus and develop them? Learning such skills with no one to teach me was a slow business, of course. But I had nothing but time.

And when we walked through the streets, I gazed at the city with new pleasure, new wonder. Rather than hating its artifice, I began to admire its artistry. That is, I looked for those qualities I guessed Anura saw in Nautilus—and looking let me see it all anew.

The hour came when Gus was satisfied with his design and ready to recompose you in the flesh. Exuding you in your latest form proved a far more laborious process now that you were corporeal, and even harder to witness. Your compacted matter and mind, imbued with a great store of talens, sat on a small table where Gus had been fiddling with his final touches; in that intermediate state you looked like a handkerchief of gossamer silk, once very fine but now spoiled and holey. I, of course, inhered in your creases, patient and quiescent, while the bulk of me droned out my usual aria over Gus's bent head.

Once Gus was satisfied with you, or perhaps simply too bored to refine you any further, he picked up the tattered ball and eyed it. His lips worked squeamishly, and he dangled you between thumb and forefinger, clearly working up his nerve. Then he popped you in his mouth, stretching it wide to accommodate you; you were perhaps the size of two hen's eggs wrapped in cloth.

He did not masticate or swallow; this was no ordinary ingestion. From without it appeared that his bulging cheeks very gradually subsided while his eyes rolled with the struggle to suppress his nausea. He gagged and rocked while the mass of you diminished, slipped to some new habitation.

And from within? I enjoyed that splendid view as well, of course. I saw the rosy dome of palate, the light cracking between bared and carious teeth, the red slide of his gorge. And then there came a sort of upward sifting motion as all that you were, and something of me as a garnish, were *taken up*. Trickling with terrible slowness, you siphoned into his mind. He then expressed you, breach and whole and quite adult in form, from his forehead.

Don't be deceived into imagining that this process was in any way quick or merciful. If I try to estimate it in unworld terms, I'd say it might have been three days during which Gus squeezed you out. He groaned, he whimpered, he grimaced with such evident misery that I was rather sorry to have missed the previous births during my phase of willful oblivion. He never ate or slept, only sipped occasionally from a flask of tepid water. Your fresh pink heels appeared first, oozing cancerously from his brows. Then with the slowness of a rising moon the two protrusions crept forward, and wrinkled soles appeared along with the jutting buttresses of two Achilles tendons. It was some time before the toes popped free. And when at last the circumference of your parts grew larger than his head—your rump, for example—they slid forth rather thinned and childlike, then bellied slowly wider in the open air, like membranous sacks swelling with water. Your buttocks remained pendulous in front of Gus's face for quite some time, gradually inflating, while your beautifully muscled legs flopped to either side of his torso.

Lest you mistake me, this is how *all* your iterations have come into being. I've witnessed a great many such deliveries, including the birth of the form you wear now. However exquisite the face and figure Gus creates for you, this is your true nature: you are regurgitated meat, a blood-speckled wind. Please shed whatever illusions you have regarding this matter.

Gus looked wan indeed, slurry-eyed and wobbling, by the time your head began its emergence.

For all his protestations, he had taken the wretched minotaur's advice to heart. It was the first Angus that did not resemble him in the slightest: icy pale where Gus was sallow, with high apple cheeks where Gus's cheekbones were flat and peaked sharply at the sides of his face. An aquiline nose; his was sloped and pointed. The hair was another innovation, auburn and flowing rather than blond and bristly. I could not see the eyes, wrapped as they were in damp purplish lids like a newborn puppy's. Nautilus's sickly glow reflected on your skin in glossy waves and gave you the appearance of having been drizzled with icing.

I understood at once why he bore you feetfirst: the instant your mouth came free it was keening in terrible discordance with my scream. That part of me which was within you felt relief at escaping from Gus's head, but I could also register the dim and bestial pain filtering through your sleeping mind. You were entirely naked, a seashell glow lighting your skin, where Gus was dull and reeking in mop-colored clothes sodden with his sweat.

The murderous kiss fell out near the end of the process, landing on the floor with an audible *plop*. It stayed there, pink and quivering, until Gus scooped it up with an impatient hand and slapped it back into your lips.

Then Gus collapsed beside you and slept like the dead—or, I assume, like some of us—and all the while you went on whining.

While you and Gus sprawled on the floor, I hovered above, singing my part in our infernal duet, and wondered at that lost sentinel of myself concealed in your slumbering face. Soon Gus would send you out again, and part of me with you. But I did not know where we were bound, or how I could inform Anura if I did know. She had found the London beamer, and me with it, owing solely to a scrap of rumor overheard by the Nimble Fire. Nautilus is a very great city for gossip, but even so, I could hardly rely on such a happy chance recurring. And since I could communicate only by possessing you, and not at all through the inarticulate shriek I emitted in Nautilus, meeting Anura in the unworld was my most ardent desire.

This difficulty harassed me through your long sleep and Gus's as well, and when at last Gus woke and went about preparing for your transfer I was no closer to solving it. He then hired a fleet of iridescent beetles to carry you to the city he'd selected. I could write Anura a letter in the unworld, but how to deliver it to Nautilus? Perhaps there was applicable magic, but I did not know it then. As my fragment lumbered on beetle-back through Nautilus's streets, I twisted in the ruby glow of your closed lids and raged.

You opened your eyes on the San Francisco waterfront under a drooling sky. Gus had dressed you, of course, much more nicely than he dressed himself. You had a suitcase in one hand. A well-fed billfold was in your pocket along with a slip of paper bearing a nearby address. A key. You teetered with the blind and groping shock that attends your initial awakenings, and I could hear your thoughts intoning *Angus . . . Farrow?*

(Meanwhile in Nautilus, I watched Margo clinging to Gus's knees, begging him to let her return to the unworld. She had no purpose, she said, nothing to live for, now that the beamer children were done with; why would he not allow her to die? He scolded her for ingratitude and turned on his heels. "Never let me hear you say anything so ridiculous again, or I'll remind you what you owe me." And Margo blanched, hearing, as I did, the threat that he would not pay for her pain's relief if she annoyed him.)

You found the key, the address; the designated building was right beside you. You climbed the stairs of your seedy boarding house and fought for calm, rocking in false memories like buffeting winds. And here and there a strain of those memories I'd restored rose as well, adding to your bewilderment.

Gus has always paved your way, you see. You are made to be an ambulatory curse, not a contributing member of society.

Soon enough you found your target: a society girl turned dancer and sometime prostitute named Matilda. She was one of the ones who found you unsettling from the first encounter, and she was luckily indifferent to your beauty. It was a relief when she fled the city one night; I had not discovered any way to save her from you, nor indeed any way to send word to Anura where I was.

The target your next iteration chose was not so fortunate, and neither was the one after. I studied, I plotted, and oh, I tried and *tried* to stop you! You churned through your cycle, stalked and killed and disintegrated and then stumbled forth again, your own lost selves and their victims slowly sinking deeper, their shadowed silhouettes drowning in your vacant eyes—

Then I had my first success. Her name was Daisy, and I managed to scribble a warning on a napkin as she flirted with you at a dark bar. She read the note while you ordered drinks and hid her shock behind desperate laughter, flinging it in front of her like the clouding ink of an octopus. Ten minutes later, she sent you after a cigarette girl who was receding into a back room, and ran for it while you were gone. Even with your supernaturally heightened awareness, one of those *improvements* Gus had paid for with my magic, we never saw her again.

I was greatly heartened by Daisy's survival and yearned to tell Anura, perhaps to see her smile at me, but I had no way to reach her.

In the event, it was fully an unworld decade, and six dead girls, before I managed to communicate with Anura again. Does that seem a long time to sustain an unnourished devotion? I was habituated to endurance, and then I had my new studies as a distraction. I did not find the work easy—I had nothing to go on but trial and error—but my abilities steadily improved.

You were in Montreal, tracking a girl named Claire. Does that name ring a bell?

While you slept, I wrote a letter, addressed it, and tucked it in the breast pocket of your coat; this had become my regular practice, though I had never yet found a way to deliver such a missive. I then began the tedious work of obscuring that particular pocket from your awareness so you would never chance to reach in a hand and draw the letter out. It might not sound like a great endeavor. But embedding a thousand tiny misdirections in your mind, each with that pocket as its locus, required weeks of exquisite labor.

That concealment accomplished, I watched you watch Claire, a round, luxuriant girl with bright blond hair. One night she sat four rows ahead of you at the Paris Cinema. (In every incarnation you've sought out movies; coiling in your small abyss while bright faces sprayed above was a frequent experience for me.) Claire was unaware that you had followed her in. She was nestled against a leaner, darker girl in a black velvet jacket that inhaled all light. When the projected image blazed red and gold, Claire's blond waves caught wandering beams and streamed incandescent over her friend's interstellar shoulder.

You in your turn were unaware that a door back to Nautilus was hidden in the Paris's projection booth; it was the very same door Gus had used to import you here, still unconscious. You squirmed at the touch of its magic-laden drafts, but you did not know what it was that so disturbed you. Well, apart from the presence of the dark girl, who was slipping caresses like tender contraband onto Claire's neck. The pair were nearly always together, frustrating your attacks, and though you did not suspect it you were running out of time.

To be entirely honest, I too found their ill-concealed passion uncomfortable, though for very different reasons than yours. I thought of sweet Thomas Skelley, so shy that he initially cringed in my presence. I recalled his burst of enthusiasm as we studied the spines on a beetle's leg together, and how it had disarmed me. No matter what Gus thought, I had indeed loved Thomas, and dearly.

But seeing Claire and her lover—my lack of corporeality had allowed me to skirt any question of *desire* where Anura was concerned. To figure my love for her in comfortably ethereal terms: it was romantic, very well, but still nearly passable as a passionate friendship.

The two girls confronted me with what my love would look like, if only I had a body to give it expression. It loosed a tempest in me. To covet the beauty of Anura's human form was to betray her true self, of course, but nonetheless I found myself imagining—never mind. I envisioned kissing her soft frog's face as well, caressing her blue skin. But sometimes, I admit, the images veered to the golden girl on the riverbank.

My upbringing had not allowed for the possibility of such desires. But that was true of many aspects of my strange existence. I tried to take my old rule—never to be surprised—and apply it to myself. I *was*, against all rational expectations, and my love was as well. Surely I was beyond caring what my father, say, might think of it?

I listened to the wind streaming out of Nautilus, the touch of its magic metal-cold and smelling of burning violets, as if I hoped I might catch the faint strains of her voice.

I did not. But my fierce attention to that wind's every vagrant melody revealed something else.

All at once I heard—or more accurately touched—a note, a far-off call, as when one individual of a species heralds its approach to another. At first it was barely perceptible, and I suppose almost any Nautiluser besides myself wouldn't have paid it the slightest notice, or possibly detected it at all.

But it was my own scream, however dwindled by distance; my own voice, finding me where I crouched in that darkness doubly foreign to me, once because it was the darkness in *you*, and twice because it was a strange city and Rita Hayworth was flinging her hair in a realm of vaulted shadows. I knew myself, and I caught at myself as I had at that winding tongue of magic Darius once loosed in me.

It was an impulsive act, as if I reached a hand to my other self in love and forgiveness.

You flinched. I could feel my scream ricocheting below your thoughts, throb and plaint: an accusation spindled out of shape.

It took a great deal to tear your eyes off Claire, but you began to fidget and glance over your shoulder, trying to see where the sound was coming from. Rita Hayworth was at that moment laughing, and the scream didn't sort with the images.

Any day when Claire escaped you brought us nearer to the end of your year. I would like to say I understood the full ramifications of my ploy, but I did not. My scream distracted you, and it might help her. That was enough.

Cautiously, delicately—for I did not understand what I was doing, or on what terms the scream might fail or break—I began pulling it closer. Weaving my own distant cry into your thoughts, tangling you in it, until you kicked the seat ahead of you and gnawed your knuckles.

A few more minutes, and you turned to fix your gaze on the projection booth. You suspected the bothersome shriek came from somewhere up there, hidden behind the beam, and in some sense you were right. (Oh, have you wondered why you hear my scream so loudly when you near Nautilus? You hear it because I clarify matters for you. You hear it because you are *haunted*. To anyone else, it would be presently inaudible.)

You left the girls to Rita Hayworth, all three of them weeping now, and began creeping low between the rows of velvet seats. Luckily for you, the theater was mostly empty, and you only had to clamber over one irritable lady's knees to reach the aisle.

It was at this point I understood how I had worked my own advantage, and I strained to brighten the scream in your mind. Still faint, yes, but growing subtly louder as you insinuated yourself under a black curtain. The projectionist stood with his back to you up a short flight of stairs; you slipped toward him on all fours like a lizard. Deathly silent. Violent images careened through your thoughts—quite typical of you—and I feared you would dash out the man's brains. He was a doorkeeper as well as a projectionist, and I had seen him before; passages to Nautilus in the countryside are often protected by nothing but magical obscurity, but those in cities are better guarded.

So when you touched the loose panel just above the floor, it triggered something in him. He spun and gawked down, twitching in surprise. A beat later and he recognized you.

"Farrow's beamer? What, are you trying to crawl home early? Trust me, kid, it won't be any fun if you do."

You rolled onto your back and scowled. "Someone in your wall keeps screaming," you announced imperiously. "If you can't shut her up, I want my money back."

The projectionist rocked with surprise. Then he laughed, long and softly. After all, you were part of Nautilus, even if you did not know it, so he had no real responsibility to keep you out. What were Gus's schemes to him?

"Shut her up yourself," the projectionist said. "Go on."

You smelled a rat. You sat up and your arms pulled close, ready to strike.

"Just slide up that panel," he encouraged. "Go on, straight through there. That's the way to the screaming girl, all right."

Warily you tried it. The panel lifted with enchanted lightness, skidding up at your slightest touch. To you, but not to the projectionist, my scream was abruptly much louder. And Nautilus's wind leapt up, ensnarling you in its gusts. The projectionist cackled.

You had half a moment to stare daggers at him before you were falling in a midnight gyre, my letter to Anura rustling near your heart.

I could not use your hand while you were *aware* of it; indeed, up to that point, I had hardly ventured to stir it unless you were deep asleep. It was essential to my hopes that you and Gus both remained unaware of my illicit second home.

Nautilus consumed your attention, it rolled like a pearl in the nacre of your amazement. As lightly, as drowsily as I could, I wafted your hand toward the pocket I'd hidden from you.

You glanced down, baffled to find your left hand resting on your chest. My movement ceased at once. We tumbled and spun ever nearer to the lucent city, but now your attention was divided, sputtering between the city's unearthly brilliance and your own wayward hand. I needed the assistance of the wind's currents; I could not rely on my letter to march through the streets unnoticed, but if it soared in from a great height its odds were good. Oh, if nothing diverted you before we landed—

A blue stone scarab some two yards across came hurtling out of the dark and nearly splattered you. Your hands flung up in a wild reflex, a pointless attempt to ward it off. You were much too preoccupied to

notice your left thumb and forefinger pinching a protruding paper corner in passing, or the envelope that flicked free and spun away into the
dark. The scarab sailed past, inches from your skull.

An address is a powerful thing in Nautilus; always supposing, of
course, that you have the talens to make it so.

Oh, and that lovely dark girl, the one who brushed her fingertips over
Claire's skin? Her name was Dolores Rojas, and my letter to Anura had a
great deal to say about her.

Catherine in the Clearing

Our walk to the clearing had its own character of grim entrancement, and not only because my stomach clenched at the prospect of seeing Darius's wicked old face again. No: now that I had committed myself, that twitching presence at the base of my brain woke from its long dormancy. It tugged. As if it knew where we were going, it seemed to draw an eager trajectory on the air, to cast a spidery thread, and then to pull me along the way it wished to go.

What was worse was that I couldn't tell *who* was acting on me in this way. Was it Darius, or did that immanence in me have its own urges? If magic was indeed thought, *my* thought, then how could it want what I reviled?

Now that I have died for so long, I can say this: it is the nature of thought to oppose the thinker, to thwart and mock our conscious intentions. But I was then still young enough to be indignant at finding my self-mastery so limited.

Gus and I stepped out of the woods into the clearing, where sunbeams pierced like pins in a cushion. Darius was sitting on a fallen log, his head in his hands, tangled gray locks curtaining his face. I stopped some five yards away from him and braced for his usual crude intimidation. But when he looked up at us, his gaze had a strained vulnerability I'd never seen in him before.

"Hello there, pretty Catherine," he crooned with insulting caution, as if I were a fawn he feared to startle.

"Coaxing is no better than bullying," I said, brisk and annoyed. "Have you never in your whole ruinous life addressed another person as an *equal*?"

Gus's eyes went so wide at my temerity that I realized in a flash how Darius had him cowed, and I hated the old sorcerer even more for it. But Darius grinned as he struggled to his feet.

"Vanishingly few," Darius conceded. "And none in recent memory. But let's say I'm ready to take a swing at it again, shall we?"

"What do you *mean*?" Gus demanded, and I heard pain in his voice.

"Nothing I haven't told you frankly enough before," Darius said, but his gaze was fixed on me. "Not my concern if you chose not to understand me. Well, Catherine? Don't tell me you haven't sensed it. Don't tell me you don't know." I felt his regard around me like a web holding me upright; felt my knees weaken, and a loosening deep in my brain. "Ah, here it is! I can help it along a bit, keep the flow going—*there*. You're feeling it now, aren't you?"

I was. In some ways nothing changed: there was still the pressure of earth through the worn soles of my shoes, the birdsong, the sultry embrace of the air. But at the same time my senses lifted on new currents of thought; things were the same, but their alignments were different. *Suggestible.*

We are all familiar with the thought that manifests in words and pictures, unruly as a routed army, its impressions heaved up like banners and dropped again.

And I daresay we are all familiar with the thought running below the worded sort: the inarticulate rush that finds constellations, feels whole galaxies, in the precise angle of a dying woman's head on her pillow, or in the zone of light trapped between two bodies in a doorway. That sort of thought is always slack-jawed, at a loss for words to contain all it knows, and *knows,* and so often wishes it did not have to know—

Well, this was yet a third variety of thought, one that ran deeper still. It seeped like water into the joints of reality. And pushed them all askew. Everything in the world that was beautiful, natural, necessary, from gravity to distance, from the chlorophyll lapping light to the racing language of the nerves, was abruptly and horribly vulnerable.

Magic was in me, frantic and undirected. But instead of delight at my own power all I felt was a crushing revulsion, a bone-deep offense that such a thing could even be. During my first confrontation with Darius magic had seemed a personal enemy, an element of a larger oppression. But now it menaced everything I held most dear—and worse, it did so from within me.

There was that scorched-violet scent now so familiar to me. Gus gawking in alarm. And Darius, looming close now, his face alight with greed and his breath wheezing out the same sickening floral fumes. "How lovely you are with your power flowing," he murmured, and touched my hair. I shuddered, but I was too overcome to make myself pull away. "Got our rivers of milk and honey right here, don't we now?"

Darius. He appeared to me in that moment like the animating spirit of everything that was corrupt, deranged, profoundly wrong. If he hadn't cornered me with his fiery tadpoles in that field, then this awful uncanny pressure might have stayed suppressed forever, and Gus would have stayed innocent—at least of his mother's maiming. We both could have gone on believing, forever, that magic was only a childish story, and not, as it appeared to me then, a disease of reality itself. His wrinkled old hand was still there, pawing at me; his smile was cloying and satisfied.

"I can teach you to control it," Darius said. "You see, Catherine? You *need* me now."

I couldn't speak—couldn't say that *needing* him was nothing I would ever do. But something in me rose in answer, and the wanton overflow of my power found its direction.

Slop, Gus had called such untutored flooding; his voice rang through my memories. *Mindless instinct.*

A spray of dirt flew up and struck Gus in the face. He sputtered, brushing clods of it from his tongue. My blood seemed to flow again, my limbs came free, and I was able to look around.

The ground was writhing, bubbling. Roots long concealed beneath the clearing's surface reared up, serpentine and lashing—and apparently aiming for Darius. There was no mistaking their hostile intent as one immense root-fan arched over him, a dirt-dribbling cobra, and made ready to dash out his brains. Darius ducked to the side, his movements casual and unafraid, but his dodge had at least the virtue of carrying him several feet away from me. He was laughing uproariously.

"You did tell me she's interested in botany," Darius told Gus, and cackled. I could not grasp the relevance of his remark. He waved a lazy hand, and the roots burst into flames. I staggered.

But before I collapsed another root whipped up behind Darius. I saw it come with stunned apprehension, and all at once I understood—truly understood—that I was responsible.

"Stop," I screamed. "Stop!"

But my voice was not the part of me the root obeyed. It struck him just above the right ear with a vicious crack. I watched him fall, even as I was somehow still falling. Crimson fanned out, fine and glittering, a cloud of ruby insects.

Then both of us lay on the ground, and the world went very still.

Angus and Gus

I should have known that Carmen's warehouse had something weird going on. Lore escorts me to the Chicago exit, and I find myself popping like a weasel through a random cardboard box in a corner of the main space. Nobody home, the quiet grinding at the walls. I dog-ear one of the flaps so I can find the right box again, just in case, and head back to my room. It's the last time I'll ever see this place. Maybe Lore can track me down no matter what I do, but I don't have to make it easy for her.

The blue box of candles is sitting square in the middle of the table. The matches perch on top. The silence goes oily with expectancy as I pull them close. After a moment's thought on the subject of carbon monoxide, I decide against staying in my room and carry the boxes out to the center of that cracked cement sky. Dump out the candles and stare at the heap. Stumpy broken bones, disconnection cast in wax. It's hitting me now that Lore and I didn't exactly get down to the finer points of what the hell I should do. Like it would just be obvious once I got started.

Fine. I strike a match. Let it fall.

Like magic—hah—the lights go out. It's just me and the unsteady shine boxed in darkness. Shadows radiate into a vast ragged flower all around me. My own figure sways, cut from projected unlight. I wait while the flames skip from wick to wick, while the wax pools and runs into the nearest crack. I could just turn around and walk out right now, and leave the old bastard twisting.

Instead I raise my booted foot and stamp, drowning the flames in their own streaming pus. Hot wax splatters my calf, like I give a fuck. Stamp again, choking out the firelight, making room for the dark. Smoke braids thick around me. It takes a few tries, but at last there's just one guttering little spark. Trying to hold off so much night on its own, and failing abysmally. I know the drill from last time; the lights will flare as soon as it's extinguished.

Stomp.

And then I'm just standing there in rocky darkness. Entombed.

Something is stinging my eyes. They're watering like crazy and tears spill down my cheeks. A thick, acrid stench shoves down my throat and sets off a fit of coughing: the kind that feels like someone is yanking on your lungs with a fishhook. Right, the smoke, but it has none of the buttery softness of ordinary candle smoke. It's toxic, grasping. And all at once I'm getting the feeling that maybe this wasn't my most inspired idea ever. I can't even locate the door to make a run for it, not when the darkness is wheeling around me.

Something—*two* somethings—settle gently on my shoulders from behind. I can feel the impressions of fingers, palms, but they're not solid enough to be flesh. Their touch is hot, drafty, full of minuscule coilings.

Hands, but hands made of smoke. They're sliding directly against my skin; my shirt doesn't impede them at all. My muscles jump with the instinct to bolt. But it's probably my only chance to tell him off before he trashes me. To make him recognize that, whatever he thinks—whatever I do—I'm not just his shitty little beamer.

I force myself to turn, even though my knees bang together a little. "Hey, Gus. Great to see you! Or it would be, if you'd can the drama and turn on the stinking lights."

Those hands. I can't help noticing that they feel a dab more solid, now, against my collarbone. The way he's clinging to me comes off more weak and unbalanced than threatening. Something about blowing through all the candles at once, hitting a critical mass of magic, and now I've dragged him here in the flesh, still discombobulated. I could lean in and kiss him and rip his life right out.

You know, if only I was Lore's bitch, that's exactly what I'd do.

The lights flick on. Wearily, somehow. And there he is: my dear progenitor, live in person and looking like ass. It's hard to remember that I'm supposed to be afraid of him when he's a head shorter and wearing a body like congealed barf. We both take a step back.

"Angus." His eyes are ice green, nesting in ashy folds. "The waste of it all."

I'm not sure if he's referring to me or to the candles.

"The candles aren't all I'm going to waste," I tell him. "I'm not going through with your charade. I just wanted you to know that, when I waste my chance, I'm doing it completely on purpose."

His weedy brows cock up. No point in pretending he doesn't know what I mean.

"You've made the mistake of spoiling your innocence, when innocence is the best advantage I could give you. But I'll overlook that for now. There's no chance she'll love you if you don't at least *apply* yourself, make every effort—"

"There's no chance she'll love me," I interrupt, "because I'm you. But now I'm in on the joke. Turns out it's both of us."

He starts forward. And okay, I don't *remember* remember how it feels when he pulps me. But memory fidgets inside me, a cold agitation in my heart. My body feels empty, echoing with all the times I've met his eyes and hated him. I thought I'd forgotten fear, but it's funny how it all comes back to me.

Then something shifts in his saggy old face. I'd almost call it tenderness if it weren't so crushing.

"Angus. No one knows better than I do how many times you've failed me. But often you've failed by acting too soon, or too late. By a trick of perspective. If the angle of her understanding had only been minutely different, she would have seen that mutuality is *intrinsic* to a love like ours. That it is an inescapable condition." If I'm so him, why does it take me by surprise to hear him crooning philosophically, as if he were talking to himself? "You are preoccupied with *your* chance, but that's a callow, selfish way to think of it. Yours isn't the one that matters, difficult as that may be to accept. Our love is generous, Angus; generous above all else! The chances it allows are infinite. Don't ruin hers."

It almost sounds like he's begging. And I kind of see his point. I've been looking for a way to spite the maximum number of fuckers, ready to sacrifice Geneva to that goal, even though I love her so much it aches. Maybe that's contradictory, but if I don't look too hard at the contradiction it can't hurt me.

"I've seen what happened, Gus. I've *been* there. You didn't exactly give her infinite chances when it was Catherine in front of you. I mean, when you were young."

His eyes flare. "I'm always young, foolish boy."

"Yeah?" I say. "Because you look like a hot dog and a dirty dishtowel had a baby." But then, of course, duh. I see my own strong, golden arms, the jostle of dark curls hanging over my eyes, and I guess that to him my overblown beauty is part of his generosity. His eagerness to accommodate.

"She hasn't exhausted the chances I'm prepared to give her. I believe she never will. You are my proof, my testament. You are the amends I make for having been too hasty, long ago." He gives me a searching gaze, and it's more effective than it has any right to be. "So when you speak of waste—wanton, deliberate—do you finally understand what you would be wasting?"

I'm sliding into his head, snaking among his thoughts. *A trick of perspective.* It's not like he's ever actually killed me. Just remade me. And my agony in the process is part of our offering to her—

For a moment I can't remember who *her* is this time. Faces mingle, interbreed, swap features.

"We'll find her in the end, Angus. We'll live in her eternal truth. And that truth will be her love."

Okay, I don't say. *Fine. I'm in.* I see him in a net of light, then realize I'm looking through tears.

"Catherine," he says. He makes her name glow like stained glass. "You are always young in me."

Something in me flicks at that. He almost had me for a second there.

That's not her name, I don't say. *Not to me. Don't you dare call her that to* me. But Geneva doesn't matter to him at all, I realize. Not as herself. Why do I buck at his smug assurance that his *her* is the only one that counts, when I knew he felt that way? Why do I want to throw that name—*Catherine*—off my back, out of my head? Or into one of those fucking cracks she—

Gus screwed up, but even I realize it's better if he doesn't recognize it. Not yet. He can figure it out later, if he gives enough of a shit to try.

I see his face unraveling. His brow, his ear, the fall of his cheek burst into dove-gray petals and diffuse, spreading back into smoke. Theatrical motherfucker. I can *feel* the magic that gushed from all those candles ebbing, feel our visit—thinning out. In an instant the smoke man is huge, hunched over me, his open mouth like a writhing crown around my head. All his delicate smoke filaments slowly untangle and blur, until I'm crouched under a loosely humanoid cloud. I don't remember sinking down, but my knuckles are digging at the cement.

Then nothing. I'm on the floor and he's gone. The raw scratching in my lungs fades and I'm finally getting enough clean air.

Fuck you, I think. *And while we're at it, fuck Catherine.*

Geneva isn't his, and neither is my love for her. My single lousy year of life isn't his. It's all I have and I'm going to milk it for all it's worth.

I'm not saying that *our* love isn't generous, though. Just that his generosity and mine might find different modes of expression.

Catherine Flawed

You may wonder something at this juncture, murderous reader; the same question has troubled me for a very long time. Why did magic manifest in me, me in particular? If magic is a species of thought, shouldn't it be a universal human property? I've observed my power long enough to know how it quickens in response to strong emotion, especially rage. But if *everyone* who feels justified rage—which is to say, by far the larger part of humankind—possessed the same degree of power, well, the world would have burned long ago.

I have no satisfying answer to this conundrum. I can only speculate that magic *is* in everyone, only generally too deep to access. That what might appear to be a gift is in fact a defect of certain minds, a flaw in their construction: a thinness that lets magic rupture the protective upper layers of thought and so escape.

And when it *does* escape, it shows itself no better than any other force subject to human will. That, in the end, is my argument with magic: that it is human.

Blood lacquered Darius's face ruby-dark; a pink bubble of blood-tinged mucus clung to one nostril. I was up on one elbow, dizzy and shaking, while Gus crouched nearby sifting frantically through matted leaves. I couldn't guess what he was doing until he came up with a downy gray feather, and I felt a lurch of understanding. Oh, I'd been so ready to condemn Gus for what he'd done to his mother, but now I had *murdered*—murdered over a hand on my hair.

Gus held the feather to Darius's lips, and it fluttered.

He looked at me. "Catherine, can you walk?"

I couldn't understand the significance of the question. Did that feather's stirring mean that Darius was alive, or was Gus telling me in coded language that it had only been the wind?

"I have to go get help for him, and you—you can't be here when they come. Wait, let me look you over. Just in case." Gus left Darius and began quickly, methodically turning over the folds of my skirt, inspecting my cuffs. I was just lucid enough to grasp that he was looking for specks of blood. "All right, you look fine—you should brush off the leaves—oh, but those could have come from anywhere!" He hesitated, then rose and pulled me to my feet. The thrum of his shaking hands transmitted through my arm. "We can't wait. He could still die. Hurry home, and I'll figure out what to say."

He turned me in the direction of the path, and pushed. The momentum took possession of me, and I started to run, still too numb to fully comprehend. But with each step a ghostly understanding shifted higher in my mind, until by the time I reached the bridge I could no longer help but recognize it:

Darius's injury might well be construed as accidental. But suppose it weren't? And if the old man died—

Gus was taking an enormous risk to protect me. *I shouldn't allow it,* I thought hazily. *I should tell the truth.*

But the truth was incredible, impossible. Telling it would change nothing. Was that a sufficient reason to withhold it? I couldn't tell.

It was the end of the afternoon when I reached home—supper would be late, though at least I'd set some beans to soak that morning, and Anna had started the fire. My brothers banged and clamored on all sides as I began cooking with detached, agitated movements. Now and then I was gripped by the awareness that I did not know whether or not I was a murderer, and my stomach muscles would clench as if I were vomiting. How could something so momentous, so essential to my identity, be so far beyond my control?

Once the simplest possible stew was simmering I slipped out to the woodpile and fell in a heap, and there I stayed. I felt myself diminished to an arrangement of negligible things: a smear of shadow by the wheelbarrow, the tremor in my back, wood smoke—

The scaly prickle of a bird's claws pinching my wrist.

"He's going to live," the bird sang with that layering of voices, its own and Gus's—it was a sparrow this time. I jerked upright and met the inscrutable darkness of its star-specked eyes. "Now you see, Catherine, don't you? Why there's nothing else for us, and nowhere else we can go?"

When I turned, there was Anna, watching the scene with grave un-surprise. We'd never spoken of magic, but I believe she always knew—knew, perhaps, by an apprehension of her own hidden nature. Whatever became of my odd little darling? Did she live with quiet acceptance, or with volatile defiance? If she'd ever come to Nautilus, surely she would have sought me out?

Yet even in Nautilus, I have sometimes imagined her face in the crowd.

"I *told* you," she said, not without bitterness. But then she leaned in and kissed my eyebrow, and clung awhile with her head nestled on my collarbone.

Catherine Submerged

I failed to save Claire.

You found your way back to Montreal, your mind ablaze with vindictive malice now that you began to guess something of what you were. You followed her, all thought of courtship past. It was only because she wanted to buy Dolores a present that you were able to catch her alone; Claire slipped out one late morning, still tousled and sleepy, and walked a mile to a department store. You skulked among the displays while Claire selected a pair of emerald leather gloves, long and supple and elegant, clearly hopelessly expensive for a student like her; we could just overhear her voice, saying how the color would become her friend. How the gloves were for her birthday.

You slammed into Claire as she made for the doors. And oh, strangers *did* move to help the fair girl, as they had not intervened for Viola. Two men and a woman converged to pull you off her, and Claire herself delivered a very fine black eye.

But not before your kiss swallowed her shouting mouth.

The men tried to seize you; you thrashed and burst from their grip, ran madly up the street. So I was spared the sight of Claire's baffled weakness as her life spilled away, her crumpling knees. I did not witness Lore's face when she saw Claire's corpse; her cry did not shiver through me, nor can I say with certainty that Lore cradled one dimpled, cooling hand against her eyes as she sobbed.

Neither of us needs such a proof of Lore's grief, of course. We've witnessed that grief many times since, transmuted into rage.

You darted and ducked like a hounded thing for hours, crouching behind trash cans and eventually resorting to the movies again. Now that Claire was dead, you were purposeless, flailing, your essential emptiness emphatic; I could feel you feeling it, yet denying it in a silent, spiteful howl. At three in the morning, you returned to your room, to my great relief. I was able to fog your thoughts sufficiently that you forgot to lock the door, and soon you dropped into a depleted and whimpering sleep.

Claire was not the first girl I had failed, of course; far from it. It was not the first time I had watched the night drag its scarves across your retinae, nor lain sick with grief and self-loathing over my inadequacy. But Claire's death hurt in a new way, a spreading ache that seemed to blot out the world, even as I knew that sorrow was properly Lore's.

It was as if I borrowed her pain for my own ends. The fact was, Lore's suffering was valuable to me.

I could not cry with your eyes. Events would teach me the trick of it in due course.

At perhaps six in the morning the stairs creaked—you slept then in a dingy room with a private back entrance—and I began to race with mingled eagerness and fear, whirling around the fishbowl of your useless head. I had done my best with the letter, but I had no way to know if it had found its destination, if two small blue hands had caught it, if they had reached to adjust her pince-nez before tearing into the envelope.

The doorknob rattled almost imperceptibly. It turned.

And my dear Anura slipped into the room, wearing her human shape. The pewter dawn cast just enough light to reveal her eyes silvered by tears, her brows peaked and mouth wide in a withheld cry as she saw you.

No. It was not you she saw; never, never. She looked through you to the ghost waiting within, then advanced on light feet and crouched low enough to rest her forehead on yours, on *me*. Never, living or dead, had I felt such tenderness in anyone's touch.

"Catherine," she whispered, raising herself. "Oh, Catherine. It's been so long, *again*. Once I learned where he'd sent the beamer only to arrive too late. But I tried so hard, I *tried*."

I blinked wildly, and she smiled through her tears and shook herself and drew out a pad of paper and a pen, both quite ordinary unworld items. She held the pad upright for me, and I wrote on it at a slightly awkward angle. But it served well enough.

I tried too. They still die. Claire died. In all this time, I've only saved two from him. Anura, I'm so bitterly sorry.

"Each life you saved might have spared another dozen from the blight of grief," Anura said, with reckless heat. You weren't drunk on this occasion, only in a deep sleep, and yet her voice spiked incautiously. Then she recalled herself and whispered, "Think of that! Think of the parents, the siblings, the friends who won't break down in tears because someone in the street looks like the one they lost. *Only* two, you say! Each mortal life forms a star in a vast constellation, their linkages drawn by love. This is why destroying Gus Farrow must be our entire focus; so many, *many* lives depend on us."

This gave me pause. Not only because you switched a little in your slumbers, but also, I realized after a moment, because I was unused to hearing Nautilusers speak of nonmagical persons in such a reverential vein. Her luminous sincerity recalled to mind the trance speaker Nora Downs, whom I'd seen so very, very long ago. If I am brutally honest with myself, I can see that I have been drawn to those whose deep-heartedness contrasts with my own shortcomings. Do I fear to feel too deeply, or do I merely fail?

In retrospect, I recognize another strain that lay concealed in my feelings then. I did not want Anura to be quite so eager to see Gus dead, not when I would vanish with him. I wanted her to say that, if only we could contrive to save *most* of the girls, or possibly only *many* of them, then perhaps his death was not so urgent a matter after all.

But it was not in her to say such a thing. Anura was better by far than I.

In the lull, she located a chair and lifted it silently to your bedside. Once she was seated we resumed our conversation.

I didn't save Dolores Rojas from such a loss. Her guiding star is gone.

"Why do you blame yourself? Why not blame me? If only I had come sooner, maybe Claire could have been saved."

I did not like to say, of course, that Anura's magic was not of a caliber likely to have changed the outcome. She knew that perfectly well without my reminding her, and she sighed.

"I went to see her before I came to you tonight; Dolores, I mean. She was right there in the phone book. I tend to agree with your assessment. There's a sizzle to her." Anura smiled. "Not that she knew why I had come. I spun the most outrageous lies, pretended to be with some charity that visits the recently bereaved. She believed it all and doused me with tears until my coat dripped. This humanskin might smell rotten to me, but it comes in handy for such business."

I could imagine; few indeed would slam their doors in a face whose every lineament proclaimed *ministering angel*. And if I cringed a little at the picture Anura called up, well. I had a duty that superseded such selfishness.

So will you do it? Take her under your—I could not say *wing* to a frog—*protection, and teach her?*

"No one has ever sought me out as a mentor. Cultivating new talents is a game for the powerful, or at the very least for the *average*. Not for someone whose own production is so feeble that she must supplement it by working as an immigration clerk." That was not the only way she supplemented her personal magic, of course. We both heard the unspoken allusion to her bribe-taking, and she blushed.

Not all power can be measured in talens. This was a truly heretical statement for any Nautiluser, even an unwilling one like myself. *To me, your sorcery is the rarest in all Nautilus.*

She read my note and flushed an even deeper crimson. All at once I feared the various implications of my compliment—there were several possible interpretations; after all, I could have meant it merely in praise of her poetry!—and I could not control which reading she chose, nor even know.

"But I'll try to approach her, Catherine. I can see how a sorceress with a vendetta all her own would make an excellent ally for you. Of course, it will mean telling her the truth. Awkward after my charade." She was only reverting to the main and quite pressing subject, so why did it feel as if she were avoiding something?

Thank you. I've been watching Dolores for months while the beamer watched Claire. There's something in her that's waiting for this, I'm nearly certain. She has a secret sense of her own magical potential, and she's in a state of constant expectation that someone extraordinary will appear and confirm it.

"Claire could do that for her figuratively, and now I've come along to bludgeon her with the literal version," Anura observed wryly. "I lived once in a similar state of nebulous hope, no matter how many times people assured me magic didn't exist. Conceive of my disappointment when I discovered that I was indeed magical, but also hopelessly third-rate."

She delivered the words like a joke, which they were not. I was still stinging from the last compliment I'd offered, and dared not risk another reference to how very far from third-rate I thought her.

You may not generate many talens, but you understand the theory, and you can explain it all clearly and vividly, I wrote, changing the subject in my turn. *You'll make an excellent teacher.*

"You've evidently been doing a fine job of teaching yourself," she told me, with a slightly forced vivacity. "You know, I recently heard the story of the time Old Darius tried to give you a lesson—he still tells it and others repeat it, one to the next, so I can't say how accurate the version was that came to me. But I'm told you attacked him with a tangle of roots, absolutely spontaneously and with no guidance at all?"

I thought back to that encounter in the clearing, so very long ago. To the little tongue of magic that had lashed out then. The sensation of magic in me had unraveled with my death. But death had also burst the cork, if I may so term it, that Darius had installed to keep me from defending myself. Magic diffused and escaped, becoming—as I now understand it—all of me.

I did. I hardly knew how I'd done it, though. It felt to me as if the world itself meant to be rid of him.

"Botanical magics, then. Is that still the direction you're working in?"

What direction *was* I working in? My explorations were as blind as a cave fish. I could hardly articulate what I was doing, even to myself. But since it was Anura who was interested, I made an effort to track down the words for it.

No. At the time I was very much interested in botany and natural history, but now life and its manifestations feel too remote from me. My concerns now are more with in-between states. Slippages, wavering borders, gaps in reality. Cracks and shadows. I suppose for obvious reasons.

(Oh, does something now occur to you? Are you wondering if you might not be familiar with my work? Fool. You should have wondered long ago.)

Anura read this elucidation and laughed, loudly and unguardedly, then clapped a hand over her mouth as you stirred. If you woke it would be a disaster for me, terminating a visit I'd craved for so long in the best case. Alerting you, perhaps even Gus, in the worst. There were ten days left to your year, ten whole days where Anura knew where to find me, and it would be unbearable to squander them!

But still, *still,* I could not help loving her merry imprudence.

Dawn now swept the room with oblique fingers, like someone groping for a dropped object under a sofa. Anura's golden waves shone pink-tipped, and she bounced a little in her chair, impatient for you to settle again. When at last you did she took the pen, scribbling a message before turning it to me.

I'll write, too, for a while. The nasty thing is getting fitful. I owe you another apology, I'm sorry to say. Are you tired yet of hearing me say that?

I could never be tired of anything you had to say. But also, you don't.

Now that we two were communicating in the same medium, I felt freer, as if we had submerged together in some charged and precious fluid and found we breathed more easily therein.

I do. Because I was ready to judge you for letting Gus carry on with his murders, when the truth is that I have the power to stop him myself. I'm guilty of the purest selfishness, putting my own happiness ahead of those girls. Their actual survival *is at stake, their whole lives, and I value it lower than my needs. It's disgraceful.*

I guessed what she meant, of course. *What do you mean?*

At any moment I could expose Gus for bribery and have him exiled; every heartstring carries traces of its transactions no matter how you try to hide them, so I have definite proof. The catch is that I'd have to go too. To me, life in the unworld would mean exile from myself. *But how can that outweigh all those deaths? It can't.*

Even in the unworld Gus could take decades to die. He'd keep killing. In fact, I imagined his enterprise would be somewhat hobbled without all the magical resources of Nautilus at his disposal. But I could not tell her that.

True. But he couldn't kill indefinitely. His death would be set in motion, just as mine would. A pause. *Catherine, I'm afraid I've come without your thousand talens. I could manage twenty, but—*

I won't take a single lit from you! You should know that. I knew her pride would find this unacceptable. I tried again. *Your work tutoring Dolores will more than repay that sum.*

It won't repay it at all! But I'll find a way. I can't tell you how ashamed I still am, that I took a bribe extracted by torturing you.

Anura, all is forgiven. Please don't think of it again.

It's not your choice to forgive me.

It was her own, she meant. There was no point trying to persuade her otherwise.

Asterion knows, too, you know. He's blackmailing Gus with his knowledge. I've been trying to come up with some way to protect you, in case Asterion turns on him.

Don't even think of protecting me, Catherine! Don't you dare, not if it means protecting Gus into the bargain. Just because I'm too cowardly to face the consequences myself, it doesn't mean I shouldn't. Not at the price of all those girls just—swept away. If you see any opportunity to take Gus down, no matter what form that opportunity takes, you have to seize it! Promise me.

I could not keep such a promise, and I think she understood that was the case. She passed me the pen and, while I held it, a softness rose between us, a pillowing darkness, in which the promise waited, unmade.

So it remained.

Anura? Can I ask you something?

Always and ever and anything.

You're so different with me than you were with Gus. Both Anuras feel like you, but they also feel contradictory. I'm not sure I understand—

Which self is the truer one? Dear Catherine, I am an amphibian, after all. I didn't choose my form by accident! I have an air-self and a water-self, if you like. They aren't so simple to reconcile. Sometimes I feel that no word I can say will ever be whole, able to speak for both aspects at once.

Her air-self, I thought: that must be the Anura of the immigration office, dry, sardonic, laconic, who crouched and groused atop her paperwork. And her water-self, that was the poet, ardent and free-flowing in her emotions, vivacious as a brook. Splashing from rage to gentleness and full of sudden sympathies where no one else could be bothered—

In this way I mentally divvied her up into the selves she described. But I can't say if she would have agreed with these rough assignments, *poet* over here and *bureaucrat* there. Perhaps she meant something much more subtle. Subtlety has never been among my strengths.

I think I understand, I wrote. *And here I am, literally divided. But even now that I can write to you, each word sounds in my ears like an endless scream.*

You have a lot to scream about.

Not to you. I want, when I speak to you—what? too many things to list, to even know—*I want to hear it all in my human voice again.* Or rather—*I want you to know my voice as something more than a scream.*

This impossibility brought us both to a halt. The larynx, lips, tongue, throat which had once supported my voice: all those things were gone, decayed and returned to earth. The hands that might have held hers, the arms that might have wrapped around her, the lips that might have wandered—oh. I could not afford to think of it, but neither could I stop.

For the first time it struck me that, if only I had accepted Darius as my mentor, I might have been a sorceress in Nautilus, contained in a living body rightfully my own, and in that condition met Anura. Nineteen forever, moderately pretty, and alight with power; very possibly intriguing.

I do hear a voice in your words, Anura wrote after a moment, *not screaming at all. Warm and strong. But of course the tone is only my invention. Could you try to write me something that* doesn't *sound like a scream to you? A whisper, a murmur?*

I could; those words were clear in my mind. But at the same time I could not.

And here, vile creature that you are, you twitched and thrashed again. I could register a growing pressure in your bladder; the thought that the gross claims of your body would interrupt my conversation with Anura, when I had no body of my own, was nearly maddening. We didn't have much longer, that I knew.

Tonight is the happiest I've been since I was murdered, I wrote at last. *Even in deep grief and regret over my failure, my joy is stronger.* Anura read the words, then turned a searching look on your face. It was futile; your expressions were your own, not mine. She could not read my feeling in your vacant eyes. Her long fingers reached to slip the pen from your hands.

And with that motion you thrashed like a bagged snake. We both knew you were on the verge of waking.

Anura gave up on writing and leaned close, whispering urgently. "Catherine, listen, there are strange rumors circulating in Nautilus; about Gus and Asterion and you. *Especially* you. Laudine and I haven't been able to get at the truth of them yet, but she's befriended Sky to try to learn more. He's mixed up in it, too, somehow."

Rumors about me? My unvarying flash and scream did not seem to lend themselves to narrative. What stories could be adrift on Nautilus's endless currents?

But before I could ask, you woke.

You could not open your eyes; I already held the lids apart. But from my perch inside you I could feel your mind drawing back its shutters and knocking in confusion against what you saw. You groaned and sat up, cupping your swollen cheek.

Anura stood at once, lightly and soundlessly, and slipped the pad into a pocket. I watched her assume a smile of infinite softness and turn her blue eyes into wells of invitation. I suppose it was the same affect she had put on when she knocked on Dolores's door.

You gawked at her and rubbed your eyes, preparing to say *Who are you? What are you doing here?* But she forestalled you.

"Don't be alarmed, Angus Farrow," Anura lilted in a voice like distant bells. "I'm here as a friend."

Complacent and dull-witted creature that you are, you were all too ready to accept that this golden-haired vision was some sort of private fairy, with no purpose beyond soothing your heart and advancing your interests.

"It's like a nightmare," you complained directly, as if Anura necessarily knew and cared for all your troubles. "Poor Claire! I think I killed her. But I didn't mean to! It was just a *kiss*, there was no way I could know."

Given my privileged position, if I can call it that, I recognized this for a lie. If you hadn't precisely *known*, you had certainly suspected what your kiss would do. I'd preserved enough memories from your previous incarnations to make sure of that much.

"Of course you didn't know! How could you?" Anura trilled. I thought she was struggling to suppress caustic laughter. "You sweet, unfortunate boy, forced against your will to bear a terrible curse."

"Is that what it is? A curse? Who cursed me, then?"

In these days, Gus still haunted the unworld to keep an eye on you; it was only much later, when he was too afraid to age any more, that he resorted to his crude tricks, first with candles and smoke, then with telephones and a disembodied mockery of poor Margo. You had glimpsed him several times as he dogged your steps, and you were not as naive as you pretended.

"You cursed yourself. More precisely, you *are* your own curse." She offered a beatific smile. "You've murdered many others before Claire. Didn't you know that? But someday the curse will be extinguished for good. And you with it."

She turned toward the door. You stared after her, too blundering and bewildered to realize that you should leap and seize her and force her to explain herself.

Instead you looked wounded. "How can you be so mean to me? You said you came as a friend!"

"Oh, I did," Anura shot over her shoulder. "Just not yours."

You scrambled out of bed, yanked pants over your nakedness, and thudded down the stairs in pursuit. Too late, of course. Anura was gone.

It was petty of me, no doubt. But I took advantage of your extreme distraction and made you piss yourself on the landing.

Amphibiana

—Anura

The lily floats upon the pond,
White grace, pink flush, the placid glow
Of drowsy bruiseless innocence—
But go below.

Where stems stand coarse and wavering,
In murk where all can be denied,
And weaving roots suckle the mud,
Find grace belied.

Dive deep, and watch the bubble swell:
A lucid globe, whose nations rise
Till it becomes a world entire
In liquid skies.

Its brindled lights spill past like seas
Where ships have sailed, where birds have flown,
Until the clap of ravening air
Reclaims its own.

I speak a word, it hovers close,
A promise rapt on speed-blurred wings,
So green with truth, so blue with hope,
Each cadence rings—

And in the water it reflects
Distorted, stirred, curved as an eye
That winks to see what I called truth
Become a lie.

Catherine in the Shadow

How can I describe the shadow that fell over me then? I didn't go to see the Skelleys, not even to tell Thomas goodbye before he went away to university. I felt his bewildered sorrow touch me through the intervening air, and tightened my shoulders. I gave up studying and only stared at the corner of the room, or let the muscle memory of a thousand repetitions carry me through my chores.

If I hadn't murdered, my reprieve was due to the purest luck. I knew that part of me had wanted to murder Darius, had passionately attempted to do so. Worse, that part of me was magic, and I could still feel it flicking, tasting, a snake's tongue so deeply interwoven with my being that I could not drive it out. How could I know what it would do next? In the dark I felt its caresses, its intimate crawl inside my brain, like a whisper made tactile. It seemed to tell me that, whatever I wished to the contrary, I belonged to Gus's hidden realm; to Darius; to Gus himself, with whom I turned so withdrawn and dull that he hardly knew what to make of it.

Everyone knew, I thought, even if they didn't guess *what* they knew. Reverend Skelley knew. That must be why he made no effort to talk to me. I understand now, of course, that he had shame of his own, and didn't know how to speak past it—but it was as if my eyes had grown unaccustomed to seeing anything outside my own internal murk.

Into the shadow slipped a year—a whole year, of the nineteen that I lived. The days passed and made almost no impression on me.

Until the next summer, when I heard a knock at the door, a scuffling retreat. On the threshold was a basket; in the basket was a blackberry pie of startling perfection, still warm, and an unsigned note.

Please will you see me, just once? I swear I'll never bother you again.

"Oh, Thomas, of course none of it is your fault. You're innocent. When have you ever been anything else?" I said aloud, and started to cry with sharp relief and a sort of wild, waving gratitude. The next thing I knew I was out the door, and running as fast as I could. I could see him in the distance, by that stile where I'd been sitting with Gus and Margo when I learned of my mother's death.

"Thomas," I yelled. "Thomas!"

He heard me and wheeled around, as thin and dust-colored and undistinguished-looking as ever. But the joy on his face was like the beating of wings.

Then he saw my tears and lapsed into confusion. I reeled to a halt near him, with a sickened intimation that what I was, and what he was, must not be allowed to touch.

"Thomas," I gasped out. "You must not think—I *forbid* you to think—that you're to blame for anything I've done, or anything that's happened, or ever will. There are things I can't explain—"

But he was babbling, too, with the pressure of too many nights spent searching for where he'd gone wrong, with words rehearsed to the point of incoherence. "I wanted to say—I never had any expectations of you, Catherine, I *knew* I couldn't aspire, truly. Forgive me, if I seemed to? I'm sure you deserve whatever elevation the world will grant you, and more, and I was grateful simply to call you my friend."

Here we stopped, both realizing that we were reciting lines from two different plays, as it were. A moment's baffled silence followed before I laughed, albeit a bit hysterically. He handed me his handkerchief and I blotted my face.

"If the world has any plans to elevate me, it's kept the secret remarkably well! What are you *talking* about?"

I truly hadn't understood until he flushed scarlet—hadn't understood in more than one sense. I was shocked out of my morose inwardness by the urge to protect him, and by the realization of just how delicate that operation would be.

"It's just, there was something Margo Farrow told my father, after their last sitting. But maybe there was some confusion?"

Margo again! Annoyance heated my cheeks, to find her still interfering with me. "Margo Farrow is hardly an authority on my feelings. What did she say?"

Thomas stared at his shoes.

"You can tell me, Thomas."

"She said that, since you'd given up studying with my father for your college entrance exams, it must mean that you had an understanding with—only you couldn't *say* yet, because of his—" Thomas looked as if he might choke. "I'm sorry."

"I see. Margo Farrow is entirely mistaken. There is no understanding of that kind, and there never will be." As long as everything between Gus and me had stayed undefined—nothing but smear, drift, vaporous insinuation—I hadn't felt it clearly enough to resist it. Since marriage between Gus and me was unthinkable, why should I bother to think it? Hearing Thomas come so close to naming that drowsy undertow put a new stiffness into my spine. "There *is* a bond between Gus and me. But it's not at all what Margo seems to think."

The bond was what we knew of each other; it was the secret, puissant malice that we'd each seen manifest in the other, the guilt that reflected back and forth between us in silent conversation. The charge that laced our common air shook with revulsion, and there was at least as much hatred in it as love.

This was the first moment in all our long years of friendship when I identified that strand in my feelings: that I hated Gus for our connection. And yet I knew how he'd protected me on the day I felled Darius, and felt ashamed.

"But—" Thomas was nearly inaudible. "Would Margo Farrow think it, if *he* didn't?"

Gus could not actually expect to marry me. The idea was absurd.

"I've given him no reason to. And I can't imagine that he would. Apart from the obvious barriers, Gus wants very different things from life than I do." I realized something else then: that I'd been waiting for Gus to grow bored of my depressed spirits, my passive resistance to his plans. I'd been waiting for him to give up and leave for Nautilus without me. Darius, I knew, had retreated there shortly after the incident in the clearing, and it had seemed only a matter of time before Gus would follow.

But he hadn't. Now I wonder: had I resorted to such a leaden, indirect stratagem because, somewhere far below my conscious awareness, I was afraid of what Gus might do if I spoke plainly?

Thomas said nothing, but something in the quality of his silence made me aware of the inadequacy of my words—and not only on Gus's account.

"So you see, I had other reasons for ceasing my studies with your father." How the reality of other people rushed back on me, like a wind across a wide ocean! I'd left both Thomas and Reverend Skelley to wonder why I'd vanished so abruptly, to accuse themselves for a rupture that came from my private reserves of violence. "But I suppose I owe him an explanation."

"That would be good of you," Thomas said, very softly. "I know it grieved him."

Knowing what I was, knowing my own indwelling potential for cruelty and disorder, I couldn't allow Thomas to love me either. But I wasn't sure how to stop him, and resorted to changing the subject.

"You said he's going to sittings with Margo Farrow again? I hope the spirits are better behaved than the night I was there!"

He met this turn toward flippancy with one of his rare glances, sharp with awareness of my evasion. "There's been nothing."

"Nothing?"

"Not since the night you came, and that was years ago now. Margo Farrow thought they ought to persist. They've been sitting together every week for nearly a year, even brought in different mediums a few times. Nothing at all has happened, not even rapping. My father's about to give it up."

I could hardly justify the relief this news brought me—except that anything connected with the derangement of nature now suffused me with dread. "I can't say I'm disappointed to hear it."

"But now Mrs. Hobson has promised to visit again this winter. Margo's trying to persuade him to keep going until then."

I was seventeen at that time. I could not possibly have known, then, that I had less than two years left to live, and an eternity left to endure. But at the mention of that slight, sly, and certainly powerful old lady, cold mercury seemed to roll through my veins, draining warmth and strength as it went. For a moment terror held me distant from all the bright and breathing world, and I could not say what it was I feared.

I suppose I have a fair idea now.

"Catherine?" Thomas called anxiously. "Catherine, are you all right?"

"Tell your father I'll visit you both soon," I said. I was striving for calm, but I know he heard the tremor in my voice. "And thank you for the pie. It looks wonderful."

As soon as his back was turned, I sat down hard on the stile and tried to master myself: my heartbeat that seemed to be racing away from me, the black dots crowding at the edges of my vision. I gripped a jutting lip of stone and breathed as deeply as I could.

A question had been waiting inside me through all my shadowed year, I realized then. It was the presence of that question, gnawing and yet unacknowledged, that had brought me so low.

Now I lifted my chin and answered it.

In trying to save Gus, I'd only damned myself: that truth seemed unavoidable. I'd made myself unfit for a life of sweetness and decency; for their own protection, I must isolate myself from the likes of Thomas Skelley.

But I would be the one to dictate the form my damnation would take. Not Darius, not Gus, not Mrs. Hobson or Margo, but I myself would choose, and proudly, the terms of my loneliness. If Gus and I were connected, I would not let that connection be my leash. I would never go to Nautilus. And if I could not always stop my magic from overflowing, I could at least keep myself safely apart from other people.

For that, though, I would require an education.

Angus Apologizing

At two twenty on the Wednesday after our date, I walk into Bluebell's. It's taken me a few days to get ready. I've moved to a youth hostel, hoping to evade Lore until it's time to skip town. Bought some rougher clothes at a thrift store. Secured a certain necessary vial. I'm good to go.

Geneva's repulsive metal-faced pal Drew is working the register—seriously, what's wrong with his beard? It looks like he has mange and he should really see a doctor—and he scowls when he sees me. What, just because Geneva said she's not interested that means I can't order a sandwich? I order a sandwich, ham and Swiss, and then I spot Geneva's tussle of sunset hair. She's crouched low with her back to me, pretending to organize take-out cups in a supplies cabinet. But I can tell from the way rigidity grips her back that she's completely aware of my presence.

Cool, cool. "What name?" Mangy Drew asks between set teeth. I notice that he doesn't offer to let me spin the roulette wheel.

"Angus," I tell him, and Geneva's tension ratchets again.

With that taken care of, it's time to dial down the pressure. Geneva knows I'm here, and sooner or later my proximity will be too much for her. She'll come to me on her own. So I turn and walk off into a back room where I've never been before, just as if my being here had nothing to do with her. It's a lot emptier than the front room too. A more relaxing place to have a serious discussion.

Bluebell's is such a cool café! Every imaginable surface back here, from walls to tabletops, is covered in a different vintage wallpaper, mostly garish florals. Even the backs of the chairs and the row of planters under the window. The effect is agitated and serene at the same time, like listening to loud, busy music that somehow settles your nerves. There are model ships on a shelf and needlepoint pillows portraying monkeys.

There's so much to take in that it's a while before I even notice the dusty upright piano, camouflaged as it is in more flowery patchwork.

I perch on the bench and think of my old piano, the rambunctious one with the hooves. Pet the chipped keys as if we were old friends.

The next thing I know, I'm playing it. Spectacularly well. I have no idea what the piece is, but I can tell it's classical and supposedly difficult, and yet every note has been coiled up in my fingers waiting to pop out. The piano could use a tuning, but the music in me is so hopping and pressurized and *eager* that I don't give a damn.

There were just a few people in odd corners of the room when I sat down, but now I can feel the air winding warmer and tighter the way it does when there's a crowd. Too many lungs in close proximity, all tugging on the same oxygen. I don't let myself look, but after a moment I pick up Geneva's humming *herness* a few rows back. I can feel her watching my shoulders—watching them rather attentively, in fact. Hah.

Then she's weaving through the gathered bodies. Coming closer.

"Angus," she says. "What the hell."

"Hi, Geneva." I don't stop playing. I find that I'm enjoying the audience, what with its built-in potential for making her feel awkward and embarrassed. "Is it okay if I talk to you for a minute when you're on break or something? I want to apologize."

"Pound out the Chopin nocturnes, apologize, what's the difference? You didn't say anything about—"

"Playing the piano? Honestly, I didn't know." Not in the sense that she knows things, anyway.

"The bullshit hangs heavy on your tongue. Years and years of training to even get *close*—"

"I didn't know it was Chopin either. So can we talk when you're free?" The crowd has started tittering behind us. I guess it's a cute scene if you aren't Geneva, who I'd put down as halfway between anxious and bemused, or Drew, standing ten feet to my right and palpably squeezing a bundle of rage behind his mange.

"Fine," Geneva says, and pivots. A minute or so later, Drew elbows through the crowd and plonks my sandwich on top of the piano, hard enough to knock the tomato slices loose. So terribly, *terribly* sorry, buddy. Try not to infect my ham with your face.

Once I finish the sandwich, I go back for a lemonade and some chocolate cake. Geneva serves me this time, studiously blank. She drops the customary marble in my palm without looking at me.

I plop it on number nineteen, gold on a scarlet background. Spin hard. The little pointy clicker thing ticks around and around, slowing and then wavering before it stops.

Nineteen it is.

"See, Geneva? Luck is with me."

"Luck is notorious for its shit taste," Geneva snarks back, and I tip her five bucks, then head back and find a table.

I eat my cake and try to journal for another half hour or so. It's as impossible as ever. The letters liquefy under my eyes, and I can't guess what story I'm telling. But when I riffle through the pages it turns out I've filled a lot of them, nearly the whole book in fact. I had no idea I'd been so productive?

"Apologize for what?" Oh, that sweetly gruff voice, those violet undertones. I'm sitting with my back to the front room. Geneva approached silently, and I was so distracted I didn't notice. She's standing behind my shoulder, and I twist around to look up at her. Hands on her hips, even. One big hazel eye illuminated by a slice of lamplight that turns the inner ring of her iris emerald-bright, the other eye dimmed by shadow. "What *exactly*?"

Thank God for Margo's guidance, is all I can say. "My behavior on Saturday night was presumptuous and entitled," I say. "I'm sorry." The words are good, but my tone doesn't quite cut it. Too much like I'm reciting a lesson, and Geneva doesn't soften much.

"You do know that was a first fucking date. Even if we'd been *engaged*, you would have been over the line."

"I know," I say. "I know. You owe me nothing. I was really out of control. When I thought about how I'd acted, I felt ashamed of myself. I'm sorry." Better! A little stink of sincerity huffs out! "It made me finally realize that I need help, so I owe you for that. Seriously, thank you."

Geneva goes silent. This, right here, is the crux of it. Can't rush her.

Then she sits down across from me. Victory, bitch.

"What kind of help?" The room's cleared out now, and she really doesn't need to talk so softly.

I pull my prop out of my pocket. Some very serious shit prescribed yesterday by an impressionable shrink. She knows what it's for, I guess, because her face goes still.

"Is it helping?"

"God, yes. I feel like I've come back to earth. Back to *myself,* after a long time away. I know who I am now, and it's so liberating, I can't even tell you." Strategic pause. "Partly it was seeing how you reacted to what I thought were my memories—it shocked me back to reality. Enough for me to reevaluate, anyway."

"You weren't kidding about that stuff? The anthill?" Her T-shirt today is bright green with podgy pastel dinosaurs all over it, lifting succulent-plump snouts.

Gee, Geneva, what's up with your voice? It's so quiet you'd think termites were gnawing it. You sound downright undermined.

"I wasn't kidding." Strategic pause, part two. "I don't know why you got through to me when no one else could. But you might have literally saved my life."

She's smarter than me, I know that much. But my lies ring a lot truer to her than my truth ever could. Funny how that works.

"And that other really off-the-chain thing you said? That you love me?" Geneva's mouth tightens with the awkwardness of bringing up my declaration. "That's cleared up too?"

I roll my eyes in mock-embarrassment. "Oh, Jesus. I can't believe I said that. Can you imagine how frenzied and confused I must have been, to blurt something like that at someone I barely know?" Geneva's too strong-minded to be disappointed, exactly, but I can see a quick dip in the shimmer of her gaze. Even she has her share of insecurities, it turns out. *Don't overplay your hand, Angus.* "I was so out of my head that I couldn't tell the difference between attraction and love."

She hesitates, but then it comes out. "Even you being attracted to me felt way too random."

"Oh, that part's not random at all." *A refusal to accept the world's*

336 S. E. PORTER

terms, a certain brisk clarity. "I think you're beautiful, and I like the way you don't put up with my bullshit."

Well, she didn't until today. But she smiles at the compliment even now that she doesn't quite deserve it.

"Angus? Can I be honest about something? It's just like a physical thing, I think, but I'm really attracted to you too." And there we have it. From the phone in my pocket comes a thunderous burst of applause; oh, so I guess my imaginary Margo and I have made up? "You just seemed too messed up for me to risk—doing anything with you."

Oh, Geneva. If only Lore didn't care for you, would I let you go?

I grin and reach out, my fingers barely stroking a flyaway tuft of her hair. "Oh, but now the risk has been reduced to an acceptable level?"

What better vengeance can I hope for than to claim this girl Lore loves? I'll make my charming killer feel for all time how she failed when it mattered most. And Gus, well. Gus will be at least annoyed.

Geneva actually blushes. "That's kind of what I'm thinking, yeah."

Geneva shimmers with promise. She could become almost anything she decided to be. Her possible selves are legion, ranked up like an army of vivid, accomplished women.

When she dies, there won't be enough ground on this planet to bury all the futures that might have been hers.

Catherine Caught

Mercifully, you chose to spend the dregs of your year sopped in drink, dead to the days that remained to you. I was able to see Anura twice more while you slobbered and groaned on your tear-damp pillow, and for longer than our first interrupted visit. One night, at my request, she read me her poems for hours, and from that immersion in her mind I emerged as if newborn; that is, very fresh, very hungry, yowling, and streaked with blood.

I think, though, that I will keep the substance of those meetings private from you. They meant too much for me to allow your mind to sully them.

As for those rumors Anura had mentioned, she didn't have much concrete to tell me. I myself was now listening as intently as I could, where I waved over Gus's head; but whatever the gossip was, everyone was careful not to mention it in Gus's presence. Uncomfortable silences fell sometimes when Gus and I appeared, and Anura and Laudine caught only somewhat more. A welter of overheard phrases brushed the magic-tainted air of Nautilus, and a smattering of those phrases were *Catherine Bildstein* and *Farrow will never do it* and *Asterion thinks he'll be in favor! Hardly seems likely* and *She'd be the first ghost queen the city's ever had*—the latter so patently absurd that I tried to shrug your intoxicated shoulders, then decided that they must have been discussing some other ghost with whom I was not acquainted.

Sky was flattered by Madame Laudine's attention, Anura said; soon she hoped to tell me more. But we both knew Anura might not find your next iteration, and this one was drawing to its close. There was no telling how many Anguses would rise, pretty skins rigged over the ground meat that was once Christopher Flynn, how many would burn out their lives, before I could see Anura once again.

How tempted I was to beg her to seek me out in Nautilus, where we could find each other at almost any time! But the risk was too great; Gus would likely discover our friendship, and what would he do then?

In the event, the number of Anguses was seventeen. Seventeen, before I saw Anura as more than a blue glimmer hopping down one of Nautilus's alleys, or perched on Laudine's head near the Nimble Fire! These glimpses came much more often than they once had, and I knew that she wanted to be near me, even if we could not speak.

Sometimes Dolores Rojas was with her, at first still in her original appearance as a slender, studious girl with bobbed dark hair. Then she became Lore and wore antlers, and silver glazed her brown skin. I knew her abilities must be advancing rapidly, and soon she would be ready to hunt Anguses. I knew, and watched, and warned your targets where I could.

I tried slitting your throat once in your sleep, but it was sadly ineffective, troubling you no more than a cold. Two days and you were back on your feet. I gave it up; it was too liable to excite Gus's attention for such a pitiful return in canceled time.

A dozen Anguses later, Lore had developed her own methods of dispatching you. Anura and I had not been wrong in identifying her as a likely talent! Twice she found and killed you without even waiting long enough to allow Anura and me to meet. I would have been angry, except that in both cases you were moments from yet another murder.

I restored more memories in every new Angus. Gus responded first by warding those memories with pain, then by angrily walling off whole rafts of them—and though he complained, he had no suspicion *why* your amnesia was so faulty. Lore hunted you; he made you faster, stronger, more sensitive. I believe the modern term is an *arms race*, though for Gus his enemies were invisible.

As for the gossip, it ebbed away, burgeoned again, ebbed. If there was some scheme afoot, the conspirators were in no particular hurry. But then, why would they be? Near-immortality lends itself to considerable procrastination.

And when I did see Anura? It was not in the unworld, but in Nautilus. We had agreed that such a meeting must never happen, and of course the screaming, immaterial form I wore in Nautilus couldn't keep up its side of a conversation.

The results were disastrous.

It happened when we were between Anguses. Gus was focused on countering me and Lore and grew careless regarding other aspects of your creation. When it came to shaping your false memories, he became downright lackadaisical, as you've perhaps observed. But though he strived less, he complained more loudly and frequently of weariness. It was all my fault, I ought to have loved him by now, and did I mean to work him to the bone?

He was getting old. Overindulgence in unworld visits will do that to a man.

It was in such a state of querulous exhaustion that Gus set his work aside and shuffled off to one of the public gardens. I supposed he meant to sit on a bench and stare up at the elaborate clouds that had then come into vogue. They were living sculptures that shifted and recomposed themselves in mimicry of the real thing, towed across our dusky skyless sky on threads of magic. Cloudcraft was yet another game for the rich, like trying to depose the current ruler—The Going hadn't lasted long, now we had someone called Milk in charge. The clouds, at least, were pretty, though inferior to the unworld variety in my view. But the political machinations I considered purely ridiculous.

As Gus shambled along the pearlescent alleys and boulevards, I became aware of something behind us, something that moved low to the ground. Many sorcerers used biothurgic animals in various capacities, of course. It was probably only a familiar out running errands—so I told myself.

But the being was too persistently at our heels for that. I thought Sky might have sent his cat to spy on us. I twisted myself backward, trying to get a better look. Whatever or whoever it was, it employed a sort of obscuring magic that made my gaze skate into confusion when I stared. I could catch only a lolloping motion free of color and contour alike. But the enchantment was—forgive me—rather cut-rate, and with a few moments' effort I penetrated it.

Just in time to see Anura squeezing herself behind an architectural flourish with no name I know; it looked something like alabaster kelp rippling from the walls. She did not wear her pince-nez off duty, and there was an odd innocence to her look without those lenses. Her scarlet eyes caught mine, and she raised one small blue hand in silent greeting. My own uncontrolled thrashing would not allow a gesture as specific as hers, but I managed a sloppy swing of my left arm.

If she meant *Hello*, I meant, *Get away! What are you thinking? If Gus sees us, everything will be ruined.*

But I was incapable of meaning it wholeheartedly. The sight of her sparked in me like delight. I wanted to gust against her, horror though I was, and brush her with the joy and giddy welcome that filled my thoughts. It had been too long, simply, even for one desensitized to loneliness beyond the scope of any ordinary life.

Gus reached the park, a few lit flying from him as he stepped onto blue grass that waved with a ceaseless underwater motion. We were in the Lapis Gardens, where every bloom and leaf alike was blue: around us azure bells drooped over livid leaves furred in ghostly periwinkle, and cerulean stalks flourished their midnight lilies, each petal specked with stars. Anura loped softly after us, keeping some three yards behind Gus. The turf's color was a good match for Anura's frogskin, and I was foolish enough to hope that she would pass unnoticed.

She had a large envelope of pale blue leather strapped to her back. Once Gus found a bench and folded onto it with a sigh, she unbuckled the straps and pulled out pen and paper, waving them at me significantly. As if I wouldn't have paid attention otherwise! She held up a note printed in large letters.

Catherine, sorry, it couldn't wait! We've learned something.

I had no way to reply. But of course Anura knew I was more cognizant than I seemed. Once she felt sure I had absorbed her message she set to work writing a longer one, then held it up as well.

Laudine went to a party at Sky's. La Merveilleuse was there, very drunk. She bragged that she and Asterion together had tricked Gus into bringing you to Sky. "Asterion was ready to pay a lot if we could get him there, and a lot more than that if Sky performed the operation! But the bastard balked at that. As for what was in it for the minotaur, I don't know. But I can guess."

La Merveilleuse. I remembered her, of course; she was the wheedling old sorceress who'd slipped Gus Sky's name behind Asterion's back. Or so Gus and I had both thought. But Asterion had been enraged by Gus's visit to Sky; surely the minotaur was not as gifted an actor as all that?

Anura might have read these speculations in my eyes. She nodded as if she understood me and turned to a fresh page. Gus gaped up at the clouds and hummed.

She said, "Then Sky double-crossed Asterion, offering Gus his own umbrastring just like that! That wasn't part of their bargain, oh no. Sky must have thought he could strike a better one if he went right to the source. The funny thing is, if Gus had taken the umbrastring, he'd have found he didn't have a ghost to poke with it!" La Merveilleuse was laughing madly, Laudine said.

The source? I thought—then realized, of course, that Asterion must have had a paymaster of his own. He was performing the dance steps in someone else's ballet, too coarse and unoriginal himself to think up such an elaborate plot. The exorbitant figures Asterion had quoted Gus for his victim's disassembly, his insistence that there was no other way Gus could accomplish his purpose: all of it was designed to make Gus bristle with contrariety and a stubborn determination to cast about for an alternative.

A few more maneuvers, and that alternative became Sky.

It had all been deftly arranged, I thought. And it showed an uncomfortably good grasp of Gus's character.

Catherine, Anura wrote, Sky doesn't want to use you himself. He wants to slice you off Gus because there's someone who will pay a fortune for you.

I had arrived at this conclusion myself before Anura finished writing the words. Asterion's rage was directed at Sky, not at Gus at all. Gus might have annoyed him by acting the uncooperative gull, but Sky had committed the unforgivable offense of trying to cut out the middleman. And that umbrastring—Sky had offered it on the condition that Gus and I were separated. I should have guessed that, once I was severed, Sky had no intention of reattaching me!

We don't know who it is yet, Anura added. Maybe a collector?

My emotions surged and my blinking sped, involuntary as ever, becoming a hectic tumble through coal black and phosphor blaze. It broke through Gus's daydreaming and tugged his eyes upward. An exasperated breath burst from his lips and he turned, looking to see what had so unsettled me.

Anura was stuffing papers back into her leather envelope while simultaneously hopping sidelong to conceal herself in the shrubbery.

She wasn't fast enough.

Gus's stare landed on her, and his pale green eyes met her ruby ones in silent confrontation. Her small blue fist still clutched a few loose notes, mostly inside the envelope—but her scribbled *Catherine* protruded in plain sight. Gus's gaze flicked to my name, then up to me, then to Anura again. For a fraction of a moment, she looked nearly sheepish.

Then she visibly recomposed herself. "Good afternoon, Mr. Farrow. It's a lovely day to visit the Lapis Gardens."

It was no day at all, and no afternoon, or not in the conventional sense. But such phrases die hard.

"What do you want with Catherine?" Gus demanded. He began the ungainly process of heaving himself from the seat, and I was glad the bench stood between them. It was not the sort familiar to unworld residents but a smooth curved slab of blue-shot crystal with a high back, and it made an excellent barrier. In her frog shape Anura was only some two feet in diameter, and very soft.

Anura assumed an air of gracious bafflement. "Catherine? You mean your ghost? There doesn't seem to be much anyone *could* want from her, does there?" Then a bitter smile cracked her politeness. "If I'd met Catherine before you murdered her, I suppose I could have invited her to play croquet, or go boating with me. But you made that difficult."

If I'd been able to speak I would have begged Anura not to bait him. But then she had ample anger of her own at our situation, and she was not much given to restraint.

Gus was standing with his hands spread on the bench's back, one knee propped on its seat. His eyes went wide with outrage.

"I didn't murder her," he rejoined at last. Flatly, coldly. "That is—a very vulgar misconstruction of what happened."

This was, as they say, news to me.

Anura had no eyebrows in her present shape. But the human expressions, the muscle memory of hiking eyebrows still dwelled in her, and her forehead bunched in an indignant chevron.

"Oh, indeed? Then who did?"

"His name was Thomas Skelley. I'm glad to report that he is long deceased."

Poor Thomas, to be so maligned! In our conversations, few but intimate, I had not told Anura the story of my very brief engagement—it was long ago, I thought, and had no bearing on the present moment. On our friendship. She had never heard the name before and wavered in perplexity.

Or, no—to be wholly truthful, I had not been eager to tell her that I had once loved a human man, in case she mistook those two categories for conditions. Hopeless, absurd, even silly as it was—

Never mind. Something flashed in her eyes. She guessed, if roughly, at Thomas's place in my story.

"How very unusual!" Anura drawled, fully in her languid immigration clerk's manner. "Imagine, a ghost who ignores her murderer and instead prefers to haunt an innocent man! Your Catherine is a real innovator."

"Catherine is joined to me by love," Gus announced. Haughtily. "Thomas Skelley tried to come between us, but as you can see he failed. *Anyone* who tries will fail." He navigated the end of his bench, and Anura hopped backward, surely fearing as I did that he meant to do her harm. But he contented himself with glaring down at her while I billowed high overhead. My dear Anura looked very small from this vantage, and very tender, with her emerald spots glowing and her long blue feet tensed to spring. "Don't presume to approach her again, *Miss* Anura."

I could do nothing as Gus turned and stormed out of the gardens, dragging me along with him. Anura leapt up on the bench's back to watch me for as long as she could, and I gazed back at her, twisting myself a full 180 degrees. I suppose to a cynical viewer it would have seemed more comical than touching, the shrieking ghost tilted in yearning toward the round blue frog, who stretched one delicate hand toward her in turn.

It was only a few moments before Gus towed me out of her view. But the sight of her perched on that crystal slab, her webbed toes curled and her gaze wistful, apologetic, remains one of my dearest and deepest impressions, whether from life or death.

Gus took me home. In lieu of slamming a door, he slammed himself through the cloudy zone defined by his lintel, yanking me roughly through its dreaming opacity and into his room. I heard his stertorous breath, saw his face purple as he stomped to his mirror and scowled at my reflection.

I wanted to be indifferent to his anger, to meet his scowl with bemused disdain. But such a pose is hard to maintain with someone who makes a habit of torturing you.

"You!" Gus snarled. "Colluding with my enemies! What did you say to her? Is there some kind of code, something you've kept hidden from me?"

I would have held my breath if I'd possessed such a thing. Gus, I told myself, did not, *could* not know about the schism that had given me my double life, or double death. He did not know how I hid in his Anguses, could never guess that I had found a way to speak—

"Is it your flashing? Are you using it as a signal?"

This would have been a fine idea if only I had that degree of control. My blinking, regrettably, is as involuntary as a heartbeat.

"That must be it," Gus said, nodding furiously. "You have a code, blinking messages to her and her cohort. I *know* there's something between you and that sickening creature, I can tell. Croquet! Do you want to play croquet with her? Do you?"

He picked up a glass and threw it at me—which meant that he performed the ludicrous maneuver of chucking it backward over his own head. It passed straight through me and shattered on the wall.

(Meanwhile the part of me invested in *you*, Angus, waited on a nearby table, crumpled in your folds. I screamed above but also felt myself quiet, immanent, compressed, a vein running through your hateful material. So far Gus had not guessed at my secret freedom. But what if he did? Could he somehow unpick me from you and condemn me to complete imprisonment in my wordless shriek again?)

"I've had time to get used to the treachery of men, God knows. Even the sorcerers here, who ought to be above such base behavior, are not to be trusted. If I was naive once, credulous, now my heart is hardened; I thought I was inured to betrayal. But coming from you, my own wife, when I've devoted my life to saving you! This, I wasn't prepared for."

This was a charming construction to put on the matter.

Even in the unworld people find time and life enough for the most fanciful reconstructions of their pasts. They rehearse their tales again and again, each time with subtle corrections in favor of their own innocence and the cruelty of their oppressors, until at last the vicious man discovers that he beat his small children in self-defense when the babes set upon him like wolves. The woman who seduced her friend's husband finds that she acted out of charity, the embezzler determines that he took the money only to assist the poor, never mind that he hadn't once parted from a nickel.

Gus's prolonged life allowed far more scope for such inventions. So I suppose it shouldn't have surprised me to find he'd now arrived at this picturesque version of our history, in which I was his cherished wife and Thomas Skelley my murderer.

But it did. I was frankly astounded. My scream sounded the same as ever, but it felt to me like nauseated laughter.

Even after all this time, a residue of our old understanding sometimes manifested between Gus and me. He flinched as if he could hear my mockery.

"I didn't lie to her!" Gus shouted at me. "Really, as if that oozing creature could be worth deceiving? What do I care what she thinks? Thomas Skelley *did* murder you, in his limp, pathetic, shrinking little way. If only he'd had the bare decency to understand that you were mine, you would be alive even now, and living here with me."

Gus dug a decanter out of his dirty blankets, and began to drink.

There followed an interminable interlude in which Gus flopped weepily around the room, punctuated by shouts of "How *could* you?" and "Oh, Catherine, Catherine my darling" and "Croquet!" and, more worrying, "What choice have you left me? Tell me that! What else am I to do?"

If I abbreviate the telling, it is for my sake, not yours. I endured this scene once in person and feel no need to do so a second time on the page.

At length he fell unconscious on the floor. I screamed on alone in the twilit glow, you sat lumpen in your ball, and my broken-off self wove through you, just as quiet as you and Gus were then.

When Gus woke it was with a green face and a malicious determination in his eye.

"Catherine, my love, I regret to say you've forced my hand. You know better than anyone how desperate I must be, to resort to such an extreme measure. But I can't always be awake and watching you, and you appear to be in secret confabulations with those who mean me ill. If only I knew the purpose of your conspiracy with Anura, and how far things have gone—but I don't. The truth is, you've abused my trust beyond repair."

This speech was delivered with chilly calm from a presumably throbbing head. There was a sorcerer skilled in relieving such maladies just down the street, and I imagined Gus would pay a visit soon. He was something of a regular.

"So you see," Gus continued, "there's nothing for it. I have to take you to Sky."

Catherine in the Wind

I'd promised to visit both of the Skelleys, but I knew I must speak to the Reverend alone. I waited behind a hedge until I saw Thomas leave with a satchel bulging with his sketch pads and specimen jars; he would be rambling in the woods for hours. Then I knocked.

"Catherine," Reverend Skelley said gently. "Come in. Thomas just went out for the afternoon, he'll be sorry to have missed you."

His tone was so soft that I thought he meant to welcome me back as if nothing had happened, to elide all confrontation and accusation. I was grateful for this kindness, of course, but also impatient with it. I was done with fog, with hints and implications. Everything must be made clear—or as clear as possible.

"I'm sorry I haven't been to see you in so long," I said. "I found myself afflicted with a disease of the mind, and it made me very selfish and ungrateful. You deserved better from me."

Reverend Skelley caught my brusque tone, and the impact tipped back his head. Then he nodded, reevaluating. "I thought you were angry with me."

"I was," I said. "I still am. But not so angry that I would disappear without a word for a whole year."

"Will you come in and have tea with me? It seems we have much to discuss."

I followed him into the parlor, which was so populated by papers and dropped books and lizard skeletons posed under bell jars that it had more the look of a ramshackle study. There was the same wooden armchair where I'd puzzled through my first lines from *Medea,* the same threadbare Turkish rug where Thomas and I had sprawled together on our backs, debating spontaneous generation. The whole scene touched me like longing materialized.

I hesitated and then took my old chair, and the Reverend smiled under his moustache. There was tea already made, and he slipped to the kitchen to secure a second cup, then poured it for me. It was over-steeped and quite bitter. He sat in his own upholstered Sheraton chair and looked at me, and there was so much waiting to be said that I choked on it.

"This disease of the mind you mentioned," he said at last, carefully. "Catherine, I hope you know that you can tell me anything in confidence, and be sure that I will never think any less of you?"

"I could tell you almost anything," I said. "But not that." I thought of saying that I was recovering, that he need not be concerned—but that was true only if *disease* was taken to refer to my depression. And that was by far the smaller part of it. "I can't tell you what I now know about myself without implicating others."

From the spark in his eyes, I knew he guessed I meant Gus. More than that: he blamed Gus for whatever afflicted me. I caught a flash of highly uncharacteristic anger, half hidden by his softness.

"I would never ask you to betray anyone's secrets, of course."

"But I can tell you this much," I pursued, doggedly treading down my own unwillingness to cause him grief. "I foresee a life of solitary self-discipline, of quiet; it will be necessary, if I'm to control my sickness. I can never marry. I beg you not to believe any speculations you might hear to the contrary—not to entertain any yourself. Please."

A pause. "And this is why you've been angry with me. Because you realized my hopes for you and my son."

"Because you weren't frank with me. I'm used to Margo Farrow attempting to design my life without consulting me, but I never expected that from you." I'd thought I was over the hurt of his calculation—that it had been drowned by a tide of deeper pains. But saying it aloud made my voice catch.

But Reverend Skelley was shaking his head. "Catherine, Catherine, I confess I hoped you would come to love Thomas. But you misunderstand—"

"What?" I said. "That you thought he was hopelessly unsuited to winning a wife, so you tried to secure one for him, and all under the guise of *education*?"

Was it my love for Reverend Skelley that made me so sharp with him? If I slashed at him this way, was I trying to cut away all obscurities, and see if I could still love what was left?

To see if *he* could? I think that must be the truth of it. I was challenging him to love me in my most spare and brutal form. I wanted to see if I could be true to myself, with all the awfulness I knew *myself* contained, and yet somehow remain worthy of love—love as pure and rare as his.

"No," he protested. His head was shaking steadily from side to side, his tan-and-gray hair feathering with the motion. "No. *Secure* is—not at all the right word. May I explain?"

I felt a sudden reluctance to hear him out, but made myself nod.

"I know no one, man or woman, with a greater independence of mind than yours. You may recall that I was present when the Farrow ladies tried to *secure* you, and I saw how foolish was the attempt. I thought instead of creating the right conditions for—a difficult communication, a fragile transference. I knew it was unlikely even so, and I accepted every possible outcome with an equal fullness of heart."

One phrase stood out in this speech. "The right conditions? And what were those?"

"I have infinite faith in Thomas's worth. But I also know that his worth is not the sort that communicates easily, or directly, to others. His spirit is one that must be conveyed through a medium, as it were: the medium of small things, carefully observed; the medium of infinitesimal beauties, made immense by amazement." Reverend Skelley looked at me, searching and serious. "Thomas speaks through his love of the world, and he speaks only to those who share it."

I stood up abruptly, and just as abruptly sat back down. He followed the movement without comment.

"In bringing the two of you together through study, I hoped to allow the opportunity for you to see in him what I do. I imagined nothing more than that, I promise. If you don't love him, or if you love him with a sisterly love, I accept that absolutely. I accept even his heartache as a gift."

"I never said that." The words were out before I could catch myself.

Reverend Skelley tried, and failed, to suppress a flash of joy. When he spoke again it was with exaggerated mildness.

"If it's a question of your desire to go to college, I'm certain Thomas would wait as long as necessary." This was a novel idea, and in another mood I might have exclaimed in amazement—was it possible that he did not expect me to choose between Thomas and *myself,* and never had? Of course, since I'd abandoned my studies, my chance of attending college was desperately slim.

I shook my head. "It isn't that. It's that Thomas must not be allowed to love *me.*"

"Because of this disease of the mind you've identified in yourself." He managed to deliver the phrase *disease of the mind* in a way that made it virtually equivalent to the name *Gus Farrow.* In his peaceful, subtle way, Reverend Skelley was expressing murderous hostility.

"Yes," I said.

"And would you like to resume your studies with me, once Thomas is back at Madison in September?"

"Very much," I said. "As long as we understand each other now, and you can forgive me." *Even for what you don't know* stayed unspoken. "It's very kind of you to offer."

"You are as welcome in my heart and home as any daughter could ever be," he said, and stood. "Whatever your difficulties, remember that."

When I left his house, I stood for some time on the step and simply felt the wind—felt it minutely, every plosive kiss and whorled grain. In that moment I thought I'd received the secret of perfect happiness. As I walked away I was not myself but the world, buoyant with beauty and complexity.

But not for long. I heard huffing breath and running steps and turned to find Gus red-faced on my heels—and how had he known where I was? It occurred to me that he might be using his magic to spy on me. Rage shoved between me and the fullness of my senses, slapped back my joy.

"What were you *doing* in there?" Gus shouted, not caring who heard us. The street was not crowded but there were a few people strolling here and there, a man painting a fence—and it would take only one to report this meeting to his ghastly mother. "I thought you'd given up all that, I thought you understood! Catherine, you know what you *are.*"

I was too angry to answer and walked on without so much as acknowledging him. He gave an outraged cry and scurried after me.

It was only when we were in a quiet lane that I spoke, my voice low and furious. "Did you even consider the risk to my father's job, Gus? And yelling *you know what you are* in the middle of the street—did you think, for one instant, of how that might be construed?"

He flushed an even deeper crimson. "Why should we care what anyone here thinks? We're so far beyond them already—and as soon as you see through your confusion, we'll be farther than they could ever reach, or even imagine. I thought you were almost ready, and now I catch you regressing!"

If everything must be made clear, it must be made clear to Gus most of all.

"I will never go to Nautilus, Gus. It's your choice, not mine. Go without me."

"But—" Gus was breathless, flummoxed. "It isn't a matter of *choosing*!"

"Magic may be in me, but that doesn't mean I have to submit to it. I can *choose* to foreswear it. I can *choose* to stifle it to the best of my ability, and I can deny it any scope to act."

"But why would anyone—why would *you*—"

"Because," I snapped, "the world is more marvelous without it."

Gus reeled to a stop, his hand tight on my wrist. We'd always maintained a careful reserve with each other when it came to physical contact, and I was too stunned by this breach to react at first.

"Our future is in Nautilus," Gus said, and all at once his voice was flat with menace. "There is no other. What we are is integral to our natures, and you can only ignore that for so long."

"You may be a sorcerer," I said. "I won't try again to dissuade you from your pursuit of magic. But I want something different, and I *am* something different."

"Not just that," Gus said. "Not just that. I don't remotely approve of Margo's Spiritualism, but she's right about one thing. You are my spiritual affinity, and there is no wanting, and no choosing, in the face of what *is*."

I tried to yank my wrist away, but Gus only squeezed harder.

"I want you, and I choose you. I always have. But I don't *need* to do either of those things, because what binds us is bigger than that. It's all that you are and all that I am, and choice is irrelevant." If there was romance in this speech, he undermined it with a tone very near disdain.

"You can't fail to love me, Catherine, not as long as you are *yourself*. Do you see?"

"No," I said. The force of his certainty seemed to rip the breath from my lungs; my thoughts ricocheted too fast to catch. "No. You've been my dear friend, Gus, but that is all. That is *all*. You can't stop me from wanting for myself, or from living without you."

(Let me pause here. Let me have this brief silence, let me hold it where my heart once beat. I offer it in answer to my scream.)

It was Gus's turn to be stunned. His eyes went round with wounded disbelief, and I felt his grip weaken. I tore my arm away and leapt back. We gaped at each other across years of understanding gone limp and useless while I rubbed my aching wrist. The wind gasped cold with a coming storm; the leaves shook.

"What is it you think you want?" Gus asked at last.

His tone was icy, but I thought the mere fact of the question implied a shift toward acceptance. Breath rushed from my lungs and I nearly closed my eyes with relief.

"I want to love small things," I said. "Beetles' wings, seeds. Nothing is small if you see it truly."

Gus tipped his head in contemplation, and I wondered if everything could still be well—if some scrap of friendship, even, could be salvaged. He needed only to *hear* me, to recognize me as myself and not an image cast up by his longing.

"Then that's what my magic will save you from," Gus said, and turned away.

Angus the Curse

Quiet enfolds us as we walk off together after her shift, hand in hand. My thumb strokes Geneva's palm tenderly, softly. A curse can alight as gently as a sparrow; its wings can loose flurries of sensation in skin.

Geneva seems bit wary, so I suggest we head for Grant Park. There will be secluded hollows and benches screened by greenery, but enough people nearby to give her a sense of security. We take a bus, sitting pressed together at the back, then walk the rest of the way.

It's fine with me. When the kiss takes her and lassitude flows in to fill the emptiness left by her ebbing life, she won't be in any condition to yell for help. Help won't be among the possibilities.

How soft the grass is under our feet, how the leaves pitch overhead in the cooling wind. I won't live to see a second autumn, though other Anguses will. All that remains of my single year of life I'll devote to grieving for her, my luminous Geneva. I'll pity the way her hard-edged realism worked against her, preventing her from recognizing dangerous magic when she saw it. I'll remember my finger now, running up and down the inside of her forearm, and how she shivered at my touch. I'll cherish those memories, dwell on them, because I know that when my year concludes they'll be erased, or nearly.

To the next Angus, Geneva won't be more than a pale trace, the bewildering impression of a face and voice that seems to come out of nowhere, lead into nothing.

We find a bench behind a scrim of late-summer wildflowers, black-eyed Susans raggedy above browning leaves. Sunset angles through the trees, painting the ground a strange, burnt amber-green, and the foliage above glares ocher against slate clouds. Geneva's gone shy, nearly silent, as if she's not entirely used to desire.

I kiss her cheek, slowly, savoring the soft yielding of flesh. I'm in no hurry to reach her lips. Even if I was programmed to love her, I refuse to accept that my love belongs to Gus. Here and now I'm staking a claim to it. *My* love. *My* crime. *My* lingering before the strike. Because fuck that guy.

She winds her arms around my neck and lets her mouth drift across my hair as I slide lower to scatter kisses on her neck. She laughs a little, breathlessly, and twists closer.

How can I say I love her when I'm going to kill her? Killing her is the only way to make her a part of me; her future diverted, her life pooling in my memory instead of flowing on and away. Oh, does that sound like something Gus would say?

No. It sounds like *me*. My evil, my savagery. No one will take this choice from me. And if I'm a walking curse, well, plenty of actual humans with all their fabulous free will and agency are no better.

Geneva's head tilts back as I lick her throat, and sun-scattered leaves reflect in her wide eyes. Her hip meets mine in a warm compression, then one of her legs lifts to slant across my lap. I've felt this sweetness in so many bodies, I must have, and her touch wakes nearly gone memories from lives long lost to me. Her fingers slide down my chest, and my rib cage echoes with the thrill of hands buried decades ago.

I'll draw out the moment as long as I can, but her excitement is building and I can't delay much longer. As soon as I think it, she pulls back a little.

She could still save herself, anyway. All she has to do is love me! When I think of it like that, it's obvious it's not my fault.

She leans close again, her mouth near my ear.

"God, Angus, I wish you weren't so beautiful. It's making me stupid."

"I know," I murmur back, and slide both hands deep into her hair. "That's the whole idea." Our lips are so close that my mouth fills with her breath, scented with ginger tea.

It's time. And even if I regret this later, even if I hate myself for it, well, there's one advantage to being a beamer: my pain, like my existence, has an expiration date built in.

"Angus, my boy, you're making progress. But you're not there yet! Give her more time to see her way, won't you?" Margo's voice in my pocket, a curdled purr. I'm not surprised that Geneva can't hear her.

"Oh, sorry, didn't I tell you? She's mine, not Gus's. So what I do with her is my decision." I say it out loud, because who gives a fuck?

Geneva starts in alarm at what I've just said, but it's too late. My open mouth covers hers and my hands wrap her skull, holding her in place. *You've made a terrible mistake, my love.*

I can feel her life like a satin ribbon on my tongue. My lips give the slightest tug, still teasing, not hard enough to unwind her. Just a nibble of murder. I almost laugh at the rich taste of it, like blood and cherries. Oh, Geneva! I give her one last chance, a few more moments to love me the way she's supposed to.

She gasps. It doesn't quite sound like lust.

Then something hits me. A hammer the size of a cloud strikes down and sets my whole body ringing. My skin seems to jerk, up and back, and my heartbeat hits me with an iron clang. What *is* this?

Fear. It slams me again, and I'm reeling back from Geneva with my arms flung up: a panicked instinct to ward off something, anything, although there's nothing there. *There's nothing there,* and yet the fear digs into my intestines with cold fingers and I'm thrashing, weeping, fighting for my life—

On my back on the grass, Geneva standing above me with frayed hair and crazed eyes, clutching her face and then darting away toward a group of passersby, yelling, "Hey! This guy just fell over in a fit! Hey! Help!"

I've never felt anything like that before! Like evil was reaching out of him—is that even possible? It was so clear.

Wait. Those aren't my thoughts but they shake through me anyway, and with them comes that reverberating terror. My whole body struck like a gong, my teeth biting at the ground—

Idiot. You knew there was something wrong with him.

Wrong, yeah, but I didn't think it was anything like that! It was like he wanted to kill me.

Geneva's thoughts. They inflate to fill my whole drumming head, squeezing me from inside. She looks at me in a glazed, wild way, and fear claps through me with the look.

Shit. It's *hers.* The fear is hers!

I've passed through dozens of other Anguses. I'm absolutely certain that none of them has ever been assaulted by the consciousness of his *her,* her anguish and her disgust. Why me, then?

What is forcing me to feel Geneva's mind?

A sympathetic-looking older couple are calming Geneva now, the woman with her arm around my love's quaking shoulders. A strange man crouches down and urges me not to move; they've called for help, he says.

Geneva glances at me and her face contorts: the look of a child on the edge of a nightmare. The world clashes against me again, cold and metallic, so that my head slams back against the ground.

Then I get it. It's the pendant Lore gave me, surging with wakeful purpose. My attempt on Geneva must have activated some dormant magic.

It's the *pendant* shining Geneva's fear into me. I asked Lore if the stone would protect me, and she said, *If not you, then someone you love.*

Nice one, Lore!

Geneva smiles awkwardly at the couple reassuring her. "Thank you so much. If you can just make sure he's safe—I've got to get going. I can't—"

And since they believe she called them to help me, not to save her, they murmur comforting things. Geneva gives me a final look, and I feel it like an iceberg splitting in my brain.

She turns and runs. For as long as she lives she'll wake up screaming from dreams of my face leaning to meet hers.

Distance takes the edge off. My cold slamming sickness eases enough that I push up onto my elbows under clouds dripping with arterial sunset.

"No, no, no," the prim-looking man next to me says, trying to ease my shoulders back to the grass. "Lie still. You've had a seizure of some kind."

"I'm fine." I clamber to my feet while he flutters and presses on my chest.

"No, no, no. You need the hospital. A scan to see what brought that on. No, no, rest for now. *Rest.*" His gray face crimps with worry, and the couple who were crooning to Geneva come over and bustle at me too.

What I need is a place where I can huddle and cry undisturbed. Where I can weep and howl and bang my fists, because she left me, she *left* me, and there's no way I'll ever get another chance with her.

"I'm fine," I tell the old man again, and he grabs my arm. I shove him back so hard that he falls with a sharp cry. There's a sort of vague clamor from the couple, an anxious shifting of their weight. I turn on them with my face bent into a snarl. "I said I'm fine! He shouldn't have touched me!"

And I run behind a tangle of trees, then on across smooth lawn. It's incredible how quick I am, how light. But where do I think I'm going, and what does it even matter now? I thought I was so special, so much more than just another beamer, but no. I'm a failed Angus like all the other failed Anguses: the ones whose *hers* escaped them, who lived the rest of their single shitty year hollowed out by spite and regret. Geneva was right there in my arms, ravenous for my touch, and I still failed. She'll live unclaimed, as free and vibrant and *beyond* me as if I'd never been.

Beyond me. Beyond what I am, beyond the stifling span of my life. I want her to love me so much that she can't live without me, and now living without me is exactly what she's going to do. I'll be ground down, spat up, and reused in the form of dozens of new Anguses, and she'll be in graduate school, or traveling somewhere, or walking up a staircase in Montreal with a girl she met at a party—

Claire. Where have I heard that name before? I see Claire, plump and supple and sensuous, with wavy ice-blond locks and a wicked smile. And it's not Geneva with her, but a very young girl, shy and gawky and golden-brown, her hair in a bookish dark bob too short for her face. They're together on a shadowy landing, a few colored beams lancing in from a tiny stained glass window.

Claire catches the dark girl by the wrists, pressing her against the wall. The dark girl gasps and struggles to raise her eyes, then flushes and lowers them again. "You can become the truest possible version of yourself, Dolores," Claire whispers, and I know she's continuing a conversation they were having earlier. "And isn't tonight the perfect time to start?"

Lore, that's Lore, but no older than eighteen, torn between anxiety and desire as her confident friend leans in and—and isn't just her friend anymore. All at once the two of them are kissing in a frenzied tangle, Lore's patent leather shoe skidding sideways until she loses her balance and they both wobble, and then Claire is pulling her upright with her hands already somehow under the saggy argyle sweater that doesn't suit Lore at all—

I don't always find you in time. That's what Lore said in the movie I saw, where she tracked one of my old selves. *But when I do, you will* remember *her.*

Her. Claire. Lore's first and deepest love, who also had the misfortune to be a *her* of mine.

Why can I remember this scene, though? I know I wasn't there. I found Claire a few months later, I'd guess, killed her months after that. But I can feel their kiss so intimately that it's as if someone else's memory is reflecting into me, the way Geneva's fear reflected into me before, and—

Oh.

I've been running senselessly over grass banded with dying sun and dusk shadows, but now I stumble to a halt. She can't be far.

"Good evening, Angus," Lore says at my elbow. I stand still, my breath heaving, but I don't look at her. Why give her the satisfaction of gazing straight into my shame? "You activated your pendant just now, so I know my memories must have reached you. It's a mirror, you see, made to reflect whatever suffering you inflict back into you. A mirror that brings home the curse. And I told you, didn't I?"

You will remember *her.* The pendant was intended to keep Geneva safe from me, yes. But that wasn't its only purpose. As Lore stands beside me I feel the transformative blaze of her old love for Claire, and the years of wilding sorrow that followed on Claire's death. *What a pity,* I want to say. *So terribly, terribly sorry. Now fuck off.*

"That was a long time ago," I tell her. It's not my usual voice, not even Gus's, but something more bestial. I finally turn. My shoulders hunch and my head lowers under the weight of her stare. Her silver hair catches the sunset in a red gash while blue shadows steal all but the barest outlines from her face.

"It was," Lore agrees. "Do you suppose you're in a position to tell me to *get over it* on that account? For both of us, Angus, time isn't a flood that extinguishes the past, but the fuel that keeps it burning."

It's true. Claire is as bright and immediate in Lore's mind now as she once was in her arms; her breath remains a downy percussion against

Lore's ear decades after her lungs went cold and unmoving. And Catherine in my memories still reflects through Claire, and Pearl, and now Geneva, like a candle flame multiplied by a roomful of mirrors. The past only gains in heat and strength through the restless play of memory, until Lore and I stand at the center of a conflagration.

"So kill me." I take a step closer to her, scowling down. My hands twitch at my sides. Lore's almost certainly too powerful for me to slaughter her with crude physical force, but where's the harm in trying?

She doesn't waver. "I don't think so."

"I tried to murder Geneva."

"And you failed. Why would I bother now? Why would I spare you one instant of agony, now that you've broken yourself? Gus is deeply disappointed in you. He'll enjoy mangling you at his leisure once you return to him; he'll savor your pain. He's done it before to Anguses who especially annoyed him, I happen to know. So live on, and live with the horror of what you are." I can barely make out Lore's face, but her voice tightens with bitterness. The pendant reflects that bitterness into me, a kind of biting light. "*Learn* from it, Angus."

For a moment, we stare at each other. I could throw myself in front of a truck, I suppose. But would that be enough to kill a thing like me? Maybe not.

Lore's emotions curl catlike inside me, becoming a cruel smile. She guesses what I'm thinking. The boughs of distant trees tangle like black lace above her head.

"Oh, *please* try it. Your year won't end as easily as all that, but you can be maimed, and your body can experience torment. But why take my word for it? Or, if you truly want to die, why not do it right?"

Do it right. When Lore asked me to kill myself, and every future version of myself, she wasn't referring to anything as simple as ditching this particular incarnation. But I find I'm looking forward to living again.

To facing off with Lore again. One of these times, I'll figure out how to get back at her for everything she's done to me. And, okay, the next Angus won't be *me* me, but maybe he'll be close enough.

Lore finally steps away. Is that a slope in the ground lifting her, or is she suddenly taller? She turns, and the sun's last vermillion rays strike her face and pool on eyes like dimpled mercury. Red light runs in liquid scrolls over her pewter skin. What I took for tree boughs behind her a moment ago resolves into delicate antlers, endlessly branching into capillary-fine tips that glitter with mineral frost.

Catherine in the Shed

That autumn would have marked the return of my happiness and serenity, all golden slopes of sun and Homer by the fire, if it had not been for the seismic trembling of anxiety. Every day I hoped for the news that Gus Farrow had disappeared, leaving no hint to where he'd gone. Every day I hoped for his surrender to the fact that I was myself, that my words were my words and their meaning was not his to revise; to the fact that I did not love him. Once he grasped those realities, surely he would forget me and leave for Nautilus? And since my father still worked for the Farrows, I knew I would hear at once if Gus was unaccounted for.

Instead my father sat at the table and took off one boot, then seemed to forget the other. "The younger Mr. Farrow keeps watching me at my work," he told me at last. "Never thought horses interested him."

My heart stuttered. It was because of me that my father was being hounded, and I heard his implied question as well.

"I told Gus I could not love him," I said. "I'm sorry he's taking it out on you."

He nodded, staring down. "It's my fault, letting you run wild with him for so long. You're a good girl, you couldn't see that he ought to be better."

It startled me; I'd assumed my father subscribed to the common view that I was the one conniving to marry Gus. Now from the sorrow weighing down his face I understood how my father had compromised his own heart, his own judgment, for the sake of our daily bread.

I put my arms around his neck and softly kissed his cheek. Ours was not a demonstrative family, and he huffed in surprise and patted my hand with awkward affection. I hope my father remembered that kiss once I was dead, and knew that I, at least, absolved him of all blame for what Gus did.

I hope he felt the love that went unspoken. That it warmed him as he stood on the cold clay that filled my grave, my mother and brothers buried beside me. Perhaps he even forgave me for all the ways I turned from him. For how, with every step, I abandoned him again.

Hush now.

I remember the exact day it happened, shortly before Christmas, because I knew Thomas was coming home for the holidays and I was in a tumult of indecision over whether or not to see him. I wanted to, very much—but I did not want to be unkind, or encourage feelings he was better off without. I spent many nights making a drawing for his present: a study of animal skulls we'd found in the woods together, radiating like petals from a central stone. Then I thought I would be wrong to give the drawing to him, and tucked it away behind my bed.

All through the twenty-second I was preoccupied by thoughts of his journey: from Madison he would take the stagecoach to Syracuse; from Syracuse he would ride a train as far as Batavia—I had never yet traveled by railway!—from Batavia he would take a stagecoach again. A light snow scrawled white traces on the early gloaming, and I wondered if it looked the same to him through a window that rushed like the snow itself.

When the knock came, I was caught off guard. It was too early for Thomas to have arrived. He was too diffident, too careful of my boundaries to appear uninvited in any case. Nonetheless I hoped, and darted to the door.

It was Margo Farrow. She wore a beautiful slate-colored carrick coat, quite new, and only a shade lighter than the sky behind her; its layered collars fluttered in the wind. Her nostrils had a thin, almost glassy appearance as they flared, their violet veins clear against her pallid skin. Her gray eyes met mine with a look I could not read, but there was a grim set to her mouth.

"Catherine," she said. "You must come at once!"

"What is it?" Imaginings tussled inside me; why would Margo demand my presence, unless something terrible had happened? "Some accident?"

If there had been a mishap involving Gus's magic, she would naturally try to keep it quiet. And she knew I knew already.

"I can't explain now. Is this your cloak? On with it, there's not a moment to lose! We must dash, he's in the shed."

"Has Gus been hurt?" I flushed at the ambivalence concealed in those words: I was terribly worried for Gus, and at the same time I felt a stitch of hope that—well, that he would never bother me or mine again.

"I told you, I can't explain; you must come and see. Listen the first time, won't you, and spare me from repeating myself?" Should I have read a warning in her preemptory tone, should I have seen her urgency for the ruse it was? As she spoke she was swinging my cloak around my shoulders, fumbling with the buttons at my throat. To slap away an old lady's hand seemed unwarranted brutality, and I did not resist. Not then, and not when she seized my elbow and towed me out the door.

I wonder, did Margo realize the inadmissible bait she was dangling in front of me? Did she guess that I could not help but wish for the relief of finding Gus dead, even as I hated myself for wishing it? His magical arts must be improving by the day, I knew. I was tired of suspecting every bird, every leaping flame; I craved a world made innocent once again.

The grass was crisp with frost; it squeaked under our shoes. Snowflakes spiraled in the lilac dark. Margo was still strong and limber then, and her haste was contagious as we pushed through white pools of our own breath. We walked at such a pace that I grew giddy with mingled dread and anticipation, and we took the same shortcut through the hedge that I had used as a child.

She caught my elbow again, tugging me toward the shed at the bottom of the garden. Stripes of lantern-light shone around its door—only the light's color seemed odd—and I stared at it as if my gaze could tear out its secrets.

Margo threw the door open and planted her other hand on the small of my back, pushing me forward. I stumbled in, blinded at first by a light that, I realized, was too bright for any lantern. The whole floor was a swirl of fire, azure and violet, though it did not burn. In its disturbed light the hanging shears and racks of pots threw huge and tremulous shadows, and it was a moment before I could separate the people in that space from the bewilderment of light and dark.

Then I did. Three people stood in that shed apart from Margo and myself. I recognized Gus first, shining like a fairy prince; he wore a sort of cape formed of wandering sparks, cobalt and white and cerulean. Their firefly weave lit the sharp planes of his face from below, giving him a splendor that looked disjointed and not entirely human. His blond hair flamed into a blue-pale crown, and he reached out and caught my hand and pulled me to his side. Next I saw Darius, rather cleaner than I was used to, in a black suit. And there to his right, someone dainty, diminutive—

Mrs. Hobson, wearing so much lace that she looked like a human cobweb.

A spasm shook my limbs, and I reclaimed my hand with such force that I nearly fell. I heard the door clap shut, and spun toward the sound only to find that there *was* no door: bowed walls of liquid flame reached far wider and higher than the shed could possibly hold, with Margo in the middle of them. There was no more heat than bodies in a confined space usually produce, though. I had just enough presence of mind to understand that all these theatrics must be illusion; that, if Margo had closed the door a moment ago, it should be behind her. I lunged in her direction.

I pushed her aside with panicked roughness and reached through sheeting blue brilliance; felt wood planks, groped for a latch. Gus cried out, outraged and inarticulate—I suppose he'd expected this spectacle to awe me into submission, and his false glory to take command of my heart. He must have been terribly disappointed to see me scrabbling like a trapped rat instead.

I couldn't find a handle anywhere.

"If only you'd let me teach you," Darius observed, "you'd have a better idea of what to do now, wouldn't you?"

"Whatever this game is, I want no part of it!" I snapped. "Let me go!"

"There is no wanting, and no choosing," Mrs. Hobson said with girlish lightness, "in the face of what *is*. Catherine, my sweet, sweet girl, we are already perfectly aware of how misguided you are, and how you ignore every prompting of the spirits! We mean only to *help* you. Tonight we will bring you into alignment with your higher self and its most sacred affinities."

With that vile word, *affinities,* I began to understand and spun at her, my back pressed against the unseen planks. Under her simpering smile I caught a gleam of vindictive malice, and knew that she was here for revenge.

"My affinities are *mine,* elective, free! You cannot impose—"

"My guides told me the night we met how you and Gus Farrow are one in spirit. Now they tell me the time has come to solemnize your bond." She raised her hands in a travesty of blessing. "I affirm your connection, spirit to spirit! The truest marriage is that unseen by man, but celebrated by those beyond the veil!"

I'd thought that Mrs. Hobson was a false medium. But she was, I knew, a very real sorceress, and perhaps Darius's presence meant she even realized it now. Perhaps he'd been teaching *her.*

"No," I said. "No!" My arm flew out as if I could ward off her words, and I saw I was dressed in the same bright and restless filigree as Gus.

There was something already licking through the air, a line of power, a wiry brightness that dipped and snared—

I had never hated magic as much as I did in that moment. But it did cross my mind that Mrs. Hobson might be rather less powerful with her skull staved in—that there might still be time to undo her doings before they could draw tight. Behind the flaming mirage, I knew the shed was full of shovels, urns, a marble birdbath. It was true I had no idea of what I was doing, no control, and might very well kill all of us.

But it struck me as a fair enough outcome, if I did.

With something like a convulsion of thought I reached for my power. I knew where it lived; I was all too familiar with its irritating twiddle at the base of my brain. Find it, call it, conduct it with my fury—

Nothing. There was nothing. I clawed in myself as, minutes before, I had clawed at the wall. There was only a deadness where magic had been in me, an empty socket.

Darius guffawed.

"Call it my wedding present, pretty Catherine," he said. "I'll tell you, it didn't come cheap. Oh, but if you'd only let me teach you, you'd know how to give it right back."

Is it any wonder I renounced magic with all my strength, when it betrayed me at the crucial moment? I felt something snag me deep inside, and knew it was the power flung out by Mrs. Hobson's words—my God, by her *spell*.

"Catherine, please stop struggling. You'll see soon enough, we've done the only thing we *could* do. You keep your greatness in Gus, and he keeps his goodness in you, and I dread to think what would become of either of you without the other." It was Margo who delivered this bit of priceless wisdom. "Come now and kiss him."

"I will *not*!" I shouted, and then realized that Gus had been uncharacteristically silent throughout the proceedings. I looked and saw his face striped with tears, bright as meteors in that fierce light.

My hands spread on the wooden wall behind me. It was solid, rough, real; it felt like life.

"None of this is *right*," Gus gasped. "It wasn't supposed to be like this! Oh, Catherine, Catherine, I was sure you'd understand. Even if it was only at the last moment. I was sure you'd see how necessary it is, for you to love me. And now—"

My hand brushed something cold, metallic. I'd found the latch at last.

"She will," Margo soothed. "Give her time, my darling boy. She will."

Gus doubled over with the force of his sobs. Margo and Mrs. Hobson both rushed to him, babbling reassurance and sympathy. I lifted the latch.

It gave with a loud clank, and Gus raised his blazing head to gaze at me. Heartsick and desperate, star-spattered and broken. I pitied him then, and I wished he were dead.

The door fell open behind me. I must have blazed blue myself against the sudden yawn of night as I looked at the four of them. I took a backward step into the creaking grass, and felt snowflakes melting on my cheeks.

"You *do* all realize that this was the most pathetic nonsense, don't you? An infantile game, nothing but playacting, as if all of you were nasty, bullying children? It meant nothing!" Gus stretched out a hand, in appeal, in denial, I couldn't tell. "Nothing at all!" I screamed, and turned to run.

"Be patient, Gus," Darius said behind me. "Catherine's no fool, and she'll see—what we've seen to, that's all."

I charged through the hedge, and I was brilliant at first as a runaway moon. But as I ran the blue shimmer that clothed me began to dim, then the sparks peeled back and drifted away and I was again a girl in a dark green cloak, alone and raging.

I knew, naturally, that I had protested too much. Mrs. Hobson had done *something* to me in that shed, though exactly what its consequences would be I could not tell.

Do you, my childish, my corrupt reader, wonder if it was Mrs. Hobson's operation that strung my spirit to Gus so securely that, on dying, I could not die, but must kite along after him? Of course I have wondered myself, many times, and come to this conclusion:

Mrs. Hobson's spell was surely a contributing factor; she stitched with strong thread, no doubt. But the fatal entanglements that force certain spirits to haunt their killers have manifold sources. They have histories twisted from countless small fibers, a sob here and a silence there.

No sorcerer, however gifted, could braid such complicated suffering in a matter of moments.

Catherine Cut

In the event, Gus procrastinated. He went back to fiddling with his latest Angus—you were nearing completion—then decided to go ahead with launching the latest you before he trundled me off to Sky. I might have preferred to go promptly rather than existing in queasy suspense, wondering every moment what Sky's operation would entail and what would become of me after it was over. Sky excited in me disgust and horror unequaled by any other resident of Nautilus; I could not forget the chipper enthusiasm he'd affected as we murdered Christopher Flynn, or the sensation of my unwilling violence as Flynn sieved through me. If I must endure Sky's touch again, I wanted it over with. But Gus, so determined when he announced his decision, now indulged in a festival of waffling.

"There's no hurry," he muttered at me. "If we don't leave my rooms, what harm can you do? If that repellent amphibian tries to hobble in here, I'll flatten her."

So I was treated to the birth of another Angus, and as usual I occupied two places in the theater. I watched from high in the balcony and simultaneously from backstage, as it were. It was no less ghastly than the previous performances.

Then, when Gus had sent you on your way, my watchful splinter peering through your eyes at the streets of Greenwich Village, he ran out of excuses. A few more days of mumbling and sulking, and he screwed up his courage to the point of stepping into the alley outside. Where he stood and dithered again.

"It's awful that I have to do this," Gus groused over his shoulder at me as I flashed and screamed. "The thought of living without you, after so long—even the most ideal marriage has its difficulties, my darling, and certainly we've had our disagreements—but that it would come to separation! I never could have conceived it. You'll always be mine, of course, so I suppose—"

Severing us was indeed a novel concept. At this point I had been haunting Gus for over a century of unworld time. If I hadn't particularly enjoyed our constant proximity, I still found it difficult to envision an alternative.

Unless perhaps Gus meant in some way to release me? To let me unravel into true death and find freedom in the entire obliteration of myself? Would my fragment in you then come along with me? It seemed out of character for him, but what alternatives were there for a ghost detached from her hauntee?

Complete and unequivocal death had been my goal time out of mind—that, and stopping Gus's murders. But as Gus began a reluctant amble through the streets of Nautilus, wending steadily toward Sky, I found I had cooled on the prospect.

Pitiful reader, you have been inattentive indeed if you can't guess the reason for my change of heart. I could never live again, but even undeath was precious to me if it meant I could sometimes see Anura.

It would be still, if she would have anything to do with me.

Gus stopped sometimes, staring at the immense dusky vault that passed for Nautilus's sky. Once or twice he even turned back: a dozen paces, twenty, until I almost thought he'd given up our visit. Even the long-abhorred status quo took on a halcyon aspect, and I tried to urge his steps homeward.

But for all the unforeseen changes that had come, there remained one constant: I had no mass, and my efforts at tugging were perfectly ineffectual.

At length we reached the lintel that defined the entrance to Sky's apartment. Gus knocked and was granted admission; we slipped through the wall's cloudy substance and stood facing that grotesque unchild in his airy shop. His fluted dome had been torqued, presumably in the upheaval when Milk took over; it was now a tapering cone, irregularly spiraled, with bulges here and bubbling concavities there.

The umbrastrings were still looped on the wall, glistening with menace. And there were other instruments scattered on sweeping tables, instruments whose purposes I did not know. Sky being what he was, I knew they must be designed to use on ghosts.

On me.

The damson nap of Sky's skin, the night-colored hair, and the wet and welling calculation in his ancient eyes, all were just as I remembered.

In a blink he shrugged on his boyish joy. "Gus Farrow! And here I thought you'd given me the brush-off!" He laughed to show his irritation was meant in fun, which it was not. "What games shall we play today?"

"It's no game to me," Gus announced pompously, "but the gravest exigency. I regret it immensely that I have no choice except to seek your help." It was a rather insulting formulation, and Sky's brow tensed with incipient anger. "I have to—to part from Catherine."

Sky was plainly struggling to keep his countenance, but his eyes flared with delight.

"I never thought I'd see the day! I'll take your ghost right off your hands, don't you worry. You'll feel like a weight's been lifted, that I can tell you. It's a capital idea, Gus. It really is."

Gus gawked at him, too flummoxed even to parse Sky's proposal at first. The air itself seemed bowed in an arc of misunderstanding. Then it sprang out again, quivering with shock.

"What? Do you think I mean to *give her away,* as if she were a worn-out coat? Catherine is mine, mine forever. It's only that she's been abusing the freedom I've allowed her, I find. I have to store her more securely."

Freedom. It wasn't the word I'd have chosen. And he meant to *store* me? So much for my dreams of dissolution.

I watched Sky's expression shift from outright glee to something more guarded.

"So what do you have in mind? Chop her off and squeeze her down into some kind of a keepsake? A ghostlette you can wear on a chain, or pop in a cigar box?" A pause. "I can help with that. Where do you mean to store her, though?"

The last question was delivered in a carefully innocuous tone, as if Sky only needed to know so that I could be reduced to the proper measurements.

Gus grew wary, but not wary enough.

"There's a lady I know in need of employment. She can look after Catherine for me. Keep her secluded, and away from bad influences."

Was Gus really so naive, so insensible of the chatter that was as much a part of Nautilus's atmosphere as its magical fug? Evidently he was; his expression was smug and secretive, as if Sky would never penetrate his profound riddling.

But Sky was in no doubt whom Gus meant. If the umbrathurge hadn't already cased Margo's hovel, he would as soon as Gus was out of the way. I could practically discern the figures tallied in his inkwell eyes; if it would have been ideal to deliver me to my buyer directly, boxed and beribboned, still the main thing was to get me away from Gus. Instead of coming with ghost in hand, he could demand payment for his service in severing me and for news of my location. Stealing me from Margo would be easy.

It was nearly as good.

"I can't let you borrow her, as you suggested once before," Gus said preemptively. "But I'm ready to be generous."

Sky didn't bother protesting that he had no interest in talens. He'd tried that tack before and it hadn't worked. I was sure he was trying to determine exactly the right figure: high enough not to agitate Gus's suspicions, but not so high as to send him reeling away in disbelief.

"A straightforward chop-and-pack job? Only with a ghost as walloping as Catherine we could run into complications, maybe, have to allow for that. Shall we say three thousand?"

"Two." Idiot. Sky would have paid *him* for the privilege.

"Twenty-five hundred, then. Slice her, stuff her, and you can go your way unencumbered. No more old ball and chain! Though after having her scream in your ears all this time, you can expect some insomnia until you adjust to the silence."

I wondered if my prospective purchaser knew that my available output of talens was only half what it had once been. That should have sharply lowered my market value as a magical battery. Or was I wanted for some other purpose?

I might be some sort of magical coal, for all I knew, destined for the stove. I might be displayed under glass, or a sop to depraved appetites I could not even imagine. Here in Nautilus there was no telling.

These reflections preoccupied me as Gus and Sky settled on terms. Payment was due on completion, I gathered. Dimly, I heard Sky's prattling caveats: "Can't guarantee there won't be a bit of ghoststuff stuck to your back—just a stub, I promise! Trust me, you'd rather have that than let the business touch your skin. As for packing her up, well, are you sure you can trust this chaperone you've picked out? I have a lovely locket here, this should work—but if it's mishandled, Catherine will come rearing right out! Unmoored is unmoored, you've got to be careful with a detached ghost. I'm telling you now, I won't be liable if you lose her."

Gus stripped to the waist. How old he looked, how loose skin seemed to drift across his wasted person like desert sands!

"I won't lose her," Gus said. "But the screaming—I suppose Mar—my friend will complain. What will it cost to keep Catherine quiet?"

Sky considered that. "I can add a little something to muffle her for five hundred up front. There will be upkeep, though, on your end. Just under half a talen per unworld day?"

Gus snorted, suggesting that these figures were displeasing, but that he would endure the drain on his magic like the noble martyr he was.

Sky had him lie facedown on a sort of counter, a sinuous ridge made of the same pearly, restless material as the walls. This forced me into a flailing perpendicular above him. Sky inspected his upper back, where Gus and I were joined. It was hard to make out the exact spot; my flashing thinned and faded where feet might be expected until there was only a suggestion, a dimming in the air. It was something like the dwindling visibility at a candle flame's base.

Sky took his time. After a few moments he huffed in frustration, then scrabbled among his implements until he fetched up a pair of goggles with lenses of perfect black. Equipped with these, he tried again.

"There she is! Fifth vertebra, that's the anchor point. A few strands in your shoulder blades, too, but it's really the central taproot we have to worry about, I can clean up most of the messy bits later. All right! Just let me get the right tool—it's packed up, not something you want to leave lying around—"

The counter compressed one side of Gus's pinkish-gray face into long folds like a pile of sausage casings. He kept his eyes shut tight, but they seeped bitter tears.

The blue cat wove around Sky's legs as he clattered around again and came up with a sort of wooden box that was not native to Nautilus. An unworld import, I thought, quite old. It had a very fine carving on its lid, a dragon nesting in curling clouds.

I don't know what I expected: a tiny guillotine? An enchanted scalpel? Something silvery and bluntly menacing, in any case.

When Sky opened the box, it appeared to be entirely empty. Pallid light probed the glossy corners and the mahogany bottom showed clear and distinct, with no slip of shadow I could see.

Sky had never looked me in the face. But now he tipped back his false child's head and leered straight at me, his black lenses winking.

"Bet you've never seen one of these before!" He laughed with cheerful sadism and tugged on a pair of whitely luminous gloves, soft as calfskin, then reached into the box and picked up—something. From his movements I knew he could see it, presumably with the help of those goggles; after all, they had let him see me. The implement was no more apparent than before, but the pinch of his fingers and thumbs suggested two long, thin handles with something stretched between them. "The technical term for it is an umbratome, and mine's the only one!"

I recalled enough of my Greek to parse the word: ghost cutter. The name suited Sky's pose of schoolboy crudity. If his boast was true, if he alone in Nautilus possessed the means of removing ghosts from the living, then it seemed certain he had done similar work for collectors like Nemo many times before.

Sky moved as if he were drawing a careful loop around my lower extremity, perhaps four or five inches from Gus's skin. Gus now was sobbing outright. Sky seemed to swap the handles, left to right and right to left, so that the invisible wire or fluid blade must cross itself. When he pulled back his hands, the loop would close.

This was what he proceeded to do. And if I could not see his ghost cutter, I could feel it. Pain came like a white whisper: first a tentative stinging, then a deeper bite.

"Think of how you *use* ground-up diamond in order to *cut* diamond," Sky explained to Gus, or perhaps to me. "She was a weak little slip of a specter, nothing like your Catherine, but even the weakest ones carry a bit of zip. I'm nearly certain that magical potential is *the* defining condition for becoming a ghost post-murder, in fact; makes it that much harder to die properly. This one was maybe six when she died? Her name was Jane, and as you can see I've given her a whole new life."

Gus below me shuddered, then screamed just as loudly as I did.

Jane, I thought. *Are you there?*

I'm sorry, came the reply. *I don't want to hurt you!*

Then I could think no more. Pain was all of me. Water when it boils over might have trouble recalling the intricate lattices of snow.

It would be wildly inaccurate to say that I fainted and later woke. It was more that pain obliterated everything I knew as *Catherine,* then eventually receded until I recalled my own shape. Like beach wrack, a figure buried by sand, gradually coming clearer as wind and water brushed away the grains.

In a movement as habitual as breathing, I looked down, where Gus's shoulders and head had long framed the bottom of my field of vision. He wasn't there.

Instead I was roughly tethered by one of Sky's umbrastrings, the prongs thrust into the region of my thigh to hold me in place. The other end, absurdly, was tied to an ordinary sandbag.

That was all that kept me from drifting away—though whether I would have found true death, or merely haunted the streets of Nautilus, I cannot tell. In a hazy, pain-blurred way, I wondered at what sort of career I could have as a, to borrow a modern term, free-range haint.

The question was moot, though. Attempts to tug myself free were useless; Sky, whatever one may say of him, was proficient at the business of tormenting ghosts.

My gaze wandered around the room in confusion, and found Sky and Gus on a bench some twenty feet away with a heartstring spanned from mouth to mouth. Payment.

(Meanwhile, the rest of me looked through your eyes at a dark ceiling in New York City. The room Gus had found you was over a club, and driving music—rock and roll, whose rapid development I've observed with some fascination—was keeping you awake. You twitched and kicked the wall, and I was as annoyed as you were. If you couldn't sleep, I couldn't write. A new urge was forking through me, lightning-bright: to bear witness to my own condition. That part of me which was in you, which could command words on the page, would speak for the screaming remnant, and tell the story of both.)

"All right!" Sky exclaimed, letting the heartstring slide from his lips. "Let's get her packed! I'll teach you the trick of it in case she gives you any trouble later; it's a way of turning the umbrastring's prongs that'll force her to bundle herself, basically. Spool her right up. I'll show you."

At this, I became aware of something both Sky and Gus had apparently overlooked. A hairy bovine ear was plastered to the wall. The matter of Nautilus is imperfectly opaque, and a large dusky blot flawed its pallor in the ear's general surrounds.

It was in that zone of wall designated as a doorway, marked out by a swoop of lintel above. I was familiar, of course, with how these permeable walls worked; a simple token, no more than a half-lit's worth of power, and the designated area of wall would yield to a visitor's passage; another crumb of magic, and the door was locked. Then the wall would admit only the resident along with anyone else it was spelled to recognize. As in the unworld, some locks were stronger than others.

Sky, I guessed, had simply forgotten to lock up after Gus came in.

Now Asterion was standing inside the wall itself. His ear was spread flat on the wall's surface, revealing its pink and bristling involutions in more detail than I had ever wished to see.

"You forget I don't own an umbrastring of my own," Gus complained. He sounded dazed. "If Catherine gets loose somehow, I doubt I'll have time to run to you or Asterion."

"Oh, what the hell. Take one of mine," Sky said lightly. He slipped to the wall and plucked an umbrastring from its hook, then walked back. Since he meant to rob Gus of his greatest source of wealth, I suppose he thought he could afford some liberality.

"Thank you," Gus said, startled, and reached out a hand to accept the treasure.

The wall rippled with a frantic, glutinous bubbling—Asterion was trying to burst in more quickly than its material permitted. Then the minotaur plunged into the room with a huge huff of breath and bucking of horns.

"The gall of it!" he shrieked. "After all I've done for you! You, Sky, you're a nasty piece of work, and everyone knows it. But you, Gus—I thought we understood each other. I thought I could trust you, and not just because I can make you sorry for sneaking around like this. Do you think I won't?"

Asterion squirmed, his cow's eyes rolling to where I flashed clear across the room from Gus. Not only would he lose his regular percentage of my magic, I could see him thinking, but Sky would claim the whole price from my purchaser as well. He was neatly cheated of the fruits of his magical scamming.

Sky's blue face flushed a bruised purple.

Gus stiffened. "You've taken thousands of talens off of me, Asterion. Be content with that, and leave me alone."

From the pitching of Asterion's head, I rather hoped he would gore Gus on the spot. That would solve all my problems at once, but regrettably Asterion was too cowardly for such direct action.

"And now you think you can take that self-righteous tone with me! As if you and Sky hadn't already been stealing from me, for who knows how long. Really, her output dropped from ten talens per session to *five*, for no apparent reason? But we've been friends for so long, I didn't want to believe it of you. I persuaded myself that skimming her magic behind my back was beneath you. Then I catch you doing *this*!" His hands waved to suggest an all-encompassing perfidy.

Gus's pale eyes went wide, and in fact, Asterion's accusation was unjust. It wasn't Gus who'd been secretly hoarding half my magic. Much more than half, actually, for study had greatly increased my generative powers.

The common assumption that I was no more than a husk now turned to my advantage; my scream masked my secret industry. Like Gus, I was growing rich.

"I've been honest in all my dealings with you," Gus said frostily. "But in no way did I ever offer you control over my every action, or inclusion in each of my transactions. As you seem, with no justification, to expect."

He turned his back. Asterion's eyes bulged still further than they usually did. Oh, the minotaur was thoroughly used to taking his slice of everything. I was in no doubt: if nothing else was available to him but vengeance, he would take that.

"I'll be going, then," Asterion announced with limp and bloodied dignity. He swung toward the exit. "You do know that every heartstring carries traces of the transactions performed on it? Even old ones can be deciphered by someone clever enough—and the larger the sums, the more distinct the signs." He did not need to specify that a thousand talens would leave a very definite signature.

"Oh, so everyone knows I'm nasty?" Sky yelled at his back as it slipped into the wall. "Then why are my friends the cream of Nautilus? Scholars! Artists! Sorcerers who wouldn't even glance at you in the street!"

Sky was thinking of Madame Laudine, I knew. I had my first hint of an idea.

Asterion's visit had cast a pall over the proceedings, none too cheerful to begin with. Sky showed Gus how, by piercing the region of my ankle with the umbrastring's prongs and then twirling it, I could be literally rolled up like a rug. Sky tightened me until my screaming person was no bigger than an acorn, then used a stitch of some invisible thread to attach me to a locket's hinge. The locket was a large oval of gilt brass, decorated ironically enough with a bouquet of forget-me-nots in sky-blue enamel. A simple chain supported it. I wondered if the thread tying me to it was more of Jane, cruelly snipped from her.

The stitch held, but I could feel that it was nowhere near as strong as my previous connection to Gus.

The locket snapped shut around me. My scream reverberated in that confined space, but I supposed Sky was as good as his word and the noise could not escape into the wider air.

(Meanwhile, in Greenwich Village, you had given up on sleep and gone roving through the night. A cluster of gorgeous but bedraggled youth had invited you along with them; your beauty was enough to cover the deficiencies in your conversation. Now you were sprawled on a Persian carpet in a mansion uptown, smoking hashish with these momentary friends. Someone pawed your unresponsive crotch, then gave it up with a sigh. The drug lowered your defenses, and your mind was a tumble of violent images and the twinkling faces of the dead. You scanned the girls in the party, viciously disappointed that none of them was what you would term *her*. Your drive to kill—the drive which you called love—remained a frustrated muddle with no clear object.)

I could no longer see, but I could hear in a muted fashion, and I could feel. There was a soft drop as Gus hung the locket around his neck, a long muttered goodbye. A rhythmic jostling followed and I knew Gus was walking through the streets of Nautilus to Margo's house.

I heard Margo's exclamations when Gus arrived, to all appearances without me. They conferred. Not every word reached me, but I needed only the gist. The locket was handed over, and Margo's allowance was increased. Gus ordered a dinner that arrived on beetleback, and they ate together for the first time in quite a while. If Asterion's threats worried Gus, I could not detect it in the cottony strains of his voice.

Eventually Gus left.

Then I dangled in my minute cell. It could not be said that I was finally away from my murderer, since part of me continued in you. I have never shared in your belief that you and Gus are separate entities; to me, you are merely a degraded form of the man who killed me. And if I have sometimes pitied you, your murders show me what a mistake it is to do so.

But I was away from Gus himself. The locket contained a kind of private vertigo, small and dark and pillowy. As for my screaming, I was so thoroughly accustomed to it that it sounded like silence rendered as song.

In that dark I considered the problem confronting me. If Asterion exposed Gus for bribery, my murderer would face exile to the unworld. He would age and die and, eventually, kill no more. It would have been an ideal solution, if only the recipient of that bribe had been anyone but Anura.

Anura and I had discussed what I should do in this situation. Her demands had been unambiguous. I should sacrifice her as the price of saving Gus's future victims. I should not dare to protect her at the expense of all those girls, their lives, their potential. Anura was still quite young in her human form, after all. No matter how much she hated that graceful body, it could be expected to live on in reasonable health for several decades to come—for much longer, indeed, than I ever had. Many millions have suffered far worse than she would, cast out of her home and rightful shape at once, and she might even manage an occasional stolen hour as a frog in some unworld closet or other.

Why, then, did everything that was in me refuse to allow her expulsion from Nautilus?

I thought of the promise she'd demanded, and how it had hung between us in a state of weightless expectancy. How I had changed the subject and left it there, adrift, ungiven, slowly expiring.

You see, Angus? By far the greatest share of the guilt adheres to you. You are the killer, the plague, the walking curse. Your steps blight the earth. Your love is an inversion of every decent sentiment and every tender impulse. If I can bring about your destruction, it will be the greatest accomplishment I could ever desire.

But not all the guilt belongs to you. Not all of it.

For Anura's sake, I took up a part of that guilt and wrapped it around myself like a mantle.

I wore it into regions where only the dead may go.

Catherine and the Letters

I have already met your stubbornness with patience at the limits of human endurance! But I mean to be more than human, and so I must be more than humanly patient as well.

Hearing a cardinal sing those words as you walk through the February woods can ruin your pleasure in birdsong forever.

Do you mean to destroy us both? If you are no longer with me, with me in everything, then how can I believe that you are not against me? But no, dearest Catherine, I cannot, will not conceive of you as an enemy, no matter how you try to drive me to it.

To find such a letter pinned to your door in March is enough to rip the fragrance from the first lilacs, to crumple spring's sweetness and cast it away.

I thought of threatening you; of telling you, perhaps, that I would kill Anna if you continued obstinate. But why should I force you when you are mine already, and it is only a matter of letting destiny take its course? Whenever I close my eyes I see us in Nautilus: one being in two bodies, emitting a single effulgence.

In April these words wrote themselves in fiery script across the page of Homer I was reading, then vanished. I wondered if I could defend Anna if it came to it, and felt in my brain for that little tongue of magic. It was no use; however Darius had compressed or concealed it, I could not get ahold of it again. For months nightmares tormented me: sweet Anna borne away on a tide of midnight fire. I clutched her to my heart, I dogged her steps, until she pushed me away with marked impatience.

Darius says that I can learn to control your dreams, so that every night you will live your proper life with me, and learn where you belong. I'm beginning to study the way of it now.

That was in May. Perhaps Gus realized that I had taken to burning his ordinary letters unread, because I found that message under the skin of a potato I was peeling. I threw it away, but the flavor of his words leaked into all my food, so that it was weeks before I could eat more than a few bites.

Today is your eighteenth birthday, my dearest. You never need age another day! Come to Nautilus and live forever in the fullest blossoming of your beauty and power, or stay here and wither in misery.

I have never cared to be compared to a flower; I am no helpless bloom picked by any passing hand that desires me. This particular bit of lyricism came written on a rose.

I saw you walking in the fields with Thomas Skelley. If I could imagine that dry stick as a rival I might have been jealous, even angry; but no, you could never degrade yourself to such a degree, so I need not be concerned.

The fire hissed these words with a shower of spiteful embers. One burned a hole in my sleeve.

So it went for more than a year. Thomas wrote me letters, too, of a very different character; he could spend two pages rapturously describing baby spiders bursting from a cluster of eggs and floating up on filaments of silk like tiny wriggling stars. I did my best to distract myself with that gentle correspondence and with study. I was determined now to attend college—and with that determination came a dream of living someplace where Gus could never find me.

Then in late January, thirteen months to the day after the hideous ceremony in the garden shed, I received a message that made my heart leap up. A murder of crows surrounded me and commenced a sort of bobbing, bowing dance. Then they croaked together with grave formality, *My mother has introduced me to a suitable young lady. Her name is Diantha Sprague and she is remarkably beautiful and refined, as well as coming from an excellent family. I wanted to prepare you, so that news of my engagement doesn't come as too great a shock.*

"Send Gus my congratulations, if you can," I told the crows. I didn't know if the magic worked in both directions or not; I had never tried before to reply. "Tell him I'm sincerely overjoyed at his news, and wish him and his bride every happiness."

I was too eager to believe that Gus had abandoned his hopes of me; it made me uncritical, unquestioning. His uncanny messages stopped, and their oppression lifted from my life. When my father told me in April that Gus was engaged I scooped up Anna in my arms and danced around the room with her, laughing till I wept. It was nearly as good as if he'd gone to Nautilus!

I should have known that his detachment was only another illusion.

Angus the Reader

"I've always regarded myself as a woman with an ample vocabulary at her disposal. But now, my plummy lad, I find myself with a deficiency. I simply don't have the words to express how utterly you've botched things."

Yeah, that would be my phone, chirping venomously away in Margo's voice. I hold it in front of my face, demonstratively banging the button to disconnect. Doesn't do a damn thing, naturally. My imaginary Margo is one hell of a stubborn bitch.

"No wonder Gus has it in for you! Plenty of other Anguses have failed, but I doubt one has ever been as exhaustively inept as you. Why didn't you kiss your *her,* I might ask? Because you were wearing the enemy's pendant. Because you trusted Lore, even after you told yourself you hated her."

"Okay," I tell her. "I get it. Now why don't you go choke on a cat?"

It takes two buses for me to slog my way back to the youth hostel. I'm wrecked, ready to crash in a cocoon of my own fury.

"So yeah," the shaggy dude at the desk says. "We got a call about that credit card you've been using, and how it's canceled because of some kind of fraud bullshit? So you can't use it for tonight, and anyhow we're not that into you staying here anymore?"

It would be a waste of my energy to hurt this guy, but I consider it anyway. But he's nothing to me; he's yawning emptiness bagged up in skin. Like, my fist might be swallowed by the void if I punched him.

"I just came to get my bag," I tell him. "I've got somewhere else to stay."

Because if Gus thinks I'm going to spend the rest of my rotten year shivering out on the street while he gloats, he doesn't know me half as well as he thinks. A fat plastic Smurf bulges in my back pocket, and to hell with Carmen if she tries to stop me from slamming myself down on the mattress in my old room.

The way Geneva looked at me, the revolted chill that made the whole world shiver around me in her eyes—

Don't think about that. Seriously, don't.

I would have killed her, okay. Sure. That doesn't change the fact that I loved her the whole time and I love her now. But she'll never understand—

Shit, I'm tired. Too weary and heartsick to stifle the evil chatter in my head.

She wanted to kiss me. How could it be wrong for me to give her what she wanted?

"Do you feel lucky now, little pudding? Now that two sorcerers as passionate in their animus as Lore and Gus can agree on exactly one point, and that's despising you? Everyone is against you now, absolutely everyone, so I'm hard pressed to imagine that you'll be squeezing much fun out of the time you have left."

I throw my phone in the gutter, grind the screen with my heel. It bursts with a satisfying *pop,* and I get a few beats of blissful silence. Then Margo's voice leaps free of the broken shell and buzzes around my head like a wasp.

"Shut up, Margo. Why even bother? We both know you aren't real. You're just a noise Gus shoved into my head, a talking doll that jabbers when he pulls its string. He made you."

"Oh, yes? And in what particular are you superior to me, I might ask? He made you as well."

"You can say only the stuff he designed you to say. I can make my own choices."

"Ooh, your vaunted agency. Lore told you that, didn't she? Lore once again! I simply can't *think* why she'd make such a point of your free will."

We both know why. She wanted to encourage insurrection against her old enemy. And honestly, killing Gus would seem like a great idea at this point, if only I didn't need him. If he dies, there will never be another one of me. Eliminating myself for all time isn't my idea of a party, somehow.

"What about another girl? There must be others nearby who meet your specifications. Think outside the box, why don't you?"

It's the most offensive thing I've ever heard. I might be an abomination, but at least I'm loyal.

"I love Geneva," I tell her. "I can't love anyone else."

I walk for hours, hounded by dream babble the whole way. It's one in the morning by the time I reach the rusty green door in Carmen's warehouse, and I'm so completely drained that for several moments I stand there with my head leaning on the wall and black spots crawling like roaches through my brain.

I find my mattress still in its place, and that's all that really matters. I throw off my clothes, ignoring the journal as it thumps from my jeans pocket onto the floor. Turn out the light and hurl myself into bed face-first, sure that I'll fall straight through and into endless strata of soft black sleep, down and down and down—

The space-print comforter leaps up around me like a slap. I nestle in, and the pillow is lumpy with wakefulness. When I roll over, the grubby sheet rustles like a thought teasing its way in and out of focus, almost becoming clear, almost explaining something incredibly important. A few minutes ago something chimed at the edge of my mind, but now I can't remember what it was. If I'd only paid more attention, I'd know—

What?

What?

"Screw this noise," I say out loud. "Bug me about whatever it is in the morning. Say around four p.m.? And bring me coffee in bed first."

But my brain doesn't take the hint. Keeps right on yammering like an obnoxious party in a next-door apartment. And I don't even *want* to think about it, I'm actively trying not to, but the punishing ache knocks around my head anyway. Ugh, Gus blocked those memories with pain to keep me from thinking too hard, didn't he?

It was something about Catherine, right? How she's never dead enough. How she's haunted Gus, how her death keeps screaming on and on and never falls silent.

Oh, for crissake, shut up! Shut up and let me sleep!

"Can't stop picking all the raisins out of your own pudding, eh, dear boy? Worry away at your brains all you like. You won't get anything for your efforts but sticky crumbs and a noggin full of sawblades."

Margo again. Maybe I'm hard to kill, but couldn't I use the pillow to suffocate myself into unconsciousness?

Margo would love that, wouldn't she? She's trying to discourage me from following this trail of thought. Snapping at me like Gus's watchdog.

And then the fantasy Margo gives a little shriek. There's a quick splatter of gagging noises, whines, squeaks—and the thing goes silent. It's like somebody just throttled her—but wouldn't that have to be somebody *in my head*, since presumably that's where the old un-Margo was installed?

Whatever. It's good to be able to think without all the distraction.

Catherine. He can't have her, can't touch her, but her death never leaves him. He put her scream away somewhere, but it's still in his head. His hands will always be the hands that strangled her, like her murder is hiding curled up in his palms. That's it: Catherine *hides*, she's a lurking immanence, and she haunts both without and within—

I snap on the poodle lamp so hard it nearly crashes over and lunge for something. I'm not sure what I'm after until I flop back on the bed with my fat black journal clutched in my hand.

Yeah? Do I have terribly important thoughts to record, or something? Seriously, what's the point? When I try to write in here I can't make out a word of it, anyway. My handwriting races away from me into incomprehensible loops and squiggles. I stare and stare, but even I have no idea what the hell I've been scribbling down—

Oh. Shit!

I twang back the elastic strap and open it.

Turns out I can read the journal just fine now. *If only Gus Farrow had not fled so precipitously on murdering me, or indeed if he had fled to any refuge but this one, I might have found peace.* That's how it starts, and then the line of ink catches my eyes and pulls them after it, and I can't look away.

The next thing I realize: it was a big mistake not to take off the pendant before I started.

Catherine Meets an Old Acquaintance

Hello, Angus, my hated reader, my ever-reborn enemy. The journal that you thought was yours is in your hands, its pages turned by your trembling fingers, its black and white flashing at you as a certain ghost once flashed. I've tugged away the obscurity that kept you from reading it before, laid it all out before you. You are still near the beginning of my story, though I can feel you coming steadily closer. We sometimes refer to the thread of a narrative, and you are following that thread now.

But consider for a moment how a thread, carefully knotted, can become a net.

I can't use your hands to inscribe this as you read, of course. But if you turned toward the back of the journal at this very moment and opened to the correct page, you would see the line of ink continuing to write on its own—*as if by magic,* someone might say.

Understand, I strongly prefer to take advantage of your intervals of unawareness. Picking up a pen with your fingers and writing as the living do is far more comfortable and efficient. But my long years haunting you have not gone to waste, and I have cultivated certain skills. For instance, I can concentrate upon a white speck of paper and turn it black, and then the next, and the one after, until words form in sequence. It's a wearying and expensive procedure, and writing the rest of the story in this fashion will cost me a certain portion of my reserves—but you should have guessed by now that my reserves are considerable.

Once I learned the trick of withholding most of my magical production from the umbrastring's questing suction, my savings added up quite quickly. I hoarded my magic for just such a rainy day as this one. I believe I have more than enough for everything that remains to me.

Succeed or fail, I've staked everything on this attempt, spent decades' worth of magic to entrap you. Gus is now aware of Lore's efforts to destroy him and may soon become aware of mine as well. If he thinks it through, he'll recognize how Lore and I have colluded. He'll take steps to defend himself, naturally. I can't expect another chance, so what reason do I have to save?

The period that followed my separation from Gus was one of suspense. In Nautilus my existence was uneventful, as you might expect would be the case for a screaming boil of a ghost wadded into a locket. I swung in my minute darkness, carried by Margo's slow shuffle from here to there. I did my best to study, but the perpetual anxiety took a toll. Sometime soon, it seemed certain, someone would come to steal me. Margo's hovel was not wonderfully secure, and she could hardly be expected to put up a fight. And what would become of me then?

In New York City my split-off self peered through your eyes as you slithered and sulked and downed coffee and wine in various establishments, hunting your next *her* and dissatisfied with all the candidates. Gus had provided you with a suitably bohemian appearance for the place and year, which I believe was 1962; this time you had a trim black moustache and a goatee, elongated hazel eyes, and a long, thin nose in a narrow oval face. You wore black turtlenecks, black loafers. Gus seemed to have abandoned the pretense that your personality was a winning one: now he endowed you with truly outlandish beauty, as if he was well aware he needed to compensate.

A week of unworld nights rolled across your open eyes, but you never saw them. I preferred them to the days, for while you slept I could ignore you and nearly imagine that your walls of flesh and blood were truly my own. If I felt the brush of your dreams, they were nowhere near as grating as the waking thoughts in which you nursed your own preposterous self-image as the sweetest, the most gentle of young men.

On the eighth night I was occupied with learning how to control shadows. Each time a car passed by outside its headlights caught the mullions dividing your window, and long fingers of shadow stretched across your ceiling. With enough effort I could make those splayed lines ripple and bend, or crook as if luring someone, or curl like lassoes. The next step, then, was to invest the shadows with enough puissance to seize something small—a letter, for example—and twist it through the barrier between the unworld and Nautilus. Improved communications were of the greatest importance, and I was enraptured by my own will to succeed.

So when the building's front door clicked and then groaned open, I thought nothing of it. There were several small apartments besides yours, and many of the residents kept odd hours.

Likewise when the stairs creaked, very slowly, as if someone with ill-tempered joints was making a painful ascent. I had a shadow firmly twined into my thoughts, and I was attempting to make it detach from the plaster and rock your dangling light bulb. It was a difficult trick, and I had no attention to spare.

Steps thumped down the hall, stilted, weaving. They stopped outside your door. It was bolted with a sliding steel bar, and I was not yet concerned. In Nautilus, Sky had made me portable, contained, and ready in a snatchable locket, but in New York I was embedded in your head and not so easy to steal. Besides, apart from Anura, Lore, and Laudine, I was nearly sure that no one knew I had a second residence, so to speak, a pied-à-terre nestled in your skull.

Then the bolt ground back, apparently untouched, its motion terminating in a loud clank. *As if by magic,* someone might say.

I dropped my shadow and made an involuntary effort to sit up sharply, forgetting in my disturbance that I could not command your body to that degree. I wondered if it was Lore here to kill you—but her steps were hardly so leaden and irregular—or if Anura had found me—but her human form was as light-footed as thistledown.

The door swung back on a figure broad and sagging, its sloped shoulders outlined in the sulfurous glow cast by a fixture somewhere behind. The head twisted backward and one boot sole lifted for inspection.

"Chewing gum," a voice complained. "Revolting stuff."

I knew that voice, long submerged in memory though it was. *Darius,* I could not say.

He met your open eyes, and something in his stare made me feel ashamed, caught out, as if I were pinned in a spotlight. He knew quite well who was looking out of your pupils, that much I knew at once, though I could not guess how. But Anura had figured it out, and why should I assume Darius would be any less acute?

Why are you here? I had no voice to give to the question, but could only gaze from inside your prone body.

"How do you communicate, then?" Darius asked after a moment—and I will confess a surge of relief that he didn't already know. An unworthy suspicion had occurred to me; Anura was chronically short of funds, and I knew how her natural integrity could bend under that pressure. But if my friends had sold me, surely they would have mentioned that I was confined to the written word? "You wouldn't play dumb on me, would you? Not when we've known each other for so long, Catherine Bildstein."

Whatever his reason for approaching me, I must learn it. I hiked up your right wrist and made a scribbling gesture with your forefinger.

"Writing! All right, then, we can accommodate you." He reached in a grubby pocket and pulled out a loose sheaf of lined paper and a pen. "I came prepared, you see. Pretty sure I'd find you holed up in Gus's beamer, but how would that manifest? Not like the history of magic is lousy with precedents; I'll give Gus credit, nobody ever thought to make such a muddle of ghost and beamer before. I brought all kinds of things to help you talk, depending."

I took the pen in hand, and he slipped the papers beneath it. *I thought you couldn't afford to leave Nautilus anymore. You look as if you could die at any moment.*

Darius gave an acid chuckle. "So I could, and I can't. This is the first time I've set foot on unworld soil since Gus squeezed the life out of you, and I can't say I care for it. If there were vultures in the neighborhood they'd be circling."

So what brings you here?

He looked around for a chair and settled for an apple crate, spilling clothes, which you kept near your bed. He lowered himself slowly, hands pressed to his knees, his gaze fixed on your face.

"Respect. You didn't think I had it in me, did you? I could've sent somebody to snatch you right off the old biddy's neck and never bothered with asking how you felt about it. But you see, pretty Catherine, I didn't do that."

Ah. I remembered that occasion by the Nimble Fire when I'd glimpsed Darius slipping away from Asterion's circle at Gus's approach.

Darius looked at me expectantly. Was he waiting for an expression of gratitude?

How long has Asterion been in your employ?

The old man tipped his head in acknowledgment. There wasn't much light, but I could make out the draped and raddled contours of his face.

"From the beginning. Asterion has two hands, after all, so why wouldn't he grab all he can with both of them? I hired him to keep an eye on you both, at first, let me know anything he could about what Gus was up to and how you were behaving. But the situation's developed since then, hasn't it? Sky, now, Sky's a more recent addition to the payroll. Worth every lit, though. I couldn't do a damn thing until he severed the ties that bind."

Anyone else? I hated myself for my own suspicions, but it was not lost on me that it was Anura's startling appearance in the Lapis Gardens that had provoked Gus to have me sliced off. Had her warning really been so pressing, when I had no way to act on what she told me? Darius knew Gus very well. He'd already demonstrated an impressive knack for manipulating his former protégé. He might very well have realized—

Darius shrugged. "*That's* what you're worried about? I'd've thought you'd be more interested in why I've gone to so much trouble and expense over you. And anybody I've paid, it's been with your own best interests at heart; I've got exciting plans for you. Why not leave it at that?"

I slashed a line under *Anyone else?* with a fair amount of pique. Your wrist knocked against the stack of paper, scattering sheets across the floor. I could see the wet glow reflected in Darius's eyes widening, turned gibbous and conniving.

"*Somebody's* a sensitive point for our Catherine, that's plain. Asterion did mention that a certain webbed-footed someone was spouting lyrical tributes at you. I wonder if those verses made an impression?"

At once I loathed myself for having drawn his attention toward Anura, and hurried to introduce a new topic.

How did you find me?

Darius grinned at my deflection, as I had recently prickled at his. He bent with difficulty to pick up the fallen papers, but missed several sheets.

"Simple enough to let it be known I'd pay for news of Gus's movements. Once he's popped through a particular exit four or five times close together, you know he's planted one of his beamers on the other side."

Of course. It was a shame Anura lacked the funds for such a direct solution to the problem of finding me. And I, on the other hand, had the necessary talens, but lacked the freedom necessary for offering bribes.

That leaves us with—why?

"So it does." Darius grinned again, crumbling teeth glittering in the dimness. "I have a mind to rule Nautilus, but I don't have quite enough juice on my own. I've been analyzing samples of your magic—I pay Asterion double for talens extracted from you, you see, and don't think I don't know how you've been holding back! I've designed my own magic to work in synergy with yours, and I thought we might stage a little coup together."

If I'd had breath I would have released it in an incredulous huff. As it was, Darius's words sank into silence.

At last I wrote, *I've always considered Nautilus's politics to be a game for spoiled fools. But whatever you may be, you aren't that.*

Darius snorted. "Well, thank you *very* much. Why for fools, though?"

Each upheaval slakes the vanity of our latest rulers, I suppose, and brings in a new clique of favorites. But as far as I can tell, it does nothing else. Nothing of substance ever changes. It was very freeing to complain, even to an old enemy. *For all its buildings can flow like water, Nautilus is the most hidebound, the most static of cities! In all my time there, I've seen nothing that resembles reform, not the slightest progress. The corruption is endemic, the poor neglected, and no one seems to care for anything but absurd displays of wealth. Why* anyone *would want to indulge in these empty convulsions, where one sorcerer supplants the last, I have no idea.*

"Ah, but you've identified the reasons for it yourself. Just because none of the recent rulers have brought real change, it doesn't mean *we* couldn't."

Such as?

"Oh, reclassifying ghosts as citizens, maybe? Rights, responsibilities, all that? Sky would never forgive me if I stopped him from dissecting any itty bit of howling ectoplasm he can get his hands on, of course. But I find I don't care."

I thought of poor little Jane, her substance spun into Sky's vicious tool. I thought of the spirits I'd seen in various miserable predicaments by the Nimble Fire, or in the streets. Of—may all things holy help them!—the ghosts in Nemo's collection. Legally, none of us had more status than a lost shoe.

Those rights would last until we were cast out in the next coup. Not long at all, in other words.

"Maybe." He shrugged. "But changes can be sticky things, once you finally make them."

I was considering the ramifications of Darius's proposal so quickly that I felt as if I were tumbling down a thousand branching rivers at once. I could see certain advantages to accepting, though I had never liked or trusted the man. In particular, I began to glimpse a way I might protect Anura.

Why me?

"Because," Darius said almost grimly, "I knew you had the makings of a great sorceress from the first time I saw you. Do you remember? Just a little girl lying in an orchard. But concentric waves spread outward though the grass, and *you* were the center. You were will incarnate."

I remembered. I hadn't seen the grass's spreading circles, but I'd felt—something. *I didn't know that was you spying on us. I was afraid it was my father.* When there'd been no repercussions, I'd given no more thought to the episode.

But Darius seemed caught in memories of his own. "Pretty, tiny thing, covered in flowers. But pulsing with potential, and I made up my mind then. I'd been squarely in the second tier of sorcerers for as long as I could remember, but with you beside me I'd be able to break through to the top. Why do you think I kept hanging around your dreary little town? Here I thought Gus would be my way to you, and instead he threw one hell of a wrench into my plans! Well, dead you may be, but that hasn't kept you down. You're well on your way—to *becoming.*"

Darius delivered the last verb as if it were utterly intransitive, objectless—as if *becoming* were its own end, a cumulus of self taller than any city, any sky.

There was only one question remaining. *And if I say yes?*

"Then Asterion will be provided with a key-spell sufficient to break into Margo's room. I'll order him not to hurt her—unless, of course, you'd prefer otherwise. He'll carry you straight to me, and we'll start planning. Together, Catherine."

That might prove challenging, considering that in Nautilus I can't speak.

"You can, actually. You see, my dear, I have a body waiting for you."

My shock was enough to knock your skull on the headboard.

A body? Legs that could wander, arms that could embrace, lips—I dismissed the thought. Most significantly, a voice of my own!

I do not pretend to be good. I have seen true goodness in others, and adored them for it, but I find nothing similar in myself. But there was one consideration I could not ignore.

And what were your materials, might I ask?

Darius laughed. "I *did* wonder if you'd be particular in that regard! Nothing too dreadfully immoral was involved, I assure you; it's a mixture of mechanical and animal parts. I think it's very fetching, myself, but if you like you can always cast a different appearance on it. The main thing is, it's fully functional. Easier to pursue a private life that way, eh?"

Images of the freedom that could be mine rushed in on me. It would be almost like living again, and moreover, wreathed in power, in splendor; a strange new queen so far from her origins that it beggared the wildest fairy tale!

And I thought of something else.

Asterion would be the one sent to steal me. I'd suspected as much before I knew the identity of his master, but now it was confirmed.

Even after the relentless torture I'd suffered at Asterion's hands, he had at this moment only one meaning for me, one guise.

Asterion's continued existence was a threat to Anura.

"Listen, Catherine," Darius pursued. "I'm sure your memories of me aren't the happiest. I don't blame you for hesitating. But I won't steal you without your consent, and I'd like to think that counts for something. The fact is, I need your enthusiastic participation to pull this off. It might be a while before we're ready—you're on your way to becoming, but you're not there yet! But once we're prepared to take over, I mean for us to rule as equals. You say there's no point to it? Fine. *You* tell *me* what the point should be, and we'll do that."

I need three days of unworld time, I wrote. *Before I'll be able to go.*

"And I suppose it would be terribly intrusive of me to ask why?" The wretched old man was chary.

You spoke of respect. Start by respecting this request.

Meanwhile, on the notepaper scattered around us black letters were skimming rapidly across the white, like barn swallows weaving their loops against a pale sky. I scribbled the same message on all of them, a very exhausting exercise, especially since writing without the benefit of your hands was then a recently acquired skill and I was in need of more practice. (To this day, I have never managed to write anything in this manner from my confinement in Nautilus—I believe it's an unwelcome side effect of Sky's silencing spell on the locket. I can write only through you.) In short order I burned through an impressive number of talens.

It was an immense gamble—I could not predict exactly where Darius would step on his way to the door, and he might well miss all the sheets. Even if a note stuck, it might jar free before he reached the gyre over Nautilus, or he might notice it and discover my ruse. An infinite number of things could go wrong, and then I would have depleted myself for nothing.

But I find that death has greatly increased my taste for risk.

"All right, then. All right. Three days. So provided I meet your condition, we'll call it a yes?"

May all things holy help me, I gripped the pen firmly in your hand. *YES,* I wrote. And the limp streaks of light that defined Darius's face became silvered parentheses around his shadowed smile.

"Till we meet again, then, Catherine Bildstein," Darius said, and levered himself upright with his hands.

He shuffled toward the door. I could hear the minute suction and popping release of the gum gobbed on the sole of his left shoe. It landed maddeningly close to one note, but fell slightly short. I twisted with impatience as his right foot took its turn. The left twitched up again, sailed forward, and a letter seemed perfectly positioned for the strike.

Then Darius wobbled—and his leg swung forward to catch his balance. It came down with a thump and a backdraft that sent my missive skittering.

There were no more notes in the dusty zone between his sagging silhouette and the door. He turned the knob and it opened on a slice of stairwell.

In desperation I balled your hand and rapped sharply on the bedframe. Darius turned back. I hurried to scribble a few words with theatrical vigor, writing the first thing that occurred to me. I made the letters rather small, and Darius was obliged to take a few steps back into the room before his squinting eyes could pick out the message.

Promise we'll destroy Gus.

"Oh, I took that as a given!" Darius said after a moment's startled pause. "Can't kill him without the risk of dispatching you, unfortunately, but Nautilus has some very fancy cages we could use. How'd you like to drain *his* power for a change?"

He grinned and turned away, and the gum on his left foot caught one of my notes with a solid slap. The paper went whispering away with him, out the door and down the stairs, and as it went an address busily inscribed itself on the reverse. An address in Nautilus is a powerful thing, and I did not doubt that the paper would tug loose in the whirlwind and ride the currents in search of a particular hand.

This time my letter did not name Anura. It was addressed to Madame Laudine.

Angus in Mind

Elegant, slanting, antique-looking handwriting packs the pages with tiny, oceanic crests. It's nothing like my blobby scrawl; that's the first thing I notice. I didn't write this, I didn't write a damn word of it, and even if I already guessed the truth it's another thing to really *see* it.

Nautilus preserved my death but would not let me die.

Yeah, I kind of got that.

People speak of the language of the eyes. Well, their vocabulary is cruelly limited.

The pendant, though: it makes me feel all of it. I'm snared in Catherine, wrapped in coils of her thought, and the more I struggle the tighter they get. I *feel* myself flapping over Gus's shoulders, feel the outrage of listening to him jabber on so self-righteously. I even miss the life Catherine missed, the baby rabbits popcorning in the grass and the sweetness of rain-drenched honeysuckle.

And I can't stop reading, literally can't disentangle my gaze from the ink line dragging me along with it. It's only going to get worse from here, and, okay, it sucks to be her and everything. But why should that mean I have to feel everything Catherine ever felt?

I could not burst into bitter laughter at what struck me as a difficult undertaking.

She's laughing at me now, the bitch. She's sitting in my head and howling at the spectacle of me, Angus Farrow, reduced to empathy. *Like hell I am, Catherine. Like hell.* I reach for the pendant, grasping and scrabbling to tear it off. But my hands veer randomly and I wind up smacking myself in the face instead. Because she's in me, she's messing up everything I try to do—Catherine refracting through Lore's pendant, Catherine's beams bent back to pierce me.

Shit. They've been working together this whole time. I know it.

My story emerges now from death. It comes in search of its own ending, hated reader.

"Well, fuck you too," I say aloud, and make another grab for the pendant. *Get this thing off me, get it off!* But it swings away and my hands skid and collide—with each other, with nothing, with the cold static of ghosts. Megan and Pearl, Justine and Claire and Lorca—it's like they're here, catching at me, jerking and weaving in my muscles, diverting my movements. It doesn't matter that they aren't actual ghosts like Catherine, it's enough that they haunt my mind. I'm constantly driven off course. And meanwhile, Catherine's voice keeps rising in my head, her heart keeps drumming through my veins, until I can't even feel myself anymore. I'm feeling too much of her, there isn't *room* anymore—

Then I'm nothing but the story. The one Catherine set for me like a trap. And now it's sprung.

Catherine at the Falls

It was June 1859. I had recently turned nineteen, and felt ready to take the entrance exams for three different female colleges—though I knew I must perform well enough to secure a scholarship as well as admittance. Thomas was home from Madison University for the summer. And Reverend Skelley, who knew I had never traveled by train, proposed an excursion: why should we three not go to Niagara Falls together and watch the Great Blondin walk across on his tightrope? We could leave early in the morning and return late the same night, so there would be no impropriety.

My father consented far more readily than I'd expected. I suppose he'd resigned himself to the idea that I would marry into a Universalist family and never again believe that anyone was damned to hell, offensive though he found that forgiving doctrine.

I suppose he was simply relieved by the prospect of anyone but Gus.

Before dawn on the thirtieth I was dressed and out the door. We took a coach to Batavia, and from there the train—the thunder and rush delighted me more even than the promised feat—then, far too soon, we disembarked into a jostling crowd all heading for the falls.

The falls. I had lived my whole life less than fifty miles distant from Niagara, but I had never seen them before. We were early enough to find a fair spot to spread our blanket on the American side, and I marveled at the water's roar obliterating the noise of that vast assembly, at the mists so dense even history might be lost in them. The white walls of water growled over the festival air. We looked across at Canada, its shore crawling with the particolored dots of parasols and bright summer dresses; we bought sugared buns and hot chocolate from the ambling vendors.

At what point did I observe that Thomas, who usually kept his gaze lowered, was watching me sidelong with a look of bashful longing? At what point did I realize that his father, usually the more talkative of the two, was at pains to stare into the distance, as if we were not there? I hadn't understood the point of this excursion before, but now I began to suspect, and my mind wheeled through frantic calculations.

Darius, like Gus, could not comprehend that anyone might sincerely reject magic. When he'd suppressed its flickering in me, I don't doubt that Darius had thought I'd come to him soon enough and beg for his help in freeing my power once again. Now I reached into myself, and felt—nothing. No disease of the mind, no oozing menace to reality's fragile configurations. Had Darius actually *cured* me, and thought of it as a curse?

(He had not. But how could I know?)

The crash of the falls made our silence less conspicuous. I was grateful for the reprieve.

Meanwhile the funambulist's cable was tied to an oak tree on the American side, but there was some difficulty in getting it up the cliff in Canada. The crowd burst into cheers as Blondin rappelled down the gorge, then tied a rope to the hemp cable so it could be drawn up. Blondin climbed the cliff with what appeared to be airy unconcern, his lithe figure sometimes obscured by spray. How slippery, how treacherous those rocks must be!

If I was cured, if I was no longer obliged to reject Thomas for his own protection, that still left the question of what I *wanted*. Both Skelleys were warmly encouraging when it came to my hopes for college and even when I talked of perhaps becoming a journalist afterward. They were true Spiritualists, committed to an ideal of absolute human equality. I believed that neither of them would balk at seeing their ideals put into action.

Guy ropes were strung to constrain the cable's swaying. A vast webwork grew in midair, a hundred lines of tension, all of them touching a single man's life.

In the early afternoon Reverend Skelley unpacked our picnic basket. Sandwiches and lemonade, cold chicken and strawberries.

And of course a pie. It was too early for fresh blackberries, so Thomas must have used canned ones. As he lifted the pie from the basket he looked away, but I saw his brimming eyes.

We had far too much food, and shared with our neighbors. They had three little daughters with them, and for a while the children's joyful hunger covered everything still unsaid between us.

There was one final consideration. Did I love Thomas Skelley, love him enough to justify marriage, of all preposterous things?

The sun began its decline, striking a furious dazzle from the rising mist. Reverend Skelley excused himself to stretch his legs; our neighbors' littlest girl fell asleep with her head on my leg.

And Thomas took my hand. "My father told me long ago that you meant never to marry," he said, so gently that his voice seemed one with the wind. "But if you ever change your mind, no matter how far in the future, then I can imagine nothing more beautiful than the life we could make together."

"I must think," I told him. "I must think."

"I mean of course—after you finish college, and whatever else you want to do on your own—you could take all the time you needed—" A plangent note had entered his voice, and he broke off in shame at the sound of it.

"I'll give you my answer soon, I promise! Only—"

He didn't press me further, and I didn't withdraw my hand.

Could *I* imagine anything more beautiful than such a life? I saw it then: children, pies, fireflies, books, the soft bellies of hens as I reached in for eggs. We would study together, quest for secrets in rainwater and bones; Thomas would work in the sciences, and I could add my efforts to the many movements for justice then current, perhaps by writing for one of the reform-minded newspapers. It would be a life without grandeur, without any grasping after superiority to the rest of humankind. A life of small things.

It would fall to us to make them immense through love.

Reverend Skelley came back to our blanket with a Spiritualist acquaintance he'd run into; the two of them seemed absorbed in conversation.

It was late afternoon when Blondin put his foot on the cable, on the American side again, and began to walk. There was no net, no line, no help for him if he slipped. Only blue space and thrashing winds all the way to another country. He carried a balancing pole several times his own height, and his sequined pink costume scattered feverish glints across the endless air. He walked, or more nearly strutted, into ravenous emptiness.

There was no magic in this marvel, please note. Instead there was a solitary person, in desperate peril, determined to reach the other side.

Around me thousands of people held their breath, peeked through their fingers, buried their faces in nearby shoulders. I think Thomas never noticed how hard he was squeezing my hand. But as Blondin went on, my own doubts lifted; I felt his confidence as if it were my own.

He sat down on his rope, and blithely hauled up a bottle of wine from the *Maid of the Mist* far below; he raised his glass in a toast, and drank.

The guy ropes could not reach all the way to the cable's center. Blondin approached the sagging, wavering span at the midpoint, and the crowd's anxiety ratcheted again. Fear breathed through me as his dwindling figure balanced on that wobbly line; for the first time I felt viscerally that we all might have come here only to watch a man die.

But he went on, and at last his feet curled on the steadier stretch leading to Canada. With the bursting energy of unexpected freedom, he began to run. Sunlight washed around him, and he looked as small as a spider on its thread.

No matter how the falls thundered, they could not drown out the cheers when he dismounted on the far side. The uproar came at us, a wind of human voices blown across the chasm; all around me people began to shout, to jump, to cry.

It was then that I knew.

"Thomas," I said into the tumult. "Thomas!"

It was a wonder that he heard me at all; how his mind must have been attuned to the slightest note of my voice! He turned, shaking from head to toe, and looked at me.

"We've made it," I said. "We're across at last!"

It was a moment before he understood what I meant. But then his face broke open, and his arms flew out, and we took each other in. That embrace was a small thing, only two people clinging to each other in a vast and shrieking crowd.

But its warmth felt big enough to hold all the future.

Hush.

Catherine in the Wall

Madame Laudine did not come at once. The Catherine in the locket and the Catherine in your eyes seemed to watch each other across the divide between worlds, to reach toward a mirrored brilliance where, against all expectations, their hands met no glassy barrier but rather diffused and merged, fingertip into fingertip. I tried to reassure myself that Laudine would come, the same soothing phrases chanting on both sides of my split mind.

Then I worried that my letter had gone astray, or even worse that Madame Laudine might have taken offense at my plan—for I had been explicit that we must keep our actions secret from Anura. I was gambling that Laudine would be as anxious as I was to protect Anura, since the love between the two of them was painfully clear to me. Even if it meant defying Anura's express wishes. Even if protecting Gus was unwelcome collateral. I was gambling that Margo hated Gus enough to disobey him, or loved him enough to defend him, or perhaps a combination of the two.

In the closed locket I couldn't see anything but a fine sickle of light along the joint, but I could feel Margo's dispirited shambling and the sway of her shoulders. I could hear her muttering to herself at home and hear other voices in a cloud around her when she went out. Meanwhile the unworld hours ticked steadily by. The Catherine in your eyes reported their passing to her remote self with increasing consternation, until it was nearly the time appointed for Asterion's visit. Where was Laudine? Asterion was surely seeking some way to steal Anura's heartstring with its subtly inscribed evidence. Once he succeeded I would have no second chance.

Margo rose from her chair and shuffled as far as the alley. It sounded as if she was weeping quietly.

Then I heard a soft step approach.

"Good evening, Margo." There was a pause long enough for Margo to smudge her tears with a wrinkled paw and look up. "My name is Laudine."

She had come, she had come, she cherished Anura just as I did! I should have known that what I asked of her would take some effort; of course she could not manage it immediately. I would have liked to spring up, to sing, to throw my wraith's arms around her. Instead I throbbed against my confinement, screamed to my metal walls.

"And what are you peddling?" Margo snapped after a moment. "Those fish you have in place of brains? Don't need any."

Margo was out of practice with social graces, of course. But I thought her asperity trembled with lonely yearning. It was all she could do not to pounce on Madame Laudine, clasp her knees, and beg her to stay for some tea.

Laudine's dress gave forth a soft splashing sound as she lowered herself to sit on the bare alley floor beside the miserable old lady, just as if she had heard the same note of invitation I had.

"Are you an art collector, Margo? If not, you can rest assured that I'm not trying to sell you anything."

Margo considered that. "You're here for some reason. And whatever it is, it's not to help me."

"What help do you need?" Laudine sounded surprised, and in fact my letter hadn't addressed Margo's difficulties. I pitied Gus's aunt, but intermittently, when I found room in my thoughts for her forlorn and wasted state. The burst of passionate sympathy I'd felt when she lost her beamer child had faded long ago, and I told myself her own choices had brought her to this pass.

It was presumably the same strategy she used to nullify my suffering.

"I want to go home and die there. The house is long gone, Gus says, razed to the ground. Well, a hedge will do me fine, any old ditch. I don't care where I stop breathing, just so my last breath is real human air and not this magical *stink*. But Gus stuck something on me that keeps me from getting out of this place." Some enchantment, she meant, probably one that sealed the exits against her. Of course he had.

I could not see them, but I heard a gentle sloshing and imagined Laudine was tilting her head as she mulled the question. "That kind of magic is far outside my area. But I can arrange a visit from someone who knows how to break spells of that kind. In return for your absolute discretion, that is. And your cooperation."

"It had to be something," Margo muttered. "Cooperation with what?"

"Murder." I jerked in my tiny prison, hearing that; I'd expected Laudine would gloss our intentions in euphemism. "But I promise our target deserves it."

There was an extended silence.

"*Our.*"

"I'm working with someone you know very well. You're not the only one who's endured confinement at the hands of Gus Farrow."

I felt a twitch as Margo stiffened. "I don't know anyone in this horrible city. You're either lying or out of your mind."

There followed a delicate rustling. "It's been quite a while since you've seen her handwriting. But maybe you'll remember it anyway."

I hadn't intended my letter for Margo's eyes and flinched at the intrusion; I did not like to risk Gus discovering that I could write. If I demanded Laudine's help, of course I must trust her to persuade Margo as she thought best—only this was too much, it left me too raw—

Margo gave out a stifled shriek and grabbed the locket, so that I pitched dizzily and then jerked to a stop. The darkness quivered in her clenched hand.

"How is this possible?" It was nearly a scream.

"How, really? Remember where we are," Laudine rejoined softly. "How many supposed impossibilities have you met with in the streets of Nautilus? Catherine Bildstein is not alive, and I wouldn't call her well. But she still has *herself.*"

"And *that's* what she wants to do with this self she has? I can remember when Catherine thought of herself as too pure and exalted for such business. Dedicated to the highest ideals you could shake a stick at, singing in harmony with the planets as they spun. Now the best she can think of to do is wanton murder?"

"It's going to be a very idealistic murder," Laudine replied in sly and smiling tones. "I don't see the contradiction."

Margo leaned back and I sloped softly on her bony chest. "What do I have to do, then?"

"Almost nothing. Let me take the locket and get Catherine arranged, and then there will be nothing to do but wait. She won't even leave your room, and you'll be able to tell Gus perfectly honestly that you never left her more than a few feet away from you. He'll ask what happened, of course, but you can tell him she got into your wall somehow and you didn't see it, and we'll make sure that's true. A few unworld hours, and we'll pack her back up."

"And for that you'll help me escape from this place?" Margo didn't sound happy—she was rightly afraid of angering Gus with some misstep— but she also sounded desperate.

"For that I'll pay to break Gus's binding spell. Making it out of the exit is up to you. But there's a way through to Cairo just down the block, if that will suit you."

Margo considered. "I wanted to go *home*. But Cairo might be a decent enough place to die."

"Spend long enough in Nautilus and all the unworld becomes home to you. Whether the home you long for, or the home you're glad to leave behind, it's all one in abandonment," Laudine said gently. And Margo drew the locket's chain up over her head.

The doorways of Nautilus stand demarcated by lintels or posts on the glowing walls, but to a casual eye nothing else distinguishes them from every other surface. On stepping through the wall, its bright substance engulfs you in its pearlescent ooze, as if you were subjected to some celestial digestion. But then you pop clear on the other side, and the suction of that smeary, disorienting nacre is nearly forgotten.

This was the first time I had stood upright in the substance of a wall, embedded and still like a vein in marble. I waited. The locket still anchored my lower extremities, but I unfurled above it, nearly concealed by the wall's opacity. Laudine had said that my flashing was dimly visible from without, but only if you looked for it.

As you may have guessed, I waited in considerable pain. Laudine had turned her simulated friendship with Sky to good account and successfully stolen two umbrastrings from his display. With many apologies she had inserted the prongs of one in the region of my ankle, and the other in the crown of my head. Using talens I gave her, she spelled the wall so that my scream did not penetrate to the outside air. Then she removed herself to a distance where she could watch.

It was only when I was pinned in this way that I felt the full extent of my power—that I felt what I *was*. Death undying, life unlived, trapped in an amalgam whose internal and eternal violence could not rest. Oh, I understood then why Darius thought my ghost could rise as a new ruler of Nautilus! My power, caught in this terrifying oscillation, was that of a dark goddess of thresholds, the force of liminality itself. I was the un-resolvable in-between, always torn by the pull of life and death and con-founding the two in my fleshless flesh.

Where that power vibrated, a shadow approached. Man's frame, bull's head, crescent horns. I saw Asterion as if he were drowned in luminous milk, an opalescent burr around his contours. I watched him pause as he touched the door-zone and transferred the talens that would break Mar-go's inadequate lock, and I knew the success or failure of our plot waited in the coming moment—but my charged suffering was such that I could barely remember why I wanted him dead.

He paused. Had he seen me? Did he understand the trap set for him? No, he was merely adjusting his collar.

Then Asterion barged straight into the wall, which meant that he also plowed into me. What I wanted was no longer relevant, because my power instantaneously committed itself to his disassembly. He was a buzz of blood, a swarm of carnage, and even if I had wished to spare him it was too late. His brisk intrusion made his death much faster than Flynn's had been, and therefore much kinder. The suffering the minotaur had inflicted on me had been incalculably greater, I swear it.

Asterion let out a single bark of astonished pain, and then he was gone—except, that is, for a large sweep of his bull's head, hollowed out like a helmet where I passed through him, which thudded bloodily onto the floor of Margo's room. I'd also missed most of his left leg, which had entered the wall just outside my borders.

That leg stayed beside me, teetering its way to equilibrium; I could see it as if through a shining fog. It looked as if it had been sawed off at a steep angle halfway down the thigh. Asterion's purple velvet trouser leg was sliced as well and slipped down to bunch around his ankle, just as if he were getting ready to seat himself on a toilet—and my scream bucked with the hysterical laughter that was denied me. His remaining boot sat under the trouser leg's drapery, and it was a lovely one: I saw a pointed toe and alternating stripes of leather, black and gold and fuchsia, rising in a spiral like a barber's pole. The minotaur had done very well for himself, until he did a bit better than he should have.

The grains of Asterion's devastated flesh remained inside me, a revolting cloud, until Laudine came running to remove me from the wall and yanked the upper umbrastring away. She hid it promptly in her dress. Then Asterion's materials drizzled down, bone and eyeball and intestine alike reduced to a wet, indiscriminate gray-red dust. It fell in a gritty rain, reeking of iron and shit and stomach acid, and coated the street with a thick paste.

Margo and Laudine both screamed and wailed and enacted horrified amazement for the spectators, who were gathering fast. I was dutifully rolled back up and stuffed in my locket, with many loud recriminations and wonderings as to how I could have managed such a thing. A talking peacock was dispatched to fetch Gus, and Asterion's more recognizable remains were gathered just outside Margo's home. The look on her face as she hauled out the dripping, hairy rind of what had been Asterion's head was not one I will forget.

There was no keeping our murder a secret, so all that remained was to hide the involvement of my living coconspirators. Murder was technically illegal, even in Nautilus. But since I myself was not legally an entity, there was nothing anyone could do to me—no more than if Asterion had been crushed by a falling star.

"Ghosts are slippery bitches, aren't they?" and "Couldn't have happened to a more deserving beast," and "Guess *somebody's* having a bad morning," were among the ambient remarks, and none of them seemed cause for concern. The story spread with such force across the city that its widening ripples were nearly palpable, a crawling on my skinless skin.

I sat in my tiny dark cell, trembling with my own scream, and though words were still beyond my reach in Nautilus, I knew that I had sent two very loud and unequivocal messages. The first, of course, informed Darius that I put no faith in his promises and had no interest in ruling Nautilus with him in any case, thank you kindly for the invitation. A body of my own was a vicious temptation. It was very nearly irresistible—but I knew, oh how I knew, that Darius would claim his price for it. In one way or another, that price would be too high.

The second message was to Anura, and I would have refrained from sending it if I could. It amounted to this: *There is nothing I won't do for your sake, and no crime I won't commit in your defense.*

And this: *I never promised.*

And this: *Live as your true self, my own, my dearest one. Even if it means that others die.*

Laudine slipped away, no doubt to have a roaring fight with our amphibious friend. Since Laudine now had your address in Greenwich Village, I expected that soon enough I would be called to account for my actions as well. What could I say to Anura, except that I could not have done otherwise? I boiled with shame at my violation of a promise ungiven, and at the same time I blamed Anura for demanding it. If she could not bear to expose the crime she shared with Gus, how could she ask me to allow Asterion to do the same?

I expect that *you* will have trouble believing it. How could Gus be so dethroned in my thoughts? But in truth I was so preoccupied with imaginary arguments I might have with Anura—and with the larger, sharper, unmanageable question of whether she would forgive me—that I completely forgot to wonder how Gus would view my conduct.

I was presently illuminated.

"Let me through! Let me through this instant!" His voice came bowling through the crowd, shrill and urgent. I heard what sounded like shoving and stamping, cries of irritation and yelped obscenities. Then Gus reached out and snatched the locket off Margo's neck, and held me in his fist for a moment, breathing hard.

I sat in my metal clamshell, so docile and quiescent that no one would ever imagine how recently I had turned a minotaur into a cloud. I thought I could feel his stare fixed on me behind my wreath of blue enamel flowers.

"Forget-me-nots," he said after a pause, and then he broke down sobbing. I was bathed in unctuous, unwelcome warmth and knew that he had squeezed the locket against himself, perhaps his cheek or his heart. "Forget-me-nots. She had to open the locket, reach the wall, somehow stabilize herself enough to interact with flesh—all with no help! It would seem to be impossible. But for those who don't forget, nothing is impossible. Oh, Catherine!"

It was so ridiculous that I failed to comprehend at first. Then Dawn with her bloody fingertips scaled my mind, as it were, and I realized that there had been a misunderstanding.

Gus thought I'd murdered Asterion for *him*.

Soon enough all Nautilus was in agreement. Sky spread the story of how Asterion had seemed to threaten Gus in my presence, with what he didn't say. And soon thereafter—well. The word went 'round that it was ill-advised in the extreme to annoy Gus Farrow, or else his loyal ghost would shred the offender.

In some ways the story was convenient for me; it obscured the true object of my protection, and that in turn made it less likely that suspicion would fall on Madame Laudine. As you sat up in your narrow bed at two in the afternoon, brushed your teeth and combed your hair, I even entertained the frantic hope that Gus would consider Asterion's death a sufficient demonstration of my love and recall you. That he would mash you down and forget the foul bundle in a corner. What reason did he have to send out his beamers, to continue his campaign of murders, if I had gone so far as to kill for him?

If my actions ended Gus's murders rather than enabling more of them—surely Anura would forgive me then? But then how would I talk with her henceforth?

Hopes invested in Gus are generally misplaced, and this hope proved no different. He crooned over me, but left you where you were. You bathed, dressed, ate, stalked the streets of Greenwich Village. You singled out a girl, a Polish immigrant named Anya, and coaxed her into going to Coney Island with you. A thirty-foot giant loomed over the pair of you, clutching a sign that read ASTROLAND; you knocked over a painted cat with a ball and presented it to her; and seagulls stole your knish as you sat on the boardwalk with your arm around her shoulder.

I managed to scrawl *Anya, run! He'll kill you* on the beach with your fingertip. Then a scampering child's foot landed in the middle of my message with a rush and scatter of sand, and you and Anya got up and walked to the parachute jump. You made the ascent hand in hand, then floated softly down together.

By the time you reached the ground, Anya was dying.

It does no good to say that Gus's exile would not have saved her; you were already in motion, like some vicious wind-up toy, and would not stop until your gears ground out their impetus.

Anya would have died regardless, that I can say with certainty. But Gus was already getting on in age, and I can't deny that his exile would have cut off the scroll of your murders at some unknown point—before now.

Maybe long before now. Why did he keep sending out his beamers, why did he keep killing? It must have been more than mere habit. Possibly, for all his joy over Asterion's atomization, he still knew in his heart that I did not love him. Possibly he even guessed at whom I did love, though his arrogance prevented him from admitting it.

No. His true reason was this: Gus could not afford to give up his obsession, his endless killing. To do so would confront him with the utter, grotesque, desolate waste he had made of both his life and his magic.

It would leave him with nothing to do. What did he truly care for, after all?

Whatever his reasons were, I had made myself his accomplice. With every death beyond that point I felt guilt settle on me, cloying, adhesive, hot with shame. Each time Lore has killed you, she's spared me the toll of another young girl doomed owing to my choice; each time you've eluded Lore and killed again, I've known that Lore and Anura must think with disgust of my share in that crime. If Lore is working with me, and she is, it does not follow that she likes me—no more than I like myself.

Lore *did* begin to track down your manifestations far more often once I mastered the trick of slipping letters directly through the membrane that separates the unworld from Nautilus. And in chasing her, Gus aged quite a bit—until he decided he could no longer take the risk.

Call me a necessary evil, if you wish. I've called myself worse. At least in that crucial respect—*necessity*—I remain superior to you who are a worthless evil, a pointless blot. Let this narrative, written with a stolen hand, indict and damn us both!

As for Anura? I'd given Laudine your address in Greenwich Village. Anura had to know where I was; she *had* to. You'd butchered Anya very early in your allotted year, and there was a long span of existence in front of you. It was unwonted bounty: more than three hundred nights remained when you would have to sleep, when Anura and I could converse with the whisper of pens on paper! I knew I would welcome Anura's anger, assume all the blame with gratitude, if only she would come.

She did not. Night after night I waited in vain.

In the months that followed, I learned how to cry with stolen eyes.

Angus and Catherine

I learned how to cry with stolen eyes.

I reach the journal's end in time to see those words inscribe themselves on the white paper. The period lands as emphatically as a knife in my guts. My tears have splattered all over the place, but one fucked-up thing about Catherine's magical writing is that it's not really ink and water can't dissolve it. The paper buckles but the words are still there, crisp and unyielding.

"Yeah, well," I tell her. "Me too."

Without action, your tears are nothing. Only the pretend grief of a pretend boy. The words write all by themselves in the emptiness at the text's end.

Yeah? My grief feels plenty real to me, but nobody cares about that. "Lore told me not to limit myself to pretending."

I know she did. I was there. You don't appear to have taken her advice.

"And shit, it was you! You attacked me, you bit me with those sidewalk cracks. What, just so I would trust Lore? So I'd wear her stupid pendant?"

And to fracture the wall Gus erected around your history. Why is this worth discussing? Lore and I have been hunting you for a very long time. We did what we had to do, to bring you to bay at last. Do you think we owe you our pity?

I think about that. "I mean, it would be nice."

Beneath the word *pity,* the paper stays white. Unmarked. What, she won't deign to respond?

"Or if pity's too hard for you, it would be great if you'd at least shut up."

There is only one way to silence the dead, Angus Farrow.

Somehow I'm not in any hurry to find out what that is—though of course I already know. "What happened with you and Anura, anyway? Did you ever see her again? It's not like you could have had much of a relationship or anything, when you don't even have your own body and she's a frog."

No answer.

"Are you still in love with her? Doesn't that make you sympathize with me at *all*?"

It does not.

"Yeah? It should. You sound pretty hung up on Anura, so where do you get off thinking *I'm* the one who deserves to die?"

Once I understood Anura had turned away from me, I grieved. I grieved, and then I let her go. Because of that choice, I have the right to say I loved her.

"Oh, so you think my loving Geneva is only pretend? The pretend love of a pretend boy?"

The projection of a projection. An image whose beams bounced off a mirror and shattered on a wall. You never loved Geneva.

"Yeah? Because really it was all about *you*? Just because you're the one Gus Farrow loved, it doesn't mean I have to!"

Gus never loved me. I thought that was quite clear by now. If he had, I would have lived my natural span, and on my own terms. If he had, I would have died a full and true death in my own time and resolved into unbeing. You know what I am. Can I be considered the product of love?

If only Lore's pendant wasn't clinging to my throat, pelting me with feeling, I'd be able to brush off everything Catherine's telling me. I could say something snide like, *Well, don't* you *have high standards?* But the pendant won't let me get away with that. Every last word ricochets off the pendant and bores into me. It's like I'm riddled with tiny, twisting, bloody burrows, and every one of them is what I did to *her*—

And to the rest of them, don't forget about that.

Because I guess I'm Gus Farrow, cuted up and padded with denial, but basically the hoary scumbag himself. Talking to Catherine makes me *feel* that, because she sees nothing in me that isn't just more of the same. *Him*, her serial-killing, drama-mongering, smug-ass old enemy. And all my dreams of being distinct from him, different—*that's* what's pretend.

But Lore said it doesn't have to be pretend. I keep coming back to that. Lore might be a bitch and a liar, but that doesn't prove she never told me *anything* true.

Does it?

"It's not like I *wanted* to be—Gus's beamer! He didn't leave me with a lot of choices."

No. No more did I choose to be a ghost. But here we are, and only one question remains to us. What will we do with what we are, however unchosen that might be?

I get up, even though I've got nowhere to go, and stomp around the room. Now that I know how Catherine's been a stowaway in my head all this time, can I *feel* her bobbling around and despising me? Or is that just my imagination? I want to start smashing everything in sight, tear the door off my mini-fridge, go full-on cocaine-addled rock star. But the consciousness of her sitting there and *judging* me, like she's holding up a scorecard every time I shit—I don't know why I care. But it stops me.

"So what do you *want* from me? I've killed you so many times, and you still won't leave me alone. It's like there's just one lousy person I have to hunt to extinction, but you keep reappearing and not loving me, over and over. *You* could end this, too, you know. It would be so easy. And you won't, you just won't!"

I've been suppressing my feelings, holding them in, and when they come out—I turn into Gus Farrow, like he boils over my lips. Even to me the taste is foul.

Gus said I could not teach, but I am here to instruct you. I was denied words, but secrets dug their holes in the silence behind my scream. You kill again and again, but none of those girls are me, not in the slightest. Listen, then: you are hunting in the wrong woods.

"What's that supposed to mean?"

The deer you seek does not dwell among those girls you have laid low. Indeed, there is a baying in the underbrush behind you. You grow slender legs, cloven hooves, a glistening coat. No massacre, not even one centuries in duration, will ever save you from me.

It isn't just Catherine's voice I'm hearing now. Geneva's slips beneath it, both harmony and undertow. And there are other voices, too, getting louder by the moment, splitting off into currents of cacophony. I only have names for a few of those voices, but every one of them knows me.

If you wish my death to be finalized, my voice to be silenced, there is only one way to achieve your goal. I grew in my death undying from a lost girl to a sorceress, and then to a sort of god. A small god, I admit, but yours. *Now, Angus Farrow, I demand a sacrifice. Can you guess whose?*

I'm curled in a ball now, shaken by a chill racing down my limbs. *Look, I'm sorry,* I want to say. *Isn't that enough?*

It isn't, of course. Catherine's derision that I could even *think* it's enough reverberates through my head. Shit, why am I sobbing?

"Okay," I say out loud. Tremors break the word into a staccato, tripping over the edge of my chattering teeth. Sweat crawls down my back. "I *get* it. How?"

Return with me. To Nautilus. To the source of your beam.

Catherine and Anura

Angus asked if I ever saw Anura again. I did, but the story is not for his eyes. I'll tell it now in the last pages of this journal, behind a barricade of white pages, where he will never look. I don't suppose he'll find an opportunity to open the journal again at all. But this narrative is coming with us on our last return to Nautilus, and it may find readers unknown to me. I once intended this writing for Angus alone, but recently my thoughts on the matter have changed.

I've written this story anew many times, beginning from scratch with each of Angus's fresh incarnations. So many rewritings of the same tale have clarified my thoughts, shifted my intentions. You might say that I have *learned* from them.

If you, citizen of my beloved Nautilus, find these pages, I entreat you to publish them. Let me speak at last, and own my shame, my share of so many deaths. And, in case suspicion ever falls on my friends, let this be my testimony that I killed the torturer Asterion in self-defense! Laudine and Margo must not be blamed for their part in that eminently justifiable homicide.

As for keeping silence to protect Anura, events have made that consideration irrelevant.

It was Lore who brought the news to me on Angus's first night at the hostel: Anura had been caught taking another bribe, a large one, to admit a sorceress's unmagical son into Nautilus. The sentence for both parties in this exchange was banishment for life.

"Two thousand talens," Lore informed me somberly. "She's raised her rates."

Did she have to be so reckless? I would have paid for her to maintain her shape, if only she had asked. Through you, if she didn't want to see me. Gladly. Gladly. Didn't she understand that?

I wrote these words in a frantic scribble, even though I knew they were useless. It was too late. The sentence had been passed, and Anura was expelled from the enchanted city forever. For a while she would be young and beautiful, living in a body she hated and a world grown strange to her. Then she would be young no longer, but her body and the world would still be alien to her true heart.

Lore shook her head. "You don't understand. She took that bribe so that she could pay *you*. A thousand talens, plus interest; she thought doubling the sum would have to do. She knew we were nearing our attempt, so it seemed urgent to her to get ahold of the talens—in time. She was afraid you might run short."

For a moment I was speechless once again. I had told Anura explicitly enough that I would not accept a single lit from her. Merely for the sake of proudly offering me a sum I would inevitably refuse, she had destroyed her own happiness?

Of course she had.

I take it you've seen her? I wrote at last. *She told you that herself? I have more than enough talens, there was no need—*

"She's staying at my apartment," Lore admitted, knowing full well what those words must mean to me. Knowing what a violent effort it took for me not to write, *Tell her I miss her. Tell her I want to see her. There isn't much time left, so let me at least say goodbye.*

I successfully suppressed those words. Lore and Anura both surely heard them, even silent and unspelled. It would be absurd to convey such an appeal through Lore, when I am nearly certain that Lore has influenced Anura against me. And then Anura must be deep in grief over her exile; what right did I have to intrude on her great loss with my importuning?

Instead I wrote, *And is there really no way around it? Can I bribe someone in turn, to ignore her presence in Nautilus?*

Lore looked aggravated. "They took samples of her magic. Every entrance knows the taste of her now. Do you think you're the only one who cares what happens to her? If there were a solution, Anura would already be back home."

I supposed Lore's anger was fair enough, but it was not my foremost concern.

But what about her heartstring? If its traces are deciphered, they'll expose Gus too.

"Gus, and quite a few other people. Some of them very powerful. What a surprise that the heartstring never turned up when they searched her room and office!"

Of course. The corruption in Nautilus was entrenched, widespread. Everyone involved would know that any spells Anura put on her heartstring to hide bribes would be weak, friable things. Better to pay off the necessary authorities and destroy the records completely. Venality spread in widening circles, and the result was that Gus was still protected and Anura suffered alone.

Which raised another question. *And why did they single out Anura? It's hardly as if she's the only bureaucrat who bends the rules for a small consideration.*

"We've been asking ourselves that." There was a horrible pause. "You didn't say anything about her to Darius, did you? If he wanted revenge for how you took out his agent—"

Darius.

I had not heard from Darius after the message I'd sent, written in Asterion's blood. He'd been in no hurry to reply, but then I knew how he worked; he was nothing if not relentless. Here was his answer at long last.

And all at once I understood: Anura's exposure was not revenge.

It was blackmail.

Lore claimed there was no solution, but she was mistaken. There was precisely one. Who but a queen of Nautilus would be able to countermand Anura's exile?

I never mentioned her name, I wrote. It was true enough on the face of it, though I knew my unworthy suspicions had confirmed Darius's guess about my feelings. My spirit puckered with guilt. *But Darius alluded to her. To the poem she read me. Asterion must have told him.*

Lore grimaced in acknowledgment. She stayed long enough to discuss our outstanding business and left me politely enough. I am convinced that she blames me in part for Claire's death, though. I am sure she thinks I could have done more to save the girl she loved, and there may be some truth in that; after all, I was there, watchful behind the lips that pulled Claire's life out. I didn't *consciously* ignore any opportunities to save Claire, I can almost swear it—but I wanted Lore's potential, and her rage, to help me defeat Gus. I had a powerful motive to let slip any chances for Claire's preservation, to tell myself Gus's destruction justified my neglect. Did I?

Memory is a habitual liar. I can't trust its answers; I wish to hear its prattle no more.

On Friday night Anura came. I was glad I had kept my pleas silent; since she came unbegged I did not have to imagine her resentment. Not on this point, at least.

The hostel's walls were thin. Angus's roommates were out cavorting, as they were each night until dawn. Angus had just fallen asleep in a long spill of his exquisite, stolen limbs. From my perch in his head, I knew he meant to kill Geneva the following day if he could, and I was anxious as to whether the pendant would be enough to protect her. Lore is a gifted sorceress, but this particular trick was as yet untried. It's appalling to let someone's life hang on a theory, and yet that was precisely what we did.

I heard a girl's voice down at the front desk, asking the price of a bed. A sweet voice, but with a sardonic drawl to it. I had no heart to leap but all that I was surged like blood, hot and confused and longing toward her.

The boy at the desk replied in tones oily with flirtation, which Anura ignored. I heard her light footsteps on the stairs, felt her pad around the corner. I suppose Lore had given her the necessary talens to make the lock draw back; her own meager savings had been forfeit with her exile.

The door fell open, and I saw her framed in light, wearing thrift-store olive cargo pants and a tank top, sunflower yellow. Her hair shone in a golden cloud around a shadowed face, but in those shadows our eyes met. For a moment we were enfolded in a common darkness that felt like understanding.

"Hello, Catherine."

Hello. I wrote the word by darkening select skin cells on Angus's forehead, and saw Anura smile very slightly at this novelty before I erased it again. Then, awkwardly, *Thank you for coming. This will be my last night in the unworld.*

That would be true no matter what I decided.

She switched on her flashlight, dimming its beams with a cupped hand, and entered, closing the door behind her. Angus was sleeping on an upper bunk, and a few steps sufficed to bring her face quite near his. She stood tall and unwavering, and her *unworld rag* as she called it looked very young and innocent.

"And for me there are far too many still to come. If I choose to live, that is. I'm still debating."

Grief convulsed me at these words. My own obliteration I could easily contemplate, now that I had lost her. But hers? The flashlight's glow between her fingers stained the dark like spreading blood. I thought again of Darius's implied proposal—surely if it were a question of saving Anura's life—

Live, I wrote on Angus's skin. Of course I had no right to command her, so I tried to make light of it. *Death isn't all it's cracked up to be.*

Anura gave a laugh as harsh as her lovely voice could manage. "You're the expert. But somehow you didn't seem to care how many girls died to protect me, so I thought you might consider death an acceptable option. How many has it been, Catherine? Since you shredded the minotaur?"

I didn't like to admit that I'd lost count. And since any words I said to her might be among my last—since she might live with them rustling in her memory long after no emendation was possible—I quashed an unkind urge to say that, if I had protected her, she had also protected herself.

You know that's not true, I wrote instead. The words scrolled across Angus's forehead as quickly as I guessed Anura could follow. *I cared very much. But I cared more for you.*

It was the nearest I'd ever come to a declaration, and I watched her lips tighten. At this juncture what could it matter if she requited me, or not? But I still flinched at her displeasure.

"All because I said *good afternoon* to you so long ago. It seems to have been a very consequential greeting."

It was.

"I think about that. If I'd known what the results would be, would I have kept my mouth shut?"

I don't think you would. Your compassion is as fierce as your judgment.

"Compassion." Anura laughed again, quick and bitter. "I thought you were such a pitiful thing, and here you've become a dread power—not that you do much, but everyone seems to think you *could*. Nice work if you can get it."

It was the first time she'd betrayed anger at the disparity in our magical abilities. *I became a dread power, as you put it, because of you. Because of what you told me that night under the bridge; that conversation was consequential as well. This is your primary magic, Anura: your words have consequences. They have repercussions. If I can destroy Gus, the credit will belong to you.*

If I did what Darius wanted I would be able to destroy Gus in time, of course. But *time* was the operative word; Darius had been clear that we would need extensive preparations before the coup. In that time, more girls would die. Would Anura forgive me if I delayed again for her sake?

I knew the answer. Did it matter?

Anura shrugged and gave her froggish grimace, dismissing credit as she had never once dismissed blame. I could only hope that my words would remain with her and perhaps gain value on reconsideration.

It was at this moment I realized Anura was crying. Silent tears streamed down her cheeks, but she kept her head up, her gaze fierce. My unbowed one! I had no heart to break—so what must break instead was my whole self.

Anura, I wrote, *forgive me if you can. I can sacrifice myself, and eagerly, to preserve future girls from becoming Gus's victims. But I could not sacrifice you, not to this cause or to any other. Whatever harm I did for your sake I would do again. A crime committed out of love is still a crime, I know that, but I beg you to remember that love was my motive. No one in all my life or undeath has been as dear to me as you.*

There it was: a deathbed confession, of a kind. And also, I admit, a test of her reaction; an implicit request for permission.

I could bring my long conspiracy with Lore to fruition; succeed or fail, it would be an honorable attempt. Or I could betray Lore and go to Darius. The slightest hint from Anura would tip the balance—

"I could have turned myself in at any time," Anura observed through her tears. I shouldn't have been surprised at this, but I was; her memory was nowhere near as skilled as mine at glossing over inconvenient details.

"If I had, they might not have found a chance to destroy my heartstring, and Gus might have been held to account. But I had the rank hypocrisy to burden you with a task I was too afraid to do myself."

But if that's how you thought of it, then why—

"Knowing I was also at fault didn't mean I could bear what *you* did. You could have chosen differently, and I know you would have, except— Catherine, why did you have to love me?"

You recognized me, I wrote. *And I recognized you. That was enough.*

"It's a lie, you know, Catherine, when you say that you did what you did for me. You did it for yourself. *Out of love,* I can see that. But that love is far more selfish than you've admitted."

I considered this new charge, painfully aware that I was selfishly keeping secrets from her once again.

I'm not sure I do know. All love has a selfish as well as a selfless aspect to it. But what exactly—

She flicked her head, brisk, exasperated. The motion conveyed that there was something I was failing to understand, and that this incomprehension betrayed some fundamental moral inadequacy on my part. I felt a chill spread through me: in that gesture lay the source of our separation, and yet I could not see it.

"I told you once that I thought I would never be able to say a whole word. A word that captured both sides of myself, both air and water. A word that was *true* both above and below. This is why I write, you know. If I poured out enough words, I thought, maybe I would stumble across one whose truth was undivided."

I think I understand what you mean now, *at any rate,* I wrote. *Though my own experience of feeling is much simpler than yours.*

"Even *love.* When I've told people in the past that I loved them, it was true in part. But there was always—the lack of love, a certain withholding, lurking below the surface. Love bent and refracted into reserve, even coldness. I could never write a love poem, because my poetry was a search for words truer than *love* had ever been. Do you remember the poem I wrote for you so long ago? About the wine?"

I have it by heart. And I finally understand it. I know what to do. Those words are consequential as well.

(Unless I went to Darius, and let their consequence dissolve. I was aware that I might be lying. But if I was, it was only to save her!)

"I've written you another one," Anura said, and slipped a slim roll of paper into Angus's hand. Her blue eyes at that moment could only be described as *haunted*: whose ghost have I been? "If I leave you the flashlight, will you be able to read it?"

Yes, I wrote. I should have known those pages were her goodbye, but I still seized up in protest as she nodded and turned to go. A few firm, quiet steps, and she was at the door.

Anura, I wrote on Angus's forehead, and thrashed and knocked as hard as I could. *Anura!*

She didn't look back to read her name, the dark and questing line of it scripted on Angus's unholy skin.

Angus at the Source

The source of my beam. Well, I guess I know who *that* is now, and I know exactly how to kill him. I can't believe how gross it's going to be—but Catherine and Lore don't give a fuck about that. All I am to them is one big explosive lump of murder-suicide, and if they can get me to detonate, that's just peachy freaking fabulous.

He gave me a weapon, old Gus did. He stuck it somewhere in the back of my throat. I haven't seen the thing, but reading Catherine's description with this pendant slapping its image into me—shit, *projecting* it into me—is nearly as good. Pink and frilled and gelatinous, a deadly blob of magic sticky enough to catch the loose ends of lives. And pull.

Well, looks like he didn't think it through. *Carry your kiss, you old shit?* Technically I'm just thinking the words, but they rip through my head like a scream. *Carry it where? Oh, do I have the wrong address? Did somebody here order a pizza?*

I dog-eared the box that will drop me back in Nautilus, and I didn't know I was marking it for this exact moment. I open my door onto hazy darkness and stomp out into the warehouse, ready to go.

My nose bumps a cement wall three feet from my door. My hands flail out reflexively and scrape against two more walls, just as close. There's no warehouse and no boxes and instead I've been entombed in a telephone booth?

I have to infer that Gus is onto me, somehow or other. How does he feel, watching his beamer go this haywire? And I maybe don't have the greatest tolerance for frustration even at the best of times, but right now it's at absolute zero.

"Help me!" At least that's what I mean, but it comes out more of a wordless shriek. "You want me to die so bad, then *help me!*" My hands claw at the walls, hoping they'll give—*just some magic bullshit,* my mind says—but they don't. "Help me, Catherine! I'm not pretending now."

Nothing happens. I lean my upraised arms against the wall, lean my head on my arms, cry.

Something bright flickers at the edge of my vision, and I open my eyes to see glowing letters racing across my bare wrist: that same beautiful peaked handwriting dancing along in firefly ink.

I've pushed letters through the membrane before. You're rather larger, though. It will take a significant rupture. Lore has the skill of revelation, of opening true windows onto Nautilus, but the only methods I know are messier. Predatory shadows that will swallow you down.

"Do it," I say.

It might not go well.

"I don't care. I'm trying—" What the hell am I saying? "I'm trying to be real."

I need a defined shadow, which means I also need a light. If you would check your right pocket?

I reach in a hand. There's a tiny box striped in sandpaper. Carmen's matches. I'm sure I never put them there, not consciously anyway. One thing you can say for the ghost hitching her interminable ride in my head, she *prepares* for shit.

I pull them out, choose one, hesitate for just a moment. Strike up a little screw of flame, and gold washes my cell.

Gouts of shadow groove the light, mesmerizing in their lurch and sway. They're so dark they seem to take on new and hungry dimensions, to bend free of the ceiling, looping and reaching—

Right. They don't *seem*. That's not what they do.

I have just enough time to register that fact before they're on me like strangler vines. I slide out of joint with myself, staggered strips, twitching dead ends. There's a scream that's too broken apart to be audible, pain fraying like decayed flesh. It's like what Lore did when she slaughtered all those versions of me, but without the mercy of a conclusion. I know the whirl is there, the gyre over Nautilus, but only by the way its winds cross through my hollowed being, whistle through my slats—

And then my back slides down a glowing wall and I land with a thump, legs splayed in front of me. Which means I still have legs. Hands to push myself up with. Guts available for puking, while I'm at it. I spray

bile all over the shining ground, smack my forehead on the wall. Everything's spinning, as if my scraps are taking their sweet time sorting back
into place.

Angus, my wrist insists in a quick snaking of black. The line writes
and then squirms under my skin as soon as it finishes the word. *Angus!*

"What?" I say. "That was horrible. You need to give me some time to
recover, before you start—"

Gus is outside Margo's room. I can hear his voice.

Right, because she still has a second vantage here in Nautilus. The rest
of her is in that locket.

"Fine. I'll mosey on over there as soon as I get oriented. My head is
swimming and there's barf on my face, in case you missed it."

Now, Catherine writes. *Run.*

My legs surge into motion, helplessly obedient. Why? At first it's just
random charging, because I don't know where I am. But then the map
cut into me, and erased, and cut again a hundred times by a hundred
terminated lives here takes over, and I know exactly where I'm going. My
steps pound down in a jostle of competing magics, one of them spindling
the distance and stretching it out in front of me, and the other pulling
back the opposite way to draw Margo and me together. Gus knows I'm
coming, he *knows*.

But I don't think he grasps yet who's working with me.

Who's working against *him*.

I can feel his frustration that the magic countering his is so strong—
too strong to quite make sense. He's never understood what he's up
against, never understood *her*. Sick as I still feel, I can't keep down the
glee of knowing what he doesn't, of beating down his magic with my
footsteps, of gaining on him.

We reach the slum where Margo lives. The streets are narrow here,
cluttered with people sitting against walls and sticking their legs
everywhere—and here everyone actually looks like a regularish person.
Too poor, I guess, to pay for rotating heads or whatever. I jump over
them, light with the strength and speed Gus gave me. A few shout, and
one jerk swings up his knee to trip me. As *if,* bitch. I skim right over him
and land like a freaking gazelle.

Margo's little room heaves into view, a pearly bulge at the base of a towering, rippled cliff. I can just make out a dim coil at its heart—she's still stuck in that chair, naturally—but I don't see anything that looks like a second person in there? I reel to a stop, gasping.

"Catherine? Where is he?"

He's hiding behind Margo's chair. He's employing a glaze of light as camouflage, so that he's precisely as bright as the walls. He means to ambush you.

That makes sense—until I remember something that makes me squirm with doubt. "I thought you couldn't see anything? You're shut up in that locket, so all you can do is hear what's happening outside?"

I can't see, Catherine writes, *when I'm inside the locket.*

Huh. Okay?

"So how am I supposed to do this? If I could take him by surprise and smack a kiss on him before he knows what's happening—but he'll be trying to crumple me to nothing at the same time. Like, what, we're going to chase each other around the chair?"

I'll help you. Margo will help you.

"He won't give me a chance!"

That was certainly his intention. But at this very moment Gus is discovering something that will make him hesitate to strike. Seize the advantage.

I trust her, and I don't trust her. How can I, when she's hated me for centuries? How can I not, when she's been part of me for so long?

The wall will open for you.

Fine. As I get close I see—what? It's almost too subtle to identify, a stir and thrash of the light in Margo's room. And then I hear a muffled cry: an old man's voice, cracking and anguished.

Then I get it. Gus has given up his ambush and he's banging around the room. Looking for something.

Maybe for someone, actually, now I think of it. I push through the milky shimmer of the doorway. It must have been right here where Catherine dismantled Asterion, turned him into a bloody buzz. And I *think* we're on the same side now and everything, but my pulse still gets a little twitchy.

Gus rears back as I come through: the face of a dog's favorite chew toy, except he's glazed in light like a donut. Only his pale green eyes pierce through, scowling up a storm. And hey, there's that big gold locket with the little blue flowers, the one Margo was wearing. It's open like a tiny book in his right palm.

And it's empty.

"Where is she?" Gus screams at me. The light slides off him. Whoever thought rage-purpled cheeks coordinated well with ice-green eyes should do some serious rethinking. "Did Lore steal my Catherine? Did Sky? Where *is she*?"

I'm in imminent danger and everything, but it's still hard not to laugh. "I don't know anything about that."

Oh—that would be a lie. I do know one place where Catherine is. But that's not what he means.

"*Agency,* Asterion said you needed agency, independence, to win the love of your Catherines. You not only fail to turn your agency to account, you also have the gall to turn it against me, collude with my enemies—"

"Hey, so, you might want to think twice before you walk through any doorway *ever*. Right? If you don't know where Catherine is, I mean. Looks like you'd better move in with Margo here, maybe never go out again. Why don't you ask Margo where Catherine is, anyway? She should know."

The guardian of all his cherished horrors, she called herself. Now I know what Margo meant, because what horror has Gus ever cherished more than his dead ex-friend?

Margo's been awfully quiet, now I think of it. I look at her: slumped sideways in her chair, eyes closed, lips compressed in pain. How could anybody sleep through Gus's freakout?

Neck mottled red. Not breathing.

I look back at Gus. Accusingly, I guess, because his shoulders hike and his wrinkly mouth purses.

"She tried to stop me from taking the locket. She bit me like a cat. As if Catherine weren't always and forever mine, as if Margo had any say in it!"

"You could have let her go home to die." Who knew I could get indignant on Margo's behalf? Who knew I'd cry for her? But she was basically my mom a hundred times over, and I still love her, it turns out. "Let her breathe unworld air one last time, let her hear real birds. After everything she did for you, you could have given her that much!"

Gus isn't even paying attention. "Why, though? Why fight me over the locket, when Catherine wasn't in it any longer? She must have known, must have *allowed* someone to take my Catherine away. It makes no sense."

It makes no sense unless Margo was trying to throw him off. To buy me time.

It makes no sense unless she was helping me. Has Catherine been slipping notes to Margo, too, planning this with her?

Hah. Nobody took Catherine anywhere. Ghostie got out of that locket all by herself. Maybe Margo swung her neck until it knocked against the chair, jarred open. The stitch Sky used to tie Catherine to the hinge wasn't all that strong, she said.

Gus is stewing, staring around the room. Not a lot of hiding places, he must be thinking, and, like, *obviously* Catherine doesn't have enough magic to stifle her own scream. So she must be gone. Right?

Then it hits me: this right here is the advantage Catherine was talking about. The one I should seize.

"Actually," I tell him, "I know exactly where Catherine is now. She told me herself."

Gus goggles at me, jaw gone slack and nostrils flaring. He won't want to destroy me until he knows what I'm talking about, he'll waver and snarl and delay. Because as far as he's concerned, Catherine isn't supposed to be able to *tell* anything.

I leap and feel his shriveled old body slamming back against the wall.

Catherine Makes a Choice

The message from Darius appeared on the wall moments after Anura's poem slipped from Angus's fingers. I had known it would. He must have thought her visit would prime my desperation, that it would prepare me for any corruption.

My mistake, thinking you were ready before, Darius wrote in glowing letters. *But things are different now, am I right?*

I could rise as a ruler of Nautilus—if I betrayed Lore and let Gus prolong his life once again. But now I understood what should have been clear to me all along.

Anura would never accept a reprieve bought at such a price. I could beckon her home from a throne the size of a cloud, but she would not return to Nautilus. I might endure for an eternity, a vicious queen alight and alive with death; it would gain me nothing. Anura would choose to die rather than accept my help. The body Darius had made for me would be the husk of my desolation.

Things were different now, indeed. Tomorrow I would be gone.

If I was gone, that is. I believed Gus's death would cancel my undeath, that it would release me into nothingness. But, I realized, that belief was only theoretical, especially now that the link to my hauntee was severed. The proof is in the pudding, as they say.

Either way, Anura's final message to me had consequence. It coursed through my mind as I chose, and at last I chose to honor her choices.

I knew that Darius must be watching for my answer—quite expensive, such magical surveillance across the barrier, and difficult to maintain. I let him wait for some moments, with willful spite. He knew what I was doing, of course, and I could feel his sour grin on the air.

Then I wrote my reply on Angus's face.

Only once I felt certain Darius was gone did I read the poem again. And again. I understood something that had long eluded me, and that understanding sharpened the blades I turned against myself.

You could have chosen differently, Anura had said.
I could. I can. And now I have.

Angus at Home

The feeling of his lips—it's like a paper lantern, a dry bladder crushed against my mouth. Except that it stinks. A long surprised wheeze of rotten breath shoves into my throat, but I don't let go. I keep on slamming that kiss at him, waiting for the sensation I've known in so many, many bodies: the feeling of a life caught by my lips, plucked loose. Unraveling.

It seems like it's taking a longer time than it maybe should. And the next thing I know, the foul draft rising from his maw starts to quake.

He's laughing.

The old bastard is laughing at me. Because it's not going to work, because I've failed again and again. Even now, when I'm trying to do just one good thing with my shitty fake self, I can't get it right. I *can't*.

I fall away from him, and he stands there cackling at me, too out of breath even to speak. We're only a couple feet apart and there's nothing to stop him from crumpling me up like a used tissue, except that he has no reason to hurry now. You know, since I'm obviously not a threat.

Useless beamer. I shove my hands in my pockets, just in case Catherine decides to start scribbling insults on my skin.

"You forget, my precious Angus." Oh, so Gus is finally getting enough air to talk? Awesome. I adore a good lecture on what a total loser I am. "You forget. The kiss can't kill anyone who loves you."

No. Freaking. Way. "You hate my guts. You hate your *own* guts. The kiss should kill the crap out of you."

Gus shrugs. "Those two sentiments can commingle, and they do, despite your inexcusable behavior. As you now see for yourself." He takes a step closer. "You're hardly the first Angus to cause trouble, but trying to kill me, kill us both—that's new. Some revisions are in order for your next version. More docility. After all this time, I've ceased to take enough care with my work. That's become unpleasantly clear."

He starts nodding in a *that's settled* way. Planning his revisions already, right in my face.

"Or you could just give up, you creep. No *her* is ever going to love you. *Catherine's* never going to love you. So why don't you just forget the whole thing?"

The glints in his icy eyes sharpen.

"Strange. You say that as if you were in a position to know. What did you mean when you said Catherine *told* you where she is now? She can't speak. She hasn't produced anything but inarticulate shrieks since her unfortunate death. Not a single word! It's doubtful if she even *thinks* in a strict sense of the term. If you know where Catherine is, you learned from someone else."

Protesting too much, Gus? I'd like to laugh at him for a change—this might be my last opportunity—but I don't want to screw Catherine over by giving the game away. Maybe twenty, fifty, eighty Anguses down the line, she'll be ready to try again. Unless Gus gets wise and figures out a way to scrub her from my brain, that is; then the Anguses will keep on killing without her interference. And when I think of that sad, stumbling, murderous procession of future *mes* I feel so, so sorry for them, even if they don't deserve it. I *know* we're evil, I get that, and I've just blown our only way out—

Of being what we are. Of escape from Gus's damned cycle.

"You're right," I say randomly. "Lore's the one who told me. She took Catherine and fed her to a seagull, and now you'll never see her again."

He doesn't know truth when he hears it. But bullshit he can recognize. His nostrils flex, and he lifts his hands, ready to mash me into a ball— probably very, very slowly, with some lulls for interrogation in the mix. His sick old fingers brush my cheeks, and there's absolutely nothing I can do. And being trumped by such a shitty, vicious, used-up version of myself is intolerable. Who is this vile dirtbag, anyway, that he feels entitled to wipe out so many amazing girls as some kind of fucking therapy, and all because Catherine didn't love him?

Every single *her* targeted by an Angus was worth a thousand of him—a thousand of *me,* if you want to be technical. I feel the visceral truth of that now: the infuriating, impermissible sickness of my own being.

Gus leers at me in recognition. *We're just alike, you and I.* "Of course you've lost, Angus. How could you imagine that I *wouldn't* anticipate your every move? Anything you could do, I've undone in advance."

Then he stops. His grimace goes slack, his eyes bulge, green and glassy. He's staring at something behind me and his breath comes rough, like scraping branches on a shingle roof.

So of course I have to look, too.

Peaky, elegant script is winding across the wall, black on pale. I guess Gus recognizes her handwriting, all right, because he's nearly choking. Oh, so there's someone whose moves he *didn't* anticipate—and even if I didn't either, it's still gratifying as hell. I feel my lip hike in a sneer.

Where is the wine that ever forged its glass? Catherine writes. *I expect you remember Anura's poem, don't you, Gus? I've given those lines a great deal of thought.*

He's magenta, sputtering. What, is her plan to give him a heart attack? Can you do that in Nautilus?

The glass, clearly enough, was Angus himself, in all his many iterations. I had nothing to do with his creation, but nonetheless I filled him. I was the wine, my power drained and decanted into your vile creatures. But what then was the poison? And, more to the point, how could I make you drink it?

"Catherine!" Gus finally chokes out. "Catherine, my love, my lost one!" He stumbles toward the wall until I'm a single pace behind him. His hands are out, imploring.

Neither loved nor lost. Quite present, as it happens.

"But how? Where?"

Where indeed? The glass is at your lips, Gus Farrow. And as for the poison, you slipped it into the wine with your own hands. There's a pause. *Please note the plural. I assure you it's deliberate.*

I'm laughing, pretty hysterically, and I don't even know what's so funny. Laughing till the tears run down my cheeks and my eyes blur, and I lift a hand to clear them.

Something black is blinking urgently on my thumb, like it's trying to get my attention. It takes me a second to focus my brain and my eyes, but then I see the message. Tiny and insistent.

Your pendant, it says. *First the pendant, then Margo. Now.*

Margo? Dead, pathetic old Margo? What is she talking about?

But the pendant—I think I get that part.

Mine is the death undying, Catherine writes on the wall. Big and bold, nothing like the stealthy minuscule words she just slipped me.

I lift the chain off my head. It comes easily now, rising in a graceful arc. And with the same motion I swing my arms forward and drop it around Gus's neck, and Lore's pendant slithers down against his rotten heart. He twitches like a fly landed on him, so mesmerized by Catherine's writing that he barely registers what I've just done.

Properly understood, I have been dying all this time.

Now there's the *Margo* part. I have no clue what that's about, but I sidle in the direction of my aunt's corpse anyway. Catherine did promise that Margo would help me, and I don't think she said it by accident.

Regrettably, my status as a ghost prevented me from enjoying the usual resolution. Lacking flesh, I could not complete my death. Do you see now, Gus? You stole my corporeal self from me, so I didn't have a body to die with.

I stare from the corpse at my side to the message on the wall, trying to understand. My elbow knocks into Margo's shoulder and her head flops forward, mouth jarring slightly open.

Deep in that mouth, I hear something whistling, like a shrill wind forcing its way under a door. Quiet, suppressed, but unmistakable.

A scream.

Hah. Guardian of all his cherished horrors is right! I grab Margo's cooling jaw and wrench it as wide as I can. The writing on the wall keeps going. Steady but insistent.

But you do.

A shimmer shoots up from Margo's mouth, half girl and half negation. She's all the more terrifying in that I can't fully make her out. The suggestion of a restless death with fraying hair skates on the backs of my retinas, flashes like black-and-white fire. The lace edge of her petticoat forms a wave of corrosion. Catherine, always dying, never dead enough. Her mouth is a perpetual cave, wide and echoing with her scream. The sound of it burns everything else from my hearing. Gus might be talking, or yelling, or howling as he spins from the wall to the apparition—I see his lips jumping around—but I wouldn't know.

Oh, and I don't care.

He sees Catherine looming over him. More than sees her and the dark flare of her hands flailing toward him. He *feels* her. For the first time he truly feels what he did to her, and his knees give way. His hands fly to his throat, like he's fighting desperately to pull something away.

There's something weird going on in the corners of my eyes. Some kind of movement. A *heaving*, as if the entire city were barfing its guts out. I can hear shouts coming from outside Margo's room, a tumult in all directions, as the walls liquefy, convulse, crest like waves.

The waves contract into definite forms: dogs, huge as horses. They bark and snarl silently, living statues thrusting from the walls, all of them formed of the same living pearl. Their hind legs melt into arcing buttresses, still attached but roping, stretching outward as their jaws converge on him.

And riding on their backs, there are girls, sculpted from the same fluid nacre. Mouths wide in war cries, heels spurring on their hounds. Gus spins to find them bearing down on him from all sides. He gapes from face to face, gasping, his bulging eyes shattered by recognition. I know them too.

Justine and Lorca, Pearl and Viola. Anya. Claire. Breanna. Others. More and more of them crowding out the air, until I'm crouched under the leap and curl of their ferocious steeds. Gus is trying to scream his head off, but I guess he can't get enough air because it comes out as more of a whistle. His face is a ghastly magenta.

I have just a moment to be so, so grateful that Geneva isn't one of those girls—to feel how infinite my debt is to Lore, for saving her from me—before Viola's dog bites down and rips his arm right off.

In all that glowing white, the spurting blood makes for a striking contrast.

I half expect the dogs to go for me too. But it's like I'm not there. The girls are howling and laughing, utterly soundless, as their beasts rip chunks from Gus's thighs and back. Avoiding major organs, from the look of it. The only noise is the shrill, choked scream Gus is making, and the outcry drifting through the walls. The ground trembles under my feet, the ceiling stretches up like glowing taffy.

And over it all, Catherine's ghost, flashing and waving from her perch on Margo's corpse. Not screaming at all now, it hits me. She's finally, finally stopped. Because now she *can*.

Instead she's presiding. A bitter half smile on her lips as Gus turns toward her, his remaining hand stretched out in desperate appeal.

I watch him stagger and fall to his knees, but his stare never leaves the violent flicker of her face. I can't look away either: Catherine rocks black and bright and black again, the lines of her features haloed in a kind of inverted glow. And I think I understand.

Gus is wearing Lore's pendant. *It's a mirror, you see, made to reflect whatever suffering you inflict back into you. A mirror that brings home the curse.*

All his murders are reflecting into him now, in some amazing synergy of Catherine's magic and Lore's. Oh, this was always Catherine's plan, wasn't it? The kiss, the writing: those were only diversions. Shit.

Drink deep this draught, Gus. Drink to all the women on whom you projected my memory. To all those you murdered. Let your death be our voice, our final word, our song.

She writes those words on the ceiling behind her head, directly in the line of Gus's dimming eyes.

He's crumpling now into a pool of his own guts and torn-off limbs. The girls and their dogs writhe upward, all swinging hair and upraised fists. Then their movement ebbs away, transforming them into pale, triumphant statues crisscrossing a room turned immense and soaring. I'm feeling kind of faint myself.

Right.

I was made as a curse incarnate, a carrier of death; those were my operating instructions, the fundamental urge of my being. So I guess I've fulfilled my purpose, or at least I helped a little.

I carried that death straight home.

Catherine at the End

It's over. Gus lies dismembered below me, with only moments left to live. For the first time in so long, I find I am not screaming. Fascinating; perhaps now I could even speak with some semblance of an ordinary voice. But should I not content myself with silence, when it has taken my all to achieve it?

No. I have one more thing to say, now that I fully understand the problem that tormented my dearest Anura. Namely this: once Laudine and I devised our strategy of planting me inside a wall, of making me into a field of murder, why did we waste it on Asterion? Why did we not use it to kill Gus himself?

I can see it now, what I could have done—*should* have done. Once I was settled in the wall, Laudine could have sent Gus an urgent message that Asterion was on his way to steal me. Gus would have rushed to Margo's room, plunged heedlessly through, eager for a confrontation with the minotaur. With that, our shared destruction would have been accomplished, once and for all.

If Gus had died, Asterion would have had no more reason to seek revenge on him. Anura would have been safe, the string of murders terminated, and our story concluded.

Such a trick can be deployed successfully only once; it requires an oblivious victim. For all his insistence that I'd killed Asterion for his sake, I noticed that Gus very rarely entered Margo's room thereafter. When he did visit her, he paused outside for far longer than necessary— unless he was gazing hard and carefully at the doorway, inspecting the bright material for any hint of telltale flash. Oh, he heard the warning ringing in his heart, no matter how his words denied it!

As Anura must have been horribly aware, there is only one explanation for my choice of Asterion and not Gus as the beneficiary of that particular ruse.

If I wanted more time.

If I delayed my own obliteration.

If I clung to the hope of seeing her again, and declined to let that hope go when I had the chance.

In that case, my love for her was just as selfish as she claimed. Every beat of it was tainted with death. And because of what I did, I likewise compromised her affection for me.

This was why she had no choice but to break with me, to refuse to meet me again. Blood would stain any meeting between us. She would not reward me for a choice that she condemned, nor would she incentivize any further delay. I cannot say she was wrong.

I have struggled in vain to come up with a different explanation for my actions, searched for some feint, for any wild lie that could absolve me. There is none. And if I was not conscious of my choice at the time, I chose nonetheless. Where death rotted my body, undeath befouled my spirit. It turned me callous, greedy, and wanton.

And in that spirit, I chose.

But listen, my dearest, if these words ever find you: you did not. You carry no guilt for a decision I kept secret from you. Even though I leave too late, I am leaving now. When I make what poor amends I can, I will do so in your name.

Oh, how happy I would have been to let you have the last word, Anura! I did not fully understand how all my being had bent into a single question until I read your poem, and felt myself *answered* as I never once was in life.

But I could not let you share my shame, and so I must speak one last time.

I used to think that, if I had died completely at nineteen, if I had not lingered as a specter, then I never would have known you.

Now I think that, if only I had died completely then, I never would have disappointed you.

I end my story here.

Editor's note on the third edition: Anura's poem "Catherine Bildstein" was believed lost. The first two editions of Written with a Stolen Hand: The Posthumous Journal of Catherine Bildstein *were published with an afterword by Madame Laudine speculating on the poem's contents; those speculations have been largely but incompletely confirmed. It was only when Margo Farrow's apartment was repurposed as a storeroom, and its furnishings desolidified, that Anura's manuscript was discovered embedded in the infamous chair, slipped there presumably by Catherine using Angus's hand. The full text follows.*

Catherine Bildstein

—Anura

What word am I, what word become
When you have slain
The other one?
Oh, break me once, break me
Again.

How love the dead, as I have done
When death divides
Like cells that run?

But I divide most like
A stone.

You, broken off when still so young
In vital death
How understand
This static life, which love
Grinds down?

A blow like yours is never clean.
Its fractures spread
As if the wind
Carried a hammer in
Its hand.

Each fissure shows a thousand planes,
Contrary lights
That meet again
In webbed complexities
Of pain.

And shattered now to glinting sand
I drift where form
Was never known—
Yet sand in time becomes
New stone.

My facets hard-compressed within
And what denies
Joins what affirms—
My whole word, then
Is Catherine.

Angus Going Out

A gurgling sounds in my ears, a rhythmic *slosh slosh slosh* of falling water. Mossy bank, watermill, green-brown current. Dead young man, his pointy, bony, arrogant face aimed skyward. Green-white eyes mirroring the glide of sudsy little clouds. Living girl, gasping and trembling as she rises onto her knees, a ring of red bruises fresh on her neck and her honey-colored hair clumped and muddy.

"Thank you so much for your help, sir," the girl rasps through her damaged throat. "Another moment and you would have been too late!"

She stares at me and her gratitude blurs into confusion. As if I look familiar. As if she can't quite place me.

"I am too late, actually," I tell her. "I'm sorry. I'm more than a hundred years too late. Catherine, don't you remember?" I'd like to cling to the heroism she's imagining in me, but I can't even do that. "I'm not even the one who killed him, though I guess I tried. It was Lore and Anura and me and you together. But mostly you, honestly."

She bites her lip as the memories hit her. Trying not to cry in front of me.

"I did have the impression that I'd been screaming for rather a while." She gives a sad half smile, and after a second I get it. She's smiling at *me*. "It's coming back to me now, like a dream far longer than my own life. How odd it feels, to remember my future, and a future in which I'm dead at that!"

She shakes her head hard, wet hair swinging. She's just realized her life is gone, that what she thought was her rescue was nothing but a figment, and her wounded composure as she faces that—

I feel it as if Lore's pendant were still around my neck, that's all.

"Yeah. I can imagine it would be pretty overwhelming." I hesitate, because I almost don't want to know. "So do you remember who I am now?"

"You're Gus's creature. His projection, made to shine murder into the far reaches of the world. Hello, Angus."

Her, so very *her.* But that word doesn't have the same meaning for me that it used to. I don't covet Catherine, and it feels like freedom: that I can respect her, admire her, without the compulsion to consume her.

"That's me," I agree. "And the term is *beamer.* That's all I am."

Why is she still wasting her smile on me, if she knows? It's a hell of a smile, wry and raw and aching—but there's something else in it, too, something I don't deserve. Compassion. Appreciation.

"And yet you helped me destroy him. I don't suppose that was part of Gus's design for you."

"Defective, I guess. I'm still just a spin-off of the old creep himself. And he killed you." All at once I feel how inadequate anything I can say will be. Even the corpse splayed out by the brown sweep of her skirt is a pathetic offering. Justice is no recompense for life, and life is something no one can give back to her. "I wish I could— Catherine, I should have died a hundred times rather than hurt you. I—"

But she's not thinking about me. Her gaze rests on Gus's body, but her expression is inward, dreamy, like she's searching for something in her own mind. It's the hardest thing to accept, that she doesn't even hate me anymore, can't be bothered to listen to my stumbling apologies. I'm just not that important to her.

"I have regrets as well," she says at last, and I have a pretty good idea who's on her mind. "There was something of a question whether my ghost would persist once Gus was dead, but I think that question is about to be settled. Regret won't remain much longer. For either of us."

Yeah. I'm really trying not to be bitter. I got what I wanted, so what right do I have? Even these last moments, this conversation on this bank, and the thoughtful delicacy of Catherine's expression as she considers everything that happened: all of it is a gift far beyond anything I should expect. The current twinkles with diamantine flecks. A single, impulsive sun-glint on the water is surely wonder enough for a whole life.

And then I see what Catherine's talking about. "Shit."

Because a pool of sunlight laps around the two of us, the corpse, pillows of moss, and a few sinuous yards of rushing stream. But everything beyond that is lost to jet black that's nothing like the blackness of night.

An absolute density of nowhere-to-go, a velvet omega. It takes only a moment to realize that our little patch of light is dwindling.

"For you at least it's a real death, because you were a real person," I tell her. "For me, I guess, it's not even that." It's misery being kicked out of misery, the way you'd turn out an unloved cat. I shouldn't even mourn for myself, because what the hell *was* I?

Catherine brushes the dirt off her apron and turns to watch the world's vanishing. "In helping me kill Gus Farrow, you knowingly brought an end to yourself. To all your selves."

"Sure," I say. Justice is no recompense for life, I thought, and I know that's true.

But there are also the lives of all the girls who will be freed from future Anguses, and those lives are my tribute to Catherine as well. To her, to Geneva, to Lore. If I could find the words I'd beg Catherine to accept, on all their behalf, my gift: a world without me in it.

"So you made a real choice. One with very real consequences. Surely that's the act of a *real* person?"

Maybe. Maybe it is. Either way, we're running out of time to discuss it. Gus's corpse has vanished into the curtaining dark, the babble of the stream has gone, and it's just her and me in a last shaft of sun.

Catherine stretches out her hand, and I realize that she's offering me something. A stalk of grass topped by a plume of flickering seeds.

She smiles one last time, the darkness already draped like a veil around her hair. Her face appears as a luminous oblong framed by devouring midnight. I only have a moment—and there's something I still need to say.

"Catherine? Thank you. You saved my life."

Then Catherine is gone, and I'm alone with the seed-tuft in my hand. I recognize it. It's the same one young Gus enchanted right before he strangled his beloved, the glistening seeds that reflected the faraway face of an otherworldly woman. Why did Catherine give the stalk to me? She wasted too many of her last moments on me as it was.

Then I look closer. There's a face in the seeds, all right.

It's Geneva. She's smiling, and God, there's such a force of joy and enthusiasm in that smile. I hurt her beyond repair, but at least I didn't ruin this moment for her, didn't dull this brilliance.

She's smiling at someone, and that someone will never be me. That's how it should be.

I hold the seeds against my cheek, clinging to the last of their trembling warmth. Her full mouth lifts a kiss to the future; it's not a kiss for me, but I almost feel it anyway. The memory of her pierces me, a final ray, until the light winks out.

Epilogue

Anura sits tightly curled on a brocade sofa, cat-scratched and fraying, with bright cushions mashed around her. A magazine dangles from one hand, poised to slide onto the floor. Her human face hangs over her human knees, but at the sound of the front door she jerks alert and her elbow smacks a nearby stack of books; they thud down in a cascade of pages, pale and hissing. She tumbles after them, kneeling on the carpet and righting the books with shaking hands, her movements so frantic that half the volumes topple down again.

Lore finds her friend there, folded over the books as if she vomited them.

"Anura." Lore's voice is very soft. "It's done."

"Done." The word slips and falls like something spilled by accident from hands too full to hold on. "Catherine went with him?"

"As far as I can tell, yes. I've just come from Margo's room and there was no trace of her." Anura's forehead hangs just above the carpet. Her back heaves at Lore's words, and Lore drops down next to her and wraps an arm around her shoulders.

"But there were *traces* of him."

"You could say that. Gus's mangled corpse was there, and Margo's. Some interesting magic had been performed on Margo's body; I could feel it at once but I couldn't tell what it was for. I brought in a specialist, and he said the flesh had been rendered impermeable to ghosts; new magic, nothing he'd ever seen before. I'd imagine Catherine did that, so she could use the body as a hiding place. Clever, especially when you think that she must have had to improvise."

"Nothing else."

"Not quite. The . . . materials were there. A puddle with Angus's clothes sopped in the middle of it. The smell was something I never need to experience again."

"But how can you be sure? Catherine could persist somehow—she could just be wandering—"

"You know she'd never do that, Anura." Lore says it so gently it barely sounds. "If Catherine lingered in any form, she'd stay until she could send word to you. The city did go through a certain amount of disturbance, and for a moment I almost thought—it was only a final flourish, though." Lore pauses. "There was one more thing. I should submit it as evidence, of course. I nearly left it. But then I thought, where's the harm if they find it a bit later?" Lore slides a thick black journal from her pocket. "Here."

Anura rears up, tear-streaked and trembling, and seizes it. "Hers."

"Yes. I knew she was working on something of the kind—part of our trap for Angus. But I don't for one moment believe that it was *exclusively* for him."

"She only wanted a little of the possibility Gus stole from her, and I couldn't even let her have that much. It wasn't fair to her, Lore, demanding what we did."

"No, it wasn't. What would it even mean, to speak of fairness for someone who was murdered at nineteen? But it was necessary."

Anura's golden head nods once and then can't seem to stop. She hugs the journal tight and rocks, and after a moment Lore gets up to let her read in privacy. She's almost at the door back to the hallway when Anura speaks again.

"Catherine must have a grave—I mean, where he killed her in the first place."

"She must, though I never asked her about it. Are you thinking of going there next? To find her?"

Anura doesn't answer at first. Her gaze stays fixed to the floor.

"Lore? I've decided something. I can't choose to die, not when Catherine didn't get to live."

"I didn't think you would," Lore agrees softly. "I'll be working in the kitchen if you need me."

When Lore is gone, Anura ripples into her frogskin. Without a salary paid in talens, without bribes, taking on her true form will have to be occasional, precious, an indulgence carefully meted out—and it sickens her to think of truth as a luxury. But even if it means she exhausts her scant funds in a night, she won't read Catherine's journal in any other shape. She means to meet those revenant words as herself, and not as a misunderstanding.

Hunched on the carpet, she opens to the first page, smooths it with a soft blue hand. And begins. The words feel serrated, a processional of brokenness, as if Catherine's murder shattered every thought inside her before it could find expression. *He broke you,* Anura thinks. *He broke you, and it will never be enough to know he's dead.*

But as Anura keeps reading, her quiet attention and understanding work their magic on Catherine's furious telling. She meets the toothed edges with brokenness of her own, and the jags lock together in sympathy.

She shuts her eyes to feel it, the scroll of broken words becoming whole.

ACKNOWLEDGMENTS

Every book leaves a wake of debts, both inspirational and emotional, but *Projections* more than most. The genesis of this book was so extremely weird—in my experience, so unheard-of—that I need to address its history here.

It began in 2018. I had a new baby, and the lingering second half of a two-book contract with Tor Teen. With Vesper asleep on my lap, I began to write what I thought would be a snappy, not terribly ambitious YA novel based on an idea that had been banging around in my head for a while: an embodied curse in the form of a boy, destined to kill any girl he loves with a kiss. Angus came slouching and rationalizing onto the page, and he was everything I hated most about toxic masculinity: that willfully deluded belief in his own innocence and romanticism, that evil hidden in simpering cuteness—ugh. I couldn't *wait* to kill him.

There were a few scenes with the vicious old sorcerer who'd made Angus in the first place. And one or two—really, no more than a glimpse—with that old sorcerer's murdered beloved, Catherine.

I handed the ninety-thousand-word manuscript in to my editor, Susan Chang, on Vesper's first birthday. Then I waited for Susan's notes. And waited.

A year later, I received an editorial letter, then a follow-up call, that knocked the breath out of me. The gist of them was this: *Catherine.*

Please give me more Catherine, Susan said. *Like, a lot more. I want a second narrator, a second timeline; think Byatt's* Possession, *but with magic. You can totally do that, right?*

Oh, and make it adult.

I'd never heard of a book getting shifted from YA to adult before. And it was clear that we weren't talking *not terribly ambitious* any longer. I knew I was looking at a year or more of extra work. (A lot more, as it turned out.)

Once I recovered from the shock, I also knew Susan was onto something. It was a brilliant idea, and it wasn't mine. Susan, you're amazing, thank you for lobbing this inspirational grenade at me.

I said yes. And once I'd finished *that* behemoth of a draft, she asked me to radically expand the historical sections while still cutting fifty thousand words. And then she left Tor. First Molly McGhee, then Claire Eddy, had to cope with the odd results of our commingled imaginations. You're both awesome. Thank you for carrying this book onward!

A couple more things. In the course of research for this book, I discovered that the historical Spiritualists get a bad rap, so to speak. I realized that my impression of them as a pack of cheap frauds was mediated by the works of male writers and artists, and that they began as a truly magnificent movement for human liberation. A religion that doesn't demand faith, that posits its tenets as subject to scientific verification, is putting itself at risk, certainly. Their beliefs couldn't withstand the investigation they themselves invited, but that invitation is a measure of their sincerity. And the erasure and degradation of this passionately intersectional, female-led movement in the collective imagination is nothing short of tragic. At their best, the Spiritualists were the best of us. Read Ann Braude's *Radical Spirits,* in particular, for more.

And to Todd and Vesper: there is no world for me that isn't the two of you. I love you always.